Nicolson.
24ᵗʰ January 1988.

Penguin Books

The New Penguin Book of
Scottish Short Stories

Ian Murray was born in Glasgow in 1935 and has lived there
ever since, except during his two years' national service. He
works as a bookseller and also writes occasional book reviews
for the *Glasgow Herald*. For four years he sat on the Scottish
Arts Council Grants to Publishers Panel.

The New Penguin Book of Scottish Short Stories

EDITED BY
IAN MURRAY

PENGUIN BOOKS

Penguin Books Ltd, Harmondsworth, Middlesex, England
Viking Penguin Inc., 40 West 23rd Street, New York, New York 10010, U.S.A.
Penguin Books Australia Ltd, Ringwood, Victoria, Australia
Penguin Books Canada Ltd, 2801 John Street, Markham, Ontario, Canada L3R 1B4
Penguin Books (N.Z.) Ltd, 182–190 Wairau Road, Auckland 10, New Zealand

First published 1983
Reprinted 1984, 1985

Set in Linotron Times by
Rowland Phototypesetting Ltd
Bury St Edmunds, Suffolk
Printed and bound in Great Britain by
Cox & Wyman Ltd, Reading

CONTENTS

F/MUR
T09093

INTRODUCTION

The modern short story can be said to have arrived early in the nineteenth century; it came as a departure from the oral tradition which encompassed the telling of tales and legends, and the ballad, and it introduced a tightness of plot and a stronger, more realistic treatment of character. The reader is given a greater insight into the behaviour and reactions of individuals in a particular incident, and the horizons are more often domestic than national, showing people in their natural habitat.

Scottish writers were very much in the vanguard of this genre. The first three stories in this collection were published in the period in which Balzac and Mérimée were writing in France, and Gogol, Pushkin and Turgenev in Russia. There were few writers in England at this time who were interested in writing short stories.

James Hogg, 'the Ettrick Shepherd', was the son of a farmer. He was for a time on the staff of *Blackwood's Magazine*, and through it he became associated with many of the literary figures of the day from both sides of the Border. 'The Brownie of the Black Haggs' first appeared in *Blackwood's* in Edinburgh in 1828. It is a sinister story, with flashes of macabre humour; the ambiguity concerning the true nature of the Brownie, apparently wished upon herself by Lady Wheelhope, remains unresolved. Here Hogg is clearly influenced by the ballad tradition, and the story is laced with proverbs, particularly in the exchange between Wattie and Bessie towards the end of the tale.

Scott's 'The Two Drovers' was published in 1827 in the first volume of *Chronicles of the Canongate*, where it appeared with 'The Highland Widow' and 'The Surgeon's Daughter'. At the time of its publication Scott was already established as a novelist, with works such as *Heart of Midlothian*, *Rob Roy* and *Ivanhoe* having brought him considerable fame and respect. The romantic fancy which characterizes many of Scott's novels is largely absent in this story; but the build-up to the final, inevitable double tragedy, and the reaction of Robin Oig to what he sees as his honour and duty, probably tell us as much about the character of the Highlander as we can discover from his longer and more ambitious works.

John Galt was a very different novelist from Scott. His best-known novels are *The Ayrshire Legatees*, *Annals of the Parish*, *The Provost* and *The Entail*, and all these present a more parochial view of small-town Scottish life and manners, particularly those of Ayrshire. Galt, like John Buchan after him, had strong links with Canada, founding one town – Guelph – and having another named after him, both in the province of Ontario. 'The Gudewife' was first published in Galt's *Stories of the Study* in 1833 and appeared again later that year in *Fraser's Magazine*. William Maginn, the editor of *Fraser's*, claimed to have made a profit of four hundred guineas by means of buying this and other stories from Galt and then re-selling them to the magazine. 'The Gudewife' is a wry and humorous tale of a nagging wife who makes a stand for women's liberation, remarkable in the first years of the nineteenth century.

These early beginnings in the development of the Scottish short story are encouraging, but the compiler of a representative anthology finds that, although the literature is extensive, a search for forgotten masterpieces is not rewarding. Many of the tales in this collection have already been anthologized elsewhere. Nevertheless, they deserve to attract a wider readership and they benefit from a chronological presentation.

Mrs Margaret Oliphant was born near Musselburgh, not far from Edinburgh. She became a widow in her thirtieth year and began to write in order to support her family. Her work follows more in a line from Galt than from Scott, and she wrote a number of novels which are undeservedly neglected today. On one level 'The Open Door' is a good ghost story, but it also tells us much about the manners and behaviour of her contemporaries.

'The Beach of Falesá' is set far from the Scottish east coast; Robert Louis Stevenson wrote it in Samoa in 1891, three years before his death, and it captures the exotic atmosphere of the South Seas. Stevenson is of course famous for his *Treasure Island*, *Kidnapped*, *Dr Jekyll and Mr Hyde* and *A Child's Garden of Verse*. Ill-health exiled him from Scotland after a youth spent there; he travelled extensively, settling eventually in Samoa where he died in 1894. 'The Beach of Falesá' is a study of the contrasting reactions of two white men, Wiltshire and Case, to the natives of the island, and it culminates in the destruction of the 'evil one', Case, who is worshipped by the natives as a devil and holds them in his power through fear. There is much in this story that anticipates Conrad.

R. B. Cunninghame-Graham was born in London of wealthy Scottish parents. He was able to travel widely, especially in South America, but later became a Scottish Member of Parliament and President of the Scottish National Party. His story 'Beattock for Moffat' confirms his Scottish roots.

John Buchan was celebrated in his lifetime as a politician and statesman, and as the author of the much-loved adventure stories which first introduced us to Richard Hannay and the Gorbals Diehards. He developed a strong interest in the supernatural and its apparent influence on Scottish character and history, and 'The Outgoing of the Tide' is taken from a collection of tales of the supernatural, *The Watcher by the Threshold*.

Neil M. Gunn was born in Caithness. He became a civil servant, but at the same time he devoted himself to writing and gained a sound reputation as a novelist. When he was forty-five he was able to resign his position and turn to writing full-time, becoming one of the most respected Scottish novelists of the twentieth century. 'The Tax-Gatherer', from his collection *The White Hour*, shows his sympathy and compassion for people living within a rural tradition and having little appreciation of the workings of bureaucracy. From a very different background, Edward Gaitens was a Clydesider who wrote of the confusion of values and priorities he saw in the people of Glasgow and its environs. 'A Wee Nip' is taken from his collection *Growing Up*, and much of the story was later used in his novel *Dance of the Apprentices* (1946).

Naomi Mitchison, born in the same year as Gaitens, contributes 'In the Family', less thematically typical than most of her writing, which does not often relate to Scotland. It is a finely written story with an element of the second-sight that preoccupies many Scottish writers.

Eric Linklater, who was born in Wales, later became an Orcadian by adoption and, like George Mackay Brown who was born in Orkney, was influenced by the wealth of legend and folklore in the islands' culture. Linklater was interested in the grey seals inhabiting the seas round Orkney and in their preservation, and he brilliantly merges this concern with fantasy in 'Sealskin Trousers'. George Mackay Brown shows us, in 'The Wireless Set', first the wonder of the villagers at this modern miracle and then their growing superstitious dislike of it, which finally results in its destruction for the bad news it carries.

Lewis Grassic Gibbon grew up in Aberdeenshire. After unsatisfactory periods spent in journalism, in the Army and the Air Force, he wrote a number of books, the finest of which must undoubtedly be his trilogy *A Scots Quair*. 'Smeddum' first appeared in his *Scottish Scene*, and he added this note at the beginning of the story: '*Smeddum* is defined by the Scots dictionaries as meaning "mettle, spirit, liveliness", but the best synonym is the colloquial "guts".'

Robert MacLellan, best known as a playwright, has also written a number of stories. Much of his writing is in Scots dialect – which may seem difficult at first for those unfamiliar with it. 'The Mennans' is a funny and touching story, not to be excluded for its use of the unfamiliar dialect.

J. F. Hendry is, of course, my distinguished predecessor as editor of *The Penguin Book of Scottish Short Stories*. 'The Disinherited' is a splendid evocation of a Glasgow now gone, and a revealing picture of growing up in a deprived environment. Fred Urquhart, in 'Alicky's Watch', gives us an insight into life in an Edinburgh long vanished; Urquhart was born there, and has distinguished himself as a novelist and short-story writer.

Muriel Spark, also born in Edinburgh, has achieved international recognition as a novelist. Many of her novels blend real and supernatural in a manner which can be disturbing; 'The House of the Famous Poet' effectively draws together these two elements. The soldier of the story is gradually revealed as being not what he first appears. The setting is London during the last war.

Elspeth Davie has three novels and three collections of short stories to her credit. 'Pedestrian' comes from her collection *The Night of the Funny Hats* (1980). She demonstrates her concern and sympathy for the outsider in this story of a pedestrian who finds himself viewed with suspicion in a motorway café.

Ian Hamilton Finlay is better known for his drawings, sculptures and concrete poetry than for his short stories. 'The Money', like Gunn's 'The Tax-Gatherer', deals with a confrontation with bureaucracy, but of a completely different kind. Here we have the confusion of an honest artist wrestling with the problem of claiming unemployment benefit.

Iain Crichton Smith was born on the island of Lewis and has lived much of his life in Oban. He has shown himself to be a master of poetry, the novel and the short story. 'Survival Without Error' appeared in his first collection of short stories (as the story of the title), published in 1970. In it we meet a lawyer who, finding it impossible to come to terms with the mindless violence of two youths he is obliged to defend in court, is reminded of his own part in causing the suicide of an army colleague.

Many of the stories in this collection contain that characteristic Scottish element of the supernatural – ghosts, brownies, second-sight; it seems to be as much of an obsession in Scottish literature as that other preoccupation, Calvinistic guilt. To balance these darker aspects, there is a good deal of humour and sensitive observation of Scottish manners and morals. Fortunately the short story is still very much alive in Scotland. There are a number of writers today whose work would not be out of place in a collection of classic Scottish short stories – young writers like Alasdair Gray, Alex Hamilton, James Kelman, Alan Spence. I think they deserve a collection to themselves. This anthology may provide an inducement for the reader unfamiliar with Scottish writing to explore further. Scotland is fortunate in having a number of small publishers who are interested in encouraging young writers and who publish innovative work (often with the help of the Scottish Arts Council) which more conventional publishers would be afraid to risk.

ACKNOWLEDGEMENTS

For permission to reprint the stories specified we are indebted to:

Gerald Duckworth & Co. Ltd for 'Beattock for Moffat' from *Scottish Stories*.

The Rt. Hon. Lord Tweedsmuir, C.B.E., and William Blackwood Ltd for 'The Outgoing of the Tide'.

Dairmid Gunn, Esq. for 'The Tax-Gatherer'.

Charles Turner, Esq. for 'A Wee Nip'.

The author and the *Scots Magazine* for 'In the Family'.

A. D. Peters & Co. Ltd for 'Sealskin Trousers'.

Curtis Brown Ltd for 'Smeddum'.

The author for 'The Mennans'.

The author for 'The Disinherited'.

The author and Methuen London Ltd for 'Alicky's Watch'.

Harold Ober Associates Incorporated for 'The House of the Famous Poet'; © 1966, 1967 by Copyright Administration Ltd.

The author and Anthony Sheil Associates Ltd for 'Pedestrian' from *The Night of the Funny Hats and Other Stories*.

The author and Hogarth Press Ltd for 'The Wireless Set' from *A Time to Keep*.

The author for 'The Money'.

The author and Victor Gollancz Ltd for 'Survival Without Error' from *Survival Without Error and Other Stories*.

James Hogg

THE BROWNIE OF THE BLACK HAGGS

When the Sprots were Lairds of Wheelhope, which is now a long time ago, there was one of the ladies who was very badly spoken of in the country. People did not just openly assert that Lady Wheelhope (for every landward laird's wife was then styled Lady) was a witch, but every one had an aversion even at hearing her named; and when by chance she happened to be mentioned, old men would shake their heads and say, 'Ah! let us alane o' her! The less ye meddle wi' her the better.' Old wives would give over spinning, and, as a pretence for hearing what might be said about her, poke in the fire with the tongs, cocking up their ears all the while; and then, after some meaning coughs, hems, and haws, would haply say, 'Hech-wow, sirs! An a' be true that's said!' or something equally wise and decisive.

In short, Lady Wheelhope was accounted a very bad woman. She was an inexorable tyrant in her family, quarrelled with her servants, often cursing them, striking them, and turning them away, especially if they were religious, for she could not endure people of that character, but charged them with everything bad. Whenever she found out that any of the servant men of the laird's establishment were religious, she gave them up to the military and got them shot, and several girls that were regular in their devotions, she was supposed to have got rid of by poison. She was certainly a wicked woman, else many good people were mistaken in her character; and the poor persecuted Covenanters were obliged to unite in their prayers against her.

As for the laird, he was a big, dun-faced, pluffy body, that cared neither for good nor evil, and did not well know the one from the other. He laughed at his lady's tantrums and barley hoods; and the greater the rage that she got into, the laird thought it the better sport. One day, when two maid-servants came running to him, in great agitation, and told him that his lady had felled one of their companions, the laird laughed heartily, and said he did not doubt it.

'Why, sir, how can you laugh?' said they; 'the poor girl is killed.'

'Very likely, very likely,' said the laird. 'Well, it will teach her to take care who she angers again.'

'And, sir, your lady will be hanged.'

'Very likely; well, it will teach her how to strike so rashly again – Ha, ha, ha! Will it not, Jessy?'

But when this same Jessy died suddenly one morning, the laird was greatly confounded, and seemed dimly to comprehend that there had been unfair play going on. There was little doubt that she was taken off by poison, but whether the lady did it through jealousy or not was never divulged; but it greatly bamboozled and astonished the poor laird, for his nerves failed him, and his whole frame became paralytic. He seems to have been exactly in the same state of mind with a collie that I once had. He was extremely fond of the gun as long as I did not kill anything with it (there being no game laws in Ettrick Forest in those days), and he got a grand chase after the hares when I missed them. But there was one day that I chanced for a marvel to shoot one dead a few paces before his nose. I'll never forget the astonishment that the poor beast manifested. He stared one while at the gun, and another while at the dead hare, and seemed to be drawing the conclusion, that if the case stood thus, there was no creature sure of its life. Finally, he took his tail between his legs and ran away home, and never would face a gun all his life again.

So was it precisely with Laird Sprot of Wheelhope. As long as his lady's wrath produced only noise and uproar among the servants, he thought it fine sport; but when he saw what he believed the dreadful effects of it, he became like a barrel organ out of tune, and could only discourse one note, which he did to every one he met. 'I wish she mayna hae gotten something she had been the waur of.' This note he repeated early and late, night and day, sleeping and waking, alone and in company, from the moment that Jessy died till she was buried; and on going to the churchyard as chief mourner, he whispered it to her relatives by the way. When they came to the grave, he took his stand at the head, nor would he give place to the girl's father; but there he stood, like a huge post, as though he neither saw nor heard; and when he had lowered her head into the grave and dropped the cord, he slowly lifted his hat with one hand, wiped his dim eyes with the back of the other, and said, in a deep tremulous tone, 'Poor lassie! I wish she didna get something she had been the waur of.'

This death made a great noise among the common people; but there was little protection for the life of the subject in those days; and provided a man or woman was a real anti-Covenanter, they might kill a good many without being quarrelled for it. So there was no one to take cognizance of the circumstances relating to the death of poor Jessy.

After this the lady walked softly for the space of two or three years. She saw that she had rendered herself odious, and had entirely lost her husband's countenance, which she liked worst of all. But the evil propensity could not be overcome; and a poor boy, whom the laird out of sheer compassion had taken into his service, being found dead one morning, the country people could no longer be restrained; so they went in a body to the sheriff, and insisted on an investigation. It was proved that she detested the boy, had often threatened him, and had given him brose and butter the afternoon before he died; but notwithstanding of all this, the cause was ultimately dismissed, and the pursuers fined.

No one can tell to what height of wickedness she might now have proceeded, had not a check of a very singular kind been laid upon her. Among the servants that came home at the next term, was one who called himself Merodach, and a strange person he was. He had the form of a boy, but the features of one a hundred years old, save that his eyes had a brilliancy and restlessness which were very extraordinary, bearing a strong resemblance to the eyes of a well-known species of monkey. He was froward and perverse, and disregarded the pleasure or displeasure of any person; but he performed his work well, and with apparent ease. From the moment he entered the house, the lady conceived a mortal antipathy against him, and besought the laird to turn him away. But the laird would not consent; he never turned away any servant, and moreover he had hired this fellow for a trivial wage, and he neither wanted activity nor perseverance. The natural consequence of this refusal was, that the lady instantly set herself to embitter Merodach's life as much as possible, in order to get early quit of a domestic every way so disagreeable. Her hatred of him was not like a common antipathy entertained by one human being against another – she hated him as one might hate a toad or an adder, and his occupation of jotteryman (as the laird termed his servant of all work) keeping him always about her hand, it must have proved highly annoying.

She scolded him, she raged at him, but he only mocked her wrath, and giggled and laughed at her, with the most provoking derision. She tried to fell him again and again, but never, with all her address, could she hit him, and never did she make a blow at him that she did not repent it. She was heavy and unwieldy, and he as quick in his motions as a monkey; besides, he generally contrived that she should be in such an ungovernable rage, that when she flew at him, she hardly knew what she was doing. At one time she guided her blow towards him, and he at the same instant avoided it with such dexterity, that she knocked down the chief hind, or fore-man, and then Merodach giggled so heartily, that, lifting the kitchen poker, she threw it at him with a full design of knocking out his brains, but the missile only broke every article of crockery on the kitchen dresser.

She then hasted to the laird, crying bitterly, and telling him she would not suffer that wretch Merodach, as she called him, to stay another night in the family.

'Why, then, put him away, and trouble me no more about him,' said the laird.

'Put him away!' exclaimed she; 'I have already ordered him away a hundred times, and charged him never to let me see his horrible face again, but he only grins, and answers with some intolerable piece of impertinence.'

The pertinacity of the fellow amused the laird: his dim eyes turned upwards into his head with delight; he then looked two ways at once, turned round his back, and laughed till the tears ran down his dun cheeks, but he could only articulate, 'You're fitted now.'

The lady's agony of rage still increasing from this derision, she upbraided the laird bitterly, and said he was not worthy the name of man, if he did not turn away that pestilence, after the way he had abused her.

'Why, Shusy, my dear, what has he done to you?'

'What done to me! has he not caused me to knock down John Thomson? and I do not know if ever he will come to life again!'

'Have you felled your favourite, John Thomson?' said the laird, laughing more heartily than before; 'you might have done a worse deed than that.'

'And has he not broke every plate and dish on the whole dresser?' continued the lady, 'and for all this devastation, he only mocks at my displeasure – absolutely mocks me; and if you do not have him turned away, and hanged or shot for his deeds, you are not worthy the name of man.'

'Oh alack! What a devastation among the cheena metal!' said the laird, and calling on Merodach, he said, 'Tell me, thou evil Merodach of Babylon, how thou darest knock down thy lady's favourite servant, John Thomson?'

'Not I, your honour. It was my lady herself, who got into such a furious rage at me, that she mistook her man, and felled Mr Thomson, and the good man's skull is fractured.'

'That was very odd,' said the laird, chuckling; 'I do not comprehend it. But then, what set you on smashing all my lady's delft and cheena ware? That was a most infamous and provoking action.'

'It was she herself, your honour. Sorry would I be to break one dish belonging to the house. I take all the house servants to witness, that my lady smashed all the dishes with a poker, and now lays the blame on me!'

The laird turned his dim eyes on his lady, who was crying with vexation and rage, and seemed meditating another personal attack on the culprit, which he did not at all appear to shun, but rather to court. She, however, vented her wrath in threatenings of the most deep and desperate revenge, the creature all the while assuring her that she would be foiled, and that in all her encounters and contests with him, she would uniformly come to the worst: he was resolved to do his duty, and there before his master he defied her.

The laird thought more than he considered it prudent to reveal; he had little doubt that his wife would find some means of wreaking her vengeance on the object of her displeasure, and he shuddered when he recollected one who had taken 'something that she had been the waur of'.

In a word, the Lady of Wheelhope's inveterate malignity against this one object was like the rod of Moses, that swallowed up the rest of the serpents. All her wicked and evil propensities seemed to be superseded if not utterly absorbed by it. The rest of the family now lived in comparative peace and quietness, for early and late her malevolence was venting itself against the jottery-man, and against him alone. It was a delirium of hatred and vengeance, on which the whole bent and bias of her inclination was set. She could not stay from the creature's presence, or, in the intervals when absent from him, she spent her breath in curses and execrations, and then, not able to rest, she ran again to seek him, her eyes gleaming with the anticipated delights of vengeance, while, ever and anon, all the ridicule and the harm redounded on herself.

Was it not strange that she could not get quit of this sole annoyance of her life? One would have thought she easily might. But by this time there was nothing further from her wishes; she wanted vengeance, full, adequate, and delicious vengeance, on her audacious opponent. But he was a strange and terrible creature, and the means of retaliation constantly came, as it were, to his hand.

Bread and sweet milk was the only fare that Merodach cared for, and having bargained for that, he would not want it, though he often got it with a curse and with ill will. The lady having, upon one occasion, intentionally kept back his wonted allowance for some days, on the Sabbath morning following, she set him down a bowl of rich sweet milk, well drugged with a deadly poison, and then she lingered in a little ante-room to watch the success of her grand plot, and prevent any other creature from tasting of the potion. Merodach came in, and the housemaid said to him, 'There is your breakfast, creature.'

'Oho! my lady has been liberal this morning,' said he, 'but I am beforehand with her. Here, little Missie, you seem very hungry to-day; take you my breakfast.' And with that he set the beverage down to the lady's little favourite spaniel. It so happened that the lady's only son came at that instant into the ante-room seeking her, and teasing his mamma about something, which withdrew her attention from the hall-table for a space. When she looked again, and saw Missie lapping up the sweet milk, she burst from her hiding-place like a fury, screaming as if her head had been on fire, kicked the remainder of its contents against the wall, and lifting Missie in her bosom, retreated hastily, crying all the way.

'Ha, ha, ha; I have you now!' cried Merodach, as she vanished from the hall.

Poor Missie died immediately, and very privately; indeed, she would have died and been buried, and never one have seen her, save her mistress, had not Merodach, by a luck that never failed him, looked over the wall of the flower garden, just as his lady was laying her favourite in a grave of her own digging. She, not perceiving her tormentor, plied on at her task, apostrophizing the insensate little carcass. 'Ah! poor dear little creature, thou hast had a hard fortune, and hast drank of the bitter potion that was not intended for thee; but he shall drink it three times double for thy sake.'

'Is that little Missie?' said the eldritch voice of the jotteryman, close at the lady's ear. She uttered a loud scream, and sank down on the bank. 'Alack for poor Missie,' continued the creature, in a tone of mockery. 'My dear heart is sorry for Missie. What has befallen her? whose breakfast cup did she drink?'

'Hence with thee, fiend!' cried the lady; 'what right hast thou to intrude on thy mistress's privacy? Thy turn is coming yet, or may the nature of woman change within me!'

'It is changed already,' said the creature, grinning with delight; 'I have thee now, I have thee now! And were it not to show my superiority over thee, which I do every hour, I should soon see thee strapped like a mad cat or a worrying bratch. What wilt thou try next?'

'I will cut thy throat, and if I die for it, will rejoice in the deed – a deed of charity to all that dwell on the face of the earth.'

'I have warned thee before, dame, and I now warn thee again, that all thy mischief meditated against me will fall double on thine own head.'

'I want none of your warning, fiendish cur. Hence with your elvish face, and take care of yourself.'

It would be too disgusting and horrible to relate or read all the incidents that fell out between this unaccountable couple. Their enmity against each other had no end and no mitigation, and scarcely a single day passed over on which the lady's acts of malevolent ingenuity did not terminate fatally for some favourite article of her own. Scarcely was there a thing, animate or inanimate, on which she set a value, left to her, that was not destroyed; and yet scarcely one hour or minute could she remain absent from her tormentor, and all the while, it seems, solely for the purpose of tormenting him. While all the rest of the establishment enjoyed peace and quietness from the fury of their termagant dame, matters still grew worse and worse between the fascinated pair. The lady haunted the menial, in the same manner as the raven haunts the eagle – for a perpetual quarrel, though the former knows that in every encounter she is to come off the loser. Noises were heard on the stairs by night, and it was whispered among the servants, that the lady had been seeking Merodach's chamber, on some horrible intent. Several of them would have sworn that they had seen her passing and repassing on the stair after midnight, when all was quiet; but then, it was likewise well known that Merodach slept with well-fastened doors, and a companion in another bed in the same room, whose bed, too, was nearest the door. Nobody cared much what became of the jotteryman, for he was an unsocial and disagreeable person; but some one told him what they had seen, and hinted a suspicion of the lady's intent. But the creature only bit his upper lip, winked with his eyes, and said, 'She had better let that alone; she will be the first to rue that.'

Not long after this, to the horror of the family and the whole country side, the laird's only son was found murdered in his bed one morning, under circumstances that manifested the most fiendish cruelty and inveteracy on the part of his destroyer. As soon as the atrocious act was divulged, the lady fell into convulsions, and lost her reason; and happy had it been for her had she never recovered the use of it, for there was blood upon her hand, which she took no care to conceal, and there was little doubt that it was the blood of her own innocent and beloved boy, the sole heir and hope of the family.

This blow deprived the laird of all power of action; but the lady had a brother, a man of the law, who came and instantly proceeded to an investigation of this unaccountable murder. Before the sheriff arrived, the housekeeper took the lady's brother aside, and told him he had better not go on with the scrutiny, for she was sure the crime would be brought home to her unfortunate mistress; and after examining into several corroborative circumstances, and viewing the state of the raving maniac, with the blood on her hand and arm, he made the investigation a very short one, declaring the domestics all exculpated.

The laird attended his boy's funeral, and laid his head in the grave, but appeared exactly like a man walking in a trance, an automaton, without feelings or sensations, oftentimes gazing at the funeral procession, as on something he could not comprehend. And when the death-bell of the parish church fell a-tolling, as the corpse approached the kirk-stile, he cast a dim eye up towards the belfry, and said hastily, 'What, what's that? Och ay, we're just in time, just in time.' And often was he hammering over the name of 'Evil Merodach, king of Babylon', to himself. He seemed to have some far-fetched conception that his unaccountable jotteryman was in some way connected with the death of his only son and other lesser calamities, although the evidence in favour of Merodach's innocence was as usual quite decisive.

This grievous mistake of Lady Wheelhope can only be accounted for, by supposing her in a state of derangement, or rather under some evil influence over which she had no control, and to a person in such a state the mistake was not so very unnatural. The mansion-house of Wheelhope was old and irregular. The stair had four acute turns, and four landing-places, all the same. In the uppermost chamber slept the two domestics, Merodach in the bed farthest in, and in the chamber immediately below that, which was exactly similar, slept the young laird and his tutor, the former in the bed farthest in, and thus, in the turmoil of her wild and raging passions, her own hand made herself childless.

Merodach was expelled the family forthwith, but refused to accept of his wages, which the man of law pressed upon him, for fear of further mischief; but he went away in apparent sullenness and discontent, no one knowing whither.

When his dismissal was announced to the lady, who was watched day and night in her chamber, the news had such an effect on her, that her whole frame seemed electrified; the horrors of remorse vanished, and another passion, which I neither can comprehend nor define, took the sole possession of her distem-

pered spirit. 'He *must* not go! He *shall* not go!' she exclaimed.
'No, no, no; he shall not, he shall not, he shall not!' and then she
instantly set herself about making ready to follow him, uttering
all the while the most diabolical expressions, indicative of anticipated vengeance. 'Oh, could I but snap his nerves one by one,
and birl among his vitals! Could I but slice his heart off piece-
meal in small messes, and see his blood lopper, and bubble, and
spin away in purple slays; and then to see him grin, and grin, and
grin, and grin! Oh – oh – oh! How beautiful and grand a sight it
would be to see him grin, and grin, and grin!' And in such a style
would she run on for hours together.

She thought of nothing, she spake of nothing, but the discarded
jotteryman, whom most people now began to regard as a creature
that was 'not canny'. They had seen him eat, and drink, and work,
like other people; still he had that about him that was not like
other men. He was a boy in form, and an antediluvian in feature.
Some thought he was a mongrel, between a Jew and an ape, some
a wizard, some a kelpie, or a fairy, but most of all, that he was
really and truly a brownie. What he was I do not know, and
therefore will not pretend to say; but be that as it may, in spite of
locks and keys, watching and waking, the Lady of Wheelhope
soon made her escape, and eloped after him. The attendants,
indeed, would have made oath that she was carried away by some
invisible hand, for it was impossible, they said, that she could have
escaped on foot like other people; and this edition of the story
took in the country, but sensible people viewed the matter in
another light.

As for instance, when Wattie Blythe, the laird's old shepherd,
came in from the hill one morning, his wife Bessie thus accosted
him: 'His presence be about us, Wattie Blythe! have you heard
what has happened at the ha'? Things are aye turning waur and
waur there, and it looks like as if Providence had gi'en up our
laird's house to destruction. This grand estate maun now gang frae
the Sprots, for it has finished them.'

'Na, na, Bessie, it isna the estate that has finished the Sprots,
but the Sprots that hae finished the estate, and themsels into the
boot. They hae been a wicked and degenerate race, and aye the
langer the waur, till they hae reached the utmost bounds o' earthly
wickedness; and its time the deil were looking after his ain.'

'Ah, Wattie Blythe, ye never said a truer say. And that's just the very point where your story ends and mine begins; for hasna the deil, or the fairies, or the brownies ta'en away our leddy bodily! and the haill country is running and riding in search o' her, and there is twenty hunder merks offered to the first that can find her and bring her safe back. They hae ta'en her away skin and bane, body and soul and a', Wattie!'

'Hech-wow, but that is awesome! And where is it thought they have ta'en her to, Bessie?'

'Oh, they hae some guess at that frae her ain hints afore. It is thought they hae carried her after that Satan of a creature wha wrought sae muckle wae about the house. It is for him they are a' looking, for they ken weel that where they get the tane they will get the tither.'

'Whew! is that the gate o't, Bessie? Why, then, the awfu' story is nouther mair nor less than this, that the leddy has made a 'lopement, as they ca't, and run away after a blackguard jottery-man. Hech-wow! wae's me for human frailty! But that's just the gate. When aince the deil gets in the point o' his finger he will soon have in his haill hand. Ay, he wants but a hair to make a tether of ony day! I hae seen her a braw sonsy lass; but even then I feared she was devoted to destruction, for she aye mockit at religion, Bessie, and that's no a good mark of a young body. And she made a' its servants her enemies; and think you these good men's prayers were a' to blaw away i' the wind, and be nae mair regarded? Na, na, Bessie, my woman, take ye this mark baith o' our ain bairns and other folk's: – If ever ye see a young body that disregards the Sabbath, and makes a mock at the ordinances o' religion, ye will never see that body come to muckle good. A braw hand our leddy has made o' her gibes and jeers at religion, and her mockeries o' the poor persecuted hill-folk! – sunk down by degrees into the very dregs o' sin and misery! run away after a scullion!'

'Fy, fy, Wattie; how can ye say sae? It was weel kenn'd that she hatit him wi' a perfect and mortal hatred, and tried to make away wi' him mae ways nor ane.'

'Aha, Bessie, but nipping and scarting is Scots folk's wooing; and though it is but right that we suspend our judgements, there will naebody persuade me, if she be found alang wi' the creature, but that she has run away after him in the natural way, on her twa shanks, without help either frae fairy or brownie.'

'I'll never believe sic a thing of ony woman born, let be a leddy weel up in years.'

' 'Od help ye, Bessie! ye dinna ken the stretch o' corrupt nature. The best o' us, when left to oursels, are nae better than strayed sheep that will never find the way back to their ain pastures; and of a' things made o' mortal flesh a wicked woman is the warst.'

'Alack-a-day! we get the blame o' muckle that we little deserve. But, Wattie, keep ye a geyan sharp look-out about the cleuchs and the caves o' our Hope, for the leddy kens them a' geyan weel; and gin the twenty hunder merks wad come our way, it might gang a waur gate. It wad tocher a' our bonny lasses.'

'Ay, weel I wat, Bessie, that's nae lee. And now when ye bring me amind o't, I'm sair mistaen if I didna hear a creature up in the Brockholes this morning skirling as if something were cutting its throat. It gars a' the hairs stand on my head when I think it may hae been our leddy, and the droich of a creature murdering her. I took it for a battle of wulcats, and wished they might pu' out ane anither's thrapples; but when I think on it again, they were unco like some o' our leddy's unearthly screams.'

'His presence be about us, Wattie! Haste ye; pit on your bonnet, tak' your staff in your hand, and gang and see what it is.'

'Shame fa' me if I daur gang, Bessie.'

'Hout, Wattie, trust in the Lord.'

'Aweel, sae I do. But ane's no to throw himsel ower a linn, and trust that the Lord will kep him in a blanket. And its nae muckle safer for an auld stiff man like me to gang away out to a wild remote place, where there is ae body murdering another. – What is that I hear, Bessie? Haud the lang tongue o' you, and rin to the door and see what noise that is.'

Bessie ran to the door, but soon returned with her mouth wide open, and her eyes set in her head.

'It is them, Wattie! it is them! His presence be about us! What will we do?'

'Them! Whaten them?'

'Why, that blackguard creature coming here leading our leddy by the hair o' the head, and yerking her wi' a stick. I am terrified out o' my wits. What will we do?'

'We'll *see* what they *say*,' said Wattie, manifestly in as great terror as his wife; and by a natural impulse or as a last resource he opened the Bible, not knowing what he did, and then hurried on his spectacles; but before he got two leaves turned over, the two entered – a frightful-looking couple indeed. Merodach, with his old withered face and ferret eyes, leading the Lady of Wheelhope by the long hair, which was mixed with grey, and whose face was all bloated with wounds and bruises, and having stripes of blood on her garments.

'How's this! how's this, sirs?' said Wattie Blythe.

'Close that book and I will tell you, goodman,' said Merodach.

'I can hear what you hae to say wi' the beuk open, sir,' said Wattie, turning over the leaves, pretending to look for some particular passage, but apparently not knowing what he was doing. 'It is a shamefu' business this, but some will hae to answer for't. My leddy, I am unco grieved to see you in sic a plight. Ye hae surely been dooms sair left to yoursel.'

The lady shook her head, uttered a feeble hollow laugh, and fixed her eyes on Merodach. But such a look! It almost frightened the simple aged couple out of their senses. It was not a look of love nor of hatred exclusively, neither was it of desire or disgust, but it was a combination of them all. It was such a look as one fiend would cast on another in whose everlasting destruction he rejoiced. Wattie was glad to take his eyes from such countenances, and look into the Bible, that firm foundation of all his hopes and all his joy.

'I request that you will shut that book, sir,' said the horrible creature, 'or if you do not, I will shut it for you with a vengeance,' and with that he seized it, and flung it against the wall. Bessie uttered a scream, and Wattie was quite paralysed; and although he seemed disposed to run after his best friend, as he called it, the hellish looks of the brownie interposed, and glued him to his seat.

'Hear what I have to say first,' said the creature, 'and then pore your fill on that precious book of yours. One concern at a time is enough. I came to do you a service. Here, take this cursed, wretched woman, whom you style your lady, and deliver her up to the lawful authorities, to be restored to her husband and her place in society. She has followed one that hates her, and never said one kind word to her in his life; and though I have beat her like a dog, still she clings to me, and will not depart, so enchanted is she with the laudable purpose of cutting my throat. Tell your master and her brother that I am not to be burdened with their maniac. I have scourged, I have spurned and kicked her, afflicting her night and day, and yet from my side she will not depart. Take her; claim the reward in full, and your fortune is made; and so farewell!'

The creature went away, and the moment his back was turned, the lady fell a-screaming and struggling, like one in an agony, and, in spite of all the couple's exertions, she forced herself out of their hands, and ran after the retreating Merodach. When he saw better would not be, he turned upon her, and, by one blow with his stick, struck her down; and, not content with that, continued to maltreat her in such a manner, as to all appearance would have killed twenty ordinary persons. The poor devoted dame could do nothing but now and then utter a squeak like a half-worried cat, and writhe and grovel on the sward, till Wattie and his wife came up, and withheld her tormentor from further violence. He then bound her hands behind her back with a strong cord, and delivered her once more to the charge of the old couple, who contrived to hold her by that means, and take her home.

Wattie was ashamed to take her into the hall, but led her into one of the out-houses, whither he brought her brother to receive her. The man of the law was manifestly vexed at her reappearance, and scrupled not to testify his dissatisfaction; for when Wattie told him how the wretch had abused his sister, and that, had it not been for Bessie's interference and his own, the lady would have been killed outright, he said, 'Why, Walter, it is a great pity that he did *not* kill her outright. What good can her life now do to her, or of what value is her life to any creature living? After one has lived to disgrace all connected with them, the sooner they are taken off the better.'

The man, however, paid old Walter down his two thousand merks, a great fortune for one like him in those days; and not to dwell longer on this unnatural story, I shall only add, very shortly, that the Lady of Wheelhope soon made her escape once more, and flew, as if drawn by an irresistible charm, to her tormentor. Her friends looked no more after her; and the last time she was seen alive, it was following the uncouth creature up the water of Daur, weary, wounded, and lame, while he was all the way beating her, as a piece of excellent amusement. A few days after that, her body was found among some wild haggs, in a place called Crook-burn, by a party of the persecuted Covenanters that were in hiding there, some of the very men whom she had exerted herself to destroy, and who had been driven, like David of old, to pray for a curse and earthly punishment upon her. They buried her like a dog at the Yetts of Keppel, and rolled three huge stones upon her grave, which are lying there to this day. When they found her corpse, it was mangled and wounded in a most shocking manner, the fiendish creature having manifestly tormented her to death. He was never more seen or heard of in this kingdom, though all that country side was kept in terror for him many years afterwards; and to this day, they will tell you of THE BROWNIE OF THE BLACK HAGGS, which title he seems to have acquired after his disappearance.

This story was told to me by an old man named Adam Halliday, whose great-grandfather, Thomas Halliday, was one of those that found the body and buried it. It is many years since I heard it; but, however ridiculous it may appear, I remember it made a dreadful impression on my young mind. I never heard any story like it, save one of an old fox-hound that pursued a fox through the Grampians for a fortnight, and when at last discovered by the Duke of Athole's people, neither of them could run, but the hound was still continuing to walk after the fox, and when the latter lay down, the other lay down beside him, and looked at him steadily all the while, though unable to do him the least harm. The passion of inveterate malice seems to have influenced these two exactly alike. But, upon the whole, I can scarcely believe the tale can be true.

Sir Walter Scott

THE TWO DROVERS

CHAPTER I

It was the day after Doune Fair when my story commences. It had
been a brisk market; several dealers had attended from the
northern and midland counties in England, and English money
had flown so merrily about as to gladden the hearts of the
Highland farmers. Many large droves were about to set off for
England, under the protection of their owners, or of the topsmen
whom they employed in the tedious, laborious, and responsible
office of driving the cattle for many hundred miles, from the
market where they had been purchased, to the fields or farm-
yards where they were to be fattened for the shambles.

The Highlanders, in particular, are masters of this difficult
trade of driving, which seems to suit them as well as the trade of
war. It affords exercise for all their habits of patient endurance
and active exertion. They are required to know perfectly the
drove-roads, which lie over the wildest tracts of the country, and
to avoid as much as possible the highways, which distress the feet
of the bullocks, and the turnpikes, which annoy the spirit of the
drover; whereas, on the broad green or grey track, which leads
across the pathless moor, the herd not only move at ease and
without taxation, but, if they mind their business, may pick up a
mouthful of food by the way. At night, the drovers usually sleep
along with their cattle, let the weather be what it will; and many of
these hardy men do not once rest under a roof during a journey on
foot from Lochaber to Lincolnshire. They are paid very highly,
for the trust reposed is of the last importance, as it depends on
their prudence, vigilance, and honesty, whether the cattle reach
the final market in good order, and afford a profit to the grazier.

But as they maintain themselves at their own expense, they are especially economical in that particular. At the period we speak of, a Highland drover was victualled for his long and toilsome journey with a few handfuls of oatmeal, and two or three onions, renewed from time to time, and a ram's horn filled with whisky, which he used regularly, but sparingly, every night and morning. His dirk, or *skene-dhu* (i.e. black-knife), so worn as to be concealed beneath the arm, or by the folds of the plaid, was his only weapon, excepting the cudgel with which he directed the movements of the cattle. A Highlander was never so happy as on these occasions. There was a variety in the whole journey, which exercised the Celt's natural curiosity and love of motion; there were the constant change of place and scene, the petty adventures incidental to the traffic, and the intercourse with the various farmers, graziers, and traders, intermingled with occasional merrymakings, not the less acceptable to Donald that they were void of expense; – and there was the consciousness of superior skill; for the Highlander, a child amongst flocks, is a prince amongst herds, and his natural habits induce him to disdain the shepherd's slothful life, so that he feels himself nowhere more at home than when following a gallant drove of his country cattle in the character of their guardian.

Of the number who left Doune in the morning, and with the purpose we described, not a *Glunamie* of them all cocked his bonnet more briskly, or gartered his tartan hose under knee over a pair of more promising *spiogs* (legs) than did Robin Oig M'Combich, called familiarly Robin Oig, that is, Young, or the Lesser, Robin. Though small of stature as the epithet Oig implies, and not very strongly limbed, he was as light and alert as one of the deer of his mountains. He had an elasticity of step which, in the course of a long march, made many a stout fellow envy him; and the manner in which he busked his plaid and adjusted his bonnet, argued a consciousness that so smart a John Highlandman as himself would not pass unnoticed among the Lowland lasses. The ruddy cheek, red lips, and white teeth, set off a countenance which had gained by exposure to the weather a healthful and hardy rather than a rugged hue. If Robin Oig did not laugh, or even smile frequently, as indeed is not the practice among his countrymen, his bright eyes usually gleamed from under his bonnet with an expression of cheerfulness ready to be turned into mirth.

The departure of Robin Oig was an incident in the little town, in and near which he had many friends, male and female. He was a topping person in his way, transacted considerable business on his own behalf, and was entrusted by the best farmers in the Highlands in preference to any other drover in that district. He might have increased his business to any extent had he condescended to manage it by deputy; but except a lad or two, sister's sons of his own, Robin rejected the idea of assistance, conscious, perhaps, how much his reputation depended upon his attending in person to the practical discharge of his duty in every instance. He remained, therefore, contented with the highest premium given to persons of his description, and comforted himself with the hopes that a few journeys to England might enable him to conduct business on his own account, in a manner becoming his birth. For Robin Oig's father, Lachlan M'Combich (or *son of my friend*, his actual clan-surname being M'Gregor), had been so called by the celebrated Rob Roy, because of the particular friendship which had subsisted between the grandsire of Robin and that renowned cateran. Some people even say that Robin Oig derived his Christian name from one as renowned in the wilds of Loch Lomond as ever was his namesake Robin Hood, in the precincts of merry Sherwood. 'Of such ancestry,' as James Boswell says, 'who would not be proud?' Robin Oig was proud accordingly; but his frequent visits to England and to the Lowlands had given him tact enough to know that pretensions, which still gave him a little right to distinction in his own lonely glen, might be both obnoxious and ridiculous if preferred elsewhere. The pride of birth, therefore, was like the miser's treasure, the secret subject of his contemplation, but never exhibited to strangers as a subject of boasting.

Many were the words of gratulation and good luck which were bestowed on Robin Oig. The judges commended his drove, especially Robin's own property, which were the best of them. Some thrust out their snuff-mulls for the parting pinch – others tendered the *doch-an-dorrach* or parting cup. All cried – 'Good luck travel out with you and come home with you. – Give you luck in the Saxon market – brave notes in the *leabhar-dhu*' (black pocket-book) 'and plenty of English gold in the *sporran*' (pouch of goatskin).

The bonny lasses made their adieus more modestly, and more than one, it was said, would have given her best brooch to be certain that it was upon her that his eye last rested as he turned towards the road.

Robin Oig had just given the preliminary '*Hoo-hoo!*' to urge forward the loiterers of the drove, when there was a cry behind him.

'Stay, Robin – bide a blink. Here is Janet of Tomahourich – auld Janet, your father's sister.'

'Plague on her, for an auld Highland witch and spaewife,' said a farmer from the Carse of Stirling; 'she'll cast some of her cantrips on the cattle.'

'She canna do that,' said another sapient of the same profession – 'Robin Oig is no the lad to leave any of them without tying St Mungo's knot on their tails, and that will put to her speed the best witch that ever flew over Dimayet upon a broomstick.'

It may not be indifferent to the reader to know that the Highland cattle are peculiarly liable to be *taken*, or infected, by spells and witchcraft; which judicious people guard against by knitting knots of peculiar complexity on the tuft of hair which terminates the animal's tail.

But the old woman who was the object of the farmer's suspicion seemed only busied about the drover, without paying any attention to the drove. Robin, on the contrary, appeared rather impatient of her presence.

'What auld-world fancy,' he said, 'has brought you so early from the ingle-side this morning, Muhme? I am sure I bid you good-even, and had your God-speed, last night.'

'And left me more siller than the useless old woman will use till you come back again, bird of my bosom,' said the sibyl. 'But it is little I would care for the food that nourishes me, or the fire that warms me, or for God's blessed sun itself, if aught but weel should happen to the grandson of my father. So let me walk the *deasil* round you, that you may go safe out into the foreign land, and come safe home.'

Robin Oig stopped, half embarrassed, half laughing, and signing to those near that he only complied with the old woman to soothe her humour. In the meantime she traced around him, with wavering steps, the propitiation, which some have thought hàs beèn derived from the Druidical mythology. It consists, as is well known, in the person who makes the *deasil* walking three times round the person who is the object of the ceremony, taking care to move according to the course of the sun. At once, however, she stopped short, and exclaimed, in a voice of alarm and horror, 'Grandson of my father, there is blood on your hand.'

'Hush, for God's sake, aunt,' said Robin Oig; 'you will bring more trouble on yourself with this *taishataragh*' (second sight) 'than you will be able to get out of for many a day.'

The old woman only repeated, with a ghastly look, 'There is blood on your hand, and it is English blood. The blood of the Gael is richer and redder. Let us see – let us –'

Ere Robin Oig could prevent her, which, indeed, could only have been done by positive violence, so hasty and peremptory were her proceedings, she had drawn from his side the dirk which lodged in the folds of his plaid, and held it up, exclaiming, although the weapon gleamed clear and bright in the sun, 'Blood, blood – Saxon blood again. Robin Oig M'Combich, go not this day to England!'

'Prutt trutt,' answered Robin Oig, 'that will never do neither – it would be next thing to running the country. For shame, Muhme – give me the dirk. You cannot tell by the colour the difference betwixt the blood of a black bullock and a white one, and you speak of knowing Saxon from Gaelic blood. All men have their blood from Adam, Muhme. Give me my skene-dhu, and let me go on my road. I should have been half-way to Stirling Brig by this time. – Give me my dirk, and let me go.'

'Never will I give it to you,' said the old woman – 'Never will I quit my hold on your plaid, unless you promise me not to wear that unhappy weapon.'

The women around him urged him also, saying few of his aunt's words fell to the ground; and as the Lowland farmers continued to look moodily on the scene, Robin Oig determined to close it at any sacrifice.

'Well, then,' said the young drover, giving the scabbard of the weapon to Hugh Morrison, 'you Lowlanders care nothing for these freats. Keep my dirk for me. I cannot give it to you, because it was my father's; but your drove follows ours, and I am content it should be in your keeping, not in mine. – Will this do, Muhme?'

'It must,' said the old woman – 'that is, if the Lowlander is mad enough to carry the knife.'

The strong westlandman laughed aloud.

'Goodwife,' said he, 'I am Hugh Morrison from Glenae, come of the Manly Morrisons of auld langsyne, that never took short weapon against a man in their lives. And neither needed they. They had their broadswords, and I have this bit supple,' showing a formidable cudgel – 'for dirking ower the board, I leave that to John Highlandman – Ye needna snort, none of you Highlanders, and you in especial, Robin. I'll keep the bit knife, if you are feared for the auld spaewife's tale, and give it back to you whenever you want it.'

Robin was not particularly pleased with some part of Hugh Morrison's speech; but he had learned in his travels more patience than belonged to his Highland constitution originally, and he accepted the service of the descendant of the Manly Morrisons without finding fault with the rather depreciating manner in which it was offered.

'If he had not had his morning in his head, and been but a Dumfriesshire hog into the boot, he would have spoken more like a gentleman. But you cannot have more of a sow than a grumph. It's shame my father's knife should ever slash a haggis for the like of him.'

Thus saying (but saying it in Gaelic) Robin drove on his cattle, and waved farewell to all behind him. He was in the greater haste, because he expected to join at Falkirk a comrade and brother in profession, with whom he proposed to travel in company.

Robin Oig's chosen friend was a young Englishman, Harry Wakefield by name, well known at every northern market, and in his way as much famed and honoured as our Highland driver of bullocks. He was nearly six feet high, gallantly formed to keep the rounds at Smithfield, or maintain the ring at a wrestling match; and although he might have been overmatched, perhaps, among the regular professors of the Fancy, yet, as a yokel, or rustic, or a chance customer, he was able to give a bellyful to any amateur of the pugilistic art. Doncaster races saw him in his glory, betting his guinea, and generally successfully; nor was there a main fought in

Yorkshire, the feeders being persons of celebrity, at which he was not to be seen, if business permitted. But though a *sprack* lad, and fond of pleasure and its haunts, Harry Wakefield was steady, and not the cautious Robin Oig M'Combich himself was more attentive to the main chance. His holidays were holidays indeed; but his days of work were dedicated to steady and persevering labour. In countenance and temper, Wakefield was the model of old England's merry yeomen, whose clothyard shafts, in so many hundred battles, asserted her superiority over the nations, and whose good sabres in our own time are her cheapest and most assured defence. His mirth was readily excited; for, strong in limb and constitution, and fortunate in circumstances, he was disposed to be pleased with everything about him; and such difficulties as he might occasionally encounter were, to a man of his energy, rather matter of amusement than serious annoyance. With all the merits of a sanguine temper, our young English drover was not without his defects. He was irascible, sometimes to the verge of being quarrelsome; and perhaps not the less inclined to bring his disputes to a pugilistic decision, because he found few antagonists able to stand up to him in the boxing ring.

It is difficult to say how Harry Wakefield and Robin Oig first became intimates; but it is certain a close acquaintance had taken place betwixt them, although they had apparently few common subjects of conversation or of interest, so soon as their talk ceased to be of bullocks. Robin Oig, indeed, spoke the English language rather imperfectly upon any other topics but stots and kyloes, and Harry Wakefield could never bring his broad Yorkshire tongue to utter a single word of Gaelic. It was in vain Robin spent a whole morning, during a walk over Minch Moor, in attempting to teach his companion to utter, with true precision, the shibboleth *Llhu*, which is the Gaelic for a calf. From Traquair to Murdercairn, the hill rang with the discordant attempts of the Saxon upon the unmanageable monosyllable, and the heartfelt laugh which followed every failure. They had, however, better modes of awakening the echoes; for Wakefield could sing many a ditty to the praise of Moll, Susan, and Cicely, and Robin Oig had a particular gift at whistling interminable pibrochs through all their involutions, and what was more agreeable to his companion's southern ear, knew many of the northern airs, both lively and pathetic, to which

Wakefield learned to pipe a bass. This, though Robin could hardly have comprehended his companion's stories about horse-racing, and cock-fighting or fox-hunting, and although his own legends of clan-fights and *creaghs*, varied with talk of Highland goblins and fairy folk, would have been caviare to his companion, they contrived nevertheless to find a degree of pleasure in each other's company, which had for three years back induced them to join company and travel together, when the direction of their journey permitted. Each, indeed, found his advantage in this companionship; for where could the Englishman have found a guide through the Western Highlands like Robin Oig M'Combich? and when they were on what Harry called the *right* side of the Border, his patronage, which was extensive, and his purse, which was heavy, were at all times at the service of his Highland friend, and on many occasions his liberality did him genuine yeoman's service.

CHAPTER II

Were ever two such loving friends! –
How could they disagree?
Oh thus it was, he loved him dear,
And thought how to requite him,
And having no friend left but he,
He did resolve to fight him.
Duke upon Duke

The pair of friends had traversed with their usual cordiality the grassy wilds of Liddesdale, and crossed the opposite part of Cumberland, emphatically called The Waste. In these solitary regions, the cattle under the charge of our drovers derived their subsistence chiefly by picking their food as they went along the drove-road, or sometimes by the tempting opportunity of a *start and owerloup*, or invasion of the neighbouring pasture, where an occasion presented itself. But now the scene changed before them; they were descending towards a fertile and enclosed country, where no such liberties could be taken with impunity, or without a previous arrangement and bargain with the possessors of the ground. This was more especially the case, as a great northern fair was upon the eve of taking place, where both the Scotch and English drover expected to dispose of a part of their cattle, which it was desirable to produce in the market, rested and in good order. Fields were therefore difficult to be obtained, and only upon high terms. This necessity occasioned a temporary separation betwixt the two friends, who went to bargain, each as he could, for the separate accommodation of his herd. Unhappily it chanced that both of them, unknown to each other, thought of bargaining for the ground they wanted on the property of a country gentleman of some fortune, whose estate lay in the neighbourhood. The English drover applied to the bailiff on the property, who was known to him. It chanced that the Cumbrian squire, who had entertained some suspicions of his manager's honesty, was taking occasional measures to ascertain how far they were well founded, and had desired that any inquiries about his enclosures, with a view to occupy them for a temporary purpose, should be referred to himself. As, however, Mr Ireby had gone the day before upon a journey of some miles' distance to the northward, the bailiff chose to consider the check upon his full powers as for the time removed, and concluded that he should best consult his master's interest, and perhaps his own, in making an agreement with Harry Wakefield. Meanwhile, ignorant of what his comrade was doing, Robin Oig, on his side, chanced to be overtaken by a good-looking smart little man upon a pony, most knowingly hogged and cropped, as was then the fashion, the rider wearing tight leather breeches and long-necked bright spurs. This cavalier asked one or two pertinent questions about markets and the price of stock. So Robin, seeing him a well-judging civil gentleman, took the freedom to ask him whether he could let him know if there was any grass-land to be let in that neighbourhood, for the temporary accommodation of his drove. He could not have put the question to more willing ears. The gentleman of the buckskin was the proprietor with whose bailiff Harry Wakefield had dealt or was in the act of dealing.

'Thou art in good luck, my canny Scot,' said Mr Ireby, 'to have spoken to me, for I see thy cattle have done their day's work, and I have at my disposal the only field within three miles that is to be let in these parts.'

'The drove can pe gang two, three, four miles very pratty weel indeed,' said the cautious Highlander; 'put what would his honour be axing for the peasts pe the head, if she was to tak the park for twa or three days?'

'We won't differ, Sawney, if you let me have six stots for winterers, in the way of reason.'

'And which peasts wad your honour pe for having?'

'Why – let me see – the two black – the dun one – yon doddy – him with the twisted horn – the brocket – How much by the head?'

'Ah,' said Robin, 'your honour is a shudge – a real shudge – I couldna have set off the pest six peasts petter mysell, me that ken them as if they were my pairns, puir things.'

'Well, how much per head, Sawney?' continued Mr Ireby.

'It was high markets at Doune and Falkirk,' answered Robin.

And thus the conversation proceeded, until they had agreed on the *prix juste* for the bullocks, the squire throwing in the temporary accommodation of the enclosure for the cattle into the boot, and Robin making, as he thought, a very good bargain, provided the grass was but tolerable. The squire walked his pony alongside of the drove, partly to show him the way, and see him put into possession of the field, and partly to learn the latest news of the northern markets.

They arrived at the field, and the pasture seemed excellent. But what was their surprise when they saw the bailiff quietly inducting the cattle of Harry Wakefield into the grassy Goshen which had just been assigned to those of Robin Oig M'Combich by the proprietor himself! Squire Ireby set spurs to his horse, dashed up to his servant, and learning what had passed between the parties, briefly informed the English drover that his bailiff had let the ground without his authority, and that he might seek grass for his cattle wherever he would, since he was to get none there. At the same time he rebuked his servant severely for having transgressed his commands, and ordered him instantly to assist in ejecting the hungry and weary cattle of Harry Wakefield, which were just beginning to enjoy a meal of unusual plenty, and to introduce those of his comrade, whom the English drover now began to consider as a rival.

The feelings which arose in Wakefield's mind would have induced him to resist Mr Ireby's decision; but every Englishman has a tolerably accurate sense of law and justice, and John Fleecebumpkin, the bailiff, having acknowledged that he had exceeded his commission, Wakefield saw nothing else for it than to collect his hungry and disappointed charge, and drive them on to seek quarters elsewhere. Robin Oig saw what had happened with regret, and hastened to offer to his English friend to share with him the disputed possession. But Wakefield's pride was severely hurt, and he answered disdainfully, 'Take it all, man – take it all – never make two bites of a cherry – thou canst talk over the gentry, and blear a plain man's eye – Out upon you, man – I would not kiss any man's dirty latchets for leave to bake in his oven.'

Robin Oig, sorry but not surprised at his comrade's displeasure, hastened to entreat his friend to wait but an hour till he had gone to the squire's house to receive payment for the cattle he had sold, and he would come back and help him to drive the cattle into some convenient place of rest, and explain to him the whole mistake they had both of them fallen into. But the Englishman continued indignant: 'Thou hast been selling, hast thou? Aye, aye, – thou is a cunning lad for kenning the hours of bargaining. Go to the devil with thyself, for I will ne'er see thy fause loon's visage again – thou should be ashamed to look me in the face.'

'I am ashamed to look no man in the face,' said Robin Oig, something moved; 'and, moreover, I will look you in the face this blessed day, if you will bide at the clachan down yonder.'

'Mayhap you had as well keep away,' said his comrade; and turning his back on his former friend, he collected his unwilling associates, assisted by the bailiff, who took some real and some affected interest in seeing Wakefield accommodated.

After spending some time in negotiating with more than one of the neighbouring farmers, who could not, or would not, afford the accommodation desired, Henry Wakefield at last, and in his necessity, accomplished his point by means of the landlord of the alehouse at which Robin Oig and he had agreed to pass the night, when they first separated from each other. Mine host was content to let him turn his cattle on a piece of barren moor, at a price little less than the bailiff had asked for the disputed enclosure; and the wretchedness of the pasture, as well as the price paid for it, were set down as exaggerations of the breach of faith and friendship of his Scottish crony. This turn of Wakefield's passions was encouraged by the bailiff (who had his own reasons for being offended against poor Robin, as having been the unwitting cause of his falling into disgrace with his master), as well as by the innkeeper, and two or three chance guests, who stimulated the drover in his resentment against his quondam associate, – some from the ancient grudge against the Scots which, when it exists anywhere, is to be found lurking in the Border counties, and some from the general love of mischief, which characterizes mankind in all ranks of life, to the honour of Adam's children be it spoken. Good John Barleycorn also, who always heightens and exaggerates the prevailing passions, be they angry or kindly, was not wanting in his offices on this occasion; and confusion to false friends and hard masters was pledged in more than one tankard.

In the meanwhile Mr Ireby found some amusement in detaining the northern drover at his ancient hall. He caused a cold round of beef to be placed before the Scot in the butler's pantry, together with a foaming tankard of home-brewed, and took pleasure in seeing the hearty appetite with which these unwonted edibles were discussed by Robin Oig M'Combich. The squire himself lighting his pipe, compounded between his patrician dignity and his love of agricultural gossip, by walking up and down while he conversed with his guest.

'I passed another drove,' said the squire, 'with one of your countrymen behind them – they were something less beasts than your drove, doddies most of them – a big man was with them – none of your kilts though, but a decent pair of breeches – D'ye know who he may be?'

'Hout aye – that might, could, and would be Hughie Morrison – I didna think he could hae peen sae weel up. He has made a day on us; but his Argyleshires will have wearied shanks. How far was he pehind?'

'I think about six or seven miles,' answered the squire, 'for I passed them at the Christenbury Crag, and I overtook you at the Hollan Bush. If his beasts be leg-weary, he will maybe be selling bargains.'

'Na, na, Hughie Morrison is no the man for pargains – ye maun come to some Highland body like Robin Oig hersell for the like of these – put I maun pe wishing you goot night, and twenty of them let alane ane, and I maun down to the clachan to see if the lad Harry Waakfelt is out of his humdudgeons yet.'

The party at the alehouse were still in full talk, and the treachery of Robin Oig still the theme of conversation, when the supposed culprit entered the apartment. His arrival, as usually happens in such a case, put an instant stop to the discussion of which he had furnished the subject, and he was received by the company assembled with that chilling silence which, more than a thousand exclamations, tells an intruder that he is unwelcome. Surprised and offended, but not appalled by the reception which he experienced, Robin entered with an undaunted and even a haughty air, attempted no greeting as he saw he was received with none, and placed himself by the side of the fire, a little apart from a table at which Harry Wakefield, the bailiff, and two or three other persons were seated. The ample Cumbrian kitchen would have afforded plenty of room, even for a larger separation.

Robin, thus seated, proceeded to light his pipe, and call for a pint of twopenny.

'We have no twopence ale,' answered Ralph Heskett, the landlord; 'but as thou findest thy own tobacco, it's like thou mayest find thy own liquor too – it's the wont of thy country, I wot.'

'Shame, goodman,' said the landlady, a blithe bustling housewife, hastening herself to supply the guest with liquor – 'Thou knowest well enow what the strange man wants, and it's thy trade to be civil, man. Thou shouldst know, that if the Scot likes a small pot, he pays a sure penny.'

Without taking any notice of this nuptial dialogue, the Highlander took the flagon in his hand, and addressing the company generally, drank the interesting toast of 'Good markets' to the party assembled.

'The better that the wind blew fewer dealers from the north,' said one of the farmers, 'and fewer Highland runts to eat up the English meadows.'

'Saul of my pody, put you are wrang there, my friend,' answered Robin, with composure, 'it is your fat Englishmen that eat up our Scots cattle, puir things.'

'I wish there was a summat to eat up their drovers,' said another; 'a plain Englishman canna make bread within a kenning of them.'

'Or an honest servant keep his master's favour, but they will come sliding in between him and the sunshine,' said the bailiff.

'If these pe jokes,' said Robin Oig, with the same composure, 'there is ower mony jokes upon one man.'

'It is no joke, but downright earnest,' said the bailiff. 'Harkye, Mr Robin Ogg, or whatever is your name, it's right we should tell you that we are all of one opinion, and that is that you, Mr Robin Ogg, have behaved to our friend Mr Harry Wakefield here, like a raff and a blackguard.'

'Nae doubt, nae doubt,' answered Robin, with great composure; 'and you are a set of very pretty judges, for whose prains or pehaviour I wad not gie a pinch of sneeshing. If Mr Harry Waakfelt kens where he is wranged, he kens where he may be righted.'

'He speaks truth,' said Wakefield, who had listened to what passed, divided between the offence which he had taken at Robin's late behaviour, and the revival of his habitual feelings of regard.

He now arose, and went towards Robin, who got up from his seat as he approached, and held out his hand.

'That's right, Harry – go it – serve him out,' resounded on all sides – 'tip him the nailer – show him the mill.'

'Hold your peace all of you, and be –' said Wakefield; and then addressing his comrade, he took him by the extended hand, with something alike of respect and defiance. 'Robin,' he said, 'thou hast used me ill enough this day; but if you mean, like a frank fellow, to shake hands, and make a tussle for love on the sod, why I'll forgie thee, man, and we shall be better friends than ever.'

'And would it not pe petter to pe cood friends without more of the matter?' said Robin; 'we will be much petter friendships with our panes hale than proken.'

Harry Wakefield dropped the hand of his friend, or rather threw it from him.

'I did not think I had been keeping company for three years with a coward.'

'Coward pelongs to none of my name,' said Robin, whose eyes began to kindle, but keeping the command of his temper. 'It was no coward's legs or hands, Harry Waakfelt, that drew you out of the fords of Frew, when you was drifting ower the plack rock, and every eel in the river expected his share of you.'

'And that is true enough, too,' said the Englishman, struck by the appeal.

'Adzooks!' exclaimed the bailiff – 'sure Harry Wakefield, the nattiest lad at Whitson Tryste, Wooler Fair, Carlisle Sands, or Stagshaw Bank, is not going to show white feather? Ah, this comes of living so long with kilts and bonnets – men forget the use of their daddles.'

'I may teach you, Master Fleecebumpkin, that I have not lost the use of mine,' said Wakefield, and then went on. 'This will never do, Robin. We must have a turn-up, or we shall be the talk of the country-side. I'll be d—d if I hurt thee – I'll put on the gloves gin thou like. Come, stand forward like a man.'

'To pe peaten like a dog,' said Robin; 'is there any reason in that? If you think I have done you wrong, I'll go before your shudge, though I neither know his law nor his language.'

A general cry of 'No, no – no law, no lawyer! a bellyful and be friends,' was echoed by the bystanders.

'But,' continued Robin, 'if I am to fight, I've no skill to fight like a jackanapes, with hands and nails.'

'How would you fight, then?' said his antagonist; 'though I am thinking it would be hard to bring you to the scratch anyhow.'

'I would fight with proadswords, and sink point on the first plood drawn, like a gentlemans.'

A loud shout of laughter followed the proposal, which indeed had rather escaped from poor Robin's swelling heart, than been the dictate of his sober judgement.

'Gentleman, quotha!' was echoed on all sides, with a shout of unextinguishable laughter; 'a very pretty gentleman, God wot – Canst get two swords for the gentlemen to fight with, Ralph Heskett?'

'No, but I can send to the armoury at Carlisle, and lend them two forks, to be making shift with in the meantime.'

'Tush, man,' said another, 'the bonny Scots come into the world with the blue bonnet on their heads, and dirk and pistol at their belt.'

'Best send post', said Mr Fleecebumpkin, 'to the squire of Corby Castle, to come and stand second to the *gentleman*.'

In the midst of this torrent of general ridicule, the Highlander instinctively griped beneath the folds of his plaid.

'But it's better not,' he said in his own language. 'A hundred curses on the swine-eaters, who know neither decency nor civility!'

'Make room, the pack of you,' he said, advancing to the door.

But his former friend interposed his sturdy bulk, and opposed his leaving the house; and when Robin Oig attempted to make his way by force, he hit him down on the floor, with as much ease as a boy bowls down a nine-pin.

'A ring, a ring!' was now shouted, until the dark rafters, and the hams that hung on them, trembled again, and the very platters on the *bink* clattered against each other. 'Well done, Harry,' – 'Give it him home, Harry,' – 'Take care of him now, – he sees his own blood!'

Such were the exclamations, while the Highlander, starting from the ground, all his coldness and caution lost in frantic rage, sprang at his antagonist with the fury, the activity, and the vindictive purpose of an incensed tiger-cat. But when could rage encounter science and temper? Robin Oig again went down in the unequal contest; and as the blow was necessarily a severe one, he lay motionless on the floor of the kitchen. The landlady ran to offer some aid, but Mr Fleecebumpkin would not permit her to approach.

'Let him alone,' he said, 'he will come to within time, and come up to the scratch again. He has not got half his broth yet.'

'He has got all I mean to give him, though,' said his antagonist, whose heart began to relent towards his old associate; 'and I would rather by half give the rest to yourself, Mr Fleecebumpkin, for you pretend to know a thing or two, and Robin had not art enough even to peel before setting to, but fought with his plaid dangling about him. – Stand up, Robin, my man! all friends now; and let me hear the man that will speak a word against you, or your country, for your sake.'

Robin Oig was still under the dominion of his passion, and eager to renew the onset; but being withheld on the one side by the peace-making Dame Heskett, and on the other, aware that Wakefield no longer meant to renew the combat, his fury sank into gloomy sullenness.

'Come, come, never grudge so much at it, man,' said the brave-spirited Englishman, with the placability of his country, 'shake hands, and we will be better friends than ever.'

'Friends!' exclaimed Robin Oig, with strong emphasis – 'friends! – Never. Look to yourself, Harry Waakfelt.'

'Then the curse of Cromwell on your proud Scots stomach, as the man says in the play, and you may do your worst, and be d—d; for one man can say nothing more to another after a tussle, than that he is sorry for it.'

On these terms the friends parted; Robin Oig drew out, in silence, a piece of money, threw it on the table, and then left the alehouse. But turning at the door, he shook his hand at Wakefield, pointing with his forefinger upwards, in a manner which might imply either a threat or a caution. He then disappeared in the moonlight.

Some words passed after his departure between the bailiff, who piqued himself on being a little of a bully, and Harry Wakefield, who, with generous inconsistency, was now not indisposed to begin a new combat in defence of Robin Oig's reputation, 'although he could not use his daddles like an Englishman, as it did not come natural to him.' But Dame Heskett prevented this second quarrel from coming to a head by her peremptory interference. 'There should be no more fighting in her house,' she said; 'there had been too much already. – And you, Mr Wakefield, may live to learn,' she added, 'what it is to make a deadly enemy out of a good friend.'

'Pshaw, dame! Robin Oig is an honest fellow, and will never keep malice.'

'Do not trust to that – you do not know the dour temper of the Scots, though you have dealt with them so often. I have a right to know them, my mother being a Scot.'

'And so is well seen on her daughter,' said Ralph Heskett.

This nuptial sarcasm gave the discourse another turn; fresh customers entered the tap-room or kitchen, and others left it. The conversation turned on the expected markets, and the report of prices from different parts both of Scotland and England – treaties were commenced, and Harry Wakefield was lucky enough to find a chap for a part of his drove, and at a very considerable profit; an event of consequence more than sufficient to blot out all remembrances of the unpleasant scuffle in the earlier part of the day. But there remained one party from whose mind that recollection could not have been wiped away by the possession of every head of cattle betwixt Esk and Eden.

This was Robin Oig M'Combich. – 'That I should have had no weapon,' he said, 'and for the first time in my life! – Blighted be the tongue that bids the Highlander part with the dirk – the dirk – ha! the English blood! – My Muhme's word – when did her word fall to the ground?'

The recollection of the fatal prophecy confirmed the deadly intention which instantly sprang up in his mind.

'Ha! Morrison cannot be many miles behind; and if it were a hundred, what then?'

His impetuous spirit had now a fixed purpose and motive of action, and he turned the light foot of his country towards the wilds, through which he knew, by Mr Ireby's report, that Morrison was advancing. His mind was wholly engrossed by the sense of injury – injury sustained from a friend; and by the desire of vengeance on one whom he now accounted his most bitter enemy. The treasured ideas of self-importance and self-opinion – of ideal birth and quality, had become more precious to him, like the hoard to the miser, because he could only enjoy them in secret. But that hoard was pillaged, the idols which he had secretly worshipped had been desecrated and profaned. Insulted, abused, and beaten, he was no longer worthy, in his own opinion, of the name he bore or the lineage which he belonged to – nothing was left to him – nothing but revenge; and, as the reflection added a galling spur to every step, he determined it should be as sudden and signal as the offence.

When Robin Oig left the door of the ale-house, seven or eight English miles at least lay betwixt Morrison and him. The advance of the former was slow, limited by the sluggish pace of his cattle; the last left behind him stubble-field and hedge-row, crag and dark heath, all glittering with frost-rime in the broad November moonlight, at the rate of six miles an hour. And now the distant lowing of Morrison's cattle is heard; and now they are seen creeping like moles in size and slowness of motion on the broad face of the moor; and now he meets them – passes them, and stops their conductor.

'May good betide us,' said the Southlander. 'Is this you, Robin M'Combich, or your wraith?'

'It is Robin Oig M'Combich,' answered the Highlander, 'and it is not. – But never mind that, put pe giving me the skene-dhu.'

'What! you are for back to the Highlands – The devil! – Have you selt all off before the fair? This beats all for quick markets!'

'I have not sold – I am not going north – May pe I will never go north again. – Give me pack my dirk, Hugh Morrison, or there will pe words petween us.'

'Indeed, Robin, I'll be better advised before I gie it back to you – it is a wanchancy weapon in a Highlandman's hand, and I am thinking you will be about some barns-breaking.'

'Prutt, trutt! let me have my weapon,' said Robin Oig, impatiently.

'Hooly, and fairly,' said his well-meaning friend. 'I'll tell you what will do better than these dirking doings – Ye ken Highlander, and Lowlander, and Border-men, are a' ae man's bairns when you are over the Scots dyke. See, the Eskdale callants, and fighting Charlie of Liddesdale, and the Lockerby lads, and the four Dandies of Lustruther, and a wheen mair grey plaids, are coming up behind, and if you are wranged, there is the hand of a Manly Morrison, we'll see you righted, if Carlisle and Stanwix baith took up the feud.'

'To tell you the truth,' said Robin Oig, desirous of eluding the suspicions of his friend, 'I have enlisted with a party of the Black Watch, and must march off to-morrow morning.'

'Enlisted! Were you mad or drunk? – You must buy yourself off – I can lend you twenty notes, and twenty to that, if the drove sell.'

'I thank you – thank ye, Hughie; but I go with good will the gate that I am going, – so the dirk – the dirk!'

'There it is for you then, since less wunna serve. But think on what I was saying. – Waes me, it will be sair news in the braes of Balquidder, that Robin Oig M'Combich should have run an ill gate, and ta'en on.'

'Ill news in Balquidder, indeed!' echoed poor Robin. 'But Cot speed you, Hughie, and send you good marcats. Ye winna meet with Robin Oig again, either at tryste or fair.'

So saying, he shook hastily the hand of his acquaintance, and set out in the direction from which he had advanced, with the spirit of his former pace.

'There is something wrang with the lad,' muttered the Morrison to himself, 'but we'll maybe see better into it the morn's morning.'

But long ere the morning dawned, the catastrophe of our tale had taken place. It was two hours after the affray had happened, and it was totally forgotten by almost every one, when Robin Oig returned to Heskett's inn. The place was filled at once by various sorts of men, and with noises corresponding to their character. There were the grave low sounds of men engaged in busy traffic, with the laugh, the song, and the riotous jest of those who had nothing to do but to enjoy themselves. Among the last was Harry Wakefield, who, amidst a grinning group of smock-frocks, hob-nailed shoes, and jolly English physiognomies, was trolling forth the old ditty,

> 'What though my name be Roger,
> Who drives the plough and cart –'

when he was interrupted by a well-known voice saying in a high and stern tone, marked by the sharp Highland accent, 'Harry Waakfelt – if you be a man, stand up!'

'What is the matter? – what is it?' the guests demanded of each other.

'It is only a d—d Scotsman,' said Fleecebumpkin, who was by this time very drunk, 'whom Harry Wakefield helped to his broth the day, who is now come to have *his cauld kail* het again.'

'Harry Waakfelt,' repeated the same ominous summons, 'stand up, if you be a man!'

There is something in the tone of deep and concentrated passion, which attracts attention and imposes awe, even by the very sound. The guests shrank back on every side, and gazed at the Highlander as he stood in the middle of them, his brows bent, and his features rigid with resolution.

'I will stand up with all my heart, Robin, my boy, but it shall be to shake hands with you, and drink down all unkindness. It is not the fault of your heart, man, that you don't know how to clench your hands.'

But this time he stood opposite to his antagonist; his open and unsuspecting look strangely contrasted with the stern purpose, which gleamed wild, dark, and vindictive in the eyes of the Highlander.

' 'Tis not thy fault, man, that, not having the luck to be an Englishman, thou canst not fight more than a schoolgirl.'

'I *can* fight,' answered Robin Oig sternly, but calmly, 'and you shall know it. You, Harry Waakfelt, showed me to-day how the Saxon churls fight – I show you now how the Highland Dunniè-wassel fights.'

He seconded the word with the action, and plunged the dagger, which he suddenly displayed, into the broad breast of the English yeoman, with such fatal certainty and force, that the hilt made a hollow sound against the breast-bone, and the double-edged point split the very heart of his victim. Harry Wakefield fell and expired with a single groan. His assassin next seized the bailiff by the collar, and offered the bloody poniard to his throat, whilst dread and surprise rendered the man incapable of defence.

'It were very just to lay you beside him,' he said, 'but the blood of a base pickthank shall never mix on my father's dirk with that of a brave man.'

As he spoke, he cast the man from him with so much force that he fell on the floor, while Robin, with his other hand, threw the fatal weapon into the blazing turf-fire.

'There,' he said, 'take me who likes – and let fire cleanse blood if it can.'

The pause of astonishment still continuing, Robin Oig asked for a peace-officer, and a constable having stepped out, he surrendered himself to his custody.

'A bloody night's work you have made of it,' said the constable.

'Your own fault,' said the Highlander. 'Had you kept his hands off me twa hours since, he would have been now as well and merry as he was twa minutes since.'

'It must be sorely answered,' said the peace-officer.

'Never you mind that – death pays all debts; it will pay that too.'

The horror of the bystanders began now to give way to indignation; and the sight of a favourite companion murdered in the midst of them, the provocation being, in their opinion, so utterly inadequate to the excess of vengeance, might have induced them to kill the perpetrator of the deed even upon the very spot. The constable, however, did his duty on this occasion, and with the assistance of some of the more reasonable persons present, procured horses to guard the prisoner to Carlisle, to abide his doom at the next assizes. While the escort was preparing, the prisoner neither expressed the least interest nor attempted the slightest reply. Only, before he was carried from the fatal apartment, he desired to look at the dead body, which, raised from the floor, had been deposited upon the large table (at the head of which Harry Wakefield had presided but a few minutes before, full of life, vigour, and animation) until the surgeons should examine the mortal wound. The face of the corpse was decently covered with a napkin. To the surprise and horror of the bystanders, which displayed itself in a general *Ah!* drawn through clenched teeth and half-shut lips, Robin Oig removed the cloth, and gazed with a mournful but steady eye on the lifeless visage, which had been so lately animated that the smile of good-humoured confidence in his own strength, of conciliation at once and contempt towards his enemy, still curled his lip. While those present expected that the wound, which had so lately flooded the apartment with gore, would send forth fresh streams at the touch of the homicide, Robin Oig replaced the covering, with the brief exclamation – 'He was a pretty man!'

My story is nearly ended. The unfortunate Highlander stood his trial at Carlisle. I was myself present, and as a young Scottish lawyer, or barrister at least, and reputed a man of some quality, the politeness of the Sheriff of Cumberland offered me a place on the bench. The facts of the case were proved in the manner I have related them; and whatever might be at first the prejudice of the audience against a crime so un-English as that of assassination from revenge, yet when the rooted national prejudices of the prisoner had been explained, which made him consider himself as stained with indelible dishonour when subjected to personal violence; when his previous patience, moderation, and endurance were considered, the generosity of the English audience was inclined to regard his crime as the wayward aberration of a false idea of honour rather than as flowing from a heart naturally savage, or perverted by habitual vice. I shall never forget the charge of the venerable judge to the jury, although not at that time liable to be much affected either by that which was eloquent or pathetic.

'We have had,' he said, 'in the previous part of our duty' (alluding to some former trials) 'to discuss crimes which infer disgust and abhorrence, while they call down the well-merited vengeance of the law. It is now our still more melancholy task to apply its salutary though severe enactments to a case of a very singular character, in which the crime (for a crime it is, and a deep one) arose less out of the malevolence of the heart, than the error of the understanding – less from any idea of committing wrong, than from an unhappily perverted notion of that which is right. Here we have two men, highly esteemed, it has been stated, in their rank of life, and attached, it seems, to each other as friends, one of whose lives has been already sacrificed to a punctilio, and the other is about to prove the vengeance of the offended laws; and yet both may claim our commiseration at least, as men acting in ignorance of each other's national prejudices, and unhappily misguided rather than voluntarily erring from the path of right conduct.

'In the original cause of the misunderstanding, we must in justice give the right to the prisoner at the bar. He had acquired possession of the enclosure, which was the object of competition, by a legal contract with the proprietor, Mr Ireby; and yet, when accosted with reproaches undeserved in themselves, and galling doubtless to a temper at least sufficiently susceptible of passion, he offered notwithstanding to yield up half his acquisition for the sake of peace and good neighbourhood, and his amicable proposal was rejected with scorn. Then follows the scene at Mr Heskett the publican's, and you will observe how the stranger was treated by the deceased, and, I am sorry to observe, by those around, who seem to have urged him in a manner which was aggravating in the highest degree. While he asked for peace and for composition, and offered submission to a magistrate, or to a mutual arbiter, the prisoner was insulted by a whole company, who seem on this occasion to have forgotten the national maxim of "fair play"; and while attempting to escape from the place in peace, he was intercepted, struck down, and beaten to the effusion of his blood.

'Gentlemen of the jury, it was with some impatience that I heard my learned brother, who opened the case for the crown, give an unfavourable turn to the prisoner's conduct on this occasion. He said the prisoner was afraid to encounter his antagonist in fair fight, or to submit to the laws of the ring; and that therefore, like a cowardly Italian, he had recourse to his fatal stiletto, to murder the man whom he dared not meet in manly encounter. I observed the prisoner shrink from this part of the accusation with the abhorrence natural to a brave man; and as I would wish to make my words impressive when I point his real crime, I must secure his opinion of my impartiality, by rebutting everything that seems to me a false accusation. There can be no doubt that the prisoner is a man of resolution – too much resolution – I wish to Heaven that he had less, or rather that he had had a better education to regulate it.

'Gentlemen, as to the laws my brother talks of, they may be known in the bull-ring, or the bear-garden, or the cockpit, but they are not known here. Or, if they should be so far admitted as furnishing a species of proof that no malice was intended in this sort of combat, from which fatal accidents do sometimes arise, it can only be so admitted when both parties are *in pari casu*, equally acquainted with, and equally willing to refer themselves to, that species of arbitrament. But will it be contended that a man of superior rank and education is to be subjected, or is obliged to subject himself, to this coarse and brutal strife, perhaps in opposition to a younger, stronger, or more skilful opponent? Certainly even the pugilistic code, if founded upon the fair play of Merry Old England, as my brother alleges it to be, can contain nothing so preposterous. And, gentlemen of the jury, if the laws would support an English gentleman, wearing, we will suppose, his sword, in defending himself by force against a violent personal aggression of the nature offered to this prisoner, they will not less protect a foreigner and a stranger, involved in the same unpleasing circumstances. If, therefore, gentlemen of the jury, when thus pressed by a *vis major*, the object of obloquy to a whole company, and of direct violence from one at least, and, as he might reasonably apprehend, from more, the panel had produced the weapon which his countrymen, as we are informed, generally carry about their persons, and the same unhappy circumstance had ensued which you have heard detailed in evidence, I could not in my conscience have asked from you a verdict of murder. The prisoner's personal defence might, indeed, even in that case, have

gone more or less beyond the *Moderamen inculpatae tutelae*,
spoken of by lawyers, but the punishment incurred would have
been that of manslaughter, not of murder. I beg leave to add that I
should have thought this milder species of charge was demanded
in the case supposed, notwithstanding the statute of James I cap.
8, which takes the case of slaughter by stabbing with a short
weapon, even without malice prepense, out of the benefit of
clergy. For this statute of stabbing, as it is termed, arose out of a
temporary cause; and as the real guilt is the same, whether the
slaughter be committed by the dagger, or by sword or pistol, the
benignity of the modern law places them all on the same, or nearly
the same, footing.

'But, gentlemen of the jury, the pinch of the case lies in the
interval of two hours interposed betwixt the reception of the
injury and the fatal retaliation. In the heat of affray and *chaude
mêlée*, law, compassionating the infirmities of humanity, makes
allowance for the passions which rule such a stormy moment – for
the sense of present pain, for the apprehension of further injury,
for the difficulty of ascertaining with due accuracy the precise
degree of violence which is necessary to protect the person of the
individual, without annoying or injuring the assailant more than is
absolutely requisite. But the time necessary to walk twelve miles,
however speedily performed, was an interval sufficient for the
prisoner to have recollected himself; and the violence with which
he carried his purpose into effect, with so many circumstances of
deliberate determination, could neither be induced by the passion
of anger, nor that of fear. It was the purpose and the act of
predetermined revenge, for which law neither can, will, nor ought
to have sympathy or allowance.

'It is true, we may repeat to ourselves, in alleviation of this poor
man's unhappy action, that his case is a very peculiar one. The
country which he inhabits was, in the days of many now alive,
inaccessible to the laws, not only of England, which have not even
yet penetrated thither, but to those to which our neighbours of
Scotland are subjected, and which must be supposed to be, and no
doubt actually are, founded upon the general principles of justice
and equity which pervade every civilized country. Amongst their
mountains, as among the North American Indians, the various
tribes were wont to make war upon each other, so that each man

was obliged to go armed for his protection. These men, from the ideas which they entertained of their own descent and of their own consequence, regarded themselves as so many cavaliers or men-at-arms, rather than as the peasantry of a peaceful country. Those laws of the ring, as my brother terms them, were unknown to the race of warlike mountaineers; that decision of quarrels by no other weapons than those which nature has given every man, must to them have seemed as vulgar and as preposterous as to the noblesse of France. Revenge, on the other hand, must have been as familiar to their habits of society as to those of the Cherokees or Mohawks. It is indeed, as described by Bacon, at bottom a kind of wild untutored justice; for the fear of retaliation must withhold the hands of the oppressor where there is no regular law to check daring violence. But though all this may be granted, and though we may allow that, such having been the case of the Highlands in the days of the prisoner's fathers, many of the opinions and sentiments must still continue to influence the present generation, it cannot, and ought not, even in this most painful case, to alter the administration of the law, either in your hands, gentlemen of the jury, or in mine. The first object of civilization is to place the general protection of the law, equally administered, in the room of that wild justice, which every man cut and carved for himself, according to the length of his sword and the strength of his arm. The law says to the subjects, with a voice only inferior to that of the Deity, 'Vengeance is mine.' The instant that there is time for passion to cool, and reason to interpose, an injured party must become aware that the law assumes the exclusive cognizance of the right and wrong betwixt the parties, and opposes her inviolable buckler to every attempt of the private party to right himself. I repeat, that this unhappy man ought personally to be the object rather of our pity than our abhorrence, for he failed in his ignorance, and from mistaken notions of honour. But his crime is not the less that of murder, gentlemen, and, in your high and important office, it is your duty so to find. Englishmen have their angry passions as well as Scots; and should this man's action remain unpunished, you may unsheath, under various pretences, a thousand daggers betwixt the Land's-end and the Orkneys.'

The venerable judge thus ended what, to judge by his apparent emotion, and by the tears which filled his eyes, was really a painful task. The jury, according to his instructions, brought in a verdict of Guilty; and Robin Oig M'Combich, *alias* M'Gregor, was sentenced to death and left for execution, which took place accordingly. He met his fate with great firmness, and acknowledged the justice of his sentence. But he repelled indignantly the observations of those who accused him of attacking an unarmed man. 'I give a life for the life I took,' he said, 'and what can I do more?'

John Galt

THE GUDEWIFE

INTRODUCTION

I am inditing the good matter of this book for the instruction of our only daughter when she comes to years of discretion, as she soon will, for her guidance when she has a house of her own, and has to deal with the kittle temper of a gudeman in so couthy a manner as to mollify his sour humour when anything out of doors troubles him. Thanks be and praise I am not ill qualified, indeed it is a clear ordinance that I was to be of such a benefit to the world; for it would have been a strange thing if the pains taken with my education had been purposeless in the decrees of Providence.

Mr Desker, the schoolmaster, was my father; and, as he was reckoned in his day a great teacher, and had a pleasure in opening my genie for learning, it is but reasonable to suppose that I in a certain manner profited by his lessons, and made a progress in parts of learning that do not fall often into the lot of womankind. This much it behoves me to say, for there are critical persons in the world that might think it very upsetting of one of my degree to write a book, especially a book which has for its end the bettering of the conjugal condition. If I did not tell them, as I take it upon me to do, how well I have been brought up for the work, they might look down upon my endeavours with a doubtful eye; but when they read this, they will have a new tout to their old horn, and reflect with more reverence of others who may be in some things their inferiors, superiors, or equals. It would not become me to say to which of these classes I belong, though I am not without an inward admonition on that head.

It fell out, when I was in my twenties, that Mr Thrifter came, in the words of the song of Auld Robin Gray, 'a-courting to me';

and, to speak a plain matter of fact, in some points he was like that bald-headed carle. For he was a man, considering my juvenility, well stricken in years; besides being a bachelor, with a natural inclination (as all old bachelors have) to be dozened, and fond of his own ayes and nays. For my part, when he first came about the house, I was as dawty as Jeanie – as I thought myself entitled to a young man, and did not relish the apparition of him coming in at the gloaming, when the day's darg was done, and before candles were lighted. However, our lot in life is not of our own choosing. I will say – for he is still to the fore – that it could not have been thought he would have proved himself such a satisfactory gudeman as he has been. To be sure, I put my shoulder to the wheel, and likewise prayed to Jupiter; for there never was a rightful head of a family without the concurrence of his wife. These are words of wisdom that my father taught, and I put in practice.

Mr Thrifter, when he first came about me, was a bein man. He had parts in two vessels, besides his own shop, and was sponsible for a nest-egg of lying money; so that he was not, though rather old, a match to be, as my father thought, discomfited with a flea in the lug instanter. I therefore, according to the best advice, so comported myself that it came to pass in the course of time that we were married; and of my wedded life and experience I intend to treat in this book.

CHAPTER I

Among the last words that my sagacious father said when I took upon me to be the wedded wife of Mr Thrifter were, that a man never throve unless his wife would let, which is a text that I have not forgotten; for though in a way, and in obedience to the customs of the world, women acknowledge men as their head, yet we all know in our hearts that this is but diplomatic. Do not we see that men work for us, which shews that they are our servants? do not we see that men protect us, are they not therefore our soldiers? do not we see that they go hither and yon at our bidding, which shews that they have that within their nature that teaches them to obey? and do not we feel that we have the command of them in all things, just as they had the upper hand in the world till woman was created? No clearer proof do I want that, although in a sense for policy we call ourselves the weaker vessels – and in that very policy there is power – we know well in our hearts that, as the last made creatures, we necessarily are more perfect, and have all that was made before us, by hook or crook, under our thumb. Well does Robin Burns sing of this truth in the song where he has –

> Her 'prentice hand she tried on man,
> And syne she made the lassies oh!

Accordingly, having a proper conviction of the superiority of my sex, I was not long of making Mr Thrifter, my gudeman, to know into what hands he had fallen, by correcting many of the bad habits of body to which he had become addicted in his bachelor loneliness. Among these was a custom that I did think ought not to be continued after he had surrendered himself into the custody of a wife, and that was an usage with him in the morning before breakfast to toast his shoes against the fender and forenent the fire. This he did not tell me till I saw it with my own eyes the morning after we were married, which, when I beheld, gave me a sore heart, because, had I known it before we were everlastingly made one, I will not say but there might have been a dubiety as to the paction; for I have ever had a natural dislike to men who toasted their shoes, thinking it was a hussie fellow's custom. However, being endowed with an instinct of prudence, I winked at it for some days; but it could not be borne any longer, and I said in a sweet manner, as it were by and by –

'Dear Mr Thrifter, that servant lass we have gotten has not a right notion of what is a genteel way of living. Do you see how the misleart creature sets up your shoes in the inside of the fender, keeping the warmth from our feet? really I'll thole this no longer; it's not a custom in a proper house. If a stranger were accidently coming in and seeing your shoes in that situation, he would not think of me as it is well known he ought to think.'

Mr Thrifter did not say much, nor could he; for I had judiciously laid all the wyte and blame of the thing to the servant; but he said, in a diffident manner, that it was not necessary to be so particular.

'No necessary! Mr Thrifter, what do you call a particularity, when you would say that toasting shoes is not one? It might do for you when you were a bachelor, but ye should remember that you're so no more, and it's a custom I will not allow.'

'But,' replied he with a smile, 'I am the head of the house; and to make few words about it, I say, Mrs Thrifter, I will have my shoes warmed anyhow, whether or no.'

'Very right, my dear,' quo' I; 'I'll ne'er dispute that you are the head of the house; but I think that you need not make a poor wife's life bitter by insisting on toasting your shoes.'

And I gave a deep sigh. Mr Thrifter looked very solemn on hearing this, and as he was a man not void of understanding, he said to me,

'My dawty,' said he, 'we must not stand on trifles; if you do not like to see my shoes within the parlour fender, they can be toasted in the kitchen.'

I was glad to hear him say this; and, ringing the bell, I told the servant-maid at once to take them away and place them before the kitchen fire, well pleased to have carried my point with such debonair suavity; for if you get the substance of a thing, it is not wise to make a piece of work for the shadow likewise. Thus it happened I was conqueror in the controversy; but Mr Thrifter's shoes have to this day been toasted every morning in the kitchen; and I daresay the poor man is vogie with the thoughts of having gained a victory; for the generality of men have, like parrots, a good conceit of themselves, and cry 'Pretty Polly!' when everybody sees they have a crooked neb.

CHAPTER II

But what I have said was nothing to many other calamities that darkened our honeymoon. Mr Thrifter having been a long-keepit bachelor, required a consideration in many things besides his shoes; for men of that stamp are so long accustomed to their own ways that it is not easy to hammer them into docility, far less to make them obedient husbands. So that although he is the best of men, yet I cannot say on my conscience that he was altogether free from an ingrained temper, requiring my canniest hand to manage properly. It could not be said that I suffered much from great faults; but he was fiky, and made more work about trifles that didna just please him than I was willing to conform to. Some excuse, however, might be pleaded for him, because he felt that infirmities were growing upon him, which was the cause that made him think of taking a wife; and I was not in my younger days quite so thoughtful, maybe, as was necessary: for I will take blame to myself, when it would be a great breach of truth in me to deny a fault that could be clearly proven.

Mr Thrifter was a man of great regularity; he went to the shop and did his business there in a most methodical manner; he returned to the house and ate his meals like clockwork; and he went to bed every night at half past nine o'clock, and slept there like a door nail. In short, all he did and said was as orderly as commodities on chandler pins; but for all that he was at times of a crunkly spirit, fractiously making faults about nothing at all: by which he was neither so smooth as oil nor so sweet as honey to me, whose duty it was to govern him.

At the first outbreaking of the original sin that was in him, I was vexed and grieved, watering the plants in the solitude of the room, when he was discoursing on the news of the day with customers in the shop. At last I said to myself, 'This will never do; one of two must obey; and it is not in the course of nature that a gudeman should rule a house, which is the province of a wife and becomes her nature to do.'

So I set a stout heart to the stey brae, and being near my time with our daughter, I thought it would be well to try how he would put up with a little sample of womanhood. So that day when he came in to his dinner, I was, maybe, more incommoded with my temper than might be, saying to him, in a way as if I could have fought with the wind, that it was very unsettled weather.

'My dawty,' said he, 'I wonder what would content you! we have had as delightful a week as ever made the sight of the sun heartsome.'

'Well, but,' said I, 'good weather that is to you may not be so to me; and I say again, that this is most ridiculous weather.'

'What would you have, my dawty? Is it not known by a better what is best for us?'

'Oh,' cried I, 'we can never speak of temporal things but you haul in the grace of the Maker by the lug and the horn. Mr

Thrifter, ye should set a watch on the door of your lips; especially as ye have now such a prospect before you of being the father of a family.'

'Mrs Thrifter,' said he, 'what has that to do with the state of the weather?'

'Everything,' said I. 'Isn't the condition that I am in a visibility that I cannot look after the house as I should do? which is the cause of your having such a poor dinner today; for the weather wiled out the servant lass, and she has in consequence not been in the kitchen to see to her duty. Doesn't that shew you that, to a woman in the state that I am, fine sunshiny weather is no comfort?'

'Well,' said he, 'though a shower is at times seasonable, I will say that I prefer days like this.'

'What you, Mr Thrifter, prefer, can make no difference to me; but I will uphold, in spite of everything you can allege to the contrary, that this is not judicious weather.'

'Really now, gudewife,' said Mr Thrifter, 'what need we quarrel about the weather? neither of us can make it better or worse.'

'That's a truth,' said I, 'but what need you maintain that dry weather is pleasant weather, when I have made it plain to you that it is a great affliction? And how can you say the contrary? does not both wet and dry come from Providence? Which of them is the evil? – for they should be in their visitations both alike.'

'Mrs Thrifter,' said he, 'what would you be at, summering and wintering on nothing?'

Upon which I said, 'Oh, Mr Thrifter, if ye were like me, ye would say anything; for I am not in a condition to be spoken to. I'll not say that ye're far wrong, but till my time is a bygone ye should not contradict me so; for I am no in a state to be contradicted: it may go hard with me if I am. So I beg you to think, for the sake of the baby unborn, to let me have my way in all things for a season.'

'I have no objection,' said he, 'if there is a necessity for complying; but really, gudewife, ye're at times a wee fashous just now; and this house has not been a corner in the kingdom of heaven for some time.'

Thus, from less to more, our argolbargoling was put an end to; and from that time I was the ruling power in our domicile, which has made it the habitation of quiet ever since; for from that

moment I never laid down the rod of authority, which I achieved
with such a womanly sleight of hand.

CHAPTER III

Though from the time of the conversation recorded in the preced-
ing chapter I was, in a certain sense, the ruling power in our house,
as a wedded wife should be, we did not slide down a glassy brae till
long after. For though the gudeman in a compassionate manner
allowed me to have my own way till my fullness of time was come,
I could discern by the tail of my eye that he meditated to usurp the
authority again, when he saw a fit time to effect the machination.
Thus it came to pass, when I was delivered of our daughter, I had,
as I lay on my bed, my own thoughts anent the evil that I saw
barming within him; and I was therefore determined to keep the
upper hand, of which I had made a conquest with such dexterity,
and the breaking down of difficulties.

So when I was some days in a recumbent posture, but in a
well-doing way, I said nothing; it made me, however, often grind
my teeth in a secrecy when I saw from the bed many a thing that I
treasured in remembrance should never be again. But I was very
thankful for my deliverance, and assumed a blitheness in my
countenance that was far from my heart. In short, I could see that
the gudeman, in whose mouth you would have thought sugar
would have melted, had from day to day a stratagem in his head
subversive of the regency that I had won in my tender state; and as
I saw it would never do to let him have his own will, I had recourse
to the usual diplomaticals of womankind.

It was a matter before the birth that we settled, him and me,
that the child should be baptized on the eighth day after, in order
that I might be up and a partaker of the ploy; which, surely, as the
mother, I was well entitled to. But from what I saw going on from
the bed and jaloused, it occurred to me that the occasion should
be postponed, and according as Mr Thrifter should give his
consent, or withhold it, I should comport myself; determined,
however, I was to have the matter postponed, just to ascertain the
strength and durability of what belonged to me.

On the fifth day I, therefore, said to him, as I was sitting in the easy chair by the fire, with a cod at my shoulders and my mother's fur cloak about me – the baby was in a cradle close by, but not rocking, for the keeper said it was yet too young – and sitting, as I have said, Mr Thrifter forenent me, 'My dear,' said I, 'it will never do to have the christening on the day we said.'

'What for no?' was the reply; 'isn't it a very good day?'

So I, seeing that he was going to be upon his peremptors, replied, with my usual meekness, 'No human being, my dear, can tell what sort of day it will be; but be it good or be it bad, the christening is not to be on that day.'

'You surprise me!' said he, 'I considered it a settled point, and have asked Mr Sweetie, the grocer, to come to his tea.'

'Dear me!' quo' I; 'ye should not have done that without my consent; for although we set the day before my time was come, it was not then in the power of man to say how I was to get through; and therefore it was just a talk we had on the subject, and by no manner of means a thing that could be fixed.'

'In some sort,' said Mr Thrifter, 'I cannot but allow that you are speaking truth; but I thought that the only impediment to the day was your illness. Now you have had a most blithe time o't, and there is nothing in the way of an obstacle.'

'Ah, Mr Thrifter!' said I, 'it's easy for you, who have such a barren knowledge of the nature of women, so to speak, but I know that I am no in a condition to have such a handling as a christening; and besides, I have a scruple of conscience well worth your attention concerning the same – and it's my opinion, formed in the watches of the night, when I was in my bed, that baby should be christened in the kirk on the Lord's day.'

'Oh,' said he, 'that's but a fashion, and you'll be quite well by the eighth; the howdie told me that ye had a most pleasant time o't, and cannot be ill on the eighth day.'

I was just provoked into contumacy to hear this; for to tell a new mother that childbirth is a pleasant thing, set me almost in a passion; and I said to him that he might entertain Mr Sweetie himself, for that I was resolved the christening should not be as had been set.

In short, from less to more, I gained my point; as, indeed, I always settled it in my own mind before broaching the subject; first, by letting him know that I had latent pains, which made me very ill, though I seemed otherwise; and, secondly, that it was very hard, and next to a martyrdom, to be controverted in religion, as I would be if the bairn was baptized anywhere but in the church.

CHAPTER IV

In due time the christening took place in the kirk, as I had made a point of having; and for some time after we passed a very happy married life. Mr Thrifter saw that it was of no use to contradict me, and in consequence we lived in great felicity, he never saying nay to me; and I, as became a wife in the rightful possession of her prerogatives, was most condescending. But still he shewed, when he durst, the bull-horn; and would have meddled with our house-holdry, to the manifest detriment of our conjugal happiness, had I not continued my interdict in the strictest manner. In truth, I was all the time grievously troubled with nursing Nance, our daughter, and could not take the same pains about things that I otherwise would have done; and it is well known that husbands are like mice, that know when the cat is out of the house or her back turned, they take their own way: and I assure the courteous reader, to say no ill of my gudeman, that he was one of the mice genus.

But at last I had a trial that was not to be endured with such a composity as if I had been a black snail. It came to pass that our daughter was to be weaned, and on the day settled – a Sabbath day – we had, of course, much to do, for it behoved in this ceremony that I should keep out of sight; and keeping out of sight it seemed but reasonable, considering his parentage to the wean, that Mr Thrifter should take my place. So I said to him in the morning that he must do so, and keep Nance for that day; and, to do the poor man justice, he consented at once, for he well knew that it would come to nothing to be contrary.

So I went to the kirk, leaving him rocking the cradle and singing hush, ba! as he saw need. But oh, dule! scarcely had I left the house when the child screamed up in a panic, and would not be pacified. He thereupon lifted it out of the cradle, and with it in his arms went about the house; but it was such a roaring buckie that for a long time he was like to go distracted. Over what ensued I draw the curtain, and must only say that, when I came from the church, there he was, a spectacle, and as sour as a crab apple, blaming me for leaving him with such a devil.

I was really woeful to see him, and sympathized in the most pitiful manner with him, on account of what had happened; but the more I condoled with him the more he would not be comforted, and for all my endeavours to keep matters in a propriety, I saw my jurisdiction over the house was in jeopardy; and every now and then the infant cried out, just as if it had been laid upon a heckle. Oh! such a day as that was for Mr Thrifter, when he heard the tyrant bairn shrieking like mad, and every now and then drumming with its wee feetie like desperation, he cried,

'For the love of God, give it a drop of the breast! or it will tempt me to wring off its ankles or its head.'

But I replied composedly that it could not be done, for the wean must be speant, and what he advised was evendown nonsense.

'What has come to pass, both my mother and other sagacious carlines told me I had to look for; and so we must bow the head of resignation to our lot. You'll just,' said I, 'keep the bairn this afternoon; it will not be a long fashery.'

He said nothing, but gave a deep sigh.

At this moment the bells of the kirk were ringing for the afternoon's discourse, and I lifted my bonnet to put it on and go; but ere I knew where I was, Mr Thrifter was out of the door and away, leaving me alone with the torment in the cradle, which the bells at that moment wakened: and it gave a yell that greatly discomposed me.

Once awa and aye awa, Mr Thrifter went into the fields, and would not come back when I lifted the window and called to him, but walked faster and faster, and was a most demented man; so that I was obligated to stay at home, and would have had my own work with the termagant baby if my mother had not come in and advised me to give it sweetened rum and water for a pacificator.

CHAPTER V

Mr Thrifter began in time to be a very complying husband, and we had, after the trial of the weaning, no particular confabulation;

indeed he was a very reasonable man, and had a rightful instinct of the reverence that is due to the opinion of a wife of discernment. I do not think, to the best of my recollection, that between the time Nance was weaned till she got her walking shoes and was learning to walk, that we had a single controversy; nor can it be said that we had a great ravelment on that occasion. Indeed, saving our daily higling about trifles not worth remembering, we passed a pleasant life. But when Nance came to get her first walking shoes, that was a catastrophe well worthy of being rehearsed for her behoof now.

It happened that for some months before, she had, in place of shoes, red worsted socks; but as she began, from the character of her capering, to kithe that she was coming to her feet, I got a pair of yellow slippers for her; and no mother could take more pains than I did to learn her how to handle her feet. First, I tried to teach her to walk by putting a thimble or an apple beyond her reach, at least a chair's breadth off; and then I endeavoured to make the cutty run from me to her father, across the hearth, and he held out his hands to catch her.

This, it will be allowed, was to us pleasant pastime. But it fell out one day, when we were diverting ourselves by making Nance run to and fro between us across the hearth, that the glaiket baudrons chanced to see the seal of her father's watch glittering, and, in coming from him to me, she drew it after her, as if it had been a turnip. He cried, 'Oh, Christal and –' I lifted my hands in wonderment; but the tottling creature, with no more sense than a sucking turkey, whirled the watch – the Almighty knows how! – into the fire, and giggled as if she had done an exploit.

'Take it out with the tongs,' said I.

'She's an ill-brought-up wean,' cried he.

The short and the long of it was, before the watch could be got out, the heat broke the glass and made the face of it dreadful; besides, he wore a riband chain – that was in a blaze before we could make a redemption.

When the straemash was over, I said to him that he could expect no better by wearing his watch in such a manner.

'It is not,' said he, 'the watch that is to blame, but your bardy bairn that ye have spoiled in the bringing up.'

'Mr Thrifter,' quo' I, 'this is not a time for upbraiding; for if ye mean to insinuate anything to my disparagement, it is what I will not submit to.'

'E'en as you like, my dawty,' said he; 'but what I say is true – that your daughter will just turn out a randy like her mother.'

'What's that ye say?' quo' I, and I began to wipe my eyes with the corner of my shawl – saying in a pathetic manner, 'If I am a randy, I ken who has made me one.'

'Ken,' said he, 'Ken! everybody kens that ye are like a clubby foot, made by the hand of God, and passed the remede of doctors.'

Was not this most diabolical to hear? Really my corruption rose at such blasphemy; and starting from my seat, I put my hands on my haunches, and gave a stamp with my foot that made the whole house dirl: 'What does the man mean?' said I.

But he replied with a composity as if he had been in liquor, saying, with an ill-faured smile, 'Sit down, my dawty; you'll do yourself a prejudice if ye allow your passion to get the better of you.'

Could mortal woman thole the like of this; it stunned me speechless, and for a time I thought my authority knocked on the head. But presently the spirit that was in my nature mustered courage, and put a new energy within me, which caused me to say nothing, but to stretch out my feet, and stiffen back, with my hands at my sides, as if I was a dead corpse. Whereupon the good man ran for a tumbler of water to jaup on my face; but when he came near me in this posture, I dauded the glass of water in his face, and drummed with my feet and hands in a delirious manner, which convinced him that I was going by myself. Oh, but he was in an awful terrification! At last, seeing his fear and contrition, I began to moderate, as it seemed; which made him as softly and kindly as if I had been a true frantic woman; which I was not, but a practiser of the feminine art, to keep the ruling power.

Thinking by my state that I was not only gone daft, but not without the need of soothing, he began to ask my pardon in a proper humility, and with a most pitiful penitence. Whereupon I said to him, that surely he had not a rightful knowledge of my nature: and then he began to confess a fault, and was such a dejected man that I took the napkin from my eyes and gave a great guffaw, telling him that surely he was silly daft and gi'en to pikery, if he thought he could daunton me. 'No, no, Mr Thrifter,' quo' I, 'while I live, and the iron tongs are by the chumly lug, never expect to get the upper hand of me.'

From that time he was as bidable a man as any reasonable woman could desire; but he gave a deep sigh, which was a testificate to me that the leaven of unrighteousness was still within him, and might break out into treason and rebellion if I was not on my guard.

Margaret Oliphant

THE OPEN DOOR

I took the house of Brentwood on my return from India in 18—, for the temporary accommodation of my family, until I could find a permanent home for them. It had many advantages which made it peculiarly appropriate. It was within reach of Edinburgh, and my boy Roland, whose education had been considerably neglected, could go in and out to school which was thought to be better for him than either leaving home altogether or staying there always with a tutor. The first of these expedients would have seemed preferable to me, the second commended itself to his mother. The doctor, like a judicious man, took the midway between. 'Put him on his pony, and let him ride into the High School every morning; it will do him all the good in the world,' Dr Simson said; 'and when it is bad weather there is the train.' His mother accepted this solution of the difficulty more easily than I could have hoped; and our pale-faced boy, who had never known anything more invigorating than Simla, began to encounter the brisk breezes of the North in the subdued severity of the month of May. Before the time of the vacation in July we had the satisfaction of seeing him begin to acquire something of the brown and ruddy complexion of his schoolfellows. The English system did not commend itself to Scotland in these days. There was no little Eton at Fettes; nor do I think, if there had been, that a genteel exotic of that class would have tempted either my wife or me. The lad was doubly precious to us, being the only one left us of many; and he was fragile in body, we believed, and deeply sensitive in mind. To keep him at home, and yet to send him to school – to combine the advantages of the two systems – seemed to be everything that could be desired. The two girls also found at Brentwood everything they wanted. They were near enough to

Edinburgh to have masters and lessons as many as they required for completing that never-ending education which the young people seem to require nowadays. Their mother married me when she was younger than Agatha, and I should like to see them improve upon their mother! I myself was then no more than twenty-five – an age at which I see the young fellows now groping about them, with no notion what they are going to do with their lives. However, I suppose every generation has a conceit of itself which elevates it, in its own opinion, above that which comes after it.

Brentwood stands on that fine and wealthy slope of country, one of the richest in Scotland, which lies between the Pentland Hills and the Firth. In clear weather you could see the blue gleam – like a bent bow, embracing the wealthy fields and scattered houses – of the great estuary on one side of you; and on the other the blue heights, not gigantic like those we had been used to, but just high enough for all the glories of the atmosphere, the play of clouds, and sweet reflections, which give to a hilly country an interest and a charm which nothing else can emulate. Edinburgh, with its two lesser heights – the Castle and the Calton Hill – its spires and towers piercing through the smoke, and Arthur's Seat lying crouched behind, like a guardian no longer very needful, taking his repose beside the well-beloved charge, which is now, so to speak, able to take care of itself without him – lay at our right hand. From the lawn and drawing-room windows we could see all these varieties of landscape. The colour was sometimes a little chilly, but sometimes, also, as animated and full of vicissitude as a drama. I was never tired of it. Its colour and freshness revived the eyes which had grown weary of arid plains and blazing skies. It was always cheery, and fresh, and full of repose.

The village of Brentwood lay almost under the house, on the other side of the deep little ravine, down which a stream – which ought to have been a lovely, wild, and frolicsome little river – flowed between its rocks and trees. The river, like so many in that district, had, however, in its earlier life been sacrificed to trade, and was grimy with paper-making. But this did not affect our pleasure in it so much as I have known it to affect other streams. Perhaps our water was more rapid – perhaps less clogged with dirt and refuse. Our side of the dell was charmingly *accidenté*, and clothed with fine trees, through which various paths wound down to the river-side and to the village bridge which crossed the stream. The village lay in the hollow, and climbed, with very prosaic houses, the other side. Village architecture does not flourish in Scotland. The blue slates and the grey stone are sworn foes to the picturesque; and though I do not, for my own part, dislike the interior of an old-fashioned pewed and galleried church, with its little family settlements on all sides, the square box outside, with its bit of a spire like a handle to lift it by, is not an improvement to the landscape. Still, a cluster of houses on differing elevations – with scraps of garden coming in between, a hedgerow with clothes laid out to dry, the opening of a street with its rural sociability, the women at their doors, the slow waggon lumbering along – give a centre to the landscape. It was cheerful to look at, and convenient in a hundred ways. Within ourselves we had walks in plenty, the glen being always beautiful in all its phases, whether the woods were green in the spring or ruddy in the autumn. In the park which surrounded the house were the ruins of the former mansion of Brentwood, a much smaller and less important house than the solid Georgian edifice which we inhabited. The ruins were picturesque, however, and gave importance to the place. Even we, who were but temporary tenants, felt a vague pride in them, as if they somehow reflected a certain consequence upon ourselves. The old building had the remains of a tower, an indistinguishable mass of mason-work, overgrown with ivy, and the shells of walls attached to this were half filled up with soil. I had never examined it closely, I am ashamed to say. There was a large room, or what had been a large room, with the lower part of the windows still existing, on the principal floor, and underneath other windows, which were perfect, though half filled up with fallen soil, and waving with a wild growth of brambles and chance growths of all kinds. This was the oldest part of all. At a little distance were some very commonplace and disjointed fragments of the building, one of them suggesting a certain pathos by its very commonness and the complete wreck which it showed. This was the end of a low gable, a bit of grey wall, all encrusted with lichens, in which was a common doorway. Probably it had been a servants' entrance, a back-door, or opening into what are called 'the offices' in Scotland. No offices remained to be entered

– pantry and kitchen had all been swept out of being; but there stood the doorway open and vacant, free to all the winds, to the rabbits, and every wild creature. It struck my eye, the first time I went to Brentwood, like a melancholy comment upon a life that was over. A door that led to nothing – closed once perhaps with anxious care, bolted and guarded, now void of any meaning. It impressed me, I remember, from the first; so perhaps it may be said that my mind was prepared to attach to it an importance which nothing justified.

The summer was a very happy period of repose for us all. The warmth of Indian suns was still in our veins. It seemed to us that we could never have enough of the greenness, the dewiness, the freshness of the northern landscape. Even its mists were pleasant to us, taking all the fever out of us, and pouring in vigour and refreshment. In autumn we followed the fashion of the time, and went away for change which we did not in the least require. It was when the family had settled down for the winter, when the days were short and dark, and the rigorous reign of frost upon us, that the incidents occurred which alone could justify me in intruding upon the world my private affairs. These incidents were, however, of so curious a character, that I hope my inevitable references to my own family and pressing personal interests will meet with a general pardon.

I was absent in London when these events began. In London an old Indian plunges back into the interests with which all his previous life has been associated, and meets old friends at every step. I had been circulating among some half-dozen of these – enjoying the return to my former life in shadow, though I had been so thankful in substance to throw it aside – and had missed some of my home letters, what with going down from Friday to Monday to old Benbow's place in the country, and stopping on the way back to dine and sleep at Sellar's and to take a look into Cross's stables, which occupied another day. It is never safe to miss one's letters. In this transitory life, as the Prayer Book says, how can one ever be certain what is going to happen? All was well at home. I knew exactly (I thought) what they would have to say to me: 'The weather has been so fine, that Roland has not once gone by train, and he enjoys the ride beyond anything.' 'Dear papa, be sure that you don't forget anything, but bring us so-and-so and so-and-so' – a list as long as my arm. Dear girls and dearer mother! I would not for the world have forgotten their commissions, or lost their little letters, for all the Benbows and Crosses in the world.

But I was confident in my home-comfort and peacefulness. When I got back to my club, however, three or four letters were lying for me, upon some of which I noticed the 'immediate', 'urgent', which old-fashioned people and anxious people still believe will influence the post office and quicken the speed of the mails. I was about to open one of these, when the club porter brought me two telegrams, one of which, he said, had arrived the night before. I opened, as was to be expected, the last first, and this was what I read: 'Why don't you come or answer? For God's sake, come. He is much worse.' This was a thunderbolt to fall upon a man's head who had one only son, and he the light of his eyes! The other telegram, which I opened with hands trembling so much that I lost time by my haste, was to much the same purport: 'No better; doctor afraid of brain-fever. Calls for you day and night. Let nothing detain you.' The first thing I did was to look up the time-tables to see if there was any way of getting off sooner than by the night-train, though I knew well enough there was not; and then I read the letters, which furnished, alas! too clearly, all the details. They told me that the boy had been pale for some time, with a scared look. His mother had noticed it before I left home, but would not say anything to alarm me. This look had increased day by day; and soon it was observed that Roland came home at a wild gallop through the park, his pony panting and in foam, himself 'as white as a sheet', but with the perspiration streaming from his forehead. For a long time he had resisted all questioning, but at length had developed such strange changes of mood, showing a reluctance to go to school, a desire to be fetched in the carriage at night – which was a ridiculous piece of luxury – an unwillingness to go out into the grounds, and nervous start at every sound, that his mother had insisted upon an explanation. When the boy – our boy Roland, who had never known what fear was – began to talk to her of voices he had heard in the park, and shadows that had appeared to him among the ruins, my wife promptly put him to bed and sent for Dr Simson – which, of course, was the only thing to do.

I hurried off that evening, as may be supposed, with an anxious heart. How I got through the hours before the starting of the train, I cannot tell. We must all be thankful for the quickness of the railway when in anxiety; but to have thrown myself into a post-chaise as soon as horses could be put to, would have been a relief. I got to Edinburgh very early in the blackness of the winter morning, and scarcely dared look the man in the face at whom I gasped, 'What news?' My wife had sent the brougham for me, which I concluded, before the man spoke, was a bad sign. His answer was that stereotyped answer which leaves the imagination so wildly free – 'Just the same.' Just the same! What might that mean? The horses seemed to me to creep along the long dark country road. As we dashed through the park, I thought I heard someone moaning among the trees, and clenched my fist at him (whoever he might be) with fury. Why had the fool of a woman at the gate allowed anyone to come in to disturb the quiet of the place? If I had not been in such hot haste to get home, I think I should have stopped the carriage and got out to see what tramp it was that had made an entrance, and chosen my grounds, of all places in the world – when my boy was ill! – to grumble and groan in. But I had no reason to complain of our slow pace here. The horses flew like lightning along the intervening path, and drew up at the door all panting, as if they had run a race. My wife stood waiting to receive me with a pale face, and a candle in her hand, which made her look paler still as the wind blew the flame about. 'He is sleeping,' she said in a whisper, as if her voice might wake him. And I replied, when I could find my voice, also in a whisper, as though the jingling of the horses' furniture and the sound of their hoofs must not have been more dangerous. I stood on the steps with her a moment, almost afraid to go in, now that I was here; and it seemed to me that I saw without observing, if I may say so, that the horses were unwilling to turn round, though their stables lay that way, or that the men were unwilling. These things occurred to me afterwards, though at the moment I was not capable of anything but to ask questions and to hear of the condition of the boy.

I looked at him from the door of his room, for we were afraid to go near, lest we should disturb that blessed sleep. It looked like actual sleep – not the lethargy into which my wife told me he would sometimes fall. She told me everything in the next room which communicated with his, rising now and then and going to the door of communication; and in this there was much that was very startling and confusing to the mind. It appeared that ever since the winter began, since it was early dark and night had fallen before his return from school, he had been hearing voices among the ruins – at first only a groaning, he said, at which his pony was as much alarmed as he was, but by degrees a voice. The tears ran down my wife's cheeks as she described to me how he would start up in the night and cry out, 'Oh, mother, let me in! Oh, mother, let me in!' with a pathos which rent her heart. And she sitting there all the time, only longing to do everything his heart could desire! But though she would try to soothe him, crying, 'You are at home, my darling. I am here. Don't you know me? Your mother is here,' he would only stare at her, and after a while spring up again with the same cry. At other times he would be quite reasonable, she said, asking eagerly when I was coming, but declaring that he must go with me as soon as I did so, 'to let them in'. 'The doctor thinks his nervous system must have received a shock,' my wife said. 'Oh, Henry, can it be that we have pushed him on too much with his work – a delicate boy like Roland? – and what is his work in comparison with his health? Even you would think little of honours or prizes if it hurt the boy's health.' Even I! as if I were an inhuman father sacrificing my child to my ambition. But I would not increase her trouble by taking any notice. After a while they persuaded me to lie down, to rest, and to eat – none of which things had been possible since I received their letters. The mere fact of being on the spot, of course, in itself was a great thing; and when I knew that I could be called in a moment, as soon as he was awake and wanted me, I felt capable, even in the dark, chill morning twilight, to snatch an hour or two's sleep. As it happened, I was so worn out with the strain of anxiety, and he so quieted and consoled by knowing I had come, that I was not disturbed till the afternoon, when the twilight had again settled down. There was just daylight enough to see his face when I went to him; and what a change in a fortnight! He was paler and more worn, I thought, than even in those dreadful days in the plains before we left India. His hair seemed to me to have grown long and lank; his eyes were like blazing lights projecting out of his white face. He got hold of my hand in a cold and tremulous clutch, and waved to everybody to go away. 'Go away – even mother,' he said – 'go away.' This went to her heart, for she did not like that even I should have more of the boy's confidence than herself; but my wife has never been a woman to think of herself, and she left us alone. 'Are they all gone?' he said eagerly. 'They would not let me speak. The doctor treated me as if I were a fool. You know I am not a fool, papa.'

'Yes, yes, my boy, I know; but you are ill, and quiet is so necessary. You are not only not a fool, Roland, but you are reasonable and understand. When you are ill you must deny yourself; you must not do everything that you might do being well.'

He waved his thin hand with a sort of indignation. 'Then, father, I am not ill,' he cried. 'Oh, I thought when you came you would not stop me – you would see the sense of it! What do you think is the matter with me, all of you? Simson is well enough, but he is only a doctor. What do you think is the matter with me? I am no more ill than you are. A doctor, of course, he thinks you are ill the moment he looks at you – that's what he's there for – and claps you into bed.'

'Which is the best place for you at present, my dear boy.'

'I made up my mind,' cried the little fellow, 'that I would stand it till you came home. I said to myself, I won't frighten mother and the girls. But now, father,' he cried, half jumping out of bed, 'it's not illness – it's a secret.'

His eyes shone so wildly, his face was so swept with strong feeling, that my heart sank within me. It could be nothing but fever that did it, and fever had been so fatal. I got him into my arms to put him back into bed. 'Roland,' I said, humouring the poor child, which I knew was the only way, 'if you are going to tell me this secret to do any good, you know you must be quite quiet, and not excite yourself. If you excite yourself, I must not let you speak.'

'Yes, father,' said the boy. He was quiet directly, like a man, as if he quite understood. When I had laid him back on his pillow, he looked up at me with that grateful sweet look with which children, when they are ill, break one's heart, the water coming into his eyes in his weakness. 'I was sure as soon as you were here you would know what to do,' he said.

'To be sure, my boy. Now keep quiet, and tell it all out like a man.' To think I was telling lies to my own child! for I did it only to humour him, thinking, poor little fellow, his brain was wrong.

'Yes, father. Father, there is someone in the park – someone that has been badly used.'

'Hush, my dear; you remember, there is to be no excitement. Well, who is this somebody, and who has been ill-using him? We will soon put a stop to that.'

'Ah,' cried Roland, 'but it is not so easy as you think. I don't know who it is. It is just a cry. Oh, if you could hear it! It gets into my head in my sleep. I heard it as clear – as clear – and they think that I am dreaming – or raving perhaps,' the boy said, with a sort of disdainful smile.

This look of his perplexed me; it was less like fever than I thought. 'Are you quite sure you have not dreamt it, Roland?' I said.

'Dreamt? – that!' he was springing up again when he suddenly bethought himself, and lay down flat with the same sort of smile on his face. 'The pony heard it too,' he said. 'She jumped as if she had been shot. If I had not grasped at the reins – for I was frightened, father –'

'No shame to you, my boy,' said I, though I scarcely knew why.

'If I hadn't held to her like a leech, she'd have pitched me over her head, and she never drew breath till we were at the door. Did the pony dream it?' he said, with a soft disdain, yet indulgence for my foolishness. Then he added slowly: 'It was only a cry the first time, and all the time before you went away. I wouldn't tell you, for it was so wretched to be frightened. I thought it might be a hare or a rabbit snared, and I went in the morning and looked, but there was nothing. It was after you went I heard it really first, and this is what he says.' He raised himself on his elbow close to me, and looked me in the face. '"Oh, mother, let me in! Oh, mother, let me in!"' As he said the words a mist came over his face, the mouth quivered, the soft features all melted and changed, and when he had ended these pitiful words, dissolved in a shower of heavy tears.

Was it a hallucination? Was it the fever of the brain? Was it the disordered fancy caused by great bodily weakness? How could I tell? I thought it wisest to accept it as if it were all true.

'This is very touching, Roland,' I said.

'Oh, if you had just heard it, father! I said to myself, if father heard it he would do something; but mamma, you know, she's given over to Simson, and that fellow's a doctor, and never thinks of anything but clapping you into bed.'

'We must not blame Simson for being a doctor, Roland.'

'No, no,' said my boy, with delightful toleration and indulgence; 'oh, no; that's the good of him – that's what he's for; I know that. But you – you are different; you are just father: and you'll do something – directly, papa, directly – this very night.'

'Surely,' I said. 'No doubt it is some little lost child.'

He gave me a sudden, swift look, investigating my face as though to see whether, after all, this was everything my eminence as 'father' came to – no more than that? Then he got hold of my shoulder, clutching it with his thin hand: 'Look here,' he said, with a quiver in his voice; 'suppose it wasn't – living at all!'

'My dear boy, how then could you have heard it?' I said.

He turned away from me with a pettish exclamation – 'As if you didn't know better than that!'

'Do you want to tell me it is a ghost?' I said.

Roland withdrew his hand; his countenance assumed an aspect of great dignity and gravity; a slight quiver remained about his lips. 'Whatever it was – you always said we were not to call names. It was something – in trouble. Oh, father, in terrible trouble!'

'But, my boy,' I said – I was at my wits' end – 'if it was a child that was lost, or any poor human creature – but, Roland, what do you want me to do?'

'I should know if I was you,' said the child eagerly. 'That is what I always said to myself – Father will know. Oh, papa, papa, to have to face it night after night, in such terrible, terrible trouble! and never to be able to do it any good. I don't want to cry; it's like a baby, I know; but what can I do else? – out there all by itself in the ruin, and nobody to help it. I can't bear it, I can't bear it!' cried my generous boy. And in his weakness he burst out, after many attempts to restrain it, into a great childish fit of sobbing and tears.

I do not know that I ever was in a greater perplexity in my life; and afterwards, when I thought of it, there was something comic in it too. It is bad enough to find your child's mind possessed with the conviction that he has seen – or heard – a ghost. But that he should require you to go instantly and help that ghost was the most bewildering experience that had ever come my way. I am a sober man myself, and not superstitious – at least any more than everybody is superstitious. Of course I do not believe in ghosts but I don't deny, any more than other people, that there are stories which I cannot pretend to understand. My blood got a sort of chill in my veins at the idea that Roland should be a ghost-seer; for that generally means a hysterical temperament and weak health, and all that men most hate and fear for their children. But that I should take up his ghost and right its wrongs and save it from its trouble, was such a mission as was enough to confuse any man. I did my best to console my boy without giving any promise of this astonishing kind; but he was too sharp for me. He would have none of my caresses. With sobs breaking in at intervals upon his voice, and the rain-drops hanging on his eyelids, he yet returned to the charge.

'It will be there now – it will be there all the night. Oh think, papa, think, if it was me! I can't rest for thinking of it. Don't!' he cried, putting away my hand – 'don't! You go and help it, and mother can take care of me.'

'But, Roland, what can I do?'

My boy opened his eyes, which were large with weakness and fever, and gave me a smile such, I think, as sick children only know the secret of. 'I was sure you would know as soon as you came. I always said – Father will know: and mother,' he cried, with a softening of repose upon his face, his limbs relaxing, his form sinking with a luxurious ease in his bed – 'mother can come and take care of me.'

I called her, and saw him turn to her with the complete dependence of a child, and then I went away and left them, as perplexed a man as any in Scotland. I must say, however, I had this consolation, that my mind was greatly eased about Roland. He might be under a hallucination, but his head was clear enough, and I did not think him so ill as everybody else did. The girls were astonished even at the ease with which I took it. 'How do you think he is?' they said in a breath, coming round me, laying hold of me. 'Not half so ill as I expected,' I said; 'not very bad at all.' 'Oh, papa, you are a darling,' cried Agatha, kissing me, and crying upon my shoulder; while little Jeanie, who was as pale as Roland, clasped both her arms round mine, and could not speak at all. I knew nothing about it, not half so much as Simson: but they believed in me; they had a feeling that all would go right now. God is very good to you when your children look to you like that. It makes one humble, not proud. I was not worthy of it; and then I recollected that I had to act the part of a father to Roland's ghost, which made me almost laugh, though I might just as well have cried. It was the strangest mission that ever was entrusted to mortal man.

It was then I remembered suddenly the looks of the men when they turned to take the brougham to the stables in the dark that morning: they had not liked it and the horses had not liked it. I remembered that even in my anxiety about Roland I had heard them tearing along the avenue back to the stables, and had made a memorandum mentally that I must speak of it. It seemed to me that the best thing I could do was to go to the stables now and make a few inquiries. It is impossible to fathom the minds of rustics; there might be some devilry or practical joking, for anything I knew, or they might have some interest in getting up a bad reputation for the Brentwood avenue. It was getting dark by the time I went out, and nobody who knows the country will need to be told how black is the darkness of a November night under high laurel bushes and yew trees. I walked into the heart of the shrubberies two or three times, not seeing a step before me, till I came out upon the broader carriage-road, where the trees opened a little, and there was a faint grey glimmer of sky visible, under which the great limes and elms stood darkling like ghosts; but it grew black again as I approached the corner where the ruins lay. Both eyes and ears were on the alert, as may be supposed; but I could see nothing in the absolute gloom, and, so far as I can recollect, I heard nothing. Nevertheless there came a strong impression upon me that somebody was there. It is a sensation which most people have felt. I have seen when it has been strong enough to awake me out of sleep, the sense of someone looking at me. I suppose my imagination had been affected by Roland's story; and the mystery of the darkness is always full of suggestions. I stamped my feet violently on the gravel to rouse myself, and called out sharply, 'Who's there?' Nobody answered, nor did I expect anyone to answer, but the impression had been made. I was so foolish that I did not like to look back, but went sideways, keeping an eye on the gloom behind. It was with great relief that I spied the light in the stables, making a sort of oasis in the darkness. I walked very quickly into the midst of that lighted and cheerful place, and thought the clank of the groom's pail one of the pleasantest sounds I had ever heard. The coachman was the head of this little colony, and it was to his house I went to pursue my investigations. He was a native of the district, and had taken care of the place in the absence of the family for years; it was impossible but that he must know everything that was going on, and all the traditions of the place. The men, I could see, eyed me anxiously when I thus appeared at such an hour among them, and followed me with their eyes to Jarvis's house, where he lived alone with his old wife, their children being all married and out in the world. Mrs Jarvis met me with anxious questions. How was the poor young gentleman? But the others knew, I could see by their faces, that not even this was the foremost thing in my mind.

'Noises? – ou ay, there'll be noises – the wind in the trees, and the water soughing down the glen. As for tramps, Cornel, no, there's little o' that kind o' cattle about here; and Merran at the gate's a careful body.' Jarvis moved about with some embarrassment from one leg to another as he spoke. He kept in the shade, and did not look at me more than he could help. Evidently his mind was perturbed, and he had reasons for keeping his own counsel. His wife sat by, giving him a quick look now and then, but saying nothing. The kitchen was very snug, and warm, and bright – as different as could be from the chill and mystery of the night outside.

'I think you are trifling with me, Jarvis,' I said.

'Triflin', Cornel? no me. What would I trifle for? If the deevil himsel was in the auld hoose, I have no interest in't one way or another –'

'Sandy, hold your peace!' cried his wife imperatively.

.'And what am I to hold my peace for, wi' the Cornel standing there asking a' thae questions? I'm saying, if the deevil himsel –'

'And I'm telling ye hold your peace!' cried the woman, in great excitement. 'Dark November weather and lang nichts, and us that ken a' we ken. How daur ye name – a name that shouldna be

spoken?' She threw down her stocking and got up, also in great
agitation. 'I tell't ye you never could keep it. It's no a thing that
will hide; and the haill toun kens as weel as you or me. Tell the
Cornel straight out – or see, I'll do it. I dinna hold wi' your secrets:
and a secret that the haill toun kens!' She snapped her fingers with
an air of large disdain. As for Jarvis, ruddy and big as he was, he
shrank to nothing before this decided woman. He repeated to her
two or three times her own adjuration, 'Hold your peace!' then,
suddenly changing his tone, cried out, 'Tell him then, confound
ye! I'll wash my hands o't. If a' the ghosts in Scotland were in the
auld hoose, is that.ony concern o' mine?'

After this I elicited without much difficulty the whole story. In
the opinion of the Jarvises, and of everybody about, the certainty
that the place was haunted was beyond all doubt. As Sandy and
his wife warmed to the tale, one tripping up another in their
eagerness to tell everything, it gradually developed as distinct a
superstition as I ever heard, and not without poetry and pathos.
How long it was since the voice had been heard first, nobody could
tell with certainty. Jarvis's opinion was that his father, who had
been coachman at Brentwood before him, had never heard
anything about it, and that the whole thing had arisen within the
last ten years, since the complete dismantling of the old house:
which was a wonderfully modern date for a tale so well authenti-
cated. According to these witnesses, and to several whom I
questioned afterwards, and who were all in perfect agreement, it
was only in the months of November and December that 'the
visitation' occurred. During these months, the darkest of the year,
scarcely a night passed without the recurrence of these inexplicable cries. Nothing, it was said, had ever been seen – at least
nothing that could be identified. Some people, bolder or more
imaginative than the others, had seen the darkness moving, Mrs
Jarvis said, with unconscious poetry. It began when night fell and
continued, at intervals, till day broke. Very often it was only an
inarticulate cry and moaning, but sometimes the words which had
taken possession of my poor boy's fancy had been distinctly
audible – 'Oh, mother, let me in!' The Jarvises were not aware
that there had ever been any investigation into it. The estate of
Brentwood had lapsed into the hands of a distant branch of the
family, who had lived but little there; and of the many people who

had taken it, as I had done, few had remained through two Decembers. And nobody had taken the trouble to make a very close examination into the facts. 'No, no,' Jarvis said, shaking his head, 'No, no, Cornel. Wha wad set themsels up for a laughin'-stock to a' the country-side, making a wark about a ghost? Naebody believes in ghosts. It bid to be the wind in the trees, the last gentleman said, or some effec' o' the water wrastlin' among the rocks. He said it was a' quite easy explained: but he gave up the hoose. And when you cam, Cornel, we were awfu' anxious you should never hear. What for should I have spoiled the bargain and hairmed the property for no-thing?'

'Do you call my child's life nothing?' I said in the trouble of the moment, unable to restrain myself. 'And instead of telling this all to me, you have told it to him – to a delicate boy, a child unable to sift evidence, or judge for himself, a tender-hearted young creature –'

I was walking about the room with an anger all the hotter that I felt it to be most likely quite unjust. My heart was full of bitterness against the stolid retainers to a family who were content to risk other people's children and comfort rather than let the house lie empty. If I had been warned I might have taken precautions, or left the place, or sent Roland away, a hundred things which now I could not do; and here I was with my boy in a brain-fever, and his life, the most precious life on earth, hanging in the balance, dependent on whether or not I could get to the reason of a commonplace ghost-story! I paced about in high wrath, not seeing what I was to do; for, to take Roland away, even if he were able to travel, would not settle his agitated mind; and I feared even that a scientific explanation of refracted sound, or reverberation, or any other of the easy certainties with which we elder men are silenced, would have very little effect upon the boy.

'Cornel,' said Jarvis solemnly, 'and *she'll* bear me witness – the young gentleman never heard a word from me – no, nor from either groom or gardener; I'll gie ye my word for that. In the first place, he's no a lad that invites ye to talk. There are some that are, and some that arena. Some will draw ye on, till ye've tellt them a' the clatter of the toun, and a' ye ken, and whiles mair. But Maister Roland, his mind's fu' of his books. He's aye civil and kind, and a fine lad; but no that sort. And ye see it's for a' our interest, Cornel, that you should stay at Brentwood. I took it upon me mysel to pass the word – "No a syllable to Maister Roland, nor to the young ieddies – no a syllable." The women-servants, that have little reason to be out at night, ken little or nothing about it. And some think it grand to have a ghost so long as they're no in the way of coming across it. If you had been tellt the story to begin with, maybe ye would have thought so yourself.'

This was true enough, though it did not throw any light upon my perplexity. If we had heard of it to start with, it is possible that all the family would have considered the possession of a ghost a distinct advantage. It is the fashion of the times. We never think what a risk it is to play with young imaginations, but cry out, in the fashionable jargon, 'A ghost! – nothing else was wanted to make it perfect.' I should not have been above this myself. I should have smiled, of course, at the idea of the ghost at all, but then to feel that it was mine would have pleased my vanity. Oh, yes, I claim no exemption. The girls would have been delighted. I could fancy their eagerness, their interest, and excitement. No; if we had been told, it would have done no good – we should have made the bargain all the more eagerly, the fools that we are. 'And there has been no attempt to investigate it,' I said, 'to see what it really is?'

'Eh, Cornel,' said the coachman's wife, 'wha would investigate, as ye call it, a thing that nobody believes in? Ye would be the laughing-stock of a' the country-side, as my man says.'

'But you believe in it,' I said, turning upon her hastily. The woman was taken by surprise. She made a step backward out of my way.

'Lord, Cornel, how ye frichten a body! Me! – there's awful strange things in this world. An unlearned person doesna ken what to think. But the minister and the gentry they just laugh in your face. Inquire into the thing that is not! Na, na, we just let it be.'

'Come with me, Jarvis,' I said hastily, 'and we'll make an attempt at least. Say nothing to the men or to anybody. I'll come back after dinner, and we'll make a serious attempt to see what it is, if it is anything. If I hear it – which I doubt – you may be sure I shall never rest till I make it out. Be ready for me about ten o'clock.'

'Me, Cornel!' Jarvis said, in a faint voice. I had not been looking at him in my own preoccupation, but when I did so, I found that the greatest change had come over that fat and ruddy coachman. 'Me, Cornel!' he repeated, wiping the perspiration from his brow. His ruddy face hung in flabby folds, his knees knocked together, his voice seemed half extinguished in his throat. Then he began to rub his hands and smile upon me in a deprecating, imbecile way. 'There's nothing I wouldna do to pleasure ye, Cornel!' taking a step further back. 'I'm sure *she* kens I've aye said I never had to do with a mair fair, weelspoken gentleman –' Here Jarvis came to a pause, again looking at me, rubbing his hands.

'Well?' I said.

'But eh, sir!' he went on, with the same imbecile yet insinuating smile, 'if ye'll reflect that I am no used to my feet. With a horse atween my legs, or the reins in my hand, I'm maybe nae worse than other men; but on fit, Cornel –. It's no the – bogles; but I've been cavalry, ye see,' with a little hoarse laugh, 'a' my life. To face a thing ye didna understan' – on your feet, Cornel.'

'Well, sir, if I do it,' said I tartly, 'why shouldn't you?'

'Eh, Cornel, there's an awfu' difference. In the first place, ye tramp about the haill country-side, and think naething of it; but a walk tires me mair than a hunard miles' drive: and then ye'e a gentleman, and do your ain pleasure; and you're no so auld as me; and it's for your ain bairn, ye see, Cornel; and then –'

'He believes in it, Cornel, and you dinna believe in it,' the woman said.

'Will you come with me?' I said, turning to her.

She jumped back, upsetting her chair in her bewilderment. 'Me!' with a scream, and then fell into a sort of hysterical laugh. 'I wouldna say but what I would go; but what would the folk say to hear of Cornel Mortimer with an auld silly woman at his heels?'

The suggestion made me laugh too, though I had little inclination for it. 'I'm sorry you have so little spirit, Jarvis,' I said. 'I must find someone else, I suppose.'

Jarvis, touched by this, began to remonstrate, but I cut him short. My butler was a soldier who had been with me in India, and was not supposed to fear anything – man or devil – certainly not the former; and I felt that I was losing time. The Jarvises were too thankful to get rid of me. They attended me to the door with the most anxious courtesies. Outside, the two grooms stood close by, a little confused by my sudden exit. I don't know if perhaps they had been listening – at least standing as near as possible, to catch any scrap of the conversation. I waved my hand to them as I went past, in answer to their salutations, and it was very apparent to me that they also were glad to see me go.

And it will be thought very strange, but it would be weak not to add, that I myself, though bent on the investigation I have spoken of, pledged to Roland to carry it out, and feeling that my boy's health, perhaps his life, depended on the result of my inquiry – I felt the most unaccountable reluctance to pass these ruins on my way home. My curiosity was intense; and yet it was all my mind could do to pull my body along. I daresay the scientific people would describe it the other way, and attribute my cowardice to the state of my stomach. I went on; but if I had followed my impulse, I should have turned and bolted. Everything in me seemed to cry out against it; my heart thumped, my pulses all began, like sledge-hammers, beating against my ears and every sensitive part. It was very dark, as I have said; the old house, with its shapeless tower, loomed a heavy mass through the darkness, which was only not entirely so solid as itself. On the other hand, the great dark cedars of which we were so proud seemed to fill up the night. My foot strayed out of the path in my confusion and the gloom together, and I brought myself up with a cry as I felt myself knock against something solid. What was it? The contact with hard stone and lime and prickly bramble bushes restored me a little to myself. 'Oh, it's only the old gable,' I said aloud, with a little laugh to reassure myself. The rough feeling of the stones reconciled me. As I groped about thus, I shook off my visionary folly. What so easily explained as that I should have strayed from the path in the darkness? This brought me back to common existence, as if I had been shaken by a wise hand out of all the silliness of superstition. How silly it was, after all! What did it matter which path I took? I laughed again, this time with better heart – when suddenly, in a moment, the blood was chilled in my veins, a shiver stole along my spine, my faculties seemed to forsake me. Close by me at my side, at my feet, there was a sigh. No, not a groan, not a moaning, not anything so tangible – a perfectly soft, faint, inarticulate sigh. I sprang back, and my heart stopped beating. Mistaken! no, mistake was impossible. I heard it as clearly as I heard myself speak; a long soft, weary sigh, as if drawn to the utmost, and emptying out a load of sadness that filled the breast. To hear this in the solitude, in the dark, in the night (though it was still early), had an effect which I cannot describe. I feel it now – something cold creeping over me, up into my hair, and down to my feet, which refused to move. I cried out, with a trembling voice, 'Who is there?' as I had done before – but there was no reply.

I got home I don't quite know how; but in my mind there was no longer any indifference as to the thing, whatever it was, that haunted these ruins. My scepticism disappeared like a mist. I was as firmly determined that there was something as Roland was. I did not for a moment pretend to myself that it was possible I could be deceived; there were movements and noises which I understood all about, cracklings of small branches in the frost, and little rolls of gravel on the path, such as have a very eerie sound sometimes, and perplex you with wonder as to who has done it, *when there is no real mystery*; but I assure you all these little movements of nature don't affect you one bit *when there is something*. I understood *them*. I did not understand the sigh. That was not simple nature; there was meaning in it – feeling, the soul of a creature invisible. This is the thing that human nature trembles at – a creature invisible, yet with sensations, feelings, a power somehow of expressing itself. I had not the same sense of unwillingness to turn my back upon the scene of the mystery which I had experienced in going to the stables; but I almost ran home, impelled by eagerness to get everything done that had to be done in order to apply myself to finding it out. Bagley was in the hall as usual when I went in. He was always there in the afternoon, always with the appearance of perfect occupation, yet, so far as I know, never doing anything. The door was open, so that I hurried in without any pause, breathless; but the sight of his calm regard, as he came to help me off with my overcoat, subdued me in a moment. Anything out of the way, anything incomprehensible, faded to nothing in the presence of Bagley. You saw and wondered how *he* was made: the parting of his hair, the tie of his white neckcloth, the fit of his trousers, all perfect as works of art; but you could see how they were done, which makes all the difference. I flung myself upon him, so to speak, without waiting to note the extreme unlikeness of the man to anything of the kind I meant.

'Bagley,' I said, 'I want you to come out with me to-night to watch for –'

'Poachers, Colonel,' he said, a gleam of pleasure running all over him.

'No, Bagley; a great deal worse,' I cried.

'Yes, Colonel; at what hour, sir?' the man said; but then I had not told him what it was.

It was ten o'clock when we set out. All was perfectly quiet indoors. My wife was with Roland, who had been quite calm, she said, and who (though, no doubt, the fever must run its course) had been better since I came. I told Bagley to put on a thick greatcoat over his evening coat, and did the same myself – with strong boots; for the soil was like a sponge, or worse. Talking to him, I almost forgot what we were going to do. It was darker even than it had been before, and Bagley kept very close to me as we went along. I had a small lantern in my hand, which gave us a partial guidance. We had come to the corner where the path turns. On one side was the bowling-green, which the girls had taken possession of for their croquet-ground – a wonderful enclosure surrounded by high hedges of holly, three hundred years old and more; on the other, the ruins. Both were black as night; but before we got so far, there was a little opening in which we could just discern the trees and the lighter line of the road. I thought it best to pause there and take breath. 'Bagley,' I said, 'there is something about these ruins I don't understand. It is there I am going. Keep your eyes open and your wits about you. Be ready to pounce upon any stranger you see – anything, man or woman. Don't hurt, but seize – anything you see.' 'Colonel,' said Bagley, with a little tremor in his breath, 'they do say there's things there – as is neither man nor woman.' There was no time for words. 'Are you game to follow me, my man? that's the question,' I said. Bagley fell in without a word, and saluted. I knew then I had nothing to fear.

We went, so far as I could guess, exactly as I had come, when I heard that sigh. The darkness, however, was so complete that all marks, as of trees or paths, disappeared. One moment we felt our feet on gravel, another sinking noiselessly into the slippery grass, that was all. I had shut up my lantern, not wishing to scare anyone, whoever it might be. Bagley followed, it seemed to me, exactly in my footsteps as I made my way, as I supposed, towards the mass of the ruined house. We seemed to take a long time groping along seeking this; the squash of the wet soil under our feet was the only thing that marked our progress. After a while I stood still to see, or rather feel, where we were. The darkness was very still, but no stiller than is usual in a winter's night. The sounds I have mentioned – the crackling of twigs, the roll of a pebble, the sound of some rustle in the dead leaves, or creeping creature on the grass – were audible when you listened, all mysterious enough when your mind is disengaged, but to me cheering now as signs of the livingness of nature, even in the death of the frost. As we stood still there came up from the trees in the glen the prolonged hoot of an owl. Bagley started with alarm, being in a state of general nervousness, and not knowing what he was afraid of. But to me the sound was encouraging and pleasant, being so comprehensible. 'An owl,' I said, under my breath. 'Y-es, Colonel,' said Bagley, his teeth chattering. We stood still about five minutes, while it broke into the still brooding of the air, the sound widening out in circles, dying upon the darkness. This sound, which is not a cheerful one, made me almost gay. It was natural, and relieved the tension of the mind. I moved on with new courage, my nervous excitement calming down.

When all at once, quite suddenly, close to us, at our feet, there broke a cry. I made a spring backwards in the first moment of surprise and horror, and in doing so came sharply against the same rough masonry and brambles that had struck me before. This new sound came upwards from the ground – a low, moaning, wailing voice, full of suffering and pain. The contrast between it and the hoot of the owl was indescribable; the one with a wholesome wildness and naturalness that hurt nobody – the other, a sound that made one's blood curdle, full of human misery. With a great deal of fumbling – for in spite of everything I could do to keep up my courage my hands shook – I managed to remove the slide of my lantern. The light leaped out like something living, and made the place visible in a moment. We were what would have been inside the ruined building had anything remained but the gable-wall which I have described. It was close to us, the vacant doorway in it going out straight into the blackness outside. The light showed the bit of wall, the ivy glistening upon it in clouds of dark green, the bramble-branches waving, and below, the open door – a door that led to nothing. It was from this the voice came which died out just as the light flashed upon this strange scene. There was a moment's silence, and then it broke forth again. The sound was so near, so penetrating, so pitiful, that, on the nervous start I gave, the light fell out of my hand. As I groped for it in the dark my hand was clutched by Bagley, who I think must have dropped upon his knees; but I was too much perturbed myself to think much of this. He clutched at me in the confusion of his terror, forgetting all his usual decorum. 'For God's sake, what is it, sir?' he gasped. If I yielded, there was evidently an end to both of us. 'I can't tell,' I said, 'any more than you; that's what we've got to find out: up, man, up!' I pulled him to his feet. 'Will you go round and examine the other side, or will you stay here with the lantern?' Bagley gasped at me with a face of horror. 'Can't we stay together, Colonel?' he said – his knees were trembling under him. I pushed him against the corner of the wall, and put the light into his hands. 'Stand fast till I come back; shake yourself together, man; let nothing pass you,' I said. The voice was within two or three feet of us, of that there could be no doubt.

I went myself to the other side of the wall, keeping close to it. The light shook in Bagley's hand, but, tremulous though it was, shone out through the vacant door, one oblong block of light marking all the crumbling corners and hanging masses of foliage. Was that something dark huddled in a heap by the side of it? I pushed forward across the light in the doorway, and fell upon it with my hands; but it was only a juniper bush growing close against the wall. Meanwhile, the sight of my figure crossing the doorway had brought Bagley's nervous excitement to a height; he flew at me, gripping my shoulder. 'I've got him, Colonel! I've got him!' he cried, with a voice of sudden exultation. He thought it was a man, and was at once relieved. But at that moment the voice burst forth again between us, at our feet – more close to us than any separate being could be. He dropped off from me, and fell against the wall, his jaw dropping as if he were dying. I suppose, at the same moment, he saw that it was me whom he had clutched. I, for my part, had scarcely more command of myself. I snatched the light out of his hand, and flashed it all about me wildly. Nothing – the juniper bush which I thought I had never seen before, the heavy growth of the glistening ivy, the brambles waving. It was close to my ears now, crying, crying, pleading as if for life. Either I heard the same words Roland had heard, or else, in my excitement, his imagination got possession of mine. The voice went on, growing into distinct articulation, but wavering about, now from one point, now from another, as if the owner of it were slowly moving back and forward – 'Mother! mother!' and then an outburst of wailing. As my mind steadied, getting accustomed (as one's mind gets accustomed to anything), it seemed to me as if some uneasy, miserable creature was pacing up and down before a closed door. Sometimes – but that must have been excitement – I thought I heard a sound like knocking, and then another burst, 'Oh, mother! mother!' All this close, close to the space where I was standing with my lantern – now before me, now behind me: a creature restless, unhappy, moaning, crying, before the vacant doorway, which no-one could either shut or open more.

'Do you hear it, Bagley? Do you hear what it is saying?' I cried, stepping in through the doorway. He was lying against the wall – his eyes glazed, half dead with terror. He made a motion of his lips as if to answer me, but no sounds came; then lifted his hand with a curious imperative movement as if ordering me to be silent and listen. And how long I did so I cannot tell. It began to have an interest, an exciting hold upon me, which I could not describe. It seemed to call up visibly a scene anyone could understand – a something shut out, restlessly wandering to and fro; sometimes the voice dropped, as if throwing itself down – sometimes wandered off a few paces, growing sharp and clear. 'Oh, mother, let me in! Oh, mother, mother, let me in! Oh, let me in!' every word was clear to me. No wonder the boy had gone wild with pity. I tried to steady my mind upon Roland, upon his conviction that I could do something, but my head swam with the excitement, even when I partially overcame the terror. At last the words died away, and there was a sound of sobs and moaning. I cried out, 'In the name of God who are you?' with a kind of feeling in my mind that to use the name of God was profane, seeing that I did not believe in ghosts or anything supernatural; but I did it all the same, and waited, my heart giving a leap of terror lest there should be a reply. Why this should have been I cannot tell, but I had a feeling that if there was an answer it would be more than I could bear. But there was no answer; the moaning went on, and then, as if it had been real, the voice rose, a little higher again, the words recommenced, 'Oh, mother, let me in! Oh, mother, let me in!' with an expression that was heart-breaking to hear.

As if it had been real! What do I mean by that? I suppose I got less alarmed as the thing went on. I began to recover the use of my senses – I seemed to explain it all to myself by saying that this had once happened, that it was a recollection of a real scene. Why there should have seemed something quite satisfactory and composing in this explanation I cannot tell, but so it was. I began to listen almost as if it had been a play, forgetting Bagley, who, I almost think, had fainted, leaning against the wall. I was startled out of this strange spectatorship that had fallen upon me by the sudden rush of something which made my heart jump once more, a large black figure in the doorway waving its arms. 'Come in! come in! come in!' it shouted out hoarsely at the top of a deep bass voice, and then poor Bagley fell down senseless across the threshold. He was less sophisticated than I – he had not been able to bear it any longer. I took him for something supernatural, as he took me, and it was some time before I awoke to the necessities of the moment. I remembered only after, that from the time I began to give my attention to the man, I heard the other voice no more. It was some time before I brought him to. It must have been a strange scene; the lantern making a luminous spot in the darkness, the man's white face lying on the black earth, I over him, doing what I could for him. Probably I should have been thought to be murdering him had anyone seen us. When at last I succeeded in pouring a little brandy down his throat he sat up and looked about him wildly. 'What's up?' he said; then recognizing me, tried to struggle to his feet with a faint 'Beg your pardon, Colonel.' I got him home as best I could, making him lean upon my arm. The great fellow was as weak as a child. Fortunately he did not for some time remember what had happened. From the time Bagley fell the voice had stopped, and all was still.

'You've got an epidemic in your house, Colonel,' Simson said to me next morning. 'What's the meaning of it all? Here's your butler raving about a voice. This will never do, you know; and so far as I can make out, you are in it too.'

'Yes, I am in it, doctor. I thought I had better speak to you. Of course you are treating Roland all right – but the boy is not raving, he is as sane as you or me. It's all true.'

'As sane as – I – or you. I never thought the boy insane. He's got cerebral excitement, fever. I don't know what you've got. There's something very queer about the look of your eyes.'

'Come,' said I, 'you can't put us all to bed, you know. You had better listen and hear the symptoms in full.'

The doctor shrugged his shoulders, but he listened to me patiently. He did not believe a word of the story, that was clear; but he heard it all from beginning to end. 'My dear fellow,' he said, 'the boy told me just the same. It's an epidemic. When one person falls a victim to this sort of thing, it's as safe as can be – there's always two or three.'

'Then how do you account for it?' I said.

'Oh, account for it! – that's a different matter; there's no accounting for the freaks our brains are subject to. If it's delusion; if it's some trick of the echoes or the winds – some phonetic disturbance or other –'

'Come with me to-night, and judge for yourself,' I said.

Upon this he laughed aloud, then said, 'That's not such a bad idea; but it would ruin me for ever if it were known that John Simson was ghost-hunting.'

'There it is,' said I; 'you dart down on us who are unlearned with your phonetic disturbances, but you daren't examine what the thing really is for fear of being laughed at. That's science!'

'It's not science – it's common sense,' said the doctor. 'The thing has delusion on the front of it. It is encouraging an unwholesome tendency even to examine. What good could come of it? Even if I am convinced, I shouldn't believe.'

'I should have said so yesterday; and I don't want you to be convinced or to believe,' said I. 'If you prove it to be a delusion, I shall be very much obliged to you for one. Come; somebody must go with me.'

'You are cool,' said the doctor. 'You've disabled this poor fellow of yours, and made him – on that point – a lunatic for life; and now you want to disable me. But for once, I'll do it. To save appearance, if you'll give me a bed, I'll come over after my last rounds.'

It was agreed that I should meet him at the gate, and that we should visit the scene of last night's occurrences before we came to the house, so that nobody might be the wiser. It was scarcely possible to hope that the cause of Bagley's sudden illness should not somehow steal into the knowledge of the servants at least, and it was better that all should be done as quietly as possible. The day seemed to me a very long one. I had to spend a certain part of it with Roland, which was a terrible ordeal for me – for what could I say to the boy? The improvement continued, but he was still in a very precarious state, and the trembling vehemence with which he turned to me when his mother left the room filled me with alarm. 'Father!' he said quietly. 'Yes, my boy; I am giving my best attention to it – all is being done that I can do. I have not come to any conclusion – yet. I am neglecting nothing you said.' I cried. What I could not do was to give his active mind any encouragement to dwell upon the mystery. It was a hard predicament, for some satisfaction had to be given him. He looked at me very wistfully, with the great blue eyes which shone so large and brilliant out of his white and worn face. 'You must trust me,' I said. 'Yes, father. Father understands,' he said to himself, as if to soothe some inward doubt. I left him as soon as I could. He was about the the most precious thing I had on earth, and his health my first thought; but yet somehow, in the excitement of this other subject, I put that aside, and preferred not to dwell upon Roland, which was the most curious part of it all.

That night at eleven I met Simson at the gate. He had come by train, and I let him in gently myself. I had been so much absorbed in the coming experiment that I passed the ruins in going to meet him, almost without thought, if you can understand that. I had my lantern; and he showed me a coil of taper which he had ready for use. 'There is nothing like light,' he said, in his scoffing tone. It was a very still night, scarcely a sound, but not so dark. We could keep the path without difficulty as we went along. As we approached the spot we could hear a low moaning, broken occasionally by a bitter cry. 'Perhaps that is your voice,' said the doctor; 'I thought it must be something of the kind. That's a poor brute caught in some of these infernal traps of yours; you'll find it among the bushes somewhere.' I said nothing. I felt no particular fear, but a triumphant satisfaction in what was to follow. I led him to the spot where Bagley and I had stood on the previous night. All was silent as a winter night could be – so silent that we heard far off the sound of the horses in the stables, the shutting of a window at the house. Simson lighted his taper and went peering about, poking into all the corners. We looked like two conspirators lying in wait for some unfortunate traveller; but not a sound broke the quiet. The moaning had stopped before we came up; a star or two shone over us in the sky, looking down as if surprised at our strange proceedings. Dr Simson did nothing but utter subdued laughs under his breath. 'I thought as much,' he said. 'It is just the same with tables and all other kinds of ghostly apparatus; a sceptic's presence stops everything. When I am present nothing ever comes off. How long do you think it will be necessary to stay here? Oh, I don't complain; only, when *you* are satisfied, *I* am – quite.'

I will not deny that I was disappointed beyond measure by this result. It made me look like a credulous fool. It gave the doctor such a pull over me as nothing else could. I should point all his morals for years to come, and his materialism, his scepticism, would be increased beyond endurance. 'It seems, indeed,' I said, 'that there is to be no –' 'Manifestation,' he said, laughing; 'that is what all the mediums say. No manifestations, in consequence of the presence of an unbeliever.' His laugh sounded very uncomfortable to me in the silence; and it was now near midnight. But that laugh seemed the signal; before it died away the moaning we had heard before was resumed. It started from some distance off, and came towards us, nearer and nearer, like someone walking along and moaning to himself. There could be no idea now that it was a hare caught in a trap. The approach was slow, like that of a weak person with little halts and pauses. We heard it coming along the grass straight towards the vacant doorway. Simson had been a little startled by the first sound. He said hastily, 'That child has no business to be out so late.' But he felt, as well as I, that this was no child's voice. As it came nearer, he grew silent, and, going to the doorway with his taper, stood looking out towards the sound. The taper being unprotected blew about in the night air, though there was scarcely any wind. I threw the light of my lantern steady and white across the same space. It was a blaze of light in the midst of the blackness. A little icy thrill had gone over me at the first sound, but as it came close, I confess that my only feeling was satisfaction. The scoffer could scoff no more. The light touched his own face, and showed a very perplexed countenance. If he was afraid, he concealed it with great success, but he was perplexed. And then all that had happened on the previous night was enacted once more. It fell strangely upon me with a sense of repetition. Every cry, every sob seemed the same as before. I listened almost without any emotion at all in my own person, thinking of its effect upon Simson. He maintained a very bold front on the whole. All that coming and going of the voice was, if our ears could be trusted, exactly in front of the vacant, blank doorway, blazing full of light, which caught and shone in the glistening leaves of the great hollies at a little distance. Not a rabbit could have crossed the turf without being seen; but there was nothing. After a time, Simson, with a certain caution and bodily reluctance, as it seemed to me, went out with his roll of taper into this space. His figure showed against the holly in full outline. Just at this moment, the voice sank, as was its custom, and seemed to fling itself down at the door. Simson recoiled violently, as if someone had come up against him, then turned, and held his taper low as if examining something. 'Do you see anybody?' I cried in a whisper, feeling the chill of nervous panic steal over me at this action. 'It's nothing but a – confounded juniper bush,' he said. This I knew very well to be nonsense, for the juniper bush was on the other side. He went about after this round and round poking his taper everywhere, then returned to me on the inner side of the wall. He scoffed no longer; his face was contracted and pale. 'How long does this go on?' he whispered to me, like a man who does not wish to interrupt someone who is speaking. I had become too much perturbed myself to remark whether the successions and changes of the voice were the same as last night. It suddenly went out in the air almost as he was speaking, with a soft reiterated sob dying away. If there had been anything to be seen, I should have said that the person was at that moment crouching on the ground close to the door.

We walked home very silent afterwards. It was only when we were in sight of the house that I said, 'What do you think of it?' 'I can't tell what to think of it,' he said quickly. He took – though he was a very temperate man – not the claret I was going to offer him,

Margaret Oliphant

but some brandy from the tray, and swallowed it almost undi-luted. 'Mind you, I don't believe a word of it,' he said, when he had lighted his candle; 'but I can't tell what to think,' he turned round to add, when he was half-way upstairs.

All of this, however, did me no good with the solution of my problem. I was to help this weeping, sobbing thing, which was already to me as distinct a personality as anything I knew – or what should I say to Roland? It was on my heart that my boy would die if I could not find some way of helping this creature. You may be surprised that I should speak of it in this way. I did not know if it was man or woman; but I no more doubted that it was a soul in pain than I doubted my own being; and it was my business to soothe this pain – to deliver it, if that was possible. Was ever such a task given to an anxious father trembling for his only boy? I felt in my heart, fantastic as it may appear, that I must fulfil this somehow, or part with my child; and you may conceive that rather than do that I was ready to die. But even my dying would not have advanced me – unless by bringing me into the same world with that seeker at the door.

Next morning Simson was out before breakfast, and came in with evident signs of the damp grass on his boots, and a look of worry and weariness, which did not say much for the night he had passed. He improved a little after breakfast, and visited his two patients, for Bagley was still an invalid. I went out with him on his way to the train, to hear what he had to say about the boy. 'He is going on very well,' he said; 'there are no complications as yet. But mind you, that's not a boy to be trifled with, Mortimer. Not a word to him about last night.' I had to tell him then of my last interview with Roland, and of the impossible demand he had made upon me – by which, though he tried to laugh, he was much discomposed, as I could see. 'We must just perjure ourselves all round,' he said, 'and swear you exorcized it'; but the man was too kind-hearted to be satisfied with that. 'It's frightfully serious for you, Mortimer. I can't laugh as I should like to. I wish I saw a way out of it, for your sake. By the way,' he added shortly, 'didn't you notice that juniper bush on the left-hand side?' 'There was one on the right hand of the door. I noticed you made that mistake last night.' 'Mistake!' he cried, with a curious low laugh, pulling up the collar of his coat as though he felt the cold – 'there's no juniper there this morning, left or right. Just go and see.' As he stepped into the train a few minutes after, he looked back upon me and beckoned me for a parting word. 'I'm coming back to-night,' he said.

I don't think I had any feeling about this as I turned away from that common bustle of the railway which made my private preoccupations feel so strangely out of date. There had been a distinct satisfaction in my mind before that his scepticism had been so entirely defeated. But the more serious part of the matter pressed upon me now. I went straight from the railway to the manse, which stood on a little plateau on the side of the river opposite to the woods of Brentwood. The minister was one of a class which is not so common in Scotland as it used to be. He was a man of good family, well educated in the Scotch way, strong in philosophy, not so strong in Greek, strongest of all in experience – a man who had 'come across', in the course of his life, most people of note that had ever been in Scotland – and who was said to be very sound in doctrine, without infringing the toleration with which old men, who are good men, are generally endowed. He was old-fashioned; perhaps he did not think so much about the troublous problems of theology as many of the young men, nor ask himself any hard questions about the Confession of Faith – but he understood human nature, which is perhaps better. He received me with a cordial welcome. 'Come away, Colonel Mortimer,' he said; 'I'm all the more glad to see you, that I feel it's a good sign for the boy. He's doing well? – God be praised – and the Lord bless him and keep him. He has many a poor body's prayers – and that can do nobody harm.'

'He will need them all, Dr Moncrieff,' I said, 'and your counsel too.' And I told him the story – more than I had told Simson. The old clergyman listened to me with many suppressed exclamations, and at the end the water stood in his eyes.

'That's just beautiful,' he said. 'I do not mind to have heard anything like it; it's as fine as Burns when he wished deliverance to one – that is prayed for in no kirk. Ay, ay! so he would have you console the poor lost spirit? God bless the boy! There's something more than common in that, Colonel Mortimer. And also the faith of him in his father! – I would like to put that into a sermon.' Then the old gentleman gave me an alarmed look, and said, 'No, no; I was not meaning a sermon; but I must write it down for the *Children's Record.*' I saw the thought that passed through his mind. Either he thought, or he feared I would think, of a funeral sermon. You may believe this did not make me more cheerful.

I can scarcely say that Dr Moncrieff gave me any advice. How could anyone advise on such a subject? But he said, 'I think I'll come too. I'm an old man; I'm less liable to be frighted than those that are further off the world unseen. It behoves me to think of my own journey there. I've no cut-and-dry beliefs on the subject. I'll come too: and maybe at the moment the Lord will put into our heads what to do.'

This gave me a little comfort – more than Simson had given me. To be clear about the cause of it was not my grand desire. It was another thing that was in my mind – my boy. As for the poor soul at the open door, I had no more doubt, as I have said, of its existence than I had of my own. It was no ghost to me. I knew the creature, and it was in trouble. That was my feeling about it, as it was Roland's. To hear it first was a great shock to my nerves, but not now; a man will get accustomed to anything. But to do something for it was the great problem; how was I to be serviceable to a being that was invisible, that was mortal no longer? 'Maybe at the moment the Lord will put it into our heads.' This is very old-fashioned phraseology, and a week before, most likely, I should have smiled (though always with kindness) at Dr Moncrieff's credulity; but there was a great comfort, whether rational or otherwise I cannot say, in the mere sound of the words.

The road to the station and the village lay through the glen – not by the ruins; but though the sunshine and the fresh air, and the beauty of the trees, and the sound of the water were all very soothing to the spirits, my mind was so full of my own subject that I could not refrain from turning to the right hand as I got to the top of the glen, and going straight to the place which I may call the scene of all my thoughts. It was lying full in the sunshine, like all the rest of the world. The ruined gable looked due east, and in the present aspect of the sun the light streamed down through the doorway as our lantern had done, throwing a flood of light upon the damp grass beyond. There was a strange suggestion in the open door – so futile, a kind of emblem of vanity – all free around, so that you could go where you pleased, and yet that semblance of an enclosure – that way of entrance, unnecessary, leading to nothing. And why any creature should pray and weep to get in – to nothing: or be kept out – by nothing! You could not dwell upon it, or it made your brain go round. I remembered, however, what Simson said about the juniper, with a little smile on my own mind as to the inaccuracy of recollection, which even a scientific man will be guilty of. I could see now the light of my lantern gleaming upon the wet glistening surface of the spiky leaves at the right hand – and he ready to go to the stake for it that it was the left! I went round to make sure. And then I saw what he had said. Right or left there was no juniper at all. I was confounded by this, though it was entirely a matter of detail: nothing at all: a bush of brambles waving, the grass growing up to the very walls. But after all, though it gave me a shock for a moment, what did that matter? There were marks as if a number of footsteps had been up and down in front of the door; but these might have been our steps; and all was bright, and peaceful, and still. I poked about the other ruin – the larger ruins of the old house – for some time, as I had done before. There were marks upon the grass here and there, I could not call them footsteps, all about; but that told for nothing one way or another. I had examined the ruined rooms closely the first day. They were half filled up with soil and *debris*, withered brackens and bramble – no refuge for anyone there. It vexed me that Jarvis should see me coming from that spot when he came up to me for his orders. I don't know whether my nocturnal expeditions had got wind among the servants. But there was a significant look in his face. Something in it I felt was like my own sensation when Simson in the midst of his scepticism was struck dumb. Jarvis felt satisfied that his veracity had been put beyond question. I never spoke to a servant of mine in such peremptory tone before. I sent him away 'with a flea in his lug', as the man described it afterwards. Interference of any kind was intolerable to me at such a moment.

But what was strangest of all was, that I could not face Roland. I did not go up to his room as I would have naturally done at once. This the girls could not understand. They saw there was some mystery in it. 'Mother has gone to lie down,' Agatha said; 'he has had such a good night.' 'But he wants you so, papa!' cried little

Jeanie, always with her two arms embracing mine in a pretty way she had. I was obliged to go at last – but what could I say? I could only kiss him, and tell him to keep still – that I was doing all I could. There is something mystical about the patience of a child. 'It will come all right, won't it, father?' he said. 'God grant it may! I hope so, Roland.' 'Oh yes, it will come all right.' Perhaps he understood that in the midst of my anxiety I could not stay with him as I should have done otherwise. But the girls were more surprised than it is possible to describe. They looked at me with wondering eyes. 'If I were ill, papa, and you only stayed with me a moment, I should break my heart,' said Agatha. But the boy had a sympathetic feeling. He knew that of my own will I would not have done it. I shut myself up in the library, where I could not rest, but kept pacing up and down like a caged beast. What could I do? and if I could do nothing, what would become of my boy? These were the questions that, without ceasing, pursued each other through my mind.

Simson came out to dinner, and when the house was all still, and most of the servants in bed, we went out and met Dr Moncrieff, as we had appointed, at the head of the glen. Simson, for his part, was disposed to scoff at the doctor. 'If there are to be any spells, you know, I'll cut the whole concern,' he said. I did not make him any reply. I had not invited him; he could go or come as he pleased. He was very talkative, far more than suited my humour, as we went on. 'One thing is certain, you know, there must be some human agency,' he said. 'It is all bosh about apparitions. I never have investigated the laws of sound to any great extent, and there's a great deal in ventriloquism that we don't know much about.' 'If it's the same to you,' I said, 'I wish you'd keep all that to yourself, Simson. It doesn't suit my state of mind.' 'Oh, I hope I know how to respect idiosyncrasy,' he said. The very tone of his voice irritated me beyond measure. These scientific fellows, I wonder people put up with them as they do, when you have no mind for their cold-blooded confidence. Dr Moncrieff met us about eleven o'clock, the same time as on the previous night. He was a large man, with a venerable countenance and white hair – old, but in full vigour, and thinking less of a cold night walk than many a younger man. He had his lantern as I had. We were fully provided with means of lighting the place, and we were all of us resolute men. We had a rapid consultation as we went up, and the result was that we divided to different posts. Dr Moncrieff remained inside the wall – if you can call that inside where there was no wall but one. Simson placed himself on the side next the ruins, so as to intercept any communication with the old house, which was what his mind was fixed upon. I was posted on the other side. To say that nothing could come near without being seen was self-evident. It had been so also on the previous night. Now, with our three lights in the midst of the darkness, the whole place seemed illuminated. Dr Moncrieff's lantern, which was a large one, without any means of shutting up – an old-fashioned lantern with a pierced and ornamental top – shone steadily, the rays shooting out of it upward into the gloom. He placed it on the grass, where the middle of the room, if this had been a room, would have been. The usual effect of the light streaming out of the doorway was prevented by the illumination which Simson and I on either side supplied. With these differences, everything seemed as on the previous night.

And what occurred was exactly the same, with the same air of repetition, point for point, as I had formerly remarked. I declare that it seemed to me as if I were pushed against, put aside, by the owner of the voice as he paced up and down in his trouble – though these are perfectly futile words, seeing that the stream of light from my lantern, and that from Simson's taper, lay broad and clear, without a shadow, without the smallest break, across the entire breadth of the grass. I had ceased even to be alarmed, for my part. My heart was rent with pity and trouble – pity for the poor suffering human creature that moaned and pleaded so, and trouble for myself and my boy. God! if I could not find any help – and what help could I find? – Roland would die.

We were all perfectly still till the first outburst was exhausted, as I knew (by experience) it would be. Dr Moncrieff, to whom it was new, was quite motionless on the other side of the wall, as we were in our places. My heart had remained almost at its usual beating during the voice. I was used to it; it did not rouse all my pulses as it did at first. But just as it threw itself sobbing at the door (I cannot use other words), there suddenly came something which sent the blood coursing through my veins and my heart into my mouth. It was a voice inside the wall – the minister's well-known voice. I would have been prepared for it in any kind of adjuration, but I was not prepared for what I heard. It came out with a sort of stammering, as if too much moved for utterance. 'Willie, Willie! Oh, God preserve us! is it you?'

These simple words had an effect upon me that the voice of the invisible creature had ceased to have. I thought the old man, whom I had brought into this danger, had gone mad with terror. I made a dash round to the other side of the wall, half crazed myself with the thought. He was standing where I had left him, his shadow thrown vague and large upon the grass by the lantern which stood at his feet. I lifted my own light to see his face as I rushed forward. He was very pale, his eyes wet and glistening, his mouth quivering with parted lips. He neither saw nor heard me. We that had gone through this experience before, had crouched towards each other to get a little strength to bear it. But he was not even aware that I was there. His whole being seemed absorbed in anxiety and tenderness. He held out his hands, which trembled, but it seemed to me with eagerness, not fear. He went on speaking all the time. 'Willie, if it is you – and it's you, if it is not a delusion of Satan – Willie, lad! why come ye here frighting them that know you not? Why came ye not to me?'

He seemed to wait for an answer. When his voice ceased, his countenance, every line moving, continued to speak. Simson gave me another terrible shock, stealing into the open doorway with his light, as much awestricken, as wildly curious, as · I. But the minister resumed, without seeing Simson, speaking to someone else. His voice took a tone of expostulation:

'Is this right to come here? Your mother's gone with your name on her lips. Do you think she would ever close her door on her own lad? Do ye think the Lord will close the door, ye faint-hearted creature? No! – I forbid ye! I forbid ye!' cried the old man. The sobbing voice had begun to resume its cries. He made a step forward, calling out the last words in a voice of command. 'I forbid ye! Cry out no more to man. Go home, ye wandering spirit! go home! Do you hear me? – me that christened ye, that have struggled with ye, that have wrestled for ye with the Lord!' Here the loud tones of his voice sank into tenderness. 'And her too, poor woman! poor woman! her you are calling upon. She's no here. You'll find her with the Lord. Go there and seek her, not here. Do you hear me, lad? go after her there. He'll let you in, though it's late. Man, take heart! if you will lie and sob and greet, let it be at heaven's gate, and no your poor mother's ruined door.'

He stopped to get his breath: and the voice had stopped, not as it had done before, when its time was exhausted and all its repetitions said, but with a sobbing catch in the breath as if over-ruled. Then the minister spoke again, 'Are you hearing me, Will? Oh, laddie, you've liked the beggarly elements all your days. Be done with them now. Go home to the Father – the Father! Are you hearing me?' Here the old man sank down upon his knees, his face raised upwards, his hands held up with a tremble in them, all white in the light in the midst of the darkness. I resisted as long as I could, though I cannot tell why – then I, too, dropped upon my knees. Simson all the time stood in the doorway, with an expression in his face such as words could not tell, his under lip dropped, his eyes wild, staring. It seemed to be to him, that image of blank ignorance and wonder, that we were praying. All the time the voice, with a low arrested sobbing, lay just where he was standing, as I thought.

'Lord,' the minister said – 'Lord, take him into Thy everlasting habitations. The mother he cries to is with Thee. Who can open to him but Thee? Lord, when is it too late for Thee, or what is too hard for Thee? Lord, let that woman there draw him inower! Let her draw him inower!'

I sprang forward to catch something in my arms that flung itself wildly within the door. The illusion was so strong, that I never paused till I felt my forehead graze against the wall and my hands clutch the ground – for there was nobody there to save from falling, as in my foolishness I thought. Simson held out his hand to me to help me up. He was trembling and cold, his lower lip hanging, his speech almost inarticulate. 'It's gone,' he said, stammering – 'it's gone!' We leant upon each other for a moment, trembling so much both of us that the whole scene trembled as if it were going to dissolve and disappear; and yet as long as I live I will never forget it – the shining of the strange lights, the blackness all round, the kneeling figure with all the whiteness of the light concentrated on its white venerable head and uplifted hands. A strange solemn stillness seemed to close all round us. By intervals a single syllable, 'Lord! Lord!' came from the old minister's lips.

He saw none of us, nor thought of us. I never knew how long we stood, like sentinels guarding him at his prayers, holding our lights in a confused, dazed way, not knowing what we did. But at last he rose from his knees, and standing up at his full height, raised his arms, as the Scotch manner is at the end of a religious service, and solemnly gave the apostolical benediction – to what? To the silent earth, the dark woods, the wide breathing atmosphere – for we were but spectators gasping an Amen!

It seemed to me that it must be the middle of the night, as we all walked back. It was in reality very late. Dr Moncrieff put his arm into mine. He walked slowly, with an air of exhaustion. It was as if we were coming from a deathbed. Something hushed and sol-emnized the very air. There was that sense of relief in it which there always is at the end of a death-struggle. And nature persis-tent, never daunted, came back in all of us, as we returned into the ways of life. We said nothing to each other, indeed, for a time; but when we got clear of the trees and reached the opening near the house, where we could see the sky, Dr Moncrieff himself was the first to speak. 'I must be going,' he said; 'it's very late, I'm afraid. I will go down the glen, as I came.'

'But not alone. I am going with you, doctor.'

'Well, I will not oppose it. I am an old man, and agitation worries more than work. Yes; I'll be thankful of your arm. To-night, Colonel, you've done me more good turns than one.'

I pressed his hand on my arm, not feeling able to speak. But Simson, who turned with us, and who had gone along all this time with his taper flaring, in entire unconsciousness, came to himself, apparently at the sound of our voices, and put out that wild little torch with a quick movement, as if of shame. 'Let me carry your lantern,' he said; 'it is heavy.' He recovered with a spring, and in a moment, from the awe-stricken spectator he had been, became himself, sceptical and cynical. 'I should like to ask you a question,' he said. 'Do you believe in Purgatory, Doctor? It's not in the tenets of the Church, so far as I know.'

'Sir,' said Dr Moncrieff, 'an old man like me is sometimes not very sure what he believes. There is just one thing I am certain of – and that is the loving kindness of God.'

'But I thought that was in this life. I am no theologian –'

'Sir,' said the old man again, with a tremor in him which I could feel going over all his frame, 'if I saw a friend of mine within the gates of hell, I would not despair but his Father would take him by the hand still – if he cried like *you.*'

'I allow it is very strange – very strange. I cannot see through it. That there must be human agency, I feel sure. Doctor, what made you decide upon the person and the name?'

The minister put out his hand with the impatience which a man might show if he were asked how he recognized his brother. 'Tuts!' he said, in familiar speech – then more solemnly, 'how should I not recognize a person that I know better – far better – than I know you?'

'Then you saw the man?'

Dr Moncrieff made no reply. He moved his hand again with a little impatient movement, and walked on, leaning heavily on my arm. And we went on for a long time without another word, threading the dark paths, which were steep and slippery with the damp of the winter. The air was very still – not more than enough to make a faint sighing in the branches, which mingled with the sound of the water to which we were descending. When we spoke again, it was about indifferent matters – about the height of the river, and the recent rains. We parted with the minister at his own door, where his old housekeeper appeared in great perturbation, waiting for him. 'Eh me, minister! the young gentleman will be worse?' she cried.

'Far from that – better. God bless him!' Dr Moncrieff said.

I think if Simson had begun again to me with his questions, I should have pitched him over the rocks as we returned up the glen; but he was silent, by a good inspiration. And the sky was clearer than it had been for many nights, shining high over the trees, with here and there a star faintly gleaming through the wilderness of dark and bare branches. The air, as I have said, was very soft in them, with a subdued and peaceful cadence. It was real, like every natural sound, and came to us like a hush of peace and relief. I thought there was a sound in it as of the breath of a sleeper, and it seemed clear to me that Roland must be sleeping, satisfied and calm. We went up to his room when we went in. There we found the complete hush of rest. My wife looked up out of a doze, and gave me a smile; 'I think he is a great deal better; but you are very late,' she said in a whisper, shading the light with her hand that the doctor might see his patient. The boy had got back something like his own colour. He woke as we stood all round his bed. His eyes had the happy half-awakened look of childhood, glad to shut again, yet pleased with the interruption and glimmer of the light. I stooped over him and kissed his forehead, which was moist and cool. 'All is well, Roland,' I said. He looked up at me with a glance of pleasure, and took my hand and laid his cheek upon it, and so went to sleep.

For some nights after, I watched among the ruins, spending all the dark hours up to midnight patrolling about the bit of wall which was associated with so many emotions; but I heard nothing, and saw nothing beyond the quiet course of nature: nor, so far as I am aware, has anything been heard again. Dr Moncrieff gave me the history of the youth, whom he never hesitated to name. I did not ask, as Simson did, how he recognized him. He had been a prodigal – weak, foolish, easily imposed upon, and 'led away', as people say. All that we had heard had passed actually in life, the Doctor said. The young man had come home thus a day or two after his mother died – who was no more than the housekeeper in the old house – and distracted with the news, had thrown himself down at the door and called upon her to let him in. The old man could scarcely speak of it for tears. To me it seemed as if – heaven help us, how little do we know about anything! – a scene like that might impress itself somehow upon the hidden heart of nature. I do not pretend to know how, but the repetition had struck me at the time as, in its terrible strangeness and incomprehensibility, almost mechanical – as if the unseen actor could not exceed or vary, but was bound to re-enact the whole. One thing that struck me, however, greatly, was the likeness between the old minister and my boy in the manner of regarding these strange phenomena. Dr Moncrieff was not terrified, as I had been myself, and all the rest of us. It was no 'ghost', as I fear we all vulgarly considered it, to him – but a poor creature whom he knew under these conditions, just as he had known him in the flesh, having no doubt of his identity. And to Roland it was the same. This spirit in pain – if it was a spirit – this voice out of the unseen – was a poor fellow-creature in misery, to be succoured and helped out of his trouble, to my boy. He spoke to me quite frankly about it when he got better. 'I knew father would find out some way,' he said. And this was when he was strong and well, and all idea that he would turn hysterical or become a seer of visions had happily passed away.

I must add one curious fact which does not seem to me to have any relation to the above, but which Simson made great use of, as the human agency which he was determined to find somehow. We had examined the ruins very closely at the time of these occurrences; but afterwards, when all was over, as we went casually about them one Sunday afternoon in the idleness of that unemployed day, Simson with his stick penetrated an old window which had been entirely blocked up with fallen soil. He jumped down into it in great excitement, and called me to follow. There we found a little hole – for it was more a hole than a room – entirely hidden under the ivy ruins, in which there was a quantity of straw laid in a corner, as if someone had made a bed there, and some remains of crusts about the floor. Someone had lodged there, and not very long before, he made out; and that this unknown being was the author of all the mysterious sounds we heard he is convinced. 'I told you it was human agency,' he said triumphantly. He forgets, I suppose, how he and I stood with our lights seeing nothing, while the space between us was audibly traversed by something that could speak, and sob, and suffer. There is no argument with men of this kind. He is ready to get up a laugh against me on this slender ground. 'I was puzzled myself – I could not make it out – but I always felt convinced human agency was at the bottom of it. And here it is – and a clever fellow he must have been,' the Doctor says.

Bagley left my service as soon as he got well. He assured me it was no want of respect; but he could not stand 'them kind of things', and the man was so shaken and ghastly that I was glad to give him a present and let him go. For my own part, I made a point of staying out the time, two years, for which I had taken Brentwood; but I did not renew my tenancy. By that time we had settled, and found for ourselves a pleasant home of our own.

I must add that when the doctor defies me, I can always bring back gravity to his countenance, and a pause in his railing, when I remind him of the juniper bush. To me that was a matter of little importance. I could believe I was mistaken. I did not care about it one way or other; but on his mind the effect was different. The miserable voice, the spirit in pain, he could think of as the result of ventriloquism, or reverberation, or – anything you please: an elaborate prolonged hoax executed somehow by the tramp that had found a lodging in the old tower. But the juniper bush staggered him. Things have effects so different on the minds of different men.

Robert Louis Stevenson

THE BEACH OF FALESÁ

CHAPTER I
A SOUTH SEA BRIDAL

I saw that island first when it was neither night nor morning. The moon was to the west, setting, but still broad and bright. To the east, and right amidships of the dawn, which was all pink, the day-star sparkled like a diamond. The land breeze blew in our faces, and smelt strong of wild lime and vanilla: other things besides, but these were the most plain; and the chill of it set me sneezing. I should say I had been for years on a low island near the line, living for the most part solitary among natives. Here was a fresh experience: even the tongue would be quite strange to me; and the look of these woods and mountains, and the rare smell of them, renewed my blood.

The captain blew out the binnacle lamp.

'There!' said he, 'there goes a bit of smoke, Mr Wiltshire, behind the break of the reef. That's Falesá, where your station is, the last village to the east; nobody lives to windward – I don't know why. Take my glass, and you can make the houses out.'

I took the glass; and the shores leaped nearer, and I saw the tangle of the woods and the breach of the surf, and the brown roofs and the black insides of houses peeped among the trees.

'Do you catch a bit of white there to the east'ard?' the captain continued. 'That's your house. Coral built, stands high, verandah you could walk on three abreast; best station in the South Pacific. When old Adams saw it, he took and shook me by the hand. "I've dropped into a soft thing here," says he. "So you have," says I, "and time too!" Poor Johnny! I never saw him again but the once, and then he had changed his tune – couldn't get on with the natives, or the whites, or something; and the next time we came round there he was dead and buried. I took and put up a bit of stick to him: "John Adams, *obiit* eighteen and sixty-eight. Go thou and do likewise." I missed that man. I never could see much harm in Johnny.'

'What did he die of?' I inquired.

'Some kind of sickness,' says the captain. 'It appears it took him sudden. Seems he got up in the night, and filled up on Pain-Killer and Kennedy's Discovery. No go: he was booked beyond Kennedy. Then he had tried to open a case of gin. No go again: not strong enough. Then he must have turned to and run out on the verandah, and capsized over the rail. When they found him, the next day, he was clean crazy – carried on all the time about somebody watering his copra. Poor John!'

'Was it thought to be the island?' I asked.

'Well, it was thought to be the island, or the trouble, or something,' he replied. 'I never could hear but what it was a healthy place. Our last man, Vigours, never turned a hair. He left because of the beach – said he was afraid of Black Jack and Case and Whistling Jimmie, who was still alive at the time, but got drowned soon afterward when drunk. As for old Captain Randall, he's been here any time since eighteen-forty, forty-five. I never could see much harm in Billy, nor much change. Seems as if he might live to be Old Kafoozleum. No, I guess it's healthy.'

'There's a boat coming now,' said I. 'She's right in the pass; looks to be a sixteen-foot whale; two white men in the stern-sheets.'

'That's the boat that drowned Whistling Jimmie!' cried the captain; 'let's see the glass. Yes, that's Case, sure enough, and the darkie. They've got a gallows bad reputation, but you know what a place the beach is for talking. My belief, that Whistling Jimmie was the worst of the trouble; and he's gone to glory, you see. What'll you bet they ain't after gin? Lay you five to two they take six cases.'

When these two traders came aboard I was pleased with the looks of them at once, or, rather, with the looks of both, and the speech of one. I was sick for white neighbours after my four years at the line, which I always counted years of prison; getting tabooed, and going down to the Speak House to see and get it taken off; buying gin and going on a break, and then repenting; sitting in the house at night with the lamp for company; or walking on the beach and wondering what kind of a fool to call myself for being where I was. There were no other whites upon my island, and when I sailed to the next, rough customers made the most of the society. Now to see these two when they came aboard was a pleasure. One was a negro, to be sure; but they were both rigged out smart in striped pyjamas and straw hats, and Case would have passed muster in a city. He was yellow and smallish, had a hawk's nose to his face, pale eyes, and his beard trimmed with scissors. No man knew his country, beyond he was of English speech; and it was clear he came of a good family and was splendidly educated. He was accomplished too; played the accordion first-rate; and give him a piece of string or a cork or a pack of cards, and he could show you tricks equal to any professional. He could speak, when he chose, fit for a drawing-room; and when he chose he could blaspheme worse than a Yankee boatswain, and talk smart to sicken a Kanaka. The way he thought would pay best at the moment, that was Case's way, and it always seemed to come natural, and like as if he was born to it. He had the courage of a lion and the cunning of a rat; and if he's not in hell to-day, there's no such place. I know but one good point to the man: that he was fond of his wife, and kind to her. She was a Samoa woman, and dyed her hair red, Samoa style; and when he came to die (as I have to tell of) they found one strange thing – that he had made a will, like a Christian, and the widow got the lot: all his, they said, and all Black Jack's, and the most of Billy Randall's in the bargain, for it was Case that kept the books. So she went off home in the schooner *Manu'a*, and does the lady to this day in her own place.

But of all this on that first morning I knew no more than a fly. Case used me like a gentleman and like a friend, made me welcome to Falesá, and put his services at my disposal, which was the more helpful from my ignorance of the native. All the better part of the day we sat drinking better acquaintance in the cabin, and I never heard a man talk more to the point. There was no smarter trader, and none dodgier, in the islands. I thought Falesá seemed to be the right kind of a place; and the more I drank the lighter my heart. Our last trader had fled the place at half an hour's notice, taking a chance passage in a labour ship from up west. The captain, when he came, had found the station closed, the keys left with the native pastor, and a letter from the runaway, confessing he was fairly frightened of his life. Since then the firm had not been represented, and of course there was no cargo. The wind, besides, was fair, the captain hoped he could make his next island by dawn, with a good tide, and the business of landing my trade was gone about lively. There was no call for me to fool with it, Case said; nobody would touch my things, every one was honest in Falesá, only about chickens or an odd knife or an odd stick of tobacco; and the best I could do was to sit quiet till the vessel left, then come straight to his house, see old Captain Randall, the father of the beach, take pot-luck, and go home to sleep when it got dark. So it was high noon, and the schooner was under way, before I set my foot on shore at Falesá.

I had a glass or two on board; I was just off a long cruise, and the ground heaved under me like a ship's deck. The world was like all new painted; my foot went along to music; Falesá might have been Fiddler's Green, if there is such a place, and more's the pity if there isn't! It was good to foot the grass, to look aloft at the green mountains, to see the men with their green wreaths and the women in their bright dresses, red and blue. On we went, in the strong sun and the cool shadow, liking both; and all the children in the town came trotting after with their shaven heads and their brown bodies, and raising a thin kind of a cheer in our wake, like crowing poultry.

'By the by,' says Case, 'we must get you a wife.'

'That's so,' said I; 'I had forgotten.'

There was a crowd of girls about us, and I pulled myself up and looked among them like a Bashaw. They were all dressed out for the sake of the ship being in; and the women of Falesá are a handsome lot to see. If they have a fault, they are a trifle broad in the beam; and I was just thinking so when Case touched me.

'That's pretty,' says he.

I saw one coming on the other side alone. She had been fishing; all she wore was a chemise, and it was wetted through. She was young and very slender for an island maid, with a long face, a high forehead, and a shy, strange, blindish look, between a cat's and a baby's.

'Who's she?' said I. 'She'll do.'

'That's Uma,' said Case, and he called her up and spoke to her in the native. I didn't know what he said; but when he was in the midst she looked up at me quick and timid, like a child dodging a blow, then down again, and presently smiled. She had a wide mouth, the lips and the chin cut like any statue's; and the smile came out for a moment and was gone. Then she stood with her head bent, and heard Case to an end, spoke back in the pretty Polynesian voice, looking him full in the face, heard him again in answer, and then with an obeisance started off. I had just a share of the bow, but never another shot of her eye, and there was no more word of smiling.

'I guess it's all right,' said Case. 'I guess you can have her. I'll make it square with the old lady. You can have your pick of the lot for a plug of tobacco,' he added, sneering.

I suppose it was the smile stuck in my memory, for I spoke back sharp. 'She doesn't look that sort,' I cried.

'I don't know that she is,' said Case. 'I believe she's as right as the mail. Keeps to herself, don't go round with the gang, and that. O no, don't you misunderstand me – Uma's on the square.' He spoke eager, I thought, and that surprised and pleased me. 'Indeed,' he went on, 'I shouldn't make so sure of getting her, only she cottoned to the cut of your jib. All you have to do is to keep dark and let me work the mother my own way; and I'll bring the girl round to the captain's for the marriage.'

I didn't care for the word marriage, and I said so.

'O, there's nothing to hurt in the marriage,' says he. 'Black Jack's the chaplain.'

By this time we had come in view of the house of these three white men; for a negro is counted a white man, and so is a Chinese! a strange idea, but common in the islands. It was a board house with a strip of rickety verandah. The store was to the front, with a counter, scales, and the poorest possible display of trade: a case or two of tinned meats, a barrel of hard bread, a few bolts of cotton stuff, not to be compared with mine; the only thing well represented being the contraband, firearms and liquor. 'If these are my only rivals,' thinks I, 'I should do well in Falesá.' Indeed, there was only the one way they could touch me, and that was with the guns and drink.

In the back room was old Captain Randall, squatting on the

floor native fashion, fat and pale, naked to the waist, grey as a badger, and his eyes set with drink. His body was covered with grey hair and crawled over by flies; one was in the corner of his eye – he never heeded; and the mosquitoes hummed about the man like bees. Any clean-minded man would have had the creature out at once and buried him; and to see him, and think he was seventy, and remember he had once commanded a ship, and come ashore in his smart togs, and talked big in bars and consulates, and sat in club verandahs, turned me sick and sober.

He tried to get up when I came in, but that was hopeless; so he reached me a hand instead, and stumbled out some salutation.

'Papa's* pretty full this morning,' observed Case. 'We've had an epidemic here; and Captain Randall takes gin for a prophylactic – don't you, Papa?'

'Never took such a thing in my life!' cried the captain indignantly. 'Take gin for my health's sake, Mr Wha's-ever-your-name –'s a precautionary measure.'

'That's all right, Papa,' said Case. 'But you'll have to brace up. There's going to be a marriage – Mr Wiltshire here is going to get spliced.'

The old man asked to whom.

'To Uma,' said Case.

'Uma!' cried the captain. 'Wha's he want Uma for? 's he come here for his health, anyway? Wha' 'n hell 's he want Uma for?'

'Dry up, Papa,' said Case. ' 'Tain't you that's to marry her. I guess you're not her godfather and godmother. I guess Mr Wiltshire's going to please himself.'

With that he made an excuse to me that he must move about the marriage, and let me alone with the poor wretch that was his partner and (to speak truth) his gull. Trade and station belonged both to Randall; Case and the negro were parasites; they crawled and fed upon him like the flies, he none the wiser. Indeed, I have no harm to say of Billy Randall beyond the fact that my gorge rose at him, and the time I now passed in his company was like a nightmare.

The room was stifling hot and full of flies; for the house was dirty and low and small, and stood in a bad place, behind the village, in the borders of the bush, and sheltered from the trade. The three men's beds were on the floor, and a litter of pans and

* Please pronounce *pappa* throughout.

dishes. There was no standing furniture; Randall, when he was violent, tearing it to laths. There I sat and had a meal which was served us by Case's wife; and there I was entertained all day by that remains of man, his tongue stumbling among low old jokes and long old stories, and his own wheezy laughter always ready, so that he had no sense of my depression. He was nipping gin all the while. Sometimes he fell asleep, and woke again, whimpering and shivering, and every now and again he would ask me why I wanted to marry Uma. 'My friend,' I was telling myself all day, 'you must not come to be an old gentleman like this.'

It might be four in the afternoon, perhaps, when the back door was thrust slowly open, and a strange old native woman crawled into the house almost on her belly. She was swathed in black stuff to her heels; her hair was grey in swatches; her face was tattooed, which was not the practice in that island; her eyes big and bright and crazy. These she fixed upon me with a rapt expression that I saw to be part acting. She said no plain words, but smacked and mumbled with her lips, and hummed aloud, like a child over its Christmas pudding. She came straight across the house, heading for me, and, as soon as she was alongside, caught up my hand and purred and crooned over it like a great cat. From this she slipped into a kind of song.

'Who the devil's this?' cried I, for the thing startled me.

'It's Fa'avao,' says Randall; and I saw he had hitched along the floor into the farthest corner.

'You ain't afraid of her?' I cried.

'Me 'fraid!' cried the captain. 'My dear friend, I defy her! I don't let her put her foot in here, only I suppose 's different to-day, for the marriage. 's Uma's mother.'

'Well, suppose it is; what's she carrying on about?' I asked, more irritated, perhaps more frightened, than I cared to show; and the captain told me she was making up a quantity of poetry in my praise because I was to marry Uma. 'All right, old lady,' says I, with rather a failure of a laugh, 'anything to oblige. But when you're done with my hand, you might let me know.'

She did as though she understood; the song rose into a cry, and stopped; the woman crouched out of the house the same way that she came in, and must have plunged straight into the bush, for when I followed her to the door she had already vanished.

'These are rum manners,' said I.

' 's a rum crowd,' said the captain, and, to my surprise, he made the sign of the cross on his bare bosom.

'Hillo!' says I, 'are you a Papist?'

He repudiated the idea with contempt. 'Hard-shell Baptis',' said he. 'But, my dear friend, the Papists got some good ideas too; and tha' 's one of 'em. You take my advice, and whenever you come across Uma or Fa'avao or Vigours, or any of that crowd, you take a leaf out o' the priests, and do what I do. Savvy,' says he, repeated the sign, and winked his dim eye at me. 'No, *sir!*' he broke out again, 'no Papists here!' and for a long time entertained me with his religious opinions.

I must have been taken with Uma from the first, or I should certainly have fled from that house, and got into the clean air, and the clean sea, or some convenient river – though, it's true, I was committed to Case; and, besides, I could never have held my head up in that island if I had run from a girl upon my wedding-night.

The sun was down, the sky all on fire, and the lamp had been some time lighted, when Case came back with Uma and the negro. She was dressed and scented; her kilt was of fine tapa, looking richer in the folds than any silk; her bust, which was of the colour of dark honey, she wore bare only for some half a dozen necklaces of seeds and flowers; and behind her ears and in her hair she had the scarlet flowers of the hibiscus. She showed the best bearing for a bride conceivable, serious and still; and I thought shame to stand up with her in that mean house and before that grinning negro. I thought shame, I say; for the mountebank was dressed with a big paper collar, the book he made believe to read from was an odd volume of a novel, and the words of his service not fit to be set down. My conscience smote me when we joined hands; and when she got her certificate I was tempted to throw up the bargain and confess. Here is the document. It was Case that wrote it, signatures and all, in a leaf out of the ledger:

This is to certify that Uma, daughter of Fa'avao of Falesá, Island of —, is illegally married to Mr John Wiltshire for one week, and Mr John Wiltshire is at liberty to send her to hell when he pleases.

JOHN BLACKAMOAR,
Chaplain to the Hulks

Extracted from the Register
by William T. Randall,
Master Mariner

A nice paper to put in a girl's hand and see her hide away like gold. A man might easily feel cheap for less. But it was the practice in these parts, and (as I told myself) not the least the fault of us white men, but of the missionaries. If they had let the natives be, I had never needed this deception, but taken all the wives I wished, and left them when I pleased, with a clear conscience.

The more ashamed I was, the more hurry I was in to be gone; and our desires thus jumping together, I made the less remark of a change in the traders. Case had been all eagerness to keep me; now, as though he had attained a purpose, he seemed all eagerness to have me go. Uma, he said, could show me to my house, and the three bade us farewell indoors.

The night was nearly come; the village smelt of trees and flowers and the sea and breadfruit-cooking; there came a fine roll of sea from the reef, and from a distance, among the woods and houses, many pretty sounds of men and children. It did me good to breathe free air; it did me good to be done with the captain and see, instead, the creature at my side. I felt for all the world as though she were some girl at home in the Old Country, and, forgetting myself for the minute, took her hand to walk with. Her fingers nestled into mine, I heard her breathe deep and quick, and all at once she caught my hand to her face and pressed it there. 'You good!' she cried, and ran ahead of me, and stopped and looked back and smiled, and ran ahead of me again, thus guiding me through the edge of the bush, and by a quiet way to my own house.

The truth is, Case had done the courting for me in style – told her I was mad to have her, and cared nothing for the consequence; and the poor soul, knowing that which I was still ignorant of, believed it, every word, and had her head nigh turned with vanity and gratitude. Now, of all this I had no guess; I was one of those most opposed to any nonsense about native women, having seen so many whites eaten up by their wives' relatives, and made fools of in the bargain; and I told myself I must make a stand at once, and bring her to her bearings. But she looked so quaint and pretty as she ran away and then awaited me, and the thing was done so like a child or a kind dog, that the best I could do was just to follow her whenever she went on, to listen for the fall of her bare feet, and to watch in the dusk for the shining of her body. And there was another thought came in my head. She played kitten with me now when we were alone; but in the house she had carried it the way a countess might, so proud and humble. And what with her dress – for all there was so little of it, and that native enough – what with her fine tapa and fine scents, and her red flowers and seeds, that were quite as bright as jewels, only larger – it came over me she was a kind of countess really, dressed to hear great singers at a concert, and no even mate for a poor trader like myself.

She was the first in the house; and while I was still without I saw a match flash and the lamplight kindle in the windows. The station was a wonderful fine place, coral built, with quite a wide veran-dah, and the main room high and wide. My chests and cases had been piled in, and made rather of a mess; and there, in the thick of the confusion, stood Uma by the table, awaiting me. Her shadow went all the way up behind her into the hollow of the iron roof; she stood against it bright, the lamplight shining on her skin. I stopped in the door, and she looked at me, not speaking, with eyes that were eager and yet daunted; then she touched herself on the bosom.

'Me – your wifie,' she said. It had never taken me like that before; but the want of her took and shook all through me, like the wind in the luff of a sail.

I could not speak if I had wanted; and if I could, I would not. I was ashamed to be so much moved about a native, ashamed of the marriage too, and the certificate she had treasured in her kilt; and I turned aside and made believe to rummage among my cases. The first thing I lighted on was a case of gin, the only one that I had brought; and, partly for the girl's sake, and partly for horror of the recollections of old Randall, took a sudden resolve. I prised the lid off. One by one I drew the bottles with a pocket corkscrew, and sent Uma out to pour the stuff from the verandah.

She came back after the last, and looked at me puzzled like.

'No good,' said I, for I was now a little better master of my tongue. 'Man he drink, he no good.'

She agreed with this, but kept considering. 'Why you bring

him?' she asked presently. 'Suppose you no want drink, you no bring him, I think.'

'That's all right,' said I. 'One time I want drink too much; now no want. You see, I no savvy I get one little wifie. Suppose I drink gin, my little wifie he 'fraid.'

To speak to her kindly was about more than I was fit for; I had made my vow I would never let on to weakness with a native, and I had nothing for it but to stop.

She stood looking gravely down at me where I sat by the open case. 'I think you good man,' she said. And suddenly she had fallen before me on the floor. 'I belong you all-e-same pig!' she cried.

CHAPTER II
THE BAN

I came on the verandah just before the sun rose on the morrow. My house was the last on the east; there was a cape of woods and cliffs behind that hid the sunrise. To the west, a swift cold river ran down, and beyond was the green of the village, dotted with cocoa-palms and breadfruits and houses. The shutters were some of them down and some open; I saw the mosquito bars still stretched, with shadows of people new-awakened sitting up inside; and all over the green others were stalking silent, wrapped in their many-coloured sleeping clothes like Bedouins in Bible pictures. It was mortal still and solemn and chilly, and the light of the dawn on the lagoon was like the shining of a fire.

But the thing that troubled me was nearer hand. Some dozen young men and children made a piece of a half-circle, flanking my house: the river divided them, some were on the near side, some on the far, and one on a boulder in the midst; and they all sat silent, wrapped in their sheets, and stared at me and my house as straight as pointer dogs. I thought it strange as I went out. When I had bathed and come back again, and found them all there, and two or three more along with them, I thought it stranger still. What could they see to gaze at in my house, I wondered, and went in.

But the thought of these starers stuck in my mind, and presently I came out again. The sun was now up, but it was still behind the cape of woods. Say a quarter of an hour had come and gone. The crowd was greatly increased, the far bank of the river was lined for quite a way – perhaps thirty grown folk, and of children twice as many, some standing, some squatted on the ground, and all staring at my house. I have seen a house in the South Sea village thus surrounded, but then a trader was thrashing his wife inside, and she singing out. Here was nothing: the stove was alight, the smoke going up in a Christian manner; all was shipshape and Bristol fashion. To be sure, there was a stranger come, but they had a chance to see that stranger yesterday, and took it quiet enough. What ailed them now? I leaned my arms on the rail and stared back. Devil a wink they had in them! Now and then I could see the children chatter, but they spoke so low not even the hum of their speaking came my length. The rest were like graven images: they stared at me, dumb and sorrowful, with their bright eyes; and it came upon me things would look not much different if I were on the platform of the gallows, and these good folk had come to see me hanged.

I felt I was getting daunted, and began to be afraid I looked it, which would never do. Up I stood, made believe to stretch myself, came down the verandah stair, and strolled towards the river. There went a short buzz from one to the other, like what you hear in theatres when the curtain goes up; and some of the nearest gave back the matter of a pace. I saw a girl lay one hand on a young man and make a gesture upward with the other; at the same time she said something in the native with a gasping voice. Three little boys sat beside my path, where I must pass within three feet of them. Wrapped in their sheets, with their shaved heads and bits of top-knots, and queer faces, they looked like figures on a chimney-piece. A while they sat their ground, solemn as judges. I came up hand over fist, doing my five knots, like a man that meant business; and I thought I saw a sort of a wink and gulp in the three faces. Then one jumped up (he was the farthest off) and ran for his mammy. The other two, trying to follow suit, got foul, came to ground together bawling, wriggled right out of their sheets mother-naked, and in a moment there were all three of them scampering for their lives and singing out like pigs. The natives, who would never let a joke slip, even at a burial, laughed and let up, as short as a dog's bark.

They say it scares a man to be alone. No such thing. What scares him in the dark or the high bush is that he can't make sure, and there might be an army at his elbow. What scares him worst is to be right in the midst of a crowd, and have no guess of what they're driving at. When that laugh stopped, I stopped too. The boys had not yet made their offing, they were still on the full stretch going the one way, when I had already gone about ship and was sheering off the other. Like a fool I had come out, doing my five knots; like a fool I went back again. It must have been the funniest thing to see, and, what knocked me silly, this time no one laughed; only one old woman gave a kind of pious moan, the way you have heard Dissenters in their chapels at the sermon.

'I never saw such fools of Kanakas as your people here,' I said once to Uma, glancing out of the window at the starers.

'Savvy nothing,' says Uma, with a kind of disgusted air that she was good at.

And that was all the talk we had upon the matter, for I was put out, and Uma took the thing so much as a matter of course that I was fairly ashamed.

All day, off and on, now fewer and now more, the fools sat about the west end of my house and across the river, waiting for the show, whatever that was – fire to come down from heaven, I suppose, and consume me, bones and baggage. But by evening, like real islanders, they had wearied of the business, and got away, and had a dance instead in the big house of the village, where I heard them singing and clapping hands till, maybe, ten at night, and the next day it seemed they had forgotten I existed. If fire had come down from heaven or the earth opened and swallowed me, there would have been nobody to see the sport or take the lesson, or whatever you like to call it. But I was to find that they hadn't forgot either, and kept an eye lifting for phenomena over my way.

I was hard at it both these days getting my trade in order and taking stock of what Vigours had left. This was a job that made me pretty sick, and kept me from thinking on much else. Ben had taken stock the trip before – I knew I could trust Ben – but it was plain somebody had been making free in the meantime. I found I was out by what might easily cover six months' salary and profit, and I could have kicked myself all round the village to have been such a blamed ass, sitting boozing with that Case instead of attending to my own affairs and taking stock.

However, there's no use crying over spilt milk. It was done now, and couldn't be undone. All I could do was to get what was left of it, and my new stuff (my own choice) in order, to go round and get after the rats and cockroaches, and to fix up that store regular Sydney style. A fine show I made of it; and the third morning when I had lit my pipe and stood in the doorway and looked in, and turned and looked far up the mountain and saw the cocoa-nuts waving and posted up the tons of copra, and over the village green and saw the island dandies and reckoned up the yards of print they wanted for their kilts and dresses, I felt as if I was in the right place to make a fortune, and go home again and start a public-house. There was I, sitting in that verandah, in as handsome a piece of scenery as you could find, a splendid sun, and a fine, fresh, healthy trade that stirred up a man's blood like sea-bathing; and the whole thing was clean gone from me, and I was dreaming England, which is, after all, a nasty, cold, muddy hole, with not enough light to see to read by; and dreaming the looks of my public, by a cant of a broad high-road like an avenue, and with the sign on a green tree.

So much for the morning; but the day passed and the devil any one looked near me, and from all I knew of natives in other islands I thought this strange. People laughed a little at our firm and their fine stations, and at this station of Falesá in particular; all the copra in the district wouldn't pay for it (I had heard them say) in fifty years, which I supposed was an exaggeration. But when the day went, and no business came at all, I began to get down-hearted; and, about three in the afternoon, I went out for a stroll to cheer me up. On the green I saw a white man coming with a cassock on, by which and by the face of him I knew he was a priest. He was a good-natured old soul to look at, gone a little grizzled, and so dirty you could have written with him on a piece of paper.

'Good day, sir,' said I.

He answered me eagerly in native.

'Don't you speak any English?' said I.

'French,' says he.

'Well,' said I, 'I'm sorry, but I can't do anything there.'

He tried me a while in the French, and then again in native, which he seemed to think was the best chance. I made out he was after more than passing the time of day with me, but had something to communicate, and I listened the harder. I heard the names of Adams and Case and of Randall – Randall the oftenest – and the word 'poison', or something like it, and a native word that he said very often. I went home, repeating it to myself.

'What does fussy-ocky mean?' I asked of Uma, for that was as near as I could come to it.

'Make dead,' said she.

'The devil it does!' says I. 'Did you ever hear that Case had poisoned Johnny Adams?'

'Every man he savvy that,' says Uma, scornful-like. 'Give him white sand – bad sand. He got the bottle still. Suppose he give you gin, you no take him.'

Now I had heard much the same sort of story in other islands, and the same white powder always to the front, which made me think the less of it. For all that, I went over to Randall's place to see what I could pick up, and found Case on the doorstep, cleaning a gun.

'Good shooting here?' says I.

'A1,' says he. 'The bush is full of all kinds of birds. I wish copra was as plenty,' says he – I thought, slyly – 'but there don't seem anything doing.'

I could see Black Jack in the store, serving a customer.

'That looks like business, though,' said I.

'That's the first sale we've made in three weeks,' said he.

'You don't tell me?' says I. 'Three weeks? Well, well.'

'If you don't believe me,' he cries, a little hot, 'you can go and look at the copra-house. It's half empty to this blessed hour.'

'I shouldn't be much the better for that, you see,' says I. 'For all I can tell, it might have been whole empty yesterday.'

'That's so,' says he, with a bit of a laugh.

'By the by,' I said, 'what sort of a party is that priest? Seems rather a friendly sort.'

At this Case laughed right out loud. 'Ah!' says he, 'I see what ails you now. Galuchet's been at you.' *Father Galoshes* was the name he went by most, but Case always gave it the French quirk, which was another reason we had for thinking him above the common.

'Yes, I have seen him,' I says. 'I made out he didn't think much of your Captain Randall.'

'That he don't!' says Case. 'It was the trouble about poor Adams. The last day, when he lay dying, there was young Buncombe round. Ever met Buncombe?'

I told him no.

'He's a cure, is Buncombe!' laughs Case. 'Well, Buncombe took it in his head that, as there was no other clergyman about, bar Kanaka pastors, we ought to call in Father Galuchet, and have the old man administered and take the sacrament. It was all the same to me, you may suppose; but I said I thought Adams was the fellow to consult. He was jawing away about watered copra and a sight of foolery. "Look here," I said. "You're pretty sick. Would you like to see Galoshes?" He sat right up on his elbow. "Get the priest," says he, "get the priest; don't let me die here like a dog!" He spoke kind of fierce and eager, but sensible enough. There was nothing to say against that, so we sent and asked Galuchet if he would come. You bet he would. He jumped in his dirty linen at the thought of it. But we had reckoned without Papa. He's a hard-shell Baptist, is Papa; no Papists need apply. And he took and locked the door. Buncombe told him he was bigoted, and I thought he would have had a fit. "Bigoted!" he says. "Me bigoted? Have I lived to hear it from a jackanapes like you?" And he made for Buncombe, and I had to hold them apart; and there was Adams in the middle, gone luny again, and carrying on about copra like a born fool. It was good as the play, and I was about knocked out of time with laughing, when all of a sudden Adams sat up, clapped his hands to his chest and went into horrors. He died hard, did John Adams,' says Case, with a kind of a sudden sternness.

'And what became of the priest?' I asked.

'The priest?' says Case. 'O! he was hammering on the door outside, and crying on the natives to come and beat it in, and singing out it was a soul he wished to save, and that. He was in a rare taking, was the priest. But what would you have? Johnny had slipped his cable: no more Johnny in the market; and the administration racket clean played out. Next thing, word came to Randall the priest was praying upon Johnny's grave. Papa was pretty full, and got a club, and lit out straight for the place, and there was Galoshes on his knees, and a lot of natives looking on. You wouldn't think Papa cared that much about anything, unless it was liquor; but he and the priest stuck to it two hours, slanging each other in native, and every time Galoshes tried to kneel down Papa went for him with the club. There never were such larks in Falesá. The end of it was that Captain Randall was knocked over with some kind of a fit or stroke, and the priest got in his goods after all. But he was the angriest priest you ever heard of, and complained to the chiefs about the outrage, as he called it. That was no account, for our chiefs are Protestant here; and, anyway, he had been making trouble about the drum for morning school, and they were glad to give him a wipe. Now he swears old Randall gave Adams poison or something, and when the two meet they grin at each other like baboons.'

He told the story as natural as could be, and like a man that enjoyed the fun; though, now I come to think of it after so long, it seems rather a sickening yarn. However, Case never set up to be soft, only to be square and hearty, and a man all round; and, to tell the truth, he puzzled me entirely.

I went home and asked Uma if she were a Popey, which I had made out to be the native word for Catholics.

'*E le ai!*' says she. She always used the native when she meant 'no' more than usually strong, and, indeed, there's more of it. 'No good Popey,' she added.

Then I asked her about Adams and the priest, and she told me much the same yarn in her own way. So that I was left not much further on, but inclined, upon the whole, to think the bottom of the matter was the row about the sacrament, and the poisoning only talk.

The next day was a Sunday, when there was no business to be looked for. Uma asked me in the morning if I was going to 'pray'; I told her she bet not, and she stopped home herself with no more words. I thought this seemed unlike a native, and a native woman, and a woman that had new clothes to show off; however, it suited me to the ground, and I made the less of it. The queer thing was that I came next door to going to church after all, a thing I'm likely to forget. I had turned out for a stroll, and heard the hymn tune up. You know how it is. If you hear folk singing, it seems to draw you: and pretty soon I found myself alongside the church. It was a little, long, low place, coral built, rounded off at both ends like a whale-boat, a big native roof on the top of it, windows without sashes and doorways without doors. I stuck my head into one of the windows, and the sight was so new to me – for things went quite different in the islands I was acquainted with – that I stayed and looked on. The congregation sat on the floor on mats, the women on one side, the men on the other, all rigged out to kill – the women with dresses and trade hats, the men in white jackets and shirts. The hymn was over; the pastor, a big buck Kanaka, was in the pulpit, preaching for his life; and by the way he wagged his hand, and worked his voice, and made his points, and seemed to argue with the folk, I made out he was a gun at the business. Well, he looked up suddenly and caught my eye, and I give you my word he staggered in the pulpit; his eyes bulged out of his head, his hand rose and pointed at me like as if against his will, and the sermon stopped right there.

It isn't a fine thing to say for yourself, but I ran away; and if the same kind of a shock was given me, I should run away again to-morrow. To see that palavering Kanaka struck all of a heap at the mere sight of me gave me a feeling as if the bottom had dropped out of the world. I went right home, and stayed there, and said nothing. You might think I would tell Uma, but that was against my system. You might have thought I would have gone over and consulted Case; but the truth was I was ashamed to speak of such a thing, I thought every one would blurt out laughing in my face. So I held my tongue, and thought all the more; and the more I thought, the less I liked the business.

By Monday night I got it clearly in my head I must be tabooed. A new store to stand open two days in a village and not a man or woman come to see the trade was past believing.

'Uma,' said I, 'I think I am tabooed.'

'I think so,' said she.

I thought a while whether I should ask her more, but it's a bad idea to set natives up with any notion of consulting them, so I went to Case. It was dark, and he was sitting alone, as he did mostly, smoking on the stairs.

'Case,' said I, 'here's a queer thing. I'm tabooed.'

'O, fudge!' says he, ' 'tain't the practice in these islands.'

'That may be, or it mayn't, said I. 'It's the practice where I was before. You can bet I know what it's like; and I tell it you for a fact, I'm tabooed.'

'Well,' said he, 'what have you been doing?'

'That's what I want to find out,' said I.

'O, you can't be,' said he; 'it ain't possible. However, I'll tell you what I'll do. Just to put your mind at rest, I'll go round and find out for sure. Just you waltz in and talk to Papa.'

'Thank you,' I said, 'I'd rather stay right out here on the verandah. Your house is so close.'

'I'll call Papa out here, then,' says he.

'My dear fellow,' I says, 'I wish you wouldn't. The fact is, I don't take to Mr Randall.'

Case laughed, took a lantern from the store, and set out into the village. He was gone perhaps a quarter of an hour, and he looked mighty serious when he came back.

'Well,' said he, clapping down the lantern on the verandah steps. 'I would never have believed it. I don't know where the impudence of these Kanakas 'll go next; they seem to have lost all idea of respect for whites. What we want is a man-of-war – a German, if we could – they know how to manage Kanakas.'

'I *am* tabooed, then?' I cried.

'Something of the sort,' said he. 'It's the worst thing of the kind I've heard of yet. But I'll stand by you, Wiltshire, man to man. You come round here to-morrow about nine, and we'll have it out with the chiefs. They're afraid of me, or they used to be; but their heads are so big by now, I don't know what to think. Understand me, Wiltshire; I don't count this your quarrel,' he went on, with a great deal of resolution, 'I count it all of our quarrel, I count it the White Man's Quarrel, and I'll stand to it through thick and thin, and there's my hand on it.'

'Have you found out what's the reason?' I asked.

'Not yet,' said Case. 'But we'll fix them down to-morrow.'

Altogether I was pretty well pleased with his attitude, and almost more the next day, when we met to go before the chiefs, to see him so stern and resolved. The chiefs awaited us in one of their big oval houses, which was marked out to us from a long way off by the crowd about the eaves, a hundred strong if there was one – men, women, and children. Many of the men were on their way to work and wore green wreaths, and it put me in thoughts of the 1st of May at home. This crowd opened and buzzed about the pair of us as we went in, with a sudden angry animation. Five chiefs were there; four mighty stately men, the fifth old and puckered. They sat on mats in their white kilts and jackets; they had fans in their hands, like fine ladies; and two of the younger ones wore Catholic medals, which gave me matter of reflection. Our place was set, and the mats laid for us over against these grandees, on the near side of the house; the midst was empty; the crowd, close at our backs, murmured, and craned, and jostled to look on, and the shadows of them tossed in front of us on the clean pebbles of the floor. I was just a hair put out by the excitement of the commons, but the quiet, civil appearance of the chiefs reassured me, all the more when their spokesman began and made a long speech in a low tone of voice, sometimes waving his hand towards Case, sometimes towards me, and sometimes knocking with his knuckles on the mat. One thing was clear: there was no sign of anger in the chiefs.

'What's he been saying?' I asked, when he had done.

'O, just that they're glad to see you, and they understand by me you wish to make some kind of complaint, and you're to fire away, and they'll do the square thing.'

'It took a precious long time to say that,' said I.

'O, the rest was sawder and *bonjour* and that,' said Case. 'You know what Kanakas are.'

'Well, they don't get much *bonjour* out of me,' said I. 'You tell them who I am. I'm a white man, and a British subject, and no end of a big chief at home; and I've come here to do them good, and bring them civilization; and no sooner have I got my trade sorted out than they go and taboo me, and no one dare come near my place! Tell them I don't mean to fly in the face of anything legal; and if what they want's a present, I'll do what's fair. I don't blame any man looking out for himself, tell them, for that's human nature; but if they think they're going to come any of their native ideas over me, they'll find themselves mistaken. And tell them plain that I demand the reason of this treatment as a white man and a British subject.'

That was my speech. I know how to deal with Kanakas: give them plain sense and fair dealing, and – I'll do them that much justice – they knuckle under every time. They haven't any real government or any real law, that's what you've got to knock into their heads; and even if they had, it would be a good joke if it was to apply to a white man. It would be a strange thing if we came all this way and couldn't do what we pleased. The mere idea has always put my monkey up, and I rapped my speech out pretty big. Then Case translated it – or made believe to, rather – and the first chief replied, and then a second, and a third, all in the same style, easy and genteel, but solemn underneath. Once a question was put to Case, and he answered it, and all hands (both chiefs and commons) laughed out aloud, and looked at me. Last of all, the puckered old fellow and the big young chief that spoke first started in to put Case through a kind of catechism. Sometimes I made out that Case was trying to fence and they stuck to him like hounds, and the sweat ran down his face, which was no very pleasant sight to me, and at some of his answers the crowd moaned and murmured, which was a worse hearing. It's a cruel shame I knew no native, for (as I now believe) they were asking Case about my marriage, and he must have had a tough job of it to clear his feet. But leave Case alone; he had the brains to run a parliament.

'Well, is that all?' I asked, when a pause came.

'Come along,' says he, mopping his face; 'I'll tell you outside.'

'Do you mean they won't take the taboo off?' I cried.

'It's something queer,' said he. 'I'll tell you outside. Better come away.'

'I won't take it at their hands,' cried I. 'I ain't that kind of a man. You don't find me turn my back on a parcel of Kanakas.'

'You'd better,' said Case.

He looked at me with a signal in his eye; and the five chiefs looked at me civilly enough, but kind of pointed; and the people looked at me, and craned and jostled. I remembered the folks that watched my house, and how the pastor had jumped in his pulpit at the bare sight of me; and the whole business seemed so out of the way that I rose and followed Case. The crowd opened again to let us through, but wider than before, the children on the skirts running and singing out, and as we two white men walked away they all stood and watched us.

'And now,' said I, 'what is all this about?'

'The truth is, I can't rightly make it out myself. They have a down on you,' says Case.

'Taboo a man because they have a down on him!' I cried. 'I never heard the like.'

'It's worse than that, you see,' said Case. 'You ain't tabooed – I told you that couldn't be. The people won't go near you, Wiltshire, and there's where it is.'

'They won't go near me? What do you mean by that? Why won't they go near me?' I cried.

Case hesitated. 'Seems they're frightened,' says he in a low voice.

I stopped dead short. 'Frightened?' I repeated. 'Are you gone crazy, Case? What are they frightened of?'

'I wish I could make out,' Case answered, shaking his head. 'Appears like one of their tomfool superstitions. That's what I don't cotton to,' he said. 'It's like the business about Vigours.'

'I'd like to know what you mean by that, and I'll trouble you to tell me,' says I.

'Well, you know, Vigours lit out and left all standing,' said he. 'It was some superstition business – I never got the hang of it; but it began to look bad before the end.'

'I've heard a different story about that,' said I, 'and I had better tell you so. I heard he ran away because of you.'

'O! well, I suppose he was ashamed to tell the truth,' says Case; 'I guess he thought it silly. And it's a fact that I packed him off. "What would you do, old man?" says he. – "Get," says I, "and not think twice about it." I was the gladdest kind of man to see him clear away. It ain't my notion to turn my back on a mate when he's in a tight place, but there was that much trouble in the village that I couldn't see where it might likely end. I was a fool to be so much about with Vigours. They cast it up to me to-day. Didn't you hear Maea – that's the young chief, the big one – ripping out about "Vika"? That was him they were after. They don't seem to forget it, somehow.'

'This is all very well,' said I, 'but it don't tell me what's wrong; it don't tell me what they're afraid of – what their idea is.'

'Well, I wish I knew,' said Case. 'I can't say fairer than that.'

'You might have asked, I think,' says I.

'And so I did,' says he. 'But you must have seen for yourself, unless you're blind, that the asking got the other way. I'll go as far as I dare for another white man; but when I find I'm in the scrape myself, I think first of my own bacon. The loss of me is I'm too good-natured. And I'll take the freedom of telling you you show a queer kind of gratitude to a man who's got into all this mess along of your affairs.'

'There's a thing I am thinking of,' said I. 'You were a fool to be so much about with Vigours. One comfort, you haven't been much about with me. I notice you've never been inside my house. Own up now; you had word of this before?'

'It's a fact I haven't been,' said he. 'It was an oversight, and I am sorry for it, Wiltshire. But about coming now, I'll be quite plain.'

'You mean you won't?' I asked.

'Awfully sorry, old man, but that's the size of it,' says Case.

'In short, you're afraid,' says I.

'In short, I'm afraid,' says he.

'And I'm still to be tabooed for nothing?' I asked.

'I tell you you're not tabooed,' said he. 'The Kanakas won't go near you, that's all. And who's to make 'em? We traders have a lot of gall, I must say; we make these poor Kanakas take back their laws, and take up their taboos, and that whenever it happens to suit us. But you don't mean to say you expect a law-obliging people to deal in your store whether they want to or not? You don't mean to tell me you've got the gall for that? And if you had, it would be a queer thing to propose to me. I would just like to point out to you, Wiltshire, that I'm a trader myself.'

'I don't think I would talk of gall if I was you,' said I. 'Here's about what it comes to, as well as I can make out: None of the people are to trade with me, and they're all to trade with you. You're to have the copra, and I'm to go to the devil and shake myself. And I don't know any native, and you're the only man here worth mention that speaks English, and you have the gall to up and hint to me my life's in danger, and all you've got to tell me is you don't know why!'

'Well, it *is* all I have to tell you,' said he. 'I don't know – I wish I did.'

'And so you turn your back and leave me to myself. Is that the position?' says I.

'If you like to put it nasty,' says he. 'I don't put it so. I say merely, "I'm going to keep clear of you; or, if I don't, I'll get in danger for myself."'

'Well' says I, 'you're a nice kind of a white man!'

'O, I understand; you're riled,' said he. 'I would be, myself. I can make excuses.'

'All right,' I said, 'go and make excuses somewhere else. Here's my way, there's yours!'

With that we parted, and I went straight home, in a hot temper, and found Uma trying on a lot of trade goods like a baby.

'Here,' I said, 'you quit that foolery! Here's a pretty mess to have made, as if I wasn't bothered enough anyway! And I thought I told you to get dinner!'

And then I believe I gave her a bit of the rough side of my tongue, as she deserved. She stood up at once, like a sentry to his officer; for I must say she was always well brought up, and had a great respect for whites.

'And now,' says I, 'you belong round here, you're bound to understand this. What am I tabooed for, anyway? Or, if I ain't tabooed, what makes the folks afraid of me?'

She stood and looked at me with eyes like saucers.

'You no savvy?' she gasps at last.

'No,' said I. 'How would you expect me to? We don't have any such craziness where I come from.'

'Ese no tell you?' she asked again.

(*Ese* was the name the natives had for Case; it may mean foreign, or extraordinary; or it might mean a mummy apple; but most like it was only his own name misheard and put in a Kanaka spelling.)

'Not much,' said I.

'Damn Ese!' she cried.

You might think it funny to hear this Kanaka girl come out with a big swear. No such thing. There was no swearing in her – no, nor anger; she was beyond anger, and meant the word simple and serious. She stood there straight as she said it. I cannot justly say that I ever saw a woman look like that before or after, and it struck me mum. Then she made a kind of an obeisance, but it was the proudest kind, and threw her hands out open.

'I'm 'shamed,' she said. 'I tnink you savvy. Ese he tell me you savvy, he tell me you no mind, tell me you love me too much. Taboo belong me,' she said, touching herself on the bosom, as she had done upon our wedding-night. 'Now I go 'way, taboo he go 'way too. Then you get too much copra. You like more better, I think. *Tofâ, alii*,' says she in the native – 'Farewell, chief!'

'Hold on!' I cried. 'Don't be in such a hurry.'

She looked at me sidelong with a smile. 'You see you get copra,' she said, the same as you might offer candies to a child.

'Uma,' said I, 'hear reason. I didn't know, and that's a fact; and Case seems to have played it pretty mean upon the pair of us. But I do know now, and I don't mind; I love you too much. You no go 'way, you no leave me, I too much sorry.'

'You no love me,' she cried, 'you talk me bad words!' And she threw herself in a corner of the floor, and began to cry.

Well, I'm no scholar, but I wasn't born yesterday, and I thought the worst of that trouble was over. However, there she lay – her back turned, her face to the wall – and shook with sobbing like a little child, so that her feet jumped with it. It's strange how it hits a man when he's in love; for there's no use mincing things – Kanaka and all, I was in love with her, or just as good. I tried to take her hand, but she would none of that. 'Uma,' I said, 'there's no sense in carrying on like this. I want you stop here, I want my little wifie, I tell you true.'

'No tell me true,' she sobbed.

'All right,' says I, 'I'll wait till you're through with this.' And I sat right down beside her on the floor, and set to smooth her hair with my hand. At first she wriggled away when I touched her; then she seemed to notice me no more; then her sobs grew gradually less, and presently stopped; and the next thing I knew, she raised her face to mine.

'You tell me true? You like me stop?' she asked.

'Uma,' I said, 'I would rather have you than all the copra in the South Seas,' which was a very big expression, and the strangest thing was that I meant it.

She threw her arms about me, sprang close up, and pressed her face to mine in the island way of kissing, so that I was all wetted with her tears, and my heart went out to her wholly. I never had anything so near me as this little brown bit of a girl. Many things went together, and all helped to turn my head. She was pretty enough to eat; it seemed she was my only friend in that queer place; I was ashamed that I had spoken rough to her: and she was a woman, and my wife, and a kind of a baby besides that I was sorry for; and the salt of her tears was in my mouth. And I forgot Case and the natives; and I forgot that I knew nothing of the story, or only remembered it to banish the remembrance; and I forgot that I was to get no copra, and so could make no livelihood; and I forgot my employers, and the strange kind of service I was doing them, when I preferred my fancy to their business; and I forgot even that Uma was no true wife of mine, but just a maid beguiled, and that in a pretty shabby style. But that is to look too far on. I will come to that part of it next.

It was late before we thought of getting dinner. The stove was out, and gone stone-cold; but we fired up after a while, and cooked each a dish, helping and hindering each other, and making a play of it like children. I was so greedy of her nearness that I sat down to dinner with my lass upon my knee, made sure of her with one hand, and ate with the other. Ay, and more than that. She was the worst cook, I suppose, God made; the things she set her hand to, it would have sickened an honest horse to eat of; yet I made my meal that day on Uma's cookery, and can never call to mind to have been better pleased.

I didn't pretend to myself, and I didn't pretend to her. I saw that I was clean gone; and if she was to make a fool of me, she must. And I suppose it was this that set her talking, for now she made sure that we were friends. A lot she told me, sitting in my lap and eating my dish, as I ate hers, from foolery – a lot about herself and her mother and Case, all which would be very tedious, and fill sheets if I set it down in Beach de Mar, but which I must give a hint of in plain English, and one thing about myself, which had a very big effect on my concerns, as you are soon to hear.

It seems she was born in one of the Line Islands; had been only two or three years in these parts, where she had come with a white man, who was married to her mother and then died; and only the one year in Falesá. Before that they had been a good deal on the move, trekking about after the white man, who was one of those rolling stones that keep going round after a soft job. They talk about looking for gold at the end of a rainbow; if a man wants an employment that'll last him till he dies, let him start out on the soft-job hunt. There's meat and drink in it too, and beer and skittles, for you never hear of them starving, and rarely see them sober; and as for steady sport, cock-fighting isn't in the same county with it. Anyway, this beachcomber carried the woman and her daughter all over the shop, but mostly to out-of-the-way islands, where there were no police, and he thought, perhaps, the soft job hung out. I've my own view of this old party; but I was just as glad he had kept Uma clear of Apia and Papeete and these flash towns. At last he struck Fale-alii on this island, got some trade – the Lord knows how! – muddled it all away in the usual style, and died worth next to nothing, bar a bit of land at Falesá that he had got for a bad debt, which was what put it in the minds of the mother and daughter to come there and live. It seems Case encouraged them all he could, and helped to get their house built. He was very kind those days, and gave Uma trade, and there is no doubt he had his eye on her from the beginning. However, they had scarce settled, when up turned a young man, a native, and wanted to marry her. He was a small chief, and had some fine mats and old songs in his family, and was 'very pretty', Uma said; and, altogether, it was an extraordinary match for a penniless girl and an out-islander.

At first word of this I got downright sick with jealousy.

'And you mean to say you would have married him?' I cried.

'*Ioe*, yes,' said she. 'I like too much!'

'Well!' I said. 'And suppose I had come round after?'

'I like you more better now,' said she. 'But, suppose I marry Ioane, I one good wife. I no common Kanaka. Good girl!' says she.

Well, I had to be pleased with that; but I promise you I didn't care about the business one little bit. And I liked the end of that yarn no better than the beginning. For it seems this proposal of marriage was the start of all the trouble. It seems, before that, Uma and her mother had been looked down upon, of course, for kinless folk and out-islanders, but nothing to hurt; and, even when Ioane came forward, there was less trouble at first than might have been looked for. And then, all of a sudden, about six months before my coming, Ioane backed out and left that part of the island, and from that day to this Uma and her mother had found themselves alone. None called at their house, none spoke to them on the roads. If they went to church, the other women drew their mats away and left them in a clear place by themselves. It was a regular excommunication, like what you read of in the

Middle Ages, and the cause or sense of it beyond guessing. It was some *tala pepelo*, Uma said, some lie, some calumny; and all she knew of it was that the girls who had been jealous of her luck with Ioane used to twit her with his desertion, and cry out, when they met her alone in the woods, that she would never be married. 'They tell me no man he marry me. He too much 'fraid,' she said.

The only soul that came about them after this desertion was Master Case. Even he was chary of showing himself, and turned up mostly by night; and pretty soon he began to table his cards and make up to Uma. I was still sore about Ioane, and when Case turned up in the same line of business I cut up downright rough.

'Well,' I said, sneering, 'and I suppose you thought Case "very pretty" and "liked too much"?'

'Now you talk silly,' said she. 'White man, he come here, I marry him all-e-same Kanaka; very well, then he marry me all-e-same white woman. Suppose he no marry, he go 'way, woman he stop. All-e-same thief, empty hand, Tonga-heart – no can love! Now you come marry me. You big heart – you no 'shamed island-girl. That thing I love you for too much. I proud.'

I don't know that ever I felt sicker all the days of my life. I laid down my fork, and I put away 'the island-girl'; I didn't seem somehow to have any use for either, and I went and walked up and down in the house, and Uma followed me with her eyes, for she was troubled, and small wonder! But troubled was no word for it with me. I so wanted, and so feared, to make a clean breast of the sweep that I had been.

And just then there came a sound of singing out of the sea; it sprang up suddenly clear and near, as the boat turned the headland, and Uma, running to the window, cried out it was 'Misi' come upon his rounds.

I thought it was a strange thing I should be glad to have a missionary: but, if it was strange, it was still true.

'Uma,' said I, 'you stop here in this room, and don't budge a foot out of it till I come back.'

CHAPTER III
THE MISSIONARY

As I came out on the verandah, the mission-boat was shooting for
the mouth of the river. She was a long whale-boat painted white; a
bit of an awning astern; a native pastor crouched on the wedge of
the poop, steering; some four-and-twenty paddles flashing and
dipping, true to the boat-song; and the missionary under the
awning, in his white clothes, reading in a book, and set him up! It
was pretty to see and hear; there's no smarter sight in the islands
than a missionary boat with a good crew and a good pipe to them;
and I considered it for half a minute, with a bit of envy perhaps,
and then strolled down towards the river.

From the opposite side there was another man aiming for the
same place, but he ran and got there first. It was Case; doubtless
his idea was to keep me apart from the missionary, who might
serve me as interpreter; but my mind was upon other things. I was
thinking how he had jockeyed us about the marriage, and tried his
hand on Uma before, and at the sight of him rage flew into my
nostrils.

'Get out of that, you low swindling thief!' I cried.

'What's that you say?' says he.

I gave him the word again, and rammed it down with a good
oath. 'And if ever I catch you within six fathoms of my house,' I
cried, 'I'll clap a bullet in your measly carcase.'

'You must do as you like about your house,' said he, 'where I
told you I have no thought of going; but this is a public place.'

'It's a place where I have private business,' said I. 'I have no
idea of a hound like you eavesdropping, and I give you notice to
clear out.'

'I don't take it, though,' says Case.

'I'll show you, then,' said I.

'We'll have to see about that,' said he.

He was quick with his hands, but he had neither the height nor
the weight, being a flimsy creature alongside a man like me, and,
besides, I was blazing to that height of wrath that I could have bit
into a chisel. I gave him first the one and then the other, so that I
could hear his head rattle and crack, and he went down straight.

'Have you had enough?' cried I. But he only looked up white

and blank, and the blood spread upon his face like wine upon a napkin. 'Have you had enough?' I cried again. 'Speak up, and don't lie malingering there, or I'll take my feet to you.'

He sat up at that, and held his head – by the look of him you could see it was spinning – and the blood poured on his pyjamas.

'I've had enough for this time,' says he, and he got up staggering, and went off by the way that he had come.

The boat was close in; I saw the missionary had laid his book to one side, and I smiled to myself. 'He'll know I'm a man, anyway,' thinks I.

This was the first time, in all my years in the Pacific, I had ever exchanged two words with any missionary, let alone asked one for a favour. I didn't like the lot – no trader does; they look down upon us, and make no concealment; and, besides, they're partly Kanakaized, and suck up with natives instead of with other white men like themselves. I had on a rig of clean striped pyjamas – for, of course, I had dressed decent to go before the chiefs; but when I saw the missionary step out of this boat in the regular uniform, white duck clothes, pith helmet, white shirt and tie, and yellow boots to his feet, I could have bunged stones at him. As he came nearer, queering me pretty curious (because of the fight, I suppose), I saw he looked mortal sick, for the truth was he had a fever on, and had just had a chill in the boat.

'Mr Tarleton, I believe?' says I, for I had got his name.

'And you, I suppose, are the new trader?' says he.

'I want to tell you first that I don't hold with missions,' I went on, 'and that I think you and the likes of you do a sight of harm, filling up the natives with old wives' tales and bumptiousness.'

'You are perfectly entitled to your opinions,' says he, looking a bit ugly, 'but I have no call to hear them.'

'It so happens that you've got to hear them,' I said. 'I'm no missionary, nor missionary lover; I'm no Kanaka, nor favourer of Kanakas – I'm just a trader; I'm just a common, low-down, God-damned white man and British subject, the sort you would like to wipe your boots on. I hope that's plain!'

'Yes, my man,' said he. 'It's more plain than creditable. When you are sober, you'll be sorry for this.'

He tried to pass on, but I stopped him with my hand. The

Kanakas were beginning to growl. Guess they didn't like my tone, for I spoke to that man as free as I would to you.

'Now, you can't say I've deceived you,' said I, 'and I can go on. I want a service – I want two services, in fact – and, if you care to give me them, I'll perhaps take more stock in what you call your Christianity.'

He was silent for a moment. Then he smiled. 'You are rather a strange sort of man,' says he.

'I'm the sort of man God made me,' says I. 'I don't set up to be a gentleman,' I said.

'I am not quite so sure,' said he. 'And what can I do for you, Mr—?'

'Wiltshire,' I says, 'though I'm mostly called Welsher; but Wiltshire is the way it's spelt, if the people on the beach could only get their tongues about it. And what do I want? Well, I'll tell you the first thing. I'm what you call a sinner – what I call a sweep – and I want you to help me make it up to a person I've deceived.'

He turned and spoke to his crew in the native. 'And now I am at your service,' said he, 'but only for the time my crew are dining. I must be much farther down the coast before night. I was delayed at Papa-malulu till this morning, and I have an engagement in Fale-alii tomorrow night.'

I led the way to my house in silence, and rather pleased with myself for the way I had managed the talk, for I like a man to keep his self-respect.

'I was sorry to see you fighting,' says he.

'O, that's part of the yarn I want to tell you,' I said. 'That's service number two. After you've heard it you'll let me know whether you're sorry or not.'

We walked right in through the store, and I was surprised to find Uma had cleared away the dinner things. This was so unlike her ways that I saw she had done it out of gratitude, and liked her the better. She and Mr Tarleton called each other by name, and he was very civil to her seemingly. But I thought little of that; they can always find civility for a Kanaka, it's us white men they lord it over. Besides, I didn't want much Tarleton just then. I was going to do my pitch.

'Uma,' said I, 'give us your marriage certificate.' She looked put out. 'Come,' said I, 'you can trust me. Hand it up.'

She had it about her person, as usual; I believe she thought it was a pass to heaven, and if she died without having it handy she would go to hell. I couldn't see where she put it the first time, I couldn't see now where she took it from; it seemed to jump into her hand like that Blavatsky business in the papers. But it's the same way with all island women, and I guess they're taught it when young.

'Now,' said I, with the certificate in my hand, 'I was married to this girl by Black Jack the negro. The certificate was wrote by Case, and it's a dandy piece of literature, I promise you. Since then I've found that there's a kind of cry in the place against this wife of mine, and so long as I keep her I cannot trade. Now, what would any man do in my place, if he was a man?' I said. 'The first thing he would do is this, I guess.' And I took and tore up the certificate and bunged the pieces on the floor.

'*Aué!*'* cried Uma, and began to clap her hands; but I caught one of them in mine.

'And the second thing he would do,' said I, 'if he was what I could call a man and you would call a man, Mr Tarleton, is to bring the girl right before you or any other missionary, and to up and say: "I was wrong married to this wife of mine, but I think a heap of her, and now I want to be married to her right." Fire away, Mr Tarleton. And I guess you'd better do it in native; it'll please the old lady,' I said, giving her the proper name of a man's wife upon the spot.

So we had in two of the crew for to witness, and were spliced in our own house; and the parson prayed a good bit, I must say – but not so long as some – and shook hands with the pair of us.

'Mr Wiltshire,' he says, when he had made out the lines and packed off the witnesses, 'I have to thank you for a very lively pleasure. I have rarely performed the marriage ceremony with more grateful emotions.'

That was what you would call talking. He was going on, besides, with more of it, and I was ready for as much taffy as he had in stock, for I felt good. But Uma had been taken up with something half through the marriage, and cut straight in.

'How your hand he get hurt?' she asked.

* Alas!

'You ask Case's head, old lady,' says I.

She jumped with joy, and sang out.

'You haven't made much of a Christian of this one,' says I to Mr Tarleton.

'We didn't think her one of our worst,' says he, 'when she was at Fale-alii; and if Uma bears malice I shall be tempted to fancy she has good cause.'

'Well, there we are at service number two,' said I. 'I want to tell you our yarn, and see if you can let a little daylight in.'

'Is it long?' he asked.

'Yes,' I cried; 'it's a goodish bit of a yarn!'

'Well, I'll give you all the time I can spare,' says he, looking at his watch. 'But I must tell you fairly, I haven't eaten since five this morning, and, unless you can let me have something, I am not likely to eat again before seven or eight to-night.'

'By God, we'll give you dinner!' I cried.

I was a little caught up at my swearing, just when all was going straight; and so was the missionary, I suppose, but he made believe to look out of the window, and thanked us.

So we ran him up a bit of a meal. I was bound to let the old lady have a hand in it, to show off, so I deputized her to brew the tea. I don't think I ever met such tea as she turned out. But that was not the worst, for she got round with the salt-box, which she considered an extra European touch, and turned my stew into sea-water. Altogether, Mr Tarleton had a devil of a dinner of it; but he had plenty entertainment by the way, for all the while that we were cooking, and afterwards, when he was making believe to eat, I kept posting him up on Master Case and the beach of Falesá, and he putting questions that showed he was following close.

'Well,' said he at last, 'I am afraid you have a dangerous enemy. This man Case is very clever, and seems really wicked. I must tell you I have had my eye on him for nearly a year, and have rather had the worst of our encounters. About the time when the last representative of your firm ran so suddenly away, I had a letter from Namu, the native pastor, begging me to come to Falesá at my earliest convenience, as his flock were all "adopting Catholic practices". I had great confidence in Namu; I fear it only shows how easily we are deceived. No one could hear him preach and not be persuaded he was a man of extraordinary parts. All our islanders easily acquire a kind of eloquence, and can roll out and illustrate, with a great deal of vigour and fancy, second-hand sermons; but Namu's sermons are his own, and I cannot deny that I have found them means of grace. Moreover, he has a keen curiosity in secular things, does not fear work, is clever at carpentering, and has made himself so much respected among the neighbouring pastors that we call him, in a jest which is half serious, the Bishop of the East. In short, I was proud of the man; all the more puzzled by his letter, and took an occasion to come this way. The morning before my arrival, Vigours had been sent on board the *Lion*, and Namu was perfectly at his ease, apparently ashamed of his letter, and quite unwilling to explain it. This, of course, I could not allow, and he ended by confessing that he had been much concerned to find his people using the sign of the cross, but since he had learned the explanation his mind was satisfied. For Vigours had the Evil Eye, a common thing in a country of Europe called Italy, where men were often struck dead by that kind of devil, and it appeared the sign of the cross was a charm against its power.

'"And I explain it, Misi," said Namu, "in this way: the country in Europe is a Popey country, and the devil of the Evil Eye may be a Catholic devil, or, at least, used to Catholic ways. So then I reasoned thus: If this sign of the cross were used in a Popey manner it would be sinful, but when it is used only to protect men from a devil, which is a thing harmless in itself, the sign too must be, as a bottle is neither good nor bad, harmless. For the sign is neither good nor bad. But if the bottle be full of gin, the gin is bad; and if the sign be made in idolatry bad, so is the idolatry." And, very like a native pastor, he had a text apposite about the casting out of devils.

'"And who has been telling you about the Evil Eye?" I asked.

'He admitted it was Case. Now, I am afraid you will think me very narrow, Mr Wiltshire, but I must tell you I was displeased, and cannot think a trader at all a good man to advise or have an influence upon my pastors. And, besides, there had been some flying talk in the country of old Adams and his being poisoned, to which I had paid no great heed; but it came back to me at the moment.

'"And is this Case a man of a sanctified life?" I asked.

'He admitted he was not; for, though he did not drink, he was profligate with women, and had no religion.

' "Then," said I, "I think the less you have to do with him the better."

'But it is not easy to have the last word with a man like Namu. He was ready in a moment with an illustration. "Misi," said he, "you have told me there were wise men, not pastors, not even holy, who knew many things useful to be taught – about trees, for instance, and beasts, and to print books, and about the stones that are burned to make knives of. Such men teach you in your college, and you learn from them, but take care not to learn to be unholy. Misi, Case is my college."

'I knew not what to say. Mr Vigours had evidently been driven out of Falesá by the machinations of Case, and with something not very unlike the collusion of my pastor. I called to mind it was Namu who had reassured me about Adams and traced the rumour to the ill-will of the priest. And I saw I must inform myself more thoroughly from an impartial source. There is an old rascal of a chief here, Faiaso, whom I daresay you saw to-day at the council; he has been all his life turbulent and sly, a great fomenter of rebellions, and a thorn in the side of the mission and the island. For all that he is very shrewd, and, except in politics or about his own misdemeanours, a teller of the truth. I went to his house, told him what I had heard, and besought him to be frank. I do not think I had ever a more painful interview. Perhaps you will understand me, Mr Wiltshire, if I tell you that I am perfectly serious in these old wives' tales with which you reproached me, and as anxious to do well for these islands as you can be to please and to protect your pretty wife. And you are to remember that I thought Namu a paragon, and was proud of the man as one of the first ripe fruits of the mission. And now I was informed that he had fallen in a sort of dependence upon Case. The beginning of it was not corrupt; it began, doubtless, in fear and respect, produced by trickery and pretence; but I was shocked to find that another element had been lately added, that Namu helped himself in the store, and was believed to be deep in Case's debt. Whatever the trader said, that Namu believed with trembling. He was not alone in this; many in the village lived in a similar subjection; but Namu's case was the most influential, it was through Namu Case had wrought most evil; and with a certain following among the chiefs, and the pastor in his pocket, the man was as good as master of the village. You know something of Vigours and Adams, but perhaps you have never heard of old Underhill, Adams' predecessor. He was a quiet, mild old fellow, I remember, and we were told he had died suddenly: white men die very suddenly in Falesá. The truth, as I now heard it, made my blood run cold. It seems he was struck with a general palsy, all of him dead but one eye, which he continually winked. Word was started that the helpless old man was now a devil, and this vile fellow Case worked upon the natives' fears, which he professed to share, and pretended he durst not go into the house alone. At last a grave was dug, and the living body buried at the far end of the village. Namu, my pastor, whom I had helped to educate, offered up a prayer at the hateful scene.

'I felt myself in a very difficult position. Perhaps it was my duty to have denounced Namu and had him deposed. Perhaps I think so now, but at the time it seemed less clear. He had a great influence, it might prove greater than mine. The natives are prone to superstition; perhaps by stirring them up I might but ingrain and spread these dangerous fancies. And Namu besides, apart from this novel and accursed influence, was a good pastor, an able man, and spiritually minded. Where should I look for a better? How was I to find as good? At that moment, with Namu's failure fresh in my view, the work of my life appeared a mockery; hope was dead in me. I would rather repair such tools as I had than go abroad in quest of others that must certainly prove worse; and a scandal is, at the best, a thing to be avoided when humanly possible. Right or wrong, then, I determined on a quiet course. All that night I denounced and reasoned with the erring pastor, twitted him with his ignorance and want of faith, twitted him with his wretched attitude, making clean the outside of the cup and platter, callously helping at a murder, childishly flying in excitement about a few childish, unnecessary, and inconvenient gestures; and long before day I had him on his knees and bathed in the tears of what seemed a genuine repentance. On Sunday I took the pulpit in the morning, and preached from First Kings, nineteenth, on the fire, the earthquake, and the voice, distinguishing the true spiritual power, and referring with such plainness as I dared to recent events in Falesá. The effect produced was great, and it was much increased when Namu rose in his turn and confessed that he had been wanting in faith and conduct, and was convinced of sin. So far, then, all was well; but there was one unfortunate circumstance. It was nearing the time of our "May" in the island, when the native contributions to the missions are received; it fell in my duty to make a notification on the subject, and this gave my enemy his chance, by which he was not slow to profit.

'News of the whole proceedings must have been carried to Case as soon as church was over, and the same afternoon he made an occasion to meet me in the midst of the village. He came up with so much intentness and animosity that I felt it would be damaging to avoid him.

' "So," says he, in native, "here is the holy man. He has been preaching against me, but that was not in his heart. He has been preaching upon the love of God; but that was not in his heart, it was between his teeth. Will you know what was in his heart?" cries he. "I will show it you!" And, making a snatch at my head he made believe to pluck out a dollar, and held it in the air.

'There went that rumour through the crowd with which Polynesians receive a prodigy. As for myself, I stood amazed. The thing was a common conjuring trick which I have seen performed at home a score of times; but how was I to convince the villagers of that? I wished I had learned legerdemain instead of Hebrew, that I might have paid the fellow out with his own coin. But there I was; I could not stand there silent, and the best I could find to say was weak.

' "I will trouble you not to lay hands on me again," said I.

' "I have no such thought," said he, "nor will I deprive you of your dollar. Here it is," he said, and flung it at my feet. I am told it lay where it fell three days.'

'I must say it was well played,' said I.

'O! he is clever,' said Mr Tarleton, 'and you can now see for yourself how dangerous. He was a party to the horrid death of the paralytic; he is accused of poisoning Adams; he drove Vigours out of the place by lies that might have led to murder; and there is no question but he has now made up his mind to rid himself of you. How he means to try we have no guess; only be sure it's something new. There is no end to his readiness and invention.'

'He gives himself a sight of trouble,' says I. 'And after all, what for?'

'Why, how many tons of copra may they make in this district?' asked the missionary.

'I daresay as much as sixty tons,' says I.

'And what is the profit to the local trader?' he asked.

'You may call it three pounds,' said I.

'Then you can reckon for yourself how much he does it for,' said Mr Tarleton. 'But the more important thing is to defeat him. It is clear he spread some report against Uma, in order to isolate and have his wicked will of her. Falling of that, and seeing a new rival come upon the scene, he used her in a different way. Now, the first point to find out is about Namu. Uma, when people began to leave you and your mother alone, what did Namu do?'

'Stop away all-e-same,' says Uma.

'I fear the dog has returned to his vomit,' said Mr Tarleton. 'And now what am I to do for you? I will speak to Namu, I will warn him he is observed; it will be strange if he allow anything to go on amiss when he is put upon his guard. At the same time, this precaution may fail, and then you must turn elsewhere. You have two people at hand to whom you might apply. There is, first of all, the priest, who might protect you by the Catholic interest; they are a wretchedly small body, but they count two chiefs. And then there is old Faiaso. Ah! if it had been some years ago you would have needed no one else; but his influence is much reduced; it has gone into Maea's hands, and Maea, I fear, is one of Case's jackals. In fine, if the worst comes to the worst, you must send up or come yourself to Fale-alii, and, though I am not due at this end of the island for a month, I will just see what can be done.'

So Mr Tarleton said farewell; and half an hour later the crew were singing and the paddles flashing in the missionary boat.

CHAPTER IV
DEVIL-WORK

Near a month went by without much doing. The same night of our marriage Galoshes called round, and made himself mighty civil, and got into a habit of dropping in about dark and smoking his pipe with the family. He could talk to Uma, of course, and started to teach me native and French at the same time. He was a kind old buffer, though the dirtiest you would wish to see, and he muddled me up with foreign languages worse than the tower of Babel.

. That was one employment we had, and it made me feel less lonesome; but there was no profit in the thing, for though the priest came and sat and yarned, none of his folks could be enticed into my store; and if it hadn't been for the other occupation I struck out there wouldn't have been a pound of copra in the house. This was the idea: Fa'avao (Uma's mother) had a score of bearing trees. Of course we could get no labour, being all as good as tabooed, and the two women and I turned to and made copra with our own hands. It was copra to make your mouth water when it was done – I never understood how much the natives cheated me till I had made that four hundred pounds of my own hand – and it weighed so light I felt inclined to take and water it myself.

When we were at the job a good many Kanakas used to put in the best of the day looking on, and once that nigger turned up. He stood back with the natives and laughed and did the big don and the funny dog till I began to get riled.

'Here, you nigger!' says I.

'I don't address myself to you, Sah,' says the nigger. 'Only speak to gen'le'um.'

'I know,' says I, 'but it happens I was addressing myself to you, Mr Black Jack. And all I want to know is just this: did you see Case's figurehead about a week ago?'

'No, Sah,' says he.

'That's all right, then,' says I; 'for I'll show you the own brother to it, only black, in the inside of about two minutes.'

And I began to walk towards him, quite slow, and my hands down; only there was trouble in my eye, if anybody took the pains to look.

'You're a low, obstropulous fellow, Sah,' says he.

'You bet!' says I.

By that time he thought I was about as near as convenient, and lit out so it would have done your heart good to see him travel. And that was all I saw of that precious gang until what I am about to tell you.

It was one of my chief employments these days to go pothunting in the woods, which I found (as Case had told me) very rich in game. I have spoken of the cape which shut up the village and my station from the east. A path went about the end of it, and led into the next bay. A strong wind blew here daily, and as the line of the barrier reef stopped at the end of the cape, a heavy surf ran on the shores of the bay. A little cliffy hill cut the valley in two parts, and stood close on the beach; and at high water the sea broke right on the face of it, so that all passage was stopped. Woody mountains hemmed the place all round; the barrier to the east was particularly steep and leafy, the lower parts of it, along the sea, falling in sheer black cliffs streaked with cinnabar; the upper part lumpy with the tops of the great trees. Some of the trees were bright green, and some red, and the sand of the beach as black as your shoes. Many birds hovered round the bay, some of them snow-white; and the flying fox (or vampire) flew there in broad daylight, gnashing its teeth.

For a long while I came as far as this shooting, and went no farther. There was no sign of any path beyond, and the cocoa-palms in the front of the foot of the valley were the last this way. For the whole 'eye' of the island, as natives call the windward end, lay desert. From Falesá round about to Papa-malulu, there was neither house, nor man, nor planted fruit-tree; and the reef being mostly absent, and the shores bluff, the sea beat direct among crags, and there was scarce a landing-place.

I should tell you that after I began to go in the woods, although no one offered to come near my store, I found people willing enough to pass the time of day with me where nobody could see them; and as I had begun to pick up native, and most of them had a word or two of English, I began to hold little odds and ends of conversation, not to much purpose to be sure, but they took off the worst of the feeling, for it's a miserable thing to be made a leper of.

It chanced one day towards the end of the month, that I was sitting in this bay in the edge of the bush, looking east, with a Kanaka. I had given him a fill of tobacco, and we were making out to talk as best we could; indeed, he had more English than most.

I asked him if there was no road going eastward.

'One time one road,' said he. 'Now he dead.'

'Nobody he go there?' I asked.

'No good,' said he. 'Too much devil he stop there.'

'Oho!' says I, 'got-um plenty devil, that bush?'

'Man devil, woman devil; too much devil,' said my friend. 'Stop there all-e-time. Man he go there, no come back.'

I thought if this fellow was so well posted on devils and spoke of them so free, which is not common, I had better fish for a little information about myself and Uma.

'You think me one devil?' I asked.

'No think devil,' said he soothingly. 'Think all-e-same fool.'

'Uma, she devil?' I asked again.

'No, no; no devil. Devil stop bush,' said the young man.

I was looking in front of me across the bay, and I saw the hanging front of the woods pushed suddenly open, and Case, with a gun in his hand, step forth into the sunshine on the black beach. He was got up in light pyjamas, near white, his gun sparkled, he looked mighty conspicuous; and the land-crabs scuttled from all round him to their holes.

'Hullo, my friend!' says I, 'you no talk all-e-same true. Ese he go, he come back.'

'Ese no all-e-same; Ese *Tiapolo*,' says my friend; and, with a 'Goodbye,' slunk off among the trees.

I watched Case all round the beach, where the tide was low; and let him pass me on the homeward way to Falesá. He was in deep thought, and the birds seemed to know it, trotting quite near him on the sand, or wheeling and calling in his ears. When he passed me I could see by the working of his lips that he was talking to himself, and, what pleased me mightily, he had still my trade mark on his brow. I tell you the plain truth: I had a mind to give him a gunful in his ugly mug, but I thought better of it.

All this time, and all the time I was following home, I kept repeating that native word, which I remembered by 'Polly, put the kettle on and make us all some tea', tea-a-pollo.

'Uma,' says I, when I got back, 'what does *Tiapolo* mean?'

'Devil,' says she.

'I thought *aitu* was the word for that,' I said.

'*Aitu* 'nother kind of devil,' said she; 'stop bush, eat Kanaka. Tiapolo big chief devil, stop home; all-e-same Christian devil.'

'Well then,' said I, 'I'm no farther forward. How can Case be Tiapolo?'

'No all-e-same,' said she. 'Ese belong Tiapolo; Tiapolo too much like; Ese all-e-same his son. Suppose Ese he wish something, Tiapolo he make him.'

'That's mighty convenient for Ese,' says I. 'And what kind of things does he make for him?'

Well out came a rigmarole of all sorts of stories, many of which (like the dollar he took from Mr Tarleton's head) were plain enough to me, but others I could make nothing of; and the thing that most surprised the Kanakas was what surprised me least – namely, that he would go in the desert among all the *aitus*. Some of the boldest, however, had accompanied him, and had heard him speak with the dead and give them orders, and, safe in his protection, had returned unscathed. Some said he had a church there, where he worshipped Tiapolo, and Tiapolo appeared to him; others swore that there was no sorcery at all, that he performed his miracles by the power of prayer, and the church was no church, but a prison, in which he had confined a dangerous *aitu*. Namu had been in the bush with him once, and returned glorifying God for these wonders. Altogether, I began to have a glimmer of the man's position, and the means by which he had acquired it, and, though I saw he was a tough nut to crack, I was noways cast down.

'Very well,' said I, 'I'll have a look at Master Case's place of worship myself, and we'll see about the glorifying.'

At this Uma fell in a terrible taking; if I went in the high bush I should never return; none could go there but by the protection of Tiapolo.

'I'll chance it on God's,' said I. 'I'm a good sort of fellow, Uma, as fellows go, and I guess God'll con me through.'

She was silent for a while. 'I think,' said she, mighty solemn – and then, presently – 'Victoreea, he big chief?'

'You bet!' said I.

'He like you too much?' she asked again.

I told her, with a grin, I believed the old lady was rather partial to me.

'All right,' said she. 'Victoreea he big chief, like you too much. No can help you here in Falesá; no can do – too far off. Maea he small chief – stop here. Suppose he like you – make you all right. All-e-same God and Tiapolo. God he big chief – got too much work. Tiapolo he small chief – he like too much make-see, work very hard.'

'I'll have to hand you over to Mr Tarleton,' said I. 'Your theology's out of its bearings, Uma.'

However, we stuck to this business all the evening, and, with the stories she told me of the desert and its dangers, she came near frightening herself into a fit. I don't remember half a quarter of them, of course, for I paid little heed; but two come back to me kind of clear.

About six miles up the coast there is a sheltered cove they call *Fanga-anaana* – 'the haven full of caves'. I've seen it from the sea myself, as near as I could get my boys to venture in; and it's a little strip of yellow sand. Black cliffs overhang it, full of the black mouths of caves; great trees overhang the cliffs, and dangle-down lianas; and in one place, about the middle, a big brook pours over in a cascade. Well, there was a boat going by here, with six young men of Falesá, 'all very pretty,' Uma said, which was the loss of them. It blew strong, there was a heavy head sea, and by the time they opened Fanga-anaana, and saw the white cascade and the shady beach, they were all tired and thirsty, and their water had run out. One proposed to land and get a drink, and, being reckless fellows, they were all of the same mind except the youngest. Lotu was his name; he was a very good young gentleman, and very wise; and he held out that they were crazy, telling them the place was given over to spirits and devils and the dead, and there were no living folk nearer than six miles the one way, and maybe twelve the other. But they laughed at his words, and, being five to one, pulled in, beached the boat, and landed. It was a wonderful pleasant place, Lotu said, and the water excellent. They walked round the beach, but could see nowhere any way to mount the cliffs, which made them easier in their mind; and at last they sat down to make a meal on the food they had brought with them. They were scarce set, when there came out of the mouth of one of the black caves six of the most beautiful ladies ever seen: they had flowers in their hair, and the most beautiful breasts, and necklaces of scarlet seeds; and began to jest with these young gentlemen, and the young gentlemen to jest back with them, all but Lotu. As for Lotu, he saw there could be no living woman in such a place, and ran, and flung himself in the bottom of the boat, and covered his face, and prayed. All the time the business lasted Lotu made one clean break of prayer, and that was all he knew of it, until his friends came back, and made him sit up, and they put to sea again out of the bay, which was now quite deserted, and no word of the six ladies. But, what frightened Lotu most, not one of the five remembered anything of what had passed, but they were all like drunken men, and sang and laughed in the boat, and skylarked. The wind freshened and came squally, and the sea rose extraordinary high; it was such weather as any man in the islands would have turned his back to and fled home to Falesá; but these five were like crazy folk, and cracked on all sail and drove their boat into the seas. Lotu went to the bailing, none of the others thought to help him, but sang and skylarked and carried on, and spoke singular things beyond a man's comprehension, and laughed out loud when they said them. So the rest of the day Lotu bailed for his life in the bottom of the boat, and was all drenched with sweat and cold sea-water; and none heeded him. Against all expectation, they came safe in a dreadful tempest to Papa-malulu, where the palms were singing out, and the cocoa-nuts flying like cannon-balls about the village green; and the same night the five young gentlemen sickened, and spoke never a reasonable word until they died.

'And do you mean to tell me you can swallow a yarn like that?' I asked.

She told me the thing was well known, and with handsome young men alone it was even common; but this was the only case where five had been slain the same day and in a company by the love of the women-devils; and it had made a great stir in the island, and she would be crazy if she doubted.

'Well, anyway,' says I, 'you needn't be frightened about me. I've no use for the women-devils. You're all the women I want, and all the devil too, old lady.'

To this she answered there were other sorts, and she had seen one with her own eyes. She had gone one day alone to the next bay, and, perhaps, got too near the margin of the bad place. The boughs of the high bush overshadowed her from the cant of the hill, but she herself was outside on a flat place, very stony, and growing full of young mummy-apples four and five feet high. It was a dark day in the rainy season, and now there came squalls that tore off the leaves and sent them flying, and now it was all still as in a house. It was in one of these still times that a whole gang of birds and flying foxes came pegging out of the bush like creatures frightened. Presently after she heard a rustle nearer hand, and saw, coming out of the margin of the trees, among the mummy-apples, the appearance of a lean grey old boar. It seemed to think as it came, like a person; and all of a sudden, as she looked at it coming, she was aware it was no boar, but a thing that was a man with a man's thoughts. At that she ran, and the pig after her, and as the pig ran it holla'd aloud, so that the place rang with it.

'I wish I had been there with my gun,' said I. 'I guess that pig would have holla'd so as to surprise himself.'

But she told me a gun was of no use with the like of these, which were the spirits of the dead.

Well, this kind of talk put in the evening, which was the best of it; but of course it didn't change my notion, and the next day, with my gun and a good knife, I set off upon a voyage of discovery. I made, as near as I could, for the place where I had seen Case come out; for if it was true he had some kind of establishment in the bush I reckoned I should find a path. The beginning of the desert was marked off by a wall to call it so, for it was more of a long mound of stones. They say it reaches right across the island, but how they know it is another question, for I doubt if anyone has made the journey in a hundred years, the natives sticking chiefly to the sea, and their little colonies along the coast, and that part being mortal high and steep and full of cliffs. Up to the west side of the wall the ground has been cleared, and there are cocoa-palms and mummy-apples and guavas, and lots of sensitive. Just across, the bush begins outright; high bush at that, trees going up like the masts of ships, and ropes of liana hanging down like a ship's rigging, and nasty orchids growing in the forks like funguses. The ground where there was no underwood looked to be a heap of boulders. I saw many green pigeons which I might have shot, only I was there with a different idea. A number of butterflies flopped up and down along the ground like dead leaves; sometimes I would hear a bird calling, sometimes the wind overhead, and always the sea along the coast.

But the queerness of the place it's more difficult to tell of, unless to one who has been alone in the high bush himself. The brightest kind of a day it is always dim down there. A man can see to the end of nothing; whichever way he looks the wood shuts up, one bough folding with another like the fingers of your hand; and whenever he listens he hears always something new – men talking, children laughing, the strokes of an axe a far way ahead of him, and sometimes a sort of a quick, stealthy scurry near at hand that makes him jump and look to his weapons. It's all very well for him to tell himself that he's alone, bar trees and birds; he can't make out to believe it; whichever way he turns the whole place seems to be alive and looking on. Don't think it was Uma's yarns that put me out; I don't value native talk a fourpenny-piece; it's a thing that's natural in the bush, and that's the end of it.

As I got near the top of the hill, for the ground of the wood goes up in this place steep as a ladder, the wind began to sound straight on, and the leaves to toss and switch open and let in the sun. This suited me better; it was the same noise all the time, and nothing to startle. Well, I had got to a place where there was an underwood of what they call wild cocoa-nut – mighty pretty with its scarlet fruit – when there came a sound of singing in the wind that I thought I had never heard the like of. It was all very fine to tell myself it was the branches; I knew better. It was all very fine to tell myself it was a bird; I knew never a bird that sang like that. It rose and swelled, and died away and swelled again; and now I thought it was like someone weeping, only prettier; and now I thought it was like harps; and there was one thing I made sure of, it was a sight too sweet to be wholesome in a place like that. You may laugh if you like; but I declare I called to mind the six young ladies that came, with their scarlet necklaces, out of the cave at Fanga-anaana, and wondered if they sang like that. We laugh at the natives and their superstitions; but see how many traders take them up, splendidly educated white men that have been book-keepers (some of them) and clerks in the old country. It's my belief a superstition grows up in a place like the different kind of weeds; and as I stood there and listened to that wailing I twittered in my shoes.

You may call me a coward to be frightened; I thought myself brave enough to go on ahead. But I went mighty carefully, with my gun cocked, spying all about me like a hunter, fully expecting to see a handsome young woman sitting somewhere in the bush, and fully determined (if I did) to try her with a charge of duck-shot. And sure enough, I had not gone far when I met with a queer thing. The wind came on the top of the wood in a strong puff, the leaves in front of me burst open, and I saw for a second something hanging in a tree. It was gone in a wink, the puff blowing by and the leaves closing. I tell you the truth: I had made up my mind to see an *aitu*; and if the thing had looked like a pig or a woman, it wouldn't have given me the same turn. The trouble was that it seemed kind of square, and the idea of a square thing that was alive and sang knocked me sick and silly. I must have stood quite a while; and I made pretty certain it was right out of the same tree that the singing came. Then I began to come to myself a bit.

'Well,' says I, 'if this is really so, if this is a place where there are square things that sing, I'm gone up anyway. Let's have my fun for my money.'

But I thought I might as well take the off-chance of a prayer being any good; so I plumped on my knees and prayed out loud; and all the time I was praying the strange sounds came out of the tree, and went up and down, and changed, for all the world like music, only you could see it wasn't human – there was nothing there that you could whistle.

As soon as I had made an end in proper style, I laid down my gun, stuck my knife between my teeth, walked right up to that tree, and began to climb. I tell you my heart was like ice. But presently, as I went up, I caught another glimpse of the thing, and that relieved me, for I thought it seemed like a box; and when I had got right up to it I near fell out of the tree with laughing.

A box it was, sure enough, and a candle-box at that, with the brand upon the side of it; and it had banjo-strings stretched so as to sound when the wind blew. I believe they call the thing a Tyrolean* harp, whatever that may mean.

'Well, Mr Case,' said I, 'you've frightened me once, but I defy you to frighten me again,' I says, and slipped down the tree, and set out again to find my enemy's head office, which I guessed would not be far away.

The undergrowth was thick in this part; I couldn't see before my

* Aeolian.

nose, and must burst my way through by main force and ply the knife as I went, slicing the cords of the lianas and slashing down whole trees at a blow. I call them trees for the bigness, but in truth they were just big weeds, and sappy to cut through like carrot. From all this crowd and kind of vegetation, I was just thinking to myself, the place might have once been cleared, when I came on my nose over a pile of stones, and saw in a moment it was some kind of a work of man. The Lord knows when it was made or when deserted, for this part of the island has lain undisturbed since long before the whites came. A few steps beyond I hit into the path I had been always looking for. It was narrow, but well beaten, and I saw that Case had plenty of disciples. It seems, indeed, it was a piece of fashionable boldness to venture up here with the trader, and a young man scarce reckoned himself grown till he had got his breech tattooed, for one thing, and seen Case's devils for another. This is mighty like Kanakas; but, if you look at it another way, it's mighty like white folks too.

A bit along the path I was brought to a clear stand, and had to rub my eyes. There was a wall in front of me, the path passing it by a gap; it was tumble-down, and plainly very old, but built of big stones very well laid; and there is no native alive to-day upon that island that could dream of such a piece of building. Along all the top of it was a line of queer figures, idols or scarecrows, or what not. They had carved and painted faces, ugly to view, their eyes and teeth were of shell, their hair and their bright clothes blew in the wind, and some of them worked with the tugging. There are islands up west where they make these kind of figures till to-day; but if ever they were made in this island, the practice and the very recollection of it are now long forgotten. And the singular thing was that all these bogies were as fresh as toys out of a shop.

Then it came in my mind that Case had let out to me the first day that he was a good forger of island curiosities, a thing by which so many traders turn an honest penny. And with that I saw the whole business, and how this display served the man a double purpose, first of all, to season his curiosities, and then to frighten those that came to visit him.

But I should tell you (what made the thing more curious) that all the time the Tyrolean harps were harping round me in the trees, and even while I looked, a green-and-yellow bird (that, I suppose, was building) began to tear the hair off the head of one of the figures.

A little farther on I found the best curiosity of the museum. The first I saw of it was a longish mound of earth with a twist to it. Digging off the earth with my hands, I found underneath tarpaulin stretched on boards, so that this was plainly the roof of a cellar. It stood right on the top of the hill, and the entrance was on the far side, between two rocks, like the entrance to a cave. I went as far in as the bend, and, looking round the corner, saw a shining face. It was big and ugly, like a pantomine mask, and the brightness of it waxed and dwindled, and at times it smoked.

'Oho!' says I, 'luminous paint!'

And I must say I rather admired the man's ingenuity. With a box of tools and a few mighty simple contrivances he had made out to have a devil of a temple. Any poor Kanaka brought up here in the dark, with the harps whining all round him, and shown that smoking face in the bottom of a hole, would make no kind of doubt but he had seen and heard enough devils for a lifetime. It's easy to find out what Kanakas think. Just go back to yourself any way round from ten to fifteen years old, and there's an average Kanaka. There are some pious, just as there are pious boys; and the most of them, like the boys again, are middling honest, and yet think it rather larks to steal, and are easy scared, and rather like to be so. I remember a boy I was at school with at home who played the Case business. He didn't know anything, that boy; he couldn't do anything; he had no luminous paint and no Tyrolean harps; he just boldly said he was a sorcerer, and frightened us out of our boots, and we loved it. And then it came in my mind how the master had once flogged that boy, and the surprise we were all in to see the sorcerer catch it and bum like anybody else. Thinks I to myself, 'I must find some way of fixing it so for Master Case.' And the next moment I had my idea.

I went back by the path, which, when once you had found it, was quite plain and easy walking; and when I stepped out on the black sands, who should I see but Master Case himself! I cocked my gun and held it handy, and we marched up and passed without a word, each keeping the tail of his eye on the other; and no sooner had we passed than we each wheeled round like fellows drilling, and stood face to face. We had each taken the same notion in his head, you see, that the other fellow might give him the load of his gun in the stern.

'You've shot nothing,' says Case.

'I'm not on the shoot to-day,' said I.

'Well, the devil go with you for me,' says he.

'The same to you,' says I.

But we stuck just the way we were; no fear of either of us moving.

Case laughed. 'We can't stop here all day, though,' said he.

'Don't let me detain you,' says I.

He laughed again. 'Look here, Wiltshire, do you think me a fool?' he asked.

'More of a knave, if you want to know,' says I.

'Well, do you think it would better me to shoot you here, on this open beach?' said he. 'Because I don't. Folks come fishing every day. There may be a score of them up the valley now, making copra; there might be half a dozen on the hill behind you, after pigeons; they might be watching us this minute, and I shouldn't wonder. I give you my word I don't want to shoot you. Why should I? You don't hinder me any. You haven't got one pound of copra but what you made with your own hands, like a negro slave. You're vegetating – that's what I call it – and I don't care where you vegetate, nor yet how long. Give me your word you don't mean to shoot me, and I'll give you a lead and walk away.'

'Well,' said I, 'you're frank and pleasant, ain't you? And I'll be the same. I don't mean to shoot you to-day. Why should I? This business is beginning; it ain't done yet, Mr Case. I've given you one turn already; I can see the marks of my knuckles on your head to this blooming hour, and I've more cooking for you. I'm not a paralee, like Underhill. My name ain't Adams, and it ain't Vigours; and I mean to show you that you've met your match.'

'This is a silly way to talk,' said he. 'This is not the talk to make me move on with.'

'All right,' said I, 'stay where you are. I ain't in any hurry, and you know it. I can put in a day on this beach and never mind. I ain't got any copra to bother with. I ain't got any luminous paint to see to.'

I was sorry I said that last, but it whipped out before I knew. I could see it took the wind out of his sails, and he stood and stared at me with his brow drawn up. Then I suppose he made up his mind he must get to the bottom of this.

'I take you at your word,' says he, and turned his back and walked right into the devil's bush.

I let him go, of course, for I had passed my word. But I watched him as long as he was in sight, and after he was gone lit out for cover as lively as you would want to see, and went the rest of the way home under the bush, for I didn't trust him sixpence-worth. One thing I saw, I had been ass enough to give him warning, and that which I meant to do I must do at once.

You would think I had had about enough excitement for one morning, but there was another turn waiting me. As soon as I got far enough round the cape to see my house I made out there were strangers there; a little farther, and no doubt about it. There was a couple of armed sentinels squatting at my door. I could only suppose the trouble about Uma must have come to a head, and the station been seized. For aught I could think, Uma was taken up already, and these armed men were waiting to do the like with me.

However, as I came nearer, which I did at top speed, I saw there was a third native sitting on the verandah like a guest, and Uma was talking with him like a hostess. Nearer still I made out it was the big young chief, Maea, and that he was smiling away and smoking. And what was he smoking? None of your European cigarettes fit for a cat, not even the genuine big, knock-me-down native article that a fellow can really put in the time with if his pipe is broke – but a cigar, and one of my Mexicans at that, that I could swear to. At sight of this my heart started beating, and I took a wild hope in my head that the trouble was over, and Maea had come round.

Uma pointed me out to him as I came up, and he met me at the head of my own stairs like a thorough gentleman.

'Vilivili,' said he, which was the best they could make of my name, 'I pleased.'

There is no doubt when an island chief wants to be civil he can do it. I saw the way things were from the word go. There was no call for Uma to say to me: 'He no 'fraid Ese now, come bring copra,' I tell you I shook hands with that Kanaka like as if he was the best white man in Europe.

The fact was, Case and he had got after the same girl; or Maea suspected it, and concluded to make hay of the trader on the chance. He had dressed himself up, got a couple of his retainers cleaned and armed to kind of make the thing more public, and, just waiting till Case was clear of the village, came round to put the whole of his business my way. He was rich as well as powerful. I suppose that man was worth fifty thousand nuts per annum. I gave him the price of the beach and a quarter cent better, and as for credit, I would have advanced him the inside of the store and the fittings besides, I was so pleased to see him. I must say he bought like a gentleman: rice and tins and biscuits enough for a week's feast, and stuffs by the bolt. He was agreeable besides; he had plenty fun to him; and we cracked jests together, mostly through the interpreter, because he had mighty little English, and my native was still off colour. One thing I made out: he could never really have thought much harm of Uma; he could never have been really frightened, and must just have made believe from dodginess, and because he thought Case had a strong pull in the village and could help him on.

This set me thinking that both he and I were in a tightish place. What he had done was to fly in the face of the whole village, and the thing might cost him his authority. More than that, after my talk with Case on the beach, I thought it might very well cost me my life. Case had as good as said he would pot me if ever I got any copra; he would come home to find the best business in the village had changed hands; and the best thing I thought I could do was to get in first with the potting.

'See here, Uma,' says I, 'tell him I'm sorry I made him wait, but I was up looking at Case's Tiapolo store in the bush.'

'He want savvy if you no 'fraid?' translated Uma.

I laughed out. 'Not much!' says I. 'Tell him the place is a blooming toy-shop! Tell him in England we give these things to the kids to play with.'

'He want savvy if you hear devil sing?' she asked next.

'Look here,' said I, 'I can't do it now because I've got no banjo-strings in stock; but the next time the ship comes round I'll have one of these same contraptions right here in my verandah, and he can see for himself how much devil there is to it. Tell him, as soon as I can get the strings I'll make one for his picaninnies.

The name of the concern is a Tyrolean harp; and you can tell him the name means in English that nobody but dam-fools give a cent for it.'

This time he was so pleased he had to try his English again: 'You talk true?' says he.

'Rather!' said I. 'Talk all-e-same Bible. – Bring out a Bible here, Uma, if you've got such a thing, and I'll kiss it. Or, I'll tell you what's better still,' says I, taking a header, 'ask him if he's afraid to go up there himself by day.'

It appeared he wasn't; he could venture as far as that by day and in company.

'That's the ticket, then!' said I. 'Tell him the man's a fraud and the place foolishness, and if he'll go up there to-morrow he'll see all that's left of it. But tell him this, Uma, and mind he understand it: If he gets talking, it's bound to come to Case, and I'm a dead man! I'm playing his game, tell him, and if he says one word my blood will be at his door and be the damnation of him here and after.'

She told him, and he shook hands with me up to the hilt, and says he: 'No talk. Go up to-mollow. You my friend?'

'No, sir,' says I, 'no such foolishness. – I've come here to trade, tell him, and not to make friends. But as to Case, I'll send that man to glory!'

So off Maea went, pretty well pleased, as I could see.

CHAPTER V
NIGHT IN THE BUSH

Well I was committed now; Tiapolo had to be smashed up before next day, and my hands were pretty full, not only with preparations, but with argument. My house was like a mechanics' debating society: Uma was so made up that I shouldn't go into the bush by night, or that, if I did, I was never to come back again. You know her style of arguing: you've had a specimen about Queen Victoria and the devil; and I leave you to fancy if I was tired of it before dark.

At last I had a good idea. What was the use of casting my pearls before her? I thought; some of her own chopped hay would be likelier to do the business.

'I'll tell you what, then,' said I. 'You fish out your Bible, and I'll take that up along with me. That'll make me right.'

She swore a Bible was no use.

'That's just your Kanaka ignorance,' said I. 'Bring the Bible out.'

She brought it, and turned to the title-page, where I thought there would likely be some English, and so there was. 'There!' said I. 'Look at that! "*London: Printed for the British and Foreign Bible Society, Blackfriars*", and the date, which I can't read, owing to its being in these X's. There's no devil in hell can look near the Bible Society, Blackfriars. Why, you silly!' I said, 'how do you suppose we get along with our own *aitus* at home? All Bible Society!'

'I think you no got any,' said she. 'White man, he tell me you no got.'

'Sounds likely, don't it?' I asked. 'Why would these islands all be chock full of them and none in Europe?'

'Well, you no got bread-fruit,' said she.

I could have torn my hair. 'Now, look here, old lady,' said I, 'you dry up, for I'm tired of you. I'll take the Bible, which'll put me as straight as the mail, and that's the last word I've got to say.'

The night fell extraordinary dark, clouds coming up with sundown and overspreading all; not a star showed; there was only an end of a moon, and that not due before the small hours. Round the village, what with the lights and the fires in the open houses, and the torches of many fishers moving on the reef, it kept as gay as an illumination; but the sea and the mountains and woods were all clean gone. I suppose it might be eight o'clock when I took the road, laden like a donkey. First there was that Bible, a book as big as your head, which I had let myself in for by my own tomfoolery. Then there was my gun, and knife, and lantern, and patent matches, all necessary. And then there was the real plant of the affair in hand, a mortal weight of gunpowder, a pair of dynamite fishing bombs, and two or three pieces of slow match that I had hauled out of the tin cases and spliced together the best way I could; for the match was only trade stuff, and a man would be crazy that trusted it. Altogether, you see, I had the materials of a pretty good blow-up! Expense was nothing to me; I wanted that thing done right.

As long as I was in the open, and had the lamp in my house to steer by, I did well. But when I got to the path, it fell so dark I could make no headway, walking into trees and swearing there, like a man looking for the matches in his bedroom. I knew it was risky to light up, for my lantern would be visible all the way to the point of the cape, and as no one went there after dark, it would be talked about, and come to Case's ears. But what was I to do? I had either to give the business over and lose caste with Maea, or light up, take my chance, and get through the thing the smartest I was able.

As long as I was on the path I walked hard, but when I came to the black beach I had to run. For the tide was now nearly flowed; and to get through with my powder dry between the surf and the steep hill, took all the quickness I possessed. As it was, even, the wash caught me to the knees, and I came near falling on a stone. All this time the hurry I was in, and the free air and smell of the sea, kept my spirits lively; but when I was once in the bush and began to climb the path I took it easier. The fearsomeness of the wood had been a good bit rubbed off for me by Master Case's banjo-strings and graven images, yet I thought it was a dreary walk, and guessed, when the disciples went up there, they must be badly scared. The light of the lantern, striking among all these trunks and forked branches and twisted rope-ends of lianas, made the whole place, or all that you could see of it, a kind of a puzzle of turning shadows. They came to meet you, solid and quick like giants, and then span off and vanished; they hove up over your head like clubs, and flew away into the night like birds. The floor of the bush glimmered with dead wood, the way the match-box used to shine after you had struck a lucifer. Big, cold drops fell on me from the branches overhead like sweat. There was no wind to mention; only a little icy breath of a land-breeze that stirred nothing; and the harps were silent.

The first landfall I made was when I got through the bush of wild cocoa-nuts, and came in view of the bogies on the wall. Mighty queer they looked by the shining of the lantern, with their painted faces and shell eyes, and their clothes and their hair hanging. One after another I pulled them all up and piled them in a bundle on the cellar roof, so as they might go to glory with the rest. Then I chose a place behind one of the big stones at the entrance, buried my powder and the two shells, and arranged my match along the passage. And then I had a look at the smoking head, just for good-bye. It was doing fine.

'Cheer up,' says I. 'You're booked.'

It was my first idea to light up and be getting homeward; for the darkness and the glimmer of the dead wood and the shadows of the lantern made me lonely. But I knew where one of the harps hung; it seemed a pity it shouldn't go with the rest; and at the same time I couldn't help letting on to myself that I was mortal tired of my employment, and would like best to be at home and have the door shut. I stepped out of the cellar and argued it fore and back. There was a sound of the sea far down below me on the coast; nearer hand not a leaf stirred; I might have been the only living creature this side of Cape Horn. Well, as I stood there thinking, it seemed the bush woke and became full of little noises. Little noises they were, and nothing to hurt – a bit of a crackle, a bit of a rush – but the breath jumped right out of me and my throat went as dry as a biscuit. It wasn't Case I was afraid of, which would have been common-sense; I never thought of Case; what took me, as sharp as the colic, was the old wives' tales, the devil-women and the man-pigs. It was the toss of a penny whether I should run: but I got a purchase on myself, and stepped out, and held up the lantern (like a fool) and looked all round.

In the direction of the village and the path there was nothing to be seen; but when I turned inland it's a wonder to me I didn't drop. There, coming right up out of the desert and the bad bush – there, sure enough, was a devil-woman, just as the way I had figured she would look. I saw the light shine on her bare arms and her bright eyes, and there went out of me a yell so big that I thought it was my death.

'Ah! No sing out!' says the devil-woman, in a kind of a high whisper. 'Why you talk big voice? Put out light! Ese he come.'

'My God Almighty, Uma, is that you?' says I.

'*Joc*,'* says she. 'I come quick. Ese here soon.'

'You come alone?' I asked. 'You no 'fraid?'

* Yes.

'Ah, too much 'fraid!' she whispered, clutching me. 'I think die.'

'Well,' says I, with a kind of a weak grin, 'I'm not the one to laugh at you, Mrs Wiltshire, for I'm about the worst scared man in the South Pacific myself.'

She told me in two words what brought her. I was scarce gone, it seems, when Fa'avao came in, and the old woman had met Black Jack running as hard as he was fit from our house to Case's. Uma neither spoke nor stopped, but lit right out to come and warn me. She was so close at my heels that the lantern was her guide across the beach, and afterwards, by the glimmer of it in the trees, she got her line up hill. It was only when I had got to the top or was in the cellar that she wandered Lord knows where! and lost a sight of precious time, afraid to call out lest Case was at the heels of her, and falling in the bush, so that she was all knocked and bruised. That must have been when she got too far to the southward, and how she came to take me in the flank at last and frighten me beyond what I've got the words to tell of.

Well, anything was better than a devil-woman, but I thought her yarn serious enough. Black Jack had no call to be about my house, unless he was set there to watch; and it looked to me as if my tomfool word about the paint, and perhaps some chatter of Maea's had got us all in a clove hitch. One thing was clear: Uma and I were here for the night; we daren't try to go home before day, and even then it would be safer to strike round up the mountain and come in by the back of the village, or we might walk into an ambuscade. It was plain, too, that the mine should be sprung immediately, or Case might be in time to stop it.

I marched into the tunnel, Uma keeping tight hold of me, opened my lantern, and lit the match. The first length of it burned like a spill of paper, and I stood stupid, watching it burn, and thinking we were going aloft with Tiapoli, which was none of my views. The second took to a better rate, though faster than I cared about; and at that I got my wits again, hauled Uma clear of the passage, blew out and dropped the lantern, and the pair of us groped our way into the bush until I thought it might be safe, and lay down together by a tree.

'Old lady,' I said, 'I won't forget this night. You're a trump, and that's what's wrong with you.'

She humped herself close up to me. She had run out the way she was, with nothing on her but her kilt; and she was all wet with the dews and the sea on the black beach, and shook straight on with cold and the terror of the dark and the devils.

'Too much 'fraid,' was all she said.

The far side of Case's hill goes down near as steep as a precipice into the next valley. We were on the very edge of it, and I could see the dead wood shine and hear the sea sound far below. I didn't care about the position, which left me no retreat, but I was afraid to change. Then I saw I had made a worse mistake about the lantern, which I should have left lighted, so that I could have had a crack at Case when he stepped into the shine of it. And even if I hadn't had the wit to do that, it seemed a senseless thing to leave the good lantern to blow up with the graven images. The thing belonged to me, after all, and was worth money, and might come in handy. If I could have trusted the match, I might have run in still and rescued it. But who was going to trust the match? You know what trade is. The stuff was good enough for Kanakas to go fishing with, where they've got to look lively anyway, and the most they risk is only to have their hand blown off. But for any one that wanted to fool around a blow-up like mine that match was rubbish.

Altogether, the best I could do was to lie still, see my shot-gun handy, and wait for the explosion. But it was a solemn kind of a business. The blackness of the night was like solid; the only thing you could see was the nasty bogy glimmer of the dead wood, and that showed you nothing but itself; and as for sounds, I stretched my ears till I thought I could have heard the match burn in the tunnel, and that bush was as silent as a coffin. Now and then there was a bit of a crack; but whether it was near or far, whether it was Case stubbing his toes within a few yards of me, or a tree breaking miles away, I knew no more than the babe unborn.

And then, all of a sudden, Vesuvius went off. It was a long time coming; but when it came (though I say it that shouldn't) no man could ask to see a better. At first it was just a son of a gun of a row, and a spout of fire, and the wood lighted up so that you could see to read. And then the trouble began. Uma and I were half buried under a wagonful of earth, and glad it was no worse, for one of the rocks at the entrance of the tunnel was fired clean into the air, fell within a couple of fathoms of where we lay, and bounded over the edge of the hill, and went pounding down into the next valley. I saw I had rather under-calculated our distance, or overdone the dynamite and powder, which you please.

And presently I saw I had made another slip. The noise of the thing began to die off, shaking the island; the dazzle was over; and yet the night didn't come back the way I expected. For the whole wood was scattered with red coals and brands from the explosion; they were all round me on the flat; some had fallen below in the valley, and some stuck and flared in the tree-tops. I had no fear of fire, for these forests are too wet to kindle. But the trouble was that the place was all lit up – not very bright, but good enough to get a shot by; and the way the coals were scattered, it was just as likely Case might have the advantage as myself. I looked all round for his white face, you may be sure; but there was not a sign of him. As for Uma, the life seemed to have been knocked right out of her by the bang and blaze of it.

There was one bad point in my game. One of the blessed graven images had come down all afire, hair and clothes and body, not four yards away from me. I cast a mighty noticing glance all round; there was still no Case, and I made up my mind I must get rid of that burning stick before he came, or I should be shot there like a dog.

It was my first idea to have crawled, and then I thought speed was the main thing, and stood half up to make the rush. The same moment from somewhere between me and the sea there came a flash and a report, and a rifle bullet screeched in my ear. I swung straight round and up with my gun, but the brute had a Winchester, and before I could as much as see him his second shot knocked me over like a nine-pin. I seemed to fly in the air, then came down by the run and lay half a minute, silly; and then I found my hands empty, and my gun had flown over my head as I fell. It makes a man mighty wide awake to be in the kind of box that I was in. I scarcely knew where I was hurt, or whether I was hurt or not, but turned right over on my face to crawl after my weapon. Unless you have tried to get about with a smashed leg you don't know what pain is, and I let out a howl like a bullock's.

This was the unluckiest noise that ever I made in my life. Up to then Uma had stuck to her tree like a sensible woman, knowing she would be only in the way; but as soon as she heard me sing out she ran forward. The Winchester cracked again and down she went.

I had sat up, leg and all, to stop her; but when I saw her tumble I clapped down again where I was, lay still, and felt the handle of my knife. I had been scurried and put out before. No more of that for me. He had knocked over my girl, I had got to fix him for it; and I lay there and gritted my teeth, and footed up the chances. My leg was broke, my gun was gone. Case had still ten shots in his Winchester. It looked a kind of hopeless business. But I never despaired nor thought upon despairing: that man had got to go.

For a goodish bit none of us let on. Then I heard Case begin to move nearer in the bush, but mighty careful. The image had burned out; there were only a few coals left here and there, and the wood was main dark, but had a kind of a low glow in it like a fire on its last legs. It was by this that I made out Case's head looking at me over a big tuft of ferns, and at the same time the brute saw me and shouldered his Winchester. I lay quite still, and as good as looked into the barrel: it was my last chance, but I thought my heart would have come right out of its bearings. Then he fired. Lucky for me it was no shot-gun, for the bullet struck within an inch of me and knocked the dirt in my eyes.

Just you try and see if you can lie quiet, and let a man take a sitting shot at you and miss you by a hair. But I did, and lucky too. A while Case stood with the Winchester at the port-arms; then he gave a little laugh to himself and stepped round the ferns.

'Laugh!' thought I. 'If you had the wit of a louse you would be praying!'

I was all as taut as a ship's hawser or the spring of a watch, and as soon as he came within reach of me I had him by the ankle, plucked the feet right out from under him, laid him out, and was upon the top of him, broken leg and all, before he breathed. His Winchester had gone the same road as my shot-gun; it was nothing to me – I defied him now. I'm a pretty strong man anyway, but I never knew what strength was till I got hold of Case. He was knocked out of time by the rattle he came down with, and threw up his hands together, more like a frightened woman, so that I caught both of them with my left. This wakened him up, and he fastened his teeth in my forearm like a weasel. Much I cared. My leg gave me all the pain I had any use for, and I drew my knife and got it in the place.

'Now,' said I, 'I've got you; and you're gone up, and a good job too! Do you feel the point of that? That's for Underhill! And there's for Adams! And now here's for Uma, and that's going to knock your blooming soul right out of you!'

With that I gave him the cold steel for all I was worth. His body kicked under me like a spring sofa; he gave a dreadful kind of a long moan, and lay still.

'I wonder if you're dead? I hope so!' I thought, for my head was swimming. But I wasn't going to take chances; I had his own example too close before me for that; and I tried to draw the knife out to give it him again. The blood came over my hands, I remember, hot as tea; and with that I fainted clean away, and fell with my head on the man's mouth.

When I came to myself it was pitch dark; the cinders had burned out; there was nothing to be seen but the shine of the dead wood, and I couldn't remember where I was nor why I was in such pain, nor what I was all wetted with. Then it came back, and the first thing I attended to was to give him the knife again a half a dozen times up to the handle. I believe he was dead already, but it did him no harm, and did me good.

'I bet you're dead now,' I said, and then I called to Uma.

Nothing answered, and I made a move to go and grope for her, fouled my broken leg, and fainted again.

When I came to myself the second time the clouds had all cleared away, except a few that sailed there, white as cotton. The moon was up – a tropic moon. The moon at home turns a wood black, but even this old butt end of a one showed up that forest as green as by day. The night birds – or, rather, they're a kind of early morning bird – sang out with their long, falling notes like nightingales. And I could see the dead man, that I was still half resting on, looking right up into the sky with his open eyes, no paler than when he was alive; and a little way off Uma tumbled on her side. I got over to her the best way I was able, and when I got there she was broad awake, and crying and sobbing to herself with no more noise than an insect. It appears she was afraid to cry out loud, because of the *aitus*. Altogether she was not much hurt, but scared beyond belief; she had come to her senses a long while ago, cried out to me, heard nothing in reply, made out we were both dead, and had lain there ever since, afraid to budge a finger. The ball had ploughed up her shoulder and she had lost a main quantity of blood; but I soon had that tied up the way it ought to be with the tail of my shirt and a scarf I had on, got her head on my sound knee and my back against a trunk, and settled down to wait for morning. Uma was for neither use nor ornament, and could only clutch hold of me and shake and cry. I don't suppose there was ever anybody worse scared, and, to do her justice, she had had a lively night of it. As for me, I was in a good bit of pain and fever, but not so bad when I sat still; and every time I looked over to Case I could have sung and whistled. Talk about meat and drink! To see that man lying there dead as a herring filled me full.

The night birds stopped after a while; and then the light began to change, the east came orange, the whole wood began to whirr with singing like a musical box, and there was the broad day.

I didn't expect Maea for a long while yet; and indeed I thought there was an off-chance he might go back on the whole idea and not come at all. I was the better pleased when, about an hour after daylight, I heard sticks smashing and a lot of Kanakas laughing and singing out to keep their courage up.

Uma sat up quite brisk at the first word of it; and presently we saw a party come stringing out of the path, Maea in front, and behind him a white man in a pith helmet. It was Mr Tarleton, who had turned up late last night in Falesá, having left his boat and walked the last stage with a lantern.

They buried Case upon the field of glory, right in the hole where he had kept the smoking head. I waited till the thing was done; and Mr Tarleton prayed, which I thought tomfoolery, but I'm bound to say he gave a pretty sick view of the dear departed's prospects, and seemed to have his own ideas of hell. I had it out with him afterwards, told him he had scamped his duty, and what he had ought to have done was to up like a man and tell the Kanakas plainly Case was damned, and a good riddance; but I never could get him to see it my way. Then they made me a litter of poles and carried me down to the station. Mr Tarleton set my leg, and made a regular missionary splice of it, so that I limp to this day. That done, he took down my evidence and Uma's, and Maea's, wrote it all out fine, and had us sign it; and then he got the chiefs and marched over to Papa Randall's to seize Case's papers.

All they found was a bit of a diary, kept for a good many years, and all about the price of copra, and chickens being stolen, and that; and the books of the business and the will I told you of in the beginning, by both of which the whole thing (stock, lock, and barrel) appeared to belong to the Samoa woman. It was I that bought her out at a mighty reasonable figure, for she was in a hurry to get home. As for Randall and the black, they had to tramp; got into some kind of a station on the Papa-malulu side; did very bad business, for the truth is neither of the pair was fit for it, and lived mostly on fish, which was the means of Randall's death. It seems there was a nice shoal in one day, and Papa went after them with the dynamite; either the match burned too fast, or Papa was full, or both, but the shell went off (in the usual way) before he threw it, and where was Papa's hand? Well, there's nothing to hurt in that; the islands up north are full of one-handed men, like the parties in the *Arabian Nights*; but either Randall was too old, or he drank too much, and the short and the long of it was that he died. Pretty soon after, the nigger was turned out of the island for stealing from white men, and went off to the west, where he found men of his own colour, in case he liked that, and the men of his own colour took and ate him at some kind of a corroborree, and I'm sure I hope he was to their fancy!

So there was I, left alone in my glory at Falesá; and when the schooner came round I felled her up, and gave her a deck-cargo half as high as the house. I must say Mr Tarleton did the right thing by us; but he took a meanish kind of a revenge.

'Now, Mr Wiltshire,' said he, 'I've put you all square with everybody here. It wasn't difficult to do, Case being gone; but I have done it, and given my pledge besides that you will deal fairly with the natives. I must ask you to keep my word.'

Well, so I did. I used to be bothered about my balances, but I reasoned it out this way: We all have queerish balances, and the natives all know it, and water their copra in a proportion so that it's fair all round; but the truth is, it did use to bother me, and, though I did well in Falesá, I was half glad when the firm moved me on to another station, where I was under no kind of a pledge and could look my balances in the face.

As for the old lady, you know her as well as I do. She's only the one fault. If you don't keep your eye lifting she would give away the roof off the station. Well, it seems it's natural in Kanakas. She's turned a powerful big woman now, and could throw a London bobby over her shoulder. But that's natural in Kanakas too, and there's no manner of doubt that she's an A1 wife.

Mr Tarleton's gone home, his trick being over. He was the best missionary I ever struck, and now, it seems, he's parsonizing down Somerset way. Well, that's best for him; he'll have no Kanakas there to get luny over.

My public-house? Not a bit of it, nor ever likely. I'm stuck here, I fancy. I don't like to leave the kids, you see: and – there's no use talking – they're better here than what they would be in a white man's country, though Ben took the eldest up to Auckland, where he's being schooled with the best. But what bothers me is the girls. They're only half-castes, of course; I know that as well as you do, and there's nobody thinks less of half-castes than I do; but they're mine, and about all I've got. I can't reconcile my mind to their taking up with Kanakas, and I'd like to know where I'm to find the whites?

R. B. Cunninghame-Graham

BEATTOCK FOR MOFFAT

The bustle on the Euston platform stopped for an instant to let the men who carried him to the third-class compartment pass along the train. Gaunt and emaciated, he looked just at death's door, and, as they propped him in the carriage between two pillows, he faintly said, 'Jock, do ye think I'll live as far as Moffat? I should na' like to die in London in the smoke.'

His cockney wife, drying her tears with a cheap hem-stitched pocket-handkerchief, her scanty town-bred hair looking like wisps of tow beneath her hat, bought from some window in which each individual article was marked at seven-and-sixpence, could only sob. His brother, with the country sun and wind burn still upon his face, and his huge hands hanging like hams in front of him, made answer.

'Andra',' he said, 'gin ye last as far as Beattock, we'll gie ye a braw hurl back to the farm, syne the bask air, ye ken, and the milk, and, and – but can ye last as far as Beattock, Andra'?'

The sick man, sitting with the cold sweat upon his face, his shrunken limbs looking like sticks inside his ill-made black slop suit, after considering the proposition on its merits, looked up, and said, 'I should na' like to bet I feel fair boss, God knows; but there, the mischief of it is, he will na' tell ye, so that, as ye may say, his knowlidge has na' commercial value. I ken I look as gash as Garscadden. Ye mind, Jock, in the braw auld times, when the auld laird just slipped awa', whiles they were birlin' at the clairet. A braw death, Jock . . . do ye think it'll be rainin' aboot Ecclefechan? Aye . . . sure to be rainin' aboot Lockerbie. Nae Christians there, Jock, a' Johnstones and Jardines, ye mind?'

The wife, who had been occupied with an air cushion and, having lost the bellows, had been blowing into it till her cheeks seemed almost bursting, and her false teeth were loosened in her head, left off her toil to ask her husband 'If'e could pick a bit of something, a pork pie, or a nice sausage roll, or something tasty,' which she could fetch from the refreshment room. The invalid having declined to eat, and his brother having drawn from his pocket a dirty bag, in which were peppermints, gave him a 'drop', telling him that he 'minded he aye used to like them weel, when the meenister had fairly got into his prelection in the auld kirk, outby.'

The train slid almost imperceptibly away, the passengers upon the platform looking after it with that half-foolish, half-astonished look with which men watch a disappearing train. Then a few sandwich papers rose with the dust almost to the level of the platform, sank again, the clock struck twelve, and the station fell into a half quiescence, like a volcano in the interval between the lava showers. Inside the third-class carriage all was quiet until the lights of Harrow shone upon the left, when the sick man, turning himself with difficulty, said, 'Good-bye, Harrow-on-the-Hill. I aye liked Harrow for the hill's sake, tho' ye can scarcely ca' yon wee bit mound a hill, Jean.'

His wife who, even in her grief, still smarted under the Scotch variant of her name, which all her life she had pronounced as 'Jayne', and who, true Cockney as she was, bounded her world within the lines of Plaistow, Peckham Rye, the Welsh 'Arp ('Endon way), and Willesden, moved uncomfortably at the depreciation of the chief mountain in her cosmos, but held her peace. Loving her husband in a sort of half-antagonistic fashion, born of the difference of type between the hard, unyielding, yet humorous and sentimental Lowland Scot, and the conglomerate of all races of the island which meet in London, and produce the weedy, shallow breed, almost incapable of reproduction, and yet high strung and nervous, there had arisen between them that intangible veil of misconception which, though not excluding love, is yet impervious to respect. Each saw the other's failings, or, perhaps, thought the good qualities which each possessed were faults, for usually men judge each other by their good points, which, seen through prejudice of race, religion, and surroundings, appear to them defects.

The brother, who but a week ago had left his farm unwillingly, just when the 'neeps were wantin' heughin and a feck o' things requirin' to be done, forby a puckle sheep waitin' for keelin',' to come and see his brother for the last time, sat in that dour and seeming apathetic attitude which falls upon the country man, torn from his daily toil, and plunged into a town. Most things in London, during the brief intervals he had passed away from the sick bed, seemed foolish to him, and of a nature such as a self-respecting Moffat man, in the hebdomadal enjoyment of the 'prelections' of a Free Church minister, could not authorize.

'Man, saw ye e'er a carter sittin' on his cart, and drivin' at a trot, instead o' walkin' in a proper manner alangside his horse?' had been his first remark.

The short-tailed sheep dogs, and the way they worked, the inferior quality of the cart horses, their shoes with hardly any calkins worth the name, all was repugnant to him.

On Sabbath, too, he had received a shock, for, after walking miles to sit under the 'brither of the U.P. minister at Symington', he had found Erastian hymn books in the pews and noticed with stern reprobation that the congregation stood to sing, and that instead of sitting solidly whilst the 'man wrastled in prayer', stooped forward in the fashion called the Nonconformist lounge.

His troubled spirit had received refreshment from the sermon, which, though short, and extending to but some five-and-forty minutes, had still been powerful, for he said:

'When yon wee, shilpit meenister – brither, ye ken, of rantin' Ferguson, out by Symington – shook the congregation ower the pit mouth, ye could hae fancied that the very sowls in hell just girned. Man, he garred the very stour to flee aboot the kirk, and, hadna' the big book been weel brass banded, he would hae dang the haricles fair oot.'

So the train slipped past Watford, swaying round the curves like a gigantic serpent, and jolting at the facing points as a horse 'pecks' in his gallop at an obstruction in the ground.

The moon shone brightly into the compartment extinguishing the flickering of the half-candle-power electric light. Rugby, the station all lit up, and with its platforms occupied but by a few belated passengers, all muffled up like race horses taking their exercise, flashed past. They slipped through Cannock Chase, which stretches down with heath and firs, clear brawling streams, and birch trees, an outpost of the north lost in the midland clay. They crossed the oily Trent, flowing through alder copses, and with its backwaters all overgrown with lilies, like an 'aguapey' in Paraguay or in Brazil.

The sick man, wrapped in cheap rugs, and sitting like Guy Fawkes, in the half comic, half pathetic way that sick folk sit, making them sport for fools, and, at the same time, moistening the eye of the judicious, who reflect that they themselves may one day sit as they do, bereft of all the dignity of strength, looked listlessly at nothing as the train sped on. His loving, tactless wife, whose cheap 'sized' handkerchief had long since become a rag with mopping up her tears, endeavoured to bring round her husband's thoughts to paradise, which she conceived a sort of music-hall, where angels sat with their wings folded, listening to sentimental songs.

Her brother-in-law, reared on the fiery faith of Moffat Calvinism, eyed her with great disfavour, as a terrier eyes a rat imprisoned in a cage.

'Jean wumman,' he burst out, 'to hear ye talk, I would jist think your meenister had been a perfectly illeeterate man, pairadise here, pairadise there; what do you think a man like Andra' could dae daunderin' aboot a garden naked, pu'in sour aipples frae the trees?'

Cockney and Scotch conceit, impervious alike to outside criticism, and each so bolstered in its pride as to be quite incapable of seeing that anything existed outside the purlieus of their sight, would soon have made the carriage into a battlefield, had not the husband, with the authority of approaching death, put in his word.

'Whist, Jeanie wumman. Jock, dae ye no ken that the Odium-Theologicum is just a curse – pairadise – set ye baith up – pairadise. I dinna' even richtly ken if I can last as far as Beattock.'

Stafford, its iron furnaces belching out flames, which burned red holes into the night, seemed to approach, rather than be approached, so smoothly ran the train. The mingled moonlight and the glare of ironworks lit the canal beside the railway, and from the water rose white vapours as from Styx or Periphlegethon. Through Cheshire ran the train, its timbered houses showing ghostly in the frost which coated all the carriage windows, and rendered them opaque. Preston, the Catholic city, lay silent in the night, its river babbling through the public park, and then the hills of Lancashire loomed lofty in the night. Past Garstang, with its water-lily-covered ponds, Garstang where, in the days gone by, Catholic squires, against their will, were forced on Sundays to 'take wine' in church on pain of fine, the puffing serpent slid.

The talk inside the carriage had given place to sleep, that is, the brother-in-law and wife slept fitfully, but the sick man looked out, counting the miles to Moffat, and speculating on his strength. Big drops of sweat stood on his forehead, and his breath came double, whistling through his lungs.

They passed by Lancaster, skirting the sea on which the moon shone bright, setting the fishing boats in silver as they lay scarcely moving on the waves. Then, so to speak, the train set its face up against Shap Fell, and, puffing heavily, drew up into the hills, the scattered grey stone houses of the north, flanked by their gnarled and twisted ash trees, hanging upon the edge of the streams, as lonely, and as cut off from the world (except the passing train) as if they had been in Central Africa. The moorland roads, winding amongst the heather, showed that the feet of generations had marked them out, and not the line, spade, and theodolite, with all the circumstance of modern road makers. They, too, looked white and unearthly in the moonlight, and now and then a sheep, aroused by the snorting of the train, moved from the heather into the middle of the road, and stood there motionless, its shadow filling the narrow track, and flickering on the heather at the edge.

The keen and penetrating air of the hills and night roused the two sleepers, and they began to talk, after the Scottish fashion, of the funeral, before the anticipated corpse.

'Ye ken, we've got a braw new hearse outby, sort of Epescopalian lookin', wi' gless a' roond, so's ye can see the kist. Very conceity too, they mak' the hearses noo-a-days. I min' when they were jist auld sort o' ruckly boxes, awfu' licht, ye ken upon the springs, and just went dodderin' alang, the body swinging to and fro, as if it would flee richt oot. The roads, ye ken, were no nigh and so richtly metalled in thae days.'

The subject of the conversation took it cheerfully, expressing pleasure at the advance of progress as typified in the new hearse, hoping his brother had a decent 'stan' o' black', and looking at his death, after the fashion of his kind, as it were something outside himself, a fact indeed, on which, at the same time, he could express himself with confidence as being in some measure interested. His wife, not being Scotch, took quite another view, and seemed to think that the mere mention of the word was impious, or, at the least, of such a nature as to bring on immediate dissolution, holding the English theory that unpleasant things should not be mentioned, and that, by this means, they can be kept at bay. Half from affection, half from the inborn love of cant, inseparable from the true Anglo-Saxon, she endeavoured to persuade her husband that he looked better, and yet would mend, once in his native air.

'At Moffit, ye'd 'ave the benefit of the 'ill breezes, and that 'ere country milk, which never 'as no cream in it, but 'olesome, as you say. Why yuss, in about eight days at Moffit, you'll be as 'earty as you ever was. Yuss, you will, you take my word.'

Like a true Londoner, she did not talk religion, being too thin in mind and body even to have grasped the dogma of any of the sects. Her heaven a music 'all, her paradise to see the King drive through the streets, her literary pleasure to read lies in newspapers, or pore on novelettes, which showed her the pure elevated lives of duchesses, placing the knaves and prostitutes within the limits of her own class; which view of life she accepted as quite natural, and as a thing ordained to be by the bright stars who write.

Just at the Summit they stopped an instant to let a goods train pass, and, in a faint voice, the consumptive said, 'I'd almost lay a wager now I'd last to Moffat, Jock. The Shap, ye ken, I aye looked at as the beginning of the run home. The hills, ye ken, are sort o' heartsome. No that they're bonny hills like Moffat hills, na', na', ill-shapen sort of things, just like Borunty tatties, awfu' puir names, too, Shap Fell and Rowland Edge, Hutton Roof Crags and Arnside Fell; heard ever onybody sich-like names for hills? Naething to fill the mooth; man, the Scotch hills jist grap ye in the mooth for a' the world like speerits.'

They stopped at Penrith, which the old castle walls make even meaner, in the cold morning light, than other stations look. Little Salkeld, and Armathwaite, Cotehill, and Scotby, all rushed past, and the train, slackening, stopped with a jerk upon the platform, at Carlisle. The sleepy porters bawled out 'change for Maryport', some drovers slouched into carriages, kicking their dogs before them, and, slamming to the doors, exchanged the time of day with others of their tribe, all carrying ash or hazel sticks, all red-faced and keen-eyed, their caps all crumpled, and their great-coat tails all creased, as if their wearers had lain down to sleep full dressed, so as to lose no time in getting to the labours of the day. The old red sandstone church, with something of a castle in its look, as well befits a shrine close to a frontier where in days gone by the priest had need to watch and pray, frowned on the passing train, and on the manufactories, whose banked-up fires sent poisonous fumes into the air, withering the trees which, in the public park, a careful council had hedged round about with wire.

The Eden ran from bank to bank, its water swirling past as wildly as when 'the Bauld Buccleugh' and his Moss Troopers, bearing the 'Kinmount' fettered in their midst, plunged in and passed it, whilst the keen Lord Scroope stood on the brink amazed and motionless. Gretna, so close to England, and yet a thousand miles away in speech and feeling, found the sands now flying through the glass. All through the mosses which once were the 'Debateable Land' on which the moss troopers of the clan Graeme were used to hide the cattle stolen from the 'auncient enemy', the now repatriated Scotchman murmured feebly 'that it was bonny scenery' although a drearier prospect of 'moss hags' and stunted birch trees is not to be found. At Ecclefechan he just raised his head, and faintly spoke of 'yon auld carle, Carlyle, ye ken, a dour thrawn body, but a gran' pheelosopher', and then lapsed into silence, broken by frequent struggles to take breath.

His wife and brother sat still, and eyed him as a cow watches a locomotive engine pass, amazed and helpless, and he himself had but the strength to whisper, 'Jock, I'm dune, I'll no see Moffat, blast it, yon smoke, ye ken, yon London smoke has been ower muckle for ma lungs.'

The tearful, helpless wife, not able even to pump up the harmful and unnecessary conventional lie, which, after all, consoles only the liar, sat pale and limp, chewing the fingers of her Berlin gloves. Upon the weather-beaten cheek of Jock glistened a tear, which he brushed off as angrily as if it had been a wasp.

'Aye, Andra',' he said, 'I would hae liket awfu' weel that ye should win to Moffat. Man, the rowan trees are a' in bloom, and there's a bonny breer upon the corn – aye, ou aye, the reid bogs are lookin' gran' the year – but, Andra', I'll tak ye east to the auld kirk-yaird, ye'll no' ken onything aboot it, but we'll hae a heartsome funeral.'

Lockerbie seemed to fly towards them, and the dying Andra' smiled as his brother pointed out the place and said, 'Ye mind, there are no ony Christians in it,' and answered, 'Aye, I mind, naething but Jardines,' as he fought for breath.

The death dews gathered on his forehead as the train shot by Nethercleugh, passed Wamphray and Dinwoodie, and with a jerk pulled up at Beattock just at the summit of the pass.

So in the cold spring morning light, the fine rain beating on the platform, as the wife and brother got their almost speechless care out of the carriage, the brother whispered, 'Dam't, ye've done it, Andra', here's Beattock; I'll tak' ye east to Moffat yet to dee.'

But on the platform, huddled on the bench to which he had been brought, Andra' sat speechless and dying in the rain. The doors banged to, the guard stepped in lightly as the train flew past, and a belated porter shouted, 'Beattock, Beattock for Moffat,' and then, summoning his last strength, Andra' smiled, and whispered faintly in his brother's ear, 'Aye, Beattock – for Moffat!' Then his head fell back, and a faint bloody foam oozed from his pallid lips. His wife stood crying helplessly, the rain beating upon the flowers of her cheap hat, rendering it shapeless and ridiculous. But Jock, drawing out a bottle, took a short dram and saying, 'Andra', man, ye made a richt gude fecht o' it,' snorted an instant in a red pocket-handkerchief, and calling up a boy, said, 'Rin, Jamie, to the toon, and tell McNicol to send up and fetch a corp.' Then, after helping to remove the body to the waiting-room, walked out into the rain, and, whistling 'Corn Rigs' quietly between his teeth, lit up his pipe, and muttered as he smoked, 'A richt gude fecht – man, aye, ou aye, a game yin Andra', puir felly. Weel, weel, he'll hae a braw hurl onyway in the new Moffat hearse.'

John Buchan

THE OUTGOING OF THE TIDE*

Men come from distant parts to admire the tides of Solloway, which race in at flood and retreat at ebb with a greater speed than a horse can follow. But nowhere are there queerer waters than in our own parish of Caulds at the place called the Sker Bay, where between two horns of land a shallow estuary receives the stream of the Sker. I never daunder by its shores, and see the waters hurrying like messengers from the great deep, without solemn thoughts and a memory of Scripture words on the terror of the sea. The vast Atlantic may be fearful in its wrath, but with us it is no clean open rage, but the deceit of the creature, the unholy ways of quicksands when the waters are gone, and their stealthy return like a thief in the night-watches. But in the times of which I write there were more awful fears than any from the violence of nature. It was before the day of my ministry in Caulds, for then I was a bit callant in short clothes in my native parish of Lesmahagow; but the worthy Doctor Chrystal, who had charge of spiritual things, has told me often of the power of Satan and his emissaries in that lonely place. It was the day of warlocks and apparitions, now happily driven out by the zeal of the General Assembly. Witches pursued their wanchancy calling, bairns were spirited away, young lassies selled their souls to the evil one, and the Accuser of the Brethren in the shape of a black tyke was seen about cottage-doors in the gloaming. Many and earnest were the prayers of good Doctor Chrystal, but the evil thing, in spite of his wrestling, grew and flourished in his midst. The parish stank of idolatry, abominable rites were practised in secret, and in all the bounds there was

* From the unpublished Remains of the Reverend John Dennistoun, sometime minister of the Gospel in the parish of Caulds, and author of *Satan's Artifices against the Elect*.

no one had a more evil name for this black traffic than one Alison Sempill, who bode at the Skerburnfoot.

The cottage stood nigh the burn in a little garden with lilyoaks and grosart-bushes lining the pathway. The Sker ran by in a linn among hollins, and the noise of its waters was ever about the place. The highroad on the other side was frequented by few, for a nearer-hand way to the west had been made through the Lowe Moss. Sometimes a herd from the hills would pass by with sheep, sometimes a tinkler or a wandering merchant, and once in a long while the laird of Heriotside on his grey horse riding to Gledsmuir. And they who passed would see Alison hirpling in her garden, speaking to herself like the illwife she was, or sitting on a cutty-stool by the doorside with her eyes on other than mortal sights. Where she came from no man could tell. There were some said she was no woman, but a ghost haunting some mortal tenement. Others would threep she was gentrice, come of a persecuting family in the west, that had been ruined in the Revolution wars. She never seemed to want for siller; the house was as bright as a new preen, the yaird better delved than the manse garden; and there was routh of fowls and doos about the small steading, forby a wheen sheep and milk-kye in the fields. No man ever saw Alison at any market in the countryside, and yet the Skerburnfoot was plenished yearly in all proper order. One man only worked on the place, a doited lad who had long been a charge to the parish, and who had not the sense to fear danger or the wit to understand it. Upon all others the sight of Alison, were it but for a moment, cast a cold grue, not to be remembered without terror. It seems she was not ordinarily ill-faured, as men use the word. She was maybe sixty years in age, small and trig, with her grey hair folded neatly under her mutch. But the sight of her eyes was not a thing to forget. John Dodds said they were the een of a deer with the devil ahint them, and indeed they would so appal an onlooker that a sudden unreasoning terror came into his heart, while his feet would impel him to flight. Once John, being overtaken in drink on the roadside by the cottage, and dreaming that he was burning in hell, woke and saw the old wife hobbling towards him. Thereupon he fled soberly to the hills, and from that day became a quiet-living humbleminded Christian. She moved about the country like a wraith, gathering herbs in dark loanings, lingering in kirkyairds, and casting a blight on innocent bairns. Once Robert Smillie found her in a ruinous kirk on the Lang Muir where of old the idolatrous rites of Rome were practised. It was a hot day, and in the quiet place the flies buzzed in crowds, and he noted that she sat clothed in them as with a garment, yet suffering no discomfort. Then he, having mind of Beelzebub, the god of flies, fled without a halt homewards; but, falling in the Coo's Loan, broke two ribs and a collar-bone, the whilk misfortune was much blessed to his soul. And there were darker tales in the countryside, of weans stolen, of lassies misguided, of innocent beasts cruelly tortured, and in one and all there came in the name of the wife of the Skerburnfoot. It was noted by them that kenned best that her cantrips were at their worst when the tides in the Sker Bay ebbed between the hours of twelve and one. At this season of the night the tides of mortality run lowest, and when the outgoing of those unco waters fell in with the setting of the current of life, then indeed was the hour for unholy revels. While honest men slept in their beds, the auld rudas carlines took their pleasure. That there is a delight in sin no man denies, but to most it is but a broken glint in the pauses of their conscience. But what must be the hellish joy of those lost beings who have forsworn God and trysted with the Prince of Darkness, it is not for a Christian to say. Certain it is that it must be great, though their master waits at the end of the road to claim the wizened things they call their souls. Serious men, notably Gidden Scott in the Back of the Hill and Simon Wauch in the sheiling of Chasehope, have seen Alison wandering on the wet sands, dancing to no earthly music, while the heavens, they said, were full of lights and sounds which betokened the presence of the prince of the powers of the air. It was a season of heart-searching for God's saints in Caulds, and the dispensation was blessed to not a few.

It will seem strange that in all this time the presbytery was idle, and no effort was made to rid the place of so fell an influence. But there was a reason, and the reason, as in most like cases, was a lassie. Forby Alison there lived at the Skerburnfoot a young maid, Ailie Sempill, who by all accounts was as good and bonnie as the other was evil. She passed for a daughter of Alison's, whether born in wedlock or nor I cannot tell; but there were some said she was no kin to the auld witch-wife, but some bairn spirited away

from honest parents. She was young and blithe, with a face like an
April morning and a voice in her that put the laverocks to shame.
When she sang in the kirk folk have told me that they had a
foretaste of the music of the New Jerusalem, and when she came
in by the village of Caulds old men stottered to their doors to look
at her. Moreover, from her earliest days the bairn had some
glimmerings of grace. Though no minister would visit the Skerburnfoot, or if he went, departed quicker than he came, the girl
Ailie attended regular at the catechizing at the Mains of Sker. It
may be that Alison thought she would be a better offering for the
devil if she were given the chance of forswearing God, or it may
be that she was so occupied in her own dark business that she had
no care of the bairn. Meanwhile the lass grew up in the nurture
and admonition of the Lord. I have heard Doctor Chrystal say
that he never had a communicant more full of the things of the
Spirit. From the day when she first declared her wish to come
forward to the hour when she broke bread at the table, she walked
like one in a dream. The lads of the parish might cast admiring
eyes on her bright cheeks and yellow hair as she sat in her white
gown in the kirk, but well they knew she was not for them. To be
the bride of Christ was the thought that filled her heart; and when
at the fencing of the tables Doctor Chrystal preached from
Matthew nine and fifteen, 'Can the children of the bride-chamber
mourn, as long as the bridegroom is with them?' it was remarked
by sundry that Ailie's face was liker the countenance of an angel
than of a mortal lass.

It is with the day of her first communion that this narrative of
mine begins. As she walked home after the morning table she
communed in secret and her heart sang within her. She had mind
of God's mercies in the past, how He had kept her feet from the
snares of evildoers which had been spread around her youth. She
had been told unholy charms like the seven south streams and the
nine rowan berries, and it was noted when she went first to the
catechizing that she prayed 'Our Father which wert in heaven,'
the prayer which the illwife Alison had taught her, meaning by it
Lucifer who had been in heaven and had been cast out therefrom.
But when she had come to years of discretion she had freely
chosen the better part, and evil had ever been repelled from her
soul like Gled water from the stones of Gled brig. Now she was in

a rapture of holy content. The drucken bell – for the ungodly fashion lingered in Caulds – was ringing in her ears as she left the village, but to her it was but a kirk-bell and a goodly sound. As she went through the woods where the primroses and whitethorn were blossoming, the place seemed as the land of Elam, wherein there were twelve wells and three-score and ten palm trees. And then, as it might be, another thought came into her head, for it is ordained that frail mortality cannot long continue in holy joy. In the kirk she had been only the bride of Christ; but as she came through the wood, with the birds lilting and the winds of the world blowing, she had mind of another lover. For this lass, though so cold to men, had not escaped the common fate. It seemed that the young Heriotside, riding by one day, stopped to speir something or other, and got a glisk of Ailie's face, which caught his fancy. He passed the road again many times, and then he would meet her in the gloaming or of a morning in the field as she went to fetch the kye. 'Blue are the hills that are far away' is an owercome in the countryside, and while at first on his side it may have been but a young man's fancy, to her he was like the god Apollo descending from the skies. He was good to look on, brawly dressed, and with a tongue in his head that would have willed the bird from the tree. Moreover, he was of gentle kin, and she was a poor lass biding in a cot-house with an ill-reputed mother. It seems that in time the young man, who had begun the affair with no good intentions, fell honestly in love, while she went singing about the doors as innocent as a bairn, thinking of him when her thoughts were not on higher things. So it came about that long ere Ailie reached home it was on young Heriotside that her mind dwelt, and it was the love of him that made her eyes glow and her cheeks redden.

Now it chanced that at that very hour her master had been with Alison, and the pair of them were preparing a deadly pit. Let no man say that the devil is not a cruel tyrant. He may give his folk some scrapings of unhallowed pleasure; but he will exact tithes, yea of anise and cummin, in return, and there is aye the reckoning to pay at the hinder end. It seems that now he was driving Alison hard. She had been remiss of late, fewer souls sent to hell, less zeal in quenching the Spirit, and above all the crowning offence that her bairn had communicated in Christ's kirk. She had waited overlong, and now it was like that Ailie would escape her toils. I have no skill of fancy to tell of that dark collogue, but the upshot was that Alison swore by her lost soul and the pride of sin to bring the lass into thrall to her master. The fiend had bare departed when Ailie came over the threshold to find the auld carline glunching by the fire.

It was plain that she was in the worst of tempers. She flyted on the lass till the poor thing's cheek paled. 'There you gang,' she cried, 'troking wi' thae wearifu' Pharisees o' Caulds, whae daurna darken your mither's door. A bonnie dutiful child, quotha! Wumman, hae ye nae pride? – no even the mense o' a tinkler-lass?' And then she changed her voice, and would be as soft as honey. 'My puir wee Ailie! was I thrawn till ye? Never mind, my bonnie. You and me are a' that's left, and we maunna be ill to ither.' And then the two had their dinner, and all the while the auld wife was crooning over the lass. 'We maun 'gree weel,' she says, 'for we're like to be our lee-lane for the rest o' our days. They tell me Heriotside is seeking Joan o' the Croft, and they're sune to be cried in Gledsmuir kirk.'

It was the first the lass had heard of it, and you may fancy she was struck dumb. And so with one thing and another the auld witch raised the fiends of jealousy in that innocent heart. She would cry out that Heriotside was an ill-doing wastrel, and had no business to come and flatter honest lasses. And then she would speak of his gentle birth and his leddy mother, and say it was indeed presumption to hope that so great a gentleman could mean all that he said. Before long Ailie was silent and white, while her mother rimed on about men and their ways. And then she could thole it no longer, but must go out and walk by the burn to cool her hot brow and calm her thoughts, while the witch indoors laughed to herself at her devices.

For days Ailie had an absent eye and a sad face, and it so fell out that in all that time young Heriotside, who had scarce missed a day, was laid up with a broken arm and never came near her. So in a week's time she was beginning to hearken to her mother when she spoke of incantations and charms for restoring love. She kenned it was sin; but though not seven days syne she had sat at the Lord's table, so strong is love in a young heart that she was on the very brink of it. But the grace of God was stronger than her weak will. She would have none of her mother's runes and philters, though her soul cried out for them. Always when she was most disposed to listen some merciful power stayed her consent. Alison grew thrawner as the hours passed. She kenned of Heriotside's broken arm, and she feared that any day he might recover and put her stratagems to shame. And then it seems that she collogued with her master and heard word of a subtler device. For it was approaching that uncanny time of year, the festival of Beltane, when the auld pagans were wont to sacrifice to their god Baal. In this season warlocks and carlines have a special dispensation to do evil, and Alison waited on its coming with graceless joy. As it happened, the tides in the Sker Bay ebbed at this time between the hours of twelve and one, and, as I have said, this was the hour above all others when the powers of darkness were most potent. Would the lass but consent to go abroad in the unhallowed place at this awful season and hour of the night, she was as firmly handfasted to the devil as if she had signed a bond with her own blood. For then, it seemed, the forces of good fled far away, the world for one hour was given over to its ancient prince, and the man or woman who willingly sought the spot was his bond-servant for ever. There are deadly sins from which God's people may recover. A man may even communicate unworthily, and yet, so be it he sin not against the Holy Ghost, he may find forgiveness. But it seems that for this Beltane sin there could be no pardon, and I can testify from my own knowledge that they who once committed it became lost souls from that day. James Deuchar, once a promising professor, fell thus out of sinful bravery and died blaspheming; and of Kate Mallison, who went the same road, no man can tell. Here, indeed, was the witch-wife's chance, and she was the more keen, for her master had warned her that this was her last. Either Ailie's soul would be his, or her auld wrinkled body and black heart would be flung from this pleasant world to their apportioned place.

Some days later it happened that young Heriotside was stepping home over the Lang Muir about ten at night – it being his first jaunt from home since his arm had mended. He had been to the supper of the Forest Club at the Cross Keys in Gledsmuir, a clamjamfry of wild young blades who passed the wine and played at cartes once a fortnight. It seems he had drunk well, so that the world ran round about and he was in the best of tempers. The moon came down and bowed to him, and he took off his hat to it. For every step he travelled miles, so that in a little he was beyond Scotland altogether and pacing the Arabian desert. He thought he was the Pope of Rome, so he held out his foot to be kissed, and rolled twenty yards to the bottom of a small brae. Syne he was the King of France, and fought hard with a whin-bush till he had banged it to pieces. After that nothing would content him but he must be a bogle, for he found his head dunting on the stars and his legs were knocking the hills together. He thought of the mischief he was doing to the auld earth, and sat down and cried at his wickedness. Then he went on, and maybe the steep road to the Moss Rig helped him, for he began to get soberer and ken his whereabouts.

On a sudden he was aware of a man linking along at his side. He cried, 'A fine night,' and the man replied. Syne, being merry from his cups, he tried to slap him on the back. The next he kenned he was rolling on the grass, for his hand had gone clean through the body and found nothing but air.

His head was so thick with wine that he found nothing droll in this. 'Faith, friend,' he says, 'that was a nasty fall for a fellow that has supped weel. Where might your road be gaun to?'

'To the World's End,' said the man, 'but I stop at the Skerburnfoot.'

'Bide the night at Heriotside,' says he. 'It's a thought out of your way, but it's a comfortable bit.'

'There's mair comfort at the Skerburnfoot,' said the dark man.

Now the mention of the Skerburnfoot brought back to him only the thought of Ailie and not of the witch-wife, her mother. So he jaloused no ill, for at the best he was slow in the uptake.

The two of them went on together for a while, Heriotside's fool head filled with the thought of the lass. Then the dark man broke silence. 'Ye're thinkin' o' the maid Ailie Sempill,' says he.

'How ken ye that?' asked Heriotside.

'It is my business to read the herts o' men,' said the other.

'And who may ye be?' said Heriotside, growing eerie.

'Just an auld packman,' said he – 'nae name ye wad ken, but kin to mony gentle houses.'

'And what about Ailie, you that ken sae muckle?' asked the young man.

'Naething,' was the answer – 'naething that concerns you, for ye'll never get the lass.'

'By God, and I will!' says Heriotside, for he was a profane swearer.

'That's the wrong name to seek her in, anyway,' said the man.

At this the young laird struck a great blow at him with his stick, but found nothing to resist him but the hill-wind.

When they had gone on a bit the dark man spoke again. 'The lassie is thirled to holy things,' says he. 'She has nae care for flesh and blood, only for devout contemplation.'

'She loves me,' says Heriotside.

'Not you,' says the other, 'but a shadow in your stead.'

At this the young man's heart began to tremble, for it seemed that there was truth in what his companion said, and he was ower drunk to think gravely.

'I kenna whatna man ye are,' he says, 'but ye have the skill of lassies' hearts. Tell me truly, is there no way to win her to common love?'

'One way there is,' said the man, 'and for our friendship's sake I will tell it you. If ye can ever tryst wi' her on Beltane's Eve on the Sker sands, at the green link o' the burn where the sands begin, on the ebb o' the tide when the midnight is bye but afore cock-crow, she'll be yours, body and soul, for this world and for ever.'

And then it appeared to the young man that he was walking his lone up the grass walk of Heriotside with the house close by him. He thought no more of the stranger he had met, but the words stuck in his heart.

It seems that about this very time Alison was telling the same tale to poor Ailie. She cast up to her every idle gossip she could think of. 'It's Joan o' the Croft,' was aye her owercome, and she would threep that they were to be cried in kirk on the first Sabbath of June. And then she would rime on about the black cruelty of it, and cry down curses on the lover, so that her daughter's heart grew cauld with fear. It is terrible to think of the power of the world even in a redeemed soul. Here was a maid who had drunk of the well of grace and tasted of God's mercies, and yet there were moments when she was ready to renounce her hope. At those awful seasons God seemed far off and the world very nigh, and to sell her soul for love looked a fair bargain. At other times she would resist the devil and comfort herself with prayer; but aye when she woke there was the sore heart, and when she went to sleep there were the weary eyes. There was no comfort in the goodliness of spring or the bright sunshine weather, and she who had been wont to go about the doors lightfoot and blithe was now as dowie as a widow woman.

And then one afternoon in the hinder end of April came young Heriotside riding to the Skerburnfoot. His arm was healed, he had got him a fine new suit of green, and his horse was a mettle beast that well set off his figure. Ailie was standing by the doorstep as he came down the road, and her heart stood still with joy. But a second thought gave her anguish. This man, so gallant and braw, would never be for her; doubtless the fine suit and the capering horse were for Joan of the Croft's pleasure. And he in turn, when he remarked her wan cheek and dowie eyes, had mind of what the dark man said on the muir, and saw in her a maid sworn to no mortal love. Yet the passion for her had grown fiercer than ever, and he swore to himself that he would win her back from her phantasies. She, one may believe, was ready enough to listen. As she walked with him by the Sker water his words were like music to her ears, and Alison within-doors laughed to herself and saw her devices prosper.

He spoke to her of love and his own heart, and the girl hearkened gladly. Syne he rebuked her coldness and cast scorn upon her piety, and so far was she beguiled that she had no answer. Then from one thing and another he spoke of some true token of their love. He said he was jealous, and craved something to ease his care. 'It's but a small thing I ask,' says he; 'but it will make me a happy man, and nothing ever shall come atween us. Tryst wi' me for Beltane's Eve on the Sker sands, at the green link o' the burn where the sands begin, on the ebb o' the tide when midnight is bye but afore cock-crow. For,' said he, 'that was our forebears' tryst for true lovers, and wherefore no for you and me?'

The lassie had grace given her to refuse, but with a woeful heart, and Heriotside rode off in black discontent, leaving poor Ailie to sigh her lone. He came back the next day and the next, but aye he got the same answer. A season of great doubt fell upon her soul. She had no clearness in her hope, nor any sense of God's promises. The Scriptures were an idle tale to her, prayer brought her no refreshment, and she was convicted in her conscience of the unpardonable sin. Had she been less full of pride she would have taken her troubles to good Doctor Chrystal and got comfort; but her grief made her silent and timorous, and she found no help anywhere. Her mother was ever at her side, seeking with coaxings and evil advice to drive her to the irrevocable step. And all the while there was her love for the man riving in her bosom and giving her no ease by night or day. She believed she had driven him away and repented her denial. Only her pride held her back from going to Heriotside and seeking him herself. She watched the road hourly for a sight of his face, and when the darkness came she would sit in a corner brooding over her sorrows.

At last he came, speiring the old question. He sought the same tryst, but now he had a further tale. It seemed he was eager to get her away from the Skerburnside and auld Alison. His aunt, the Lady Balcrynie, would receive her gladly at his request till the day of their marriage. Let her but tryst with him at the hour and place he named, and he would carry her straight to Balcrynie, where she would be safe and happy. He named that hour, he said, to escape men's observation for the sake of her own good name. He named that place, for it was near her dwelling, and on the road between Balcrynie and Heriotside, which fords the Sker Burn. The temptation was more than mortal heart could resist. She gave him the promise he sought, stifling the voice of conscience; and as she clung to his neck it seemed to her that heaven was a poor thing compared with a man's love.

Three days remained till Beltane's Eve, and throughout the time it was noted that Heriotside behaved like one possessed. It may be that his conscience pricked him, or that he had a glimpse of his sin and its coming punishment. Certain it is that, if he had been daft before, he now ran wild in his pranks, and an evil report of him was in every mouth. He drank deep at the Cross Keys, and fought two battles with young lads that angered him. One he let off with a touch in the shoulder, the other goes lame to this day from a wound he got in the groin. There was a word of the procurator-fiscal taking note of his doings, and troth, if they had continued long he must have fled the country. For a wager he rode his horse down the Dow Craig, wherefore the name of the place is the Horseman's Craig to this day. He laid a hundred guineas with the laird of Slipperfield that he would drive four horses through the Slipperfield loch, and in the prank he had his bit chariot dung to pieces and a good mare killed. And all men observed that his eyes were wild and his face grey and thin, and that his hand would twitch as he held the glass, like one with the palsy.

The eve of Beltane was lown and hot in the low country, with fire hanging in the clouds and thunder grumbling about the heavens. It seems that up in the hills it had been an awesome deluge of rain, but on the coast it was still dry and lowering. It is a long road from Heriotside to the Skerburnfoot. First you go down the Heriot Water, and syne over the Lang Muir to the edge of Mucklewham. When you pass the steadings of Mirehope and Cockmalane you turn to the right and ford the Mire Burn. That brings you on to the turnpike road, which you will ride till it bends inland, while you keep on straight over the Whinny Knowes to the Sker Bay. There, if you are in luck, you will find the tide out and the place fordable dryshod for a man on a horse. But if the tide runs, you will do well to sit down on the sands and content yourself till it turn, or it will be the solans and scarts of the Solloway that will be seeing the next of you. On this Beltane's Eve the young man, after supping with some wild young blades, bade his horse be saddled about ten o'clock. The company were eager to ken his errand, but he waved them back. 'Bide here,' he says, 'and birl the wine till I return. This is a ploy of my own on which no man follows me.' And there was that in his face as he spoke which chilled the wildest, and left them well content to keep to the good claret and the soft seat and let the daft laird go his own ways.

Well and on, he rode down the bridlepath in the wood, along the top of the Heriot glen, and as he rode he was aware of a great noise beneath him. It was not wind, for there was none, and it was not the sound of thunder, and aye as he speired at himself what it was it grew louder till he came to a break in the trees. And then he saw the cause, for Heriot was coming down in a furious flood, sixty yards wide, tearing at the roots of the aiks, and flinging red waves against the dry-stone dykes. It was a sight and sound to solemnize a man's mind, deep calling unto deep, the great waters of the hills running to meet with the great waters of the sea. But Heriotside recked nothing of it, for his heart had but one thought and the eye of his fancy one figure. Never had he been so filled with love of the lass, and yet it was not happiness but a deadly secret fear.

As he came to the Lang Muir it was geyan dark, though there was a moon somewhere behind the clouds. It was little he could see of the road, and ere long he had tried many mosspools and sloughs, as his braw new coat bare witness. Aye in front of him was the great hill of Mucklewham, where the road turned down by the Mire. The noise of the Heriot had not long fallen behind him ere another began, the same eerie sound of burns crying to ither in the darkness. It seemed that the whole earth was overrun with waters. Every little runnel in the bog was astir, and yet the land around him was as dry as flax, and no drop of rain had fallen. As he rode on the din grew louder, and as he came over the top of Mirehope he kenned by the mighty rushing noise that something uncommon was happening with the Mire Burn. The light from Mirehope sheiling twinkled on his left, and had the man not been dozened with his fancies he might have observed that the steading was deserted and men were crying below in the fields. But he rode on, thinking of but one thing, till he came to the cot-house of Cockmalane, which is nigh the fords of the Mire.

John Dodds, the herd who bode in the place, was standing at the door, and he looked to see who was on the road so late.

'Stop,' says he, 'stop, Laird Heriotside. I kenna what your errand is, but it is to no holy purpose that ye're out on Beltane Eve. D'ye no hear the warning o' the waters?'

And then in the still night came the sound of Mire like the clash of armies.

'I must win over the ford,' says the laird quietly, thinking of another thing.

'Ford!' cried John in scorn. 'There'll be nae ford for you the nicht unless it be the ford o' the River Jordan. The burns are up, and bigger than man ever saw them. It'll be a Beltane's Eve that a' folk will remember. They tell me that Gled valley is like a loch, and that there's an awesome folk drooned in the hills. Gin ye were ower the Mire, what about crossin' the Caulds and the Sker?' says he, for he jaloused he was going to Gledsmuir.

And then it seemed that that word brought the laird to his

senses. He looked the airt the rain was coming from, and he saw it was the airt the Sker flowed. In a second, he has told me, the works of the devil were revealed to him. He saw himself a tool in Satan's hands, he saw his tryst a device for the destruction of the body, as it was assuredly meant for the destruction of the soul, and there came on his mind the picture of an innocent lass borne down by the waters with no place for repentance. His heart grew cold in his breast. He had but one thought, a sinful and reckless one – to get to her side, that the two might go together to their account. He heard the roar of the Mire as in a dream, and when John Dodds laid hands on his bridle he felled him to the earth. And the next seen of it was the laird riding the floods like a man possessed.

The horse was the grey stallion he aye rode, the very beast he had ridden for many a wager with the wild lads of the Cross Keys. No man but himself durst back it, and it had lamed many a hostler lad and broke two necks in its day. But it seemed it had the mettle for any flood, and took the Mire with little spurring. The herds on the hillside looked to see man and steed swept into eternity; but though the red waves were breaking about his shoulders and he was swept far down, he aye held on for the shore. The next thing the watchers saw was the laird struggling up the far bank, and casting his coat from him, so that he rode in his sark. And then he set off like wildfire across the muir towards the turnpike road. Two men saw him on the road and have recorded their experience. One was a gangrel, by name M'Nab, who was travelling from Gledsmuir to Allerkirk with a heavy pack on his back and a bowed head. He heard a sound like wind afore him, and, looking up, saw coming down the road a grey horse stretched out to a wild gallop and a man on its back with a face like a soul in torment. He kenned not whether it was the devil or mortal, but flung himself on the roadside, and lay like a corp for an hour or more till the rain aroused him. The other was one Sim Doolittle, the fish-hawker from Allerfoot, jogging home in his fish-cart from Gledsmuir fair. He had drunk more than was fit for him, and he was singing some light song, when he saw approaching, as he said, the pale horse mentioned in the Revelations, with Death seated as the rider. Thoughts of his sins came on him like a thunderclap, fear loosened his knees, he leaped from the cart to the road, and from the road to the back of a dyke. Thence he flew to the hills, and was found the next morning far up among the Mire Craigs, while his horse and cart were gotten on the Aller sands, the horse lamed and the cart without the wheels.

At the tollhouse the road turns inland to Gledsmuir, and he who goes to Sker Bay must leave it and cross the wild land called the Whinny Knowes, a place rough with bracken and foxes' holes and old stone cairns. The tollman, John Gilzean, was opening his window to get a breath of air in the lown night when he heard and saw the approaching horse. He kenned the beast for Heriotside's, and, being a friend of the laird's, he ran down in all haste to open the yett, wondering to himself about the laird's errand on this night. A voice came down the road to him bidding him hurry; but John's old fingers were slow with the keys, and so it happened that the horse had to stop, and John had time to look up at the gash and woful face.

'Where away the nicht sae late, laird?' says John.

'I go to save a soul from hell,' was the answer.

And then it seems that through the open door there came the chapping of a clock.

'Whatna hour is that?' asks Heriotside.

'Midnicht,' says John, trembling, for he did not like the look of things.

There was no answer but a groan, and horse and man went racing down the dark hollows of the Whinny Knowes.

How he escaped a broken neck in that dreadful place no human being will ever tell. The sweat, he has told me, stood in cold drops upon his forehead; he scarcely was aware of the saddle in which he sat; and his eyes were stelled in his head, so that he saw nothing but the sky ayont him. The night was growing colder, and there was a small sharp wind stirring from the east. But, hot or cold, it was all one to him, who was already cold as death. He heard not the sound of the sea nor the peesweeps startled by his horse, for the sound that ran in his ears was the roaring Sker Water and a girl's cry. The thought kept goading him, and he spurred the grey till the creature was madder than himself. It leaped the hole which they call the Devil's Mull as I would step over a thistle, and the next he kenned he was on the edge of the Sker Bay.

It lay before him white and ghastly, with mist blowing in wafts across it and a slow swaying of the tides. It was the better part of a mile wide, but save for some fathoms in the middle where the Sker current ran, it was no deeper even at flood than a horse's fetlocks. It looks eerie at bright midday when the sun is shining and whaups are crying among the seaweeds; but think what it was on that awesome night with the powers of darkness brooding over it like a cloud. The rider's heart quailed for a moment in natural fear. He stepped his beast a few feet in, still staring afore him like a daft man. And then something in the sound or the feel of the waters made him look down, and he perceived that the ebb had begun and the tide was flowing out to sea.

He kenned that all was lost, and the knowledge drove him to stark despair. His sins came in his face like birds of night, and his heart shrank like a pea. He knew himself for a lost soul, and all that he loved in the world was out in the tides. There, at any rate, he could go too, and give back that gift of life he had so blackly misused. He cried small and soft like a bairn, and drove the grey out into the waters. And aye as he spurred it the foam should have been flying as high as his head; but in that uncanny hour there was no foam, only the waves running sleek like oil. It was not long ere he had come to the Sker channel, where the red moss-waters were roaring to the sea, an ill place to ford in midsummer heat, and certain death, as folks reputed it, in the smallest spate. The grey was swimming, but it seemed the Lord had other purposes for him than death, for neither man nor horse could drown. He tried to leave the saddle, but he could not; he flung the bridle from him, but the grey held on, as if some strong hand were guiding. He cried out upon the devil to help his own, he renounced his Maker and his God; but whatever his punishment, he was not to be drowned. And then he was silent, for something was coming down the tide.

It came down as quiet as a sleeping bairn, straight for him as he sat with his horse breasting the waters, and as it came the moon crept out of a cloud and he saw a glint of yellow hair. And then his madness died away and he was himself again, a weary and stricken man. He hung down over the tides and caught the body in his arms and then let the grey make for the shallows. He cared no more for the devil and all his myrmidons, for he kenned brawly he was damned. It seemed to him that his soul had gone from him and he was as toom as a hazel-shell. His breath rattled in his throat, the tears were dried up in his head, his body had lost its strength, and yet he clung to the drowned maid as to a hope of salvation. And then he noted something at which he marvelled dumbly. Her hair was drookit back from her clay-cold brow, her eyes were shut, but in her face there was the peace of a child. It seemed even that her lips were smiling. Here, certes, was no lost soul, but one who had gone joyfully to meet her Lord. It may be that in that dark hour at the burn-foot, before the spate caught her, she had been given grace to resist her adversary and flung herself upon God's mercy.

And it would seem that it had been granted, for when he came to the Skerburnfoot there in the corner sat the weird-wife Alison, dead as a stone and shrivelled like a heather-birn.

For days Heriotside wandered the country or sat in his own house with vacant eye and trembling hands. Conviction of sin held him like a vice: he saw the lassie's death laid at his door, her face haunted him by day and night, and the word of the Lord dirled in his ears telling of wrath and punishment. The greatness of his anguish wore him to a shadow, and at last he was stretched on his bed and like to perish. In his extremity worthy Doctor Chrystal went to him unasked and strove to comfort him. Long, long the good man wrestled, but it seemed as if his ministrations were to be of no avail. The fever left his body, and he rose to stotter about the doors; but he was still in his torments, and the mercy-seat was far from him. At last in the back-end of the year came Mungo Muirhead to Caulds to the autumn communion, and nothing would serve him but he must try his hand at this storm-tossed soul. He spoke with power and unction, and a blessing came with his words, the black cloud lifted and showed a glimpse of grace, and in a little the man had some assurance of salvation. He became a pillar of Christ's Kirk, prompt to check abominations, notably the sin of witchcraft, foremost in good works; but with it all a humble man, who walked contritely till his death. When I came first to Caulds I sought to prevail upon him to accept the eldership, but he aye put me by, and when I heard his tale I saw that he had done wisely. I mind him well as he sat in his chair or daundered through

Caulds, a kind word for every one and sage counsel in time of distress, but withal a severe man to himself and a crucifier of the body. It seems that this severity weakened his frame, for three years syne come Martinmas he was taken ill with a fever, and after a week's sickness he went to his account, where I trust he is accepted.

Neil M. Gunn

THE TAX-GATHERER

'Blast it,' he muttered angrily. 'Where is the accursed place?'

He looked at the map again spread before him on the steering-wheel. Yes, it should be just here. There was the cross-roads. He threw a glance round the glass of his small saloon car and saw a man's head bobbing beyond the hedge. At once he got out and walked along the side of the road.

'Excuse me,' he cried. The face looked at him over the hedge. 'Excuse me, but can you tell me where Mrs Martha Williamson stays?'

'Mrs Who?'

'Mrs Martha Williamson.'

'No,' said the face slowly, and moved away. He followed it for a few paces to a gap in the hedge. 'No,' said the man again, and turned to call a spaniel out of the turnips. He had a gun under his arm and was obviously a gamekeeper.

'Well, she lives about here, at Ivy Cottage.'

'Ivy Cottage? Do you mean the tinkers?' And the gamekeeper regarded him thoughtfully.

'Yes. I suppose so.'

'I see,' said the gamekeeper, looking away. 'Turn up to your right at the cross-roads there and you'll see it standing back from the road.'

He thanked the gamekeeper and set off, walking quickly so that he needn't think too much about his task, for it was new to him.

When he saw the cottage, over amongst some bushes with a rank growth of nettles at one end, he thought it a miserable place, but when he came close to the peeling limewash, the torn-down ivy, the sagging roof, the broken stone doorstep thick with trampled mud, he saw that it was a wretched hovel.

The door stood half-open, stuck. He knocked on it and listened to the acute silence. He knocked again firmly and thought he heard thin whisperings. He did not like the hushed fear in the sounds, and was just about to knock peremptorily when there was a shuffling, and, quietly as an apparition, a woman was there.

She stood twisted, lax, a slim, rather tall figure, with a face the colour of the old limewash. She clung to the edge of the door in a manner unhumanly pathetic, and looked at him out of dark, soft eyes.

'Are you Mrs Williamson?'

After a moment she said, 'Yes.'

'Well, I've come about that dog. Have you taken out the licence yet?'

'No.'

'Well, it's like this,' he said, glancing away from her. 'We don't want to get you into trouble. But the police reported to us that you had the dog. Now, you can't have a dog without paying a licence. You know that. So, in all the circumstances, the authorities decided that if you paid a compromise fine of seven-and-six, and took out the licence, no more would be said about it. You would not be taken to court.' He looked at her again, and saw no less than five small heads poking round her ragged dark skirt. 'We don't want you to get into trouble,' he said. 'But you've got to pay by Friday – or you'll be summonsed. There's no way out.'

She did not speak, stood there unmoving, clinging to the door, a feminine creature waiting dumbly for the blow.

'Have you a husband?' he asked.

'Yes,' she said, after a moment.

'Where is he?'

'I don't know,' she answered, in her soft, hopeless voice. He wanted to ask her if he had left her for good, but could not, and this irritated him, so he said calmly, 'Well, that's the position, as you know. I was passing, and, seeing we had got no word of your payment, I thought I'd drop in and warn you. We don't want to take you to court. So my advice to you is to pay up – and at once, or it will be too late.'

She did not answer. As he was about to turn away the dregs of his irritation got the better of him. 'Why on earth did you want to keep the dog, anyway?'

'We tried to put him away, but he wouldn't go,' she said.

His brows gathered. 'Oh, well, it's up to you,' he replied coldly, and he turned and strode back to his car. Slamming the door after him, he gripped the wheel, but could not, at the last instant, press the self-starter. He swore to himself in a furious rage. Damn it all, what concern was it of his? None at all. As a public official he had to do his job. It was nothing to him. If a person wanted to enjoy the luxury of keeping a dog, he or she had to pay for it. That's all. And he looked for the self-starter, but, with his finger on the button, again could not press it. He twisted in his seat. Fifteen bob! he thought. Go back and slip her fifteen bob? Am I mad? He pressed the self-starter and set the engine off in an unnecessary roar. As he turned at the cross-roads he hesitated before shoving the gear lever into first, then shoved it and set off. If a fellow was to start paying public fines where would it end? Sentimental? Absolutely.

By the following Tuesday it was clear she had not paid.

'The case will go on,' said his chief in the office.

'It's a hard case,' he answered. 'She won't be able to pay.' His voice was calm and official.

'She'll have to pay – one way or the other,' answered his chief, with the usual trace of official satire in his voice.

'She's got a lot of kids,' said the young man.

'Has she?' said the chief. 'Perhaps she could not help having them – but the dog is another matter.' He smiled, and glanced at the young man, who awkwardly smiled back.

There was nothing unkindly in the chief's attitude, merely a complete absence of feeling. He was dealing with 'a file', and had no sympathy for anyone who tried to evade the law. He prosecuted with lucid care, and back in his office smiled with satisfaction when he got a conviction. For to fail in getting a conviction was to be inept in his duty. Those above him frowned upon such ineptitude.

All the same, the young man felt miserable. If he hadn't gone to the cottage it would have been all right. But the chief had had no unnecessary desire for a court case – particularly one of those hard cases that might get into the press. Not that that mattered really, for the law had to be carried out. Than false sentiment against the law of the land there could, properly regarded, be nothing more reprehensible – because it was so easy to indulge.

'By the way,' said the chief, as he was turning away, 'I see the dog has been shot. You didn't mention that?'

'No. I –' He had forgotten to ask the woman if the dog was still with her. 'I – as a matter of fact, I didn't think about it, seeing it was a police report, and therefore no evidence from us needed.'

'Quite so,' said his chief reticently, as he turned to his file.

'Who shot it?' the young man could not help asking.

'A gamekeeper, apparently.'

The young man withdrew, bit on his embarrassment at evoking the chief's 'reticence', and thought of the gamekeeper who might believe that if the dog was shot nothing more could be done about the case. As if the liability would thereby be wiped out! As if it would make the slightest difference to the case!

In his own room he remembered the gamekeeper and his curious look. Decent of him all the same to have tried to help. If the children's faces had been sallow and hollow from underfeeding, what could the dog have got? Nothing, unless – The thought dawned: the gamekeeper had probably shot the brute without being asked. Poaching rabbits and game? Perhaps the mainstay of the family? He laughed in his nostrils. When you're down you're right down, down and out. Absolutely. With a final snort of satire, he took some papers from the 'pending' cover and tried to concentrate on an old woman's application for a pension. It seemed quite straightforward, though he would have to investigate her circumstances. Then he saw the children's faces again.

He had hardly been conscious of looking at them at the time. In fact, after that first glance of surprise he had very definitely not looked at them. The oldest was a girl of nine or ten, thin and watery, fragile, with her mother's incredible pallor and black eyes. The stare from those considering eyes, blank and dumb, and yet wary. They didn't appeal: trust could not touch them; they waited, just waited, for – the only hope – something less than the worst.

And the little fellow of seven or eight – sandy hair, inflamed eyelids, and that something about the expression, the thick, half-open mouth, suggesting the mental deficient. Obviously from the father's side, physically. The father had deserted them. Was perhaps in quod somewhere else, for they had only recently returned from their travels to the cottage. How did they manage even to live in it without being turned out? But the police would have that in hand as well! There was something too soft about the woman. She would never face up to her husband. When he was drunk, her softness would irritate him; he would clout her one. She was feckless. Her body had slumped into a pliant line, utterly hopeless, against the door. All at once he saw the line as graceful, and this unexpected vision added the last touch to derision.

The young man had observed in his life already that if his mind was keen on some subject he would come across references to it in the oddest places, in books dealing with quite other matters, from the most unlikely people. But this, carefully considered, was not altogether fortuitous. For example, when the old woman who had applied for the Old Age Pension asked him if he would have a cup of tea, he hesitated, not because he particularly wanted to have a cup of tea, but because he vaguely wanted to speak to her about the ways of tinkers, for Ivy Cottage was little more than a mile away.

His hesitation, however, the hesitation of an important official who had arrived in a motor-car and upon whom the granting of her pension depended (as she thought), excited her so much that before she quite knew what she was doing she was on her knees before the fire, flapping the dull peat embers with her apron, for she did not like, in front of him, to bend her old grey head and blow the embers to a flame. As he was watching her she suddenly stopped flapping, with an expression of almost ludicrous dismay, and mumbled something about not having meant to do that. At once he was interested, for clearly there was something involved beyond mere politeness. The old folk in this northern land, he had found, were usually very polite, and he liked their ways and curious beliefs. The fact that they had a Gaelic language of their own attracted him, for he was himself a student of French, and, he believed, somewhat of an authority on Balzac.

Fortunately for the old lady, a sprightly tongue of flame ran up the dry peat at that moment, and she swung the kettle over it. 'Now it won't be long,' she said, carefully backing up the flame with more peat.

She was a quick-witted, bright-eyed old woman, and as she hurried to and fro getting the tea things on the table they chatted pleasantly. Presently, when she seated herself and began to pour the tea, he asked her in the friendliest way why she had stopped flapping her apron.

She glanced at him and then said, 'Och, just an old woman's way.'

But he would not have that, and rallied her. 'Come, now, there was something more to it than that.'

And at last she said: 'It's just an old story in this part of the world and likely it will not be true. But I will tell it to you, seeing you say you like stories of the kind, but you will have to take it as you get it, for that's the way I got it myself, more years ago now than I can remember. It is a story about our Lord at the time of His crucifixion. You will remember that when our Lord was being crucified they nailed Him to the Cross. But before they could do that they needed the nails, and the nails were not in it. So they tried to get the nails made, but no one would make them. They asked the Roman soldiers to make them, but they would not. Perhaps it was not their business to make the nails. Anyway, they would not make them. So they asked the Jews to make the nails, but they would not make them either. No, they would not make them. No one would make the nails that were needed to crucify our Lord. And when they were stuck now, and did not know what to do, who should they see coming along but a tinker with his little leather apron on him. So they asked him if he would make the nails. And he said yes, he would make them. And to make the nails he needed a fire. So a fire was made, but it would not go very well, so he bent down in front of it and flapped it with his leather apron. In that way the fire went and the nails were made. And so it came about that the tinkers became wanderers, and were never liked by the people of the world anywhere. And that's the story.'

When at last he drove away from the old woman's house he came to the cross-roads and, a few yards beyond, drew up. This is the place, he thought, and he felt it about him, gripped the wheel hard, and sat still. Irritation began to get the better of him. Anyone could see he was a fool. He got out and stretched his legs and lit a cigarette. There was no one in the turnip field, no one anywhere. All at once he walked back quickly to the cross-roads, turned right, and again saw the cottage. It was looking at him with a still, lopsided, idiotic expression. His flesh quickened and drew taut in cool anger. He threw the cigarette away, emptied his mind, and came to the door, which was exactly as it had been before, half-open and stuck.

When he had knocked once, and no one answered, he felt like retreating, so he knocked very loudly the second time, and the woman materialized. There was no other word for it. There she was, with the graceful twist in her dejected body, attached to the edge of the door. Was she expecting the blow? Was there something not so much antagonistic as withdrawn, prepared to endure, in the pathos of her attitude? She knew how to wait, in any case.

'I see you didn't pay,' he said.

She did not answer. She could not have been more than thirty.

'Well, you have got to appear before the court now,' he asserted, and added, with a lighthearted brutality, 'or the police will come and fetch you. Hadn't you the money to pay?' And he looked at her.

'No,' she said, looking back at him.

'So you hadn't the money,' he said, glancing away with the smile of official satire. 'And what are you going to do now – go to prison?'

The children were poking their heads round her skirts again. Their fragility appeared extreme, possibly because they were unwashed. Obviously they were famished.

She did not answer.

'Look here,' he said, 'this is no business of mine.' He took out his pocket-book. His hands shook as he extracted a pound note. 'Here's something for you. That'll pay for everything. The only thing I want you *never* to do is to mention that I gave it to you. Do you understand?'

She could not answer for looking at the pound note. If he had been afraid of a rush of gratitude he might have saved himself the worry. She took it stupidly and glanced at him as if there might be a trick in all this somewhere. Then he saw a stirring in her eyes, a woman's divination of character, a slow welling of understanding in the black deeps. It was pathetic.

'That's all right,' he said, and turned away as if she had thanked him.

When he got back into his car he felt better. That was all over, anyway. She was just stupid, a weak, stupid woman who had got trodden down. Tough luck on her. But she certainly wouldn't give him away. Perhaps he ought to have emphasized that part of it more? By God, I would never live it down in the office! Never! He began to laugh as he bowled along. He felt he could trust her. She was not the sort to give anything away. Too frightened. Experience had taught her how to hold her tongue before the all-important males of the world – not to mention the all-important females! She knew the old conspiracy all right and then some! His mirth increased. That he had felt he could not afford the pound – a pound is a pound, by heavens! – added now to the fun of the whole affair.

He did not go to court. After all, he might feel embarrassed; and the silly woman might, if she saw him, turn to him or depend on him or something. Moreover, he did not know how these affairs were conducted. So far it had not been his business. Besides, he disliked the whole idea of court proceedings. Time enough for that when he *had* to turn up.

Before lunch the chief came into his room for some papers. The young man repressed his excitement, for he had been wondering how the case had gone, having, only a few minutes before, remembered the possibility of court expenses. He could not bring himself to ask the result, but the chief, as he was going out, paused and said: 'That woman from Ivy Cottage, the dog case, she was convicted.'

'Oh. I'm glad you got the case through.'

'Yes. A silly woman. The bench was very considerate in the circumstances. Didn't put on any extra fine. No expenses. Take out the licence and pay the seven-and-six compromise fine – or five days. She was asked if she could pay. She said no. So they gave her time to pay.'

The young man regarded the point of his pen. 'So she's off again,' he said, with official humour.

'No. She elected to go to prison. She put the bench rather in a difficulty, but she was obdurate.'

'You mean – they've put her in prison?'

'Presumably. There was no other course at the time.'

'But the children – what'll happen to them?'

'No doubt the police will give the facts to the Inspector of Poor. It's up to the local authorities now. We wash our hands of it. If people will keep dogs they must know what to expect!' He smiled dryly and withdrew.

The young man sat back in his chair and licked his dry lips. She had cheated him. She had . . . she preferred . . . let him think. Clearly the pound mattered more than the five days. His money she would have left with the eldest girl, or some of it, with instructions what to buy and how to feed the children. She would have said to the eldest girl, 'I'll be away for a few days, but don't worry, I'll be back. And meantime . . .'

But no, she would tell the eldest everything, by the pressure of instinct, of reality. That would bring the eldest into it; make her feel responsible for the young ones. And food . . . food . . . the overriding avid interest in food. Food – it was everything. The picture formed in his mind of the mother taking leave of her children.

It was pretty hellish, really. By God, he thought, we're as hard as nails. He threw his pen down, shoved his chair back, and strolled to the window.

The people passed on the pavement, each for himself or herself, upright, straight as nails, straight as spikes.

He turned from them, looked at his watch, feeling weary and gloomy, and decided he might as well go home to lunch, though it was not yet ten minutes to one. Automatically taking the white towel from its nail on the far side of the cupboard, he went out to wash his hands.

Edward Gaitens

A WEE NIP

A Macdonnel party was nearly always an informal affair. Guests were never invited by card or telephone. They just 'got to know' and drifted in, irresistibly drawn by the prospect of free drink and uproarious song. John Macdonnel always insisted that there were people in the Gorbals who possessed second-sight in the matter of parties. Fellows like Squinty Traynor, Baldy, Flynn and bowleg-ged Rab Macpherson and ladies like wee Mrs Rombach, Tittering Tessie and wee Minnie Milligan – though why she always showed up at parties when she was a Rechabite and never touched a drop, he couldn't understand – could smell a wake or a wedding a mile off and always crept in at the exact moment when there was still plenty of drink going and everybody was too drunk to ask or care if they had been invited.

Sometimes the nucleus of a Macdonnel party was formed in the Ladies' Parlour of a local pub from which Mrs Macdonnel would emerge with some shawled cronies and confer on the pavement, deciding whether they should continue their tippling in another Ladies' Parlour or in one of their own kitchens. Owing to this erratic behaviour on the part of his wife, Mr Macdonnel oc-casionally returned from his day's work to find her absent – when he went round her friends' kitchens in search of her – or at home with several lady friends all jolly and mildly drunk. If he was hungry and in sober mood his icy glare sent all his wife's friends flying like snow in a wintry blast, but if he yearned for spirits he thawed and deferred his displeasure till the following morning when the mere thought of work was a nightmare to his aching head.

Every time Jimmy Macdonnel came home from sea there was a party and a few more after it till his pay of several months was burned right up. Even if Mrs Macdonnel had been six months teetotal, she couldn't resist taking one wee nip to celebrate her son's return and that wee nip somehow multiplied, had bairns, as she would laughingly tell you herself.

Returning from his last voyage before World War I, Jimmy Macdonnel, after a year's absence as cook on a tramp steamship, was the originator of a famous Macdonnel party. It was a bright July Saturday afternoon when Jimmy unexpectedly arrived. A delicious smell of Irish stew was still hanging around the Macdonnel kitchen. Mrs Macdonnel was a rare cook and Mr Macdonnel who loved her cooking had dropped into a smiling drowse, dazed by his enormous meal. At the open window Eddy Macdonnel was seated on the dishboard of the sink muttering to himself the Rules of Syntax out of an English Grammar, asking himself how it was that Donald Hamilton could repeat from memory whole pages of the Grammar and yet couldn't write a grammatical sentence, while he, who could hardly memorize a couple of Rules, could write perfect English with the greatest of ease. But he drove himself to the unpleasant exercise of memorizing, resisting the temptation to bask in the powerful sunshine and listen to the children playing at an old singing-game. 'The Bonny Hoose O' Airlie O'. The children were gathered near the backcourt washhouse, round the robber and his wife. First the little girl sang:

> 'Ah'll no' be a robber's wife,
> Ah'll no' die wi' your penknife
> Ah'll no' be a robber's wife
> Doon b' the bonny hoose o' Airlie, O.'

then the boy answered, taking her hand,

> 'Oh you sall be a robber's wife,
> An' ye'll die wi' my penknife
> You sall be a robber's wife
> Doon b' the bonny hoose o' Airlie, O.'

The old ballad tune seemed to come out of the heart of young Scotland, out of the childhood of his country's life. Eddy wanted to dream into that bygone poetry. Ach! He drove his mind again to memorizing the lesson for his night-school class. Mr Henderson, the English teacher, had a biting tongue for lazy students. He turned back the page, started again, and his muttered Rules mingled with the snores of his father and his mother's whispers as she sat at the table scribbling a shopping-list on a scrap of paper and continually pausing to count the silver in her purse.

Just then there was a knock at the stairhead door and Mrs Macdonnel, touching back her greying, reddish hair, rose in a fluster to open, exclaimed, 'My Goad, it's Jimmy!' and returned followed by a slim, dapper young man of twenty-nine, with bronzed features, in the uniform of a petty-officer of the Merchant Service and carrying a sailor's kitbag which he dumped on the floor.

'Did ye no' ken Ah was comin' hame the day?' he asked resentfully; 'Ah sent ye a postcard fae Marsels.'

'Och, no son!' said his mother, blaming in her heart those 'forrin' postcairds' which always bewildered her. 'Shure yer da would hiv come tae meet the boat. Ye said the twenty-seeventh,' and she began searching in a midget bureau on the dresser to prove her words, then she gazed mystified at the 'Carte Postale' with the view of Marseilles Harbour. 'Och, Ah'm haverin'!' she cried, 'it says here the seeventeenth!'

'Ach away! Ye're daft!' said Jimmy. 'How could ye mistake a "one" for a "two"?'

Mr Macdonnel woke up, rubbing his eyes, Eddy got down from the dishboard, closing his Grammar; and they all stared at Jimmy in silent wonder. He certainly looked trim as a yacht in his blue reefer suit, white shirt, collar and black tie, but they weren't amazed at his spruceness nor by his unexpected arrival but by the fact that he stood there as sober as a priest. For ten years Jimmy had been coming home from sea at varying intervals and had never been able to get up the stairs unassisted; and here he was, after á six months voyage, not even giving off a smell of spirits. Mr Macdonnel put on his glasses to have a better look at him. What was wrong with Jimmy? They wondered if he was ill, then the agonizing thought that he had been robbed occurred simultaneously to the old folk, and Jimmy was about to ask them what they were all looking at when his mother collected herself and embraced him and his father shook his hand, patting his shoulder.

Jimmy flushed with annoyance at his mother's sentiment as he produced from his kitbag a large plug of ship's tobacco for his da, a

Spanish shawl of green silk, with big crimson roses on it for his mother, and a coloured plaster-of-paris plaque of Cologne Cathedral for his Aunt Kate, then, blushing slightly, he took his seaman's book from his pocket and showed them the photograph of a young woman. 'That's Meg,' he said, 'Meg Macgregor. She's a fisher-girl. I met her at the herring-boats when ma ship called in at Peterhead.'

His mother was delighted with his taste and knew immediately why he had arrived sober. She passed the photograph to her husband, who beamed at it and said heartily, 'My, she's a stunner, Jimmy boy! A proper stunner! She'll create a sensation roun' here!' Mr Macdonnel usually awoke ill-tempered from his after-dinner naps, but his indigestion vanished like magic as he imagined the glorious spree they were going to have on Jimmy's six months' pay; and he swore he had never seen such a beautiful young woman as Meg Macgregor. Then Jimmy startled them all by announcing, as if he was forcing it out of himself: 'Meg's awfu' good-livin', mother, an' she's asked me tae stoap drinkin' for the rest o' ma life. Ah've promised her Ah will.'

Mr Macdonnel glared wildly at his son, then gave a sour look at the portrait and, handing it back without a word, rolled down his sleeves and pulled up his braces. He was dumbfounded. What had come over his son Jimmy? Teetotal for the rest of his life! Was he going to lose his head over that silly-faced girl? Mrs Macdonnel studied Jimmy with plaintive anxiety while he described Meg's beauty and goodness. 'Ach, she was made tae be adored b' everybody!' he said, and warned his mother to steer clear of the drink and keep her house in order to receive his beloved, whom he had invited to come and stay with the family.

His mother promised to love Meg as a daughter and silently hoped that the girl would stay at home. She was too old now to be bothered by a healthy young woman with managing ways. Jimmy swore he hadn't touched a drop since he had sailed from Peterhead and described the tortures of his two days' self-denial so vividly that his father shivered and hurried into the parlour to get his coat and vest. Jimmy said he was finished with the sea and booze; sick of squandering money. He was determined to settle on shore, get married, and spend all his money on Meg's happiness.

A miserly gleam beamed in his mother's eye when he said that and she wondered how much his new devotion would limit his contribution to her purse. Jimmy took a bundle of notes from his inside breast-pocket and handed her thirty pounds, reminding her that she had already drawn advance-sums from his shipping office. Mrs Macdonnel said he was too kind and offered to return five notes with a drawing-back movement, but Jimmy refused them with a bluff, insincere gesture, for there was a flash of regret in his eye as she tucked the wad in her purse, but, with genuine feeling he invited her and his da out to drink him welcome home. 'Ah'll have a lemonade,' he said, gazing piously at the ceiling as though at the Holy Grail. His mother thought he was being too harsh with himself. 'Shure ye'll hiv a wee nip wi' me an' yer da, son. A wee nip won't kill ye!' she laughed slyly, and Jimmy promised to drink a shandygaff just to please her, sighing with relief when he thought of the dash of beer in the lemonade. He called his father who came in from the parlour wrestling with a white dickey which he was trying to dispose evenly on his chest. 'Ah won't keep ye a jiffy, laddie!' he said, facing the mirror and fervently praying that the smell of the pub would restore poor Jimmy to his senses.

As she put on her old brown shawl Mrs Macdonnel was disappointed at Jimmy's insistence that they should go to an out-of-the-way pub. She wanted to show off her bonny son; he was so braw; so like a captain! She imagined the greetings they would get going down the long street.

'Ay, ye've won hame, Jimmy, boay? My, ye're lookin' fine, mun! Goash, ye oaght tae be a prood wumman the day, Mrs Macdonnel! Jimmy's a credit tae ye!' and she foretasted the old sweet thrill of envy and flattery. But Jimmy said he would never drink again with the corner-boys. Love had made a new man of him!

When they had all gone out Eddy Macdonnel hurried into the small side bedroom to read the book on PSYCHOLOGY AND MORALS he had borrowed from the Corporation Library. Inspired by Jimmy's miraculous conversion he crouched over the volume, concentrating fiercely on the chapters headed WILL POWER AND SIN, and his heart swelled with a reformer's zeal as he saw himself one day applying all these marvellous laws to the human race, hypnotizing countless millions of people into sobriety.

Three hours later he heard a loud clamour in the street below. Throwing his book on the bed he raised the window and looked over and his uplifted heart sank down, for he saw Jimmy stumbling happily up the street with his Aunt Kate's hat on his head and his arm round his father's neck. They were lustily singing 'The Bonny Lass O' Ballochmyle'. Mr Macdonnel's dickey was sticking out like the wings of a moulted swan and large bottles of whisky waggled from the pockets of the two men. Behind them, laughing like witches, came Mrs Macdonnel and Aunt Kate with the sailor's cap on, followed by six of Jimmy's pals who were carrying between them three large crates of bottled beer.

Eddy closed the window quickly and stared sadly at the wall. Jimmy, the idol of his dream, himself had shattered it! As he turned into the lobby, Jimmy opened the stairhead door and thrust his pals into the kitchen, which already seemed crowded with only two members of the family. John Macdonnel, now a fair young man of twenty-five, just home from overtime at the shipyards, leant in his oil-stained working clothes against the gas stove, reading about the Celtic and Rangers match in the Glasgow *Evening Times* and regretting that he had missed a hard-fought game which his team had won. With a wild 'whoopee' Jimmy embraced his brothers, who smiled with embarrassment. John was proud of Jimmy's prestige with the corner-boys, though he knew it was the worthless esteem for a fool and his money; Eddy saw Jimmy as a grand romantic figure, a great chef who had cooked for a millionaire on his yacht and had seen all the capital cities of the world, and Jimmy's kitbag, lying against a home-made stool by the dresser, stuffed with cook's caps and jackets, radiated the fascination of travel.

Aunt Kate, a tiny, dark woman of remarkable vitality, went kissing all her nephews in turn and the party got into full swing. Liquor was soon winking from tumblers, teacups, egg-cups – anything that could hold drink – and Aunt Kate, while directing the young men to bring chairs from the parlour, sang 'A Guid New Year Tae Ane an' A'', disregarding the fact that it was only summer-time, and Jimmy, thinking a nautical song was expected from him, sang 'A Life On The Ocean Wave!' in a voice as flat as stale beer that drowned his Aunt's pleasant treble. But somebody shouted that he sang as well as John McCormack and he sat down with a large tumbler of whisky, looking as if he thought so himself.

Then Aunt Kate told everybody about her marvellous meeting with Jimmy whose voice she had heard through the partition as she sat in the Ladies' Parlour in The Rob Roy Arms and Eddy learned how his brother had fallen. Jimmy, it appeared, felt he must toast Meg Macgregor in just one glass of something strong; that dash of beer in lemonade had infuriated his thirst and in a few minutes he had downed several glasses of the right stuff to his sweetheart, proving to his aunt's delight that he was still the same old jovial Jimmy.

John Macdonnel, all this while, was going to and fro, stumbling over out-thrust feet between the small bedroom and kitchen, sprucing himself up to go out and meet his girl. From feet to waist he was ready for love. His best brown trousers with shoes to match adorned his lower half, while his torso was still robed in a shirt blackened with shipyard oil and rust. He washed himself at the sink, laughing at his Aunt's story, then turned, drying himself, to argue with his mother about his 'clean change'. Mrs Macdonnel waved her cup helplessly, saying she couldn't help the indifference of laundrymen, and John implored Eddy to shoot downstairs and find if the family washing had arrived at the receiving-office of the Bonnyburn Laundries.

Visitors kept dropping in for a word with the sailor and delayed their departure while the drinks went round. Rumour had spread the report that Jimmy Macdonnel was home flush with money and a Macdonnel party was always a powerful attraction. The gathering was livening up. Two quart bottles of whisky had been absorbed and beer was frothing against every lip when Eddy returned triumphantly waving a big brown paper parcel in John's direction.

It was at the right psychological moment, when a slight lull in the merriment was threatening, that Rab Macpherson romped from his hiding-place in the doorway into the middle of the kitchen and suddenly burst out singing at the top of his voice:

> 'Le – et Kings an' courteers rise an' fa'
> This wurrld has minny turns,
> But brighter beams abune them a'
> The star o' Rabbie Burns!'

Rab's legs were very bow and wee Tommy Mohan, who was talking to his pal John Macdonnel at the sink, sunk down on his hunkers and gazed under his palm, like a sailor looking over the sea, away through Rab's legs all the time he was singing. Everybody was convulsed with laughter and Mrs Macdonnel was so pleased with Rab, that she got up, still laughing, and with her arm around his neck, gave him a good measure of whisky in a small cream jug.

Suddenly everybody fell silent to listen to Jimmy Macdonnel, who had been up since three that morning and half-asleep was trolling away to himself 'The Lass That Made The Bed For Me', and Mrs Steedman, a big-bosomed Orangewoman, startled the company by shouting, 'Good aul' Rabbie Burns! He ken't whit a wumman likes the maist!' There was a roar of laughter at this reminder of the poet's lechery, then Aunt Kate insisted that Mr Macdonnel should sing 'I Dreamt That I Dwelt In Marble Halls', while her sister, Mrs Macdonnel, asked him for 'The Meeting Of The Waters' because it reminded her of their honeymoon in Ireland. Mr Macdonnel, assisted by the table, swayed to his feet as pompously as Signor Caruso, twirled his moustache, stuck his thumbs behind his lapels, like the buskers of Glasgow backcourts, and 'hemmed' very loudly to silence the arguing sisters. He always sang with his eyes closed and when the gaslight shone on his glasses he looked like a man with four eyes, one pair shut, the other brilliantly open. He honestly believed he had a fine tenor voice and with swelled chest he bellowed:

> 'Yes! Let me like a soldier fall, upon some open plain!
> Me breast boldly bared to meet the ball
> That blots out every stain!'

The china shivered on the shelves above the dresser and Eddy Macdonnel, lost in some vision of bravery, stared with pride at his father. Halfway through the ballad, Mr Macdonnel forgot the words but sang on, 'tra-laing' here, pushing in his own words there, and sat down well satisfied to a din of handclaps and stamping feet.

Jimmy was blasted into wakefulness by his father's song and he washed himself sober and led out all the young men to help him buy more drink. When they returned, well-stocked, half an hour later, Mr Macdonnel had the whole crowd singing.

'I'll knock a hole in McCann for knocking a hole in me can!
McCann knew me can was new
I'd only had it a day or two,
I gave McCann me can to fetch me a pint of stout
An' McCann came running in an' said
That me can was running out!'

This was Mr Macdonnel's winning number at every spree and the refrain had echoed several times through the open windows to the street and backcourt before the young men returned. In the comparative silence of clinking bottles and glasses, Jimmy told his laughing guests of the night when he had served up beer in chamber-pots to a party of corner-boys. A dozen chamber-pots were arrayed round the table and twelve youths sat gravely before them while Jimmy muttered a Turkish grace over the beer and told them that was the way the Turks drank their drink and they believed him because he had been six times round the world.

When Aunt Kate had recovered from her delight in this story she asked Eddy to run up and see if her 'bonny wee man' was home from the gasworks. Eddy raced up to the top storey, knocked on a door, and started back as his uncle's gargoyle face thrust out at him and barked, 'Where's Katey? Am Oi a man or a mouse? B' the Holy Saint Pathrick Oi'll murther the lazy cow!' Eddy said faintly, 'Jimmy's home an' we're having a party. Will ye come down?' and Mr Hewes followed him downstairs muttering threats of vengeance on his wife for neglecting his tea.

The gathering had overflowed into the parlour when Eddy returned with the gasworker behind him; the lobby was crowded with newly-arrived guests listening to Aunt Kate singing 'The Irish Emigrant's Farewell'; the eyes of all the women were wet with film-star tears and the singer herself seemed to be seeing a handsome Irish youth as she looked straight at her husband standing in the kitchen doorway and returning her stare with a malignant leer. Aunt Kate filled a large cup with whisky from a bottle on the dresser and, still singing, handed it to him with a mock bow. On similar occasions Mr Hewes had been known to dash the cup from her hand and walk out and desert her for six months, but this time he seized it, swallowed the drink in one gulp, hitched up his belt and joined the party.

Eddy crushed a way through to his seat on the sink and watched his uncle, who, seated beside Mr Macdonnel, eyed with hostility every move of his popular wife. There was an excess of spite in Mr Hewes and he loved to hate people. Time, accident and ill-nature had ruined his face. A livid scar streamed from his thin hair down his right temple to his lip; his broken nose had reset all to one side, his few teeth were black and his little moustache as harsh as barbed wire; and with a blackened sweatrag round his neck he looked like a being from some underworld come to spy on human revels. He was called upon for a song when the applause for his wife had ended, and he stood up and roared, glaring at her:

> 'Am Oi a man, or am Oi a mouse
> Or am I a common artful dodger?
> Oi want to know who is master of my house!
> Is ut me or Micky Flanagan the lodger?'

Shouts of 'ongcore!' egged him on to sing the verse several times, his glare at his smiling wife intensifying with each repetition. He was suspected of having composed the song himself and the neighbours always knew he was going to desert his wife when he came up the stairs singing it. His whole body was humming like a dynamo after two large cups of Heather Dew and as his wife began chanting an old Irish jig he started to dance. Throwing off his jacket he roared 'B' Jasus!' tightened his belt and rolled up his sleeves, revealing thick leather straps round his wrists, and his hob-nailed boots beat a rapid deafening tattoo on the spot of floor inside the surrounding feet. His wife's chant became shriller and the whole company began clapping hands, stamping and yelling wild 'hoochs!' that drove the little gasworker to frenzy. John Macdonnel, all dressed to go out with a new bowler hat perched on his head, lifted a poker from the grate and thrust it into the dancer's hand. Mr Hewes tried to twirl it round his head between finger and thumb like a drum-major, then smashed it on the floor in passionate chagrin at his failure. 'B' Jasus Oi could dance ye'se all under the table!' he yelled, and with head and torso held stiff and arms working like pistons across his middle, he pranced like an enraged cockerel.

Faster he hopped from heel to heel, still packed with energy after a hard day shovelling in a hot atmosphere; sweat glistened on his grey hair and beaded his blackened cheeks; he twisted his feet in and out in awkward attempts at fancy steps and looked as if he would fly asunder in his efforts to beat the pace of his accompanists; then, with a despairing yell of 'B' Jasus!' he stopped suddenly, gasped, 'Och, Oi 'm bate!' and hurled dizzily behind foremost into his chair.

It was a hefty piece of furniture but it couldn't stand up to his violence; with a loud crack its four legs splayed out and the gasworker crashed like a slung sack into the hearth, smashing the polished plate-shelf sticking out beneath the oven; his head struck heavily the shining bevel of the range; the snapped chair-back lay over his head, and there was a roar of laughter which stopped when he was seen to lie still among the wreckage.

His wife and Mr Macdonnel bent over him, but he pushed them away, staggered erect and, shaking himself like a dog after a fight, snatched and swallowed the cup of whisky which Mrs Macdonnel had poured quickly for him while looking ruefully at her shattered chair and plate-shelf. The blow had hardly affected him and, as Mrs Hewes anxiously examined his head, he pushed her rudely aside, shouting, 'B' Jasus! Oi'll give ye'se "The Enniskillen's Farewell"!' and he roared boastfully the Boer War song of an Irish regiment's departure. Suddenly he realized that attention was diverted from him; someone in the packed lobby was crying, 'Here's Big Mary! Make way for Blind Mary!' and Mr Hewes, grasping his jacket from Mr Macdonnel's hand, slung it across his shoulder, stared malignantly at everyone and pushed uncivilly out of the house.

The Widow Loughran, who was being guided in by Jerry Delaney and his wife, was a magnificent Irishwoman, well over six feet, round about forty, and round about considerably more at waist and bosom. The habit of raising the head in the manner of the blind made her appear taller and gave her a haughty look, but she was a jolly, kind woman in robust health, and her rosy face and glossy, jet hair, her good-humoured laughter, caused one to forget her blindness. Blind Mary was the wonder of the Gorbals. She drank hard and regularly and stood it better than the toughest men. 'Mary's never up nor doon,' they said, and she boasted that she had never known a 'bad moarnin'' in her life. She also wore a tartan shoulder-shawl of the Gordon clan, a widow's bonnet, and a bright print apron over her skirt. Mrs Macdonnel led her to a seat and she stood up, her hands searching around for Jerry Delaney when she heard there wasn't a chair for him. He was pushed into her arms and she pulled him into a tight embrace on her ample knees. Mr Delaney, popularly known as 'One-Eyed Jerry' since a flying splinter, at his work as a ship's carpenter, had deprived him of his right eye, was no light weight, but Mary handled him like a baby, and Mrs Macdonnel shrieked with laughter: 'Blind Mary's stole yer man, Bridget!' and Mrs Delaney, a dark beauty of five-and-thirty, laughed back, 'Ach away! She's welcome tae him! Shure they're weel matched wi' yin eye atween them!' This so tickled Mary and Jerry that they almost rolled on the floor with helpless laughter, and Mrs Macdonnel looked very worried, expecting every minute to see another of her chairs smashed to smithereens.

Aunt Kate had vanished in pursuit of her man and returned at this moment, pale with anger, to announce publicly that he had skedaddled, but that she would set the police at his heels and make him support her; then she sang in her sweetest voice, 'O My Love Is Like A Red, Red Rose!' followed by a delicate rendering of 'Ae Fond Kiss'. But no one was surprised by her instant change from wrath to tenderness, except young Eddy, who felt that this was his most profitable 'psychological' evening as he watched Blind Mary with her hands boldly grasping Mr Delaney's thighs and began excitedly composing an essay on 'Psychology And The Blind' for his night-school class.

Someone called for a song from Blind Mary, and One-Eyed Jerry courteously handed her to her feet. She stood dominating the whole room, protesting that she couldn't sing a note, but everyone cried: 'Strike up, Mary! Ye sing like a lark!' and she began singing 'Bonny Mary O' Argyle' to the unfailing amazement of young Eddy, who could never understand why her voice that was so melodious in speech was so hideous when she sang. In his boyhood Eddy had always loved to see her in the house, finding a strange sense of comfort in her strength and cheerful vitality. Coming in from school his heart had always rippled with delight to see her gossiping and drinking with his mother and some neighbours. Her rich brogue always welcomed him, 'Ach, it's me wee Edward. Come here, ye darlin'!' and there was always a penny or sixpenny bit for him, hot from her fat hand, or a bag of sweets, warm from her placket-pocket, their colours blushing through the paper. He enjoyed the strong smell of snuff from her soft fingers when they fondled his hair or read his face and the smell of her kiss, scented with whisky or beer, had never repelled him.

Mary had only sung two lines, when she was sensationally interrupted by Bridget Delaney, who suddenly leapt from her feet and shrieked indignantly: 'Ach, don't talk tae me about legs! Is there a wumman in this house has a better leg than meself? Tae hell wi' Bonny Mary O' Argyle! I'll show ye'se the finest leg on the South Side this night!' and she bent and pulled her stocking down her left leg to the ankle, whipped up her blue satinette skirt and pulled up a blue leg of bloomer so fiercely that she revealed a handsome piece of behind. 'There ye are!' cried Bridget, holding forth her leg. 'Ah defy a wumman among ye'se tae shake as good a wan!'

Blind Mary stood silent and trembling in a strange listening attitude, thinking a fight had begun, and everyone was astounded. Jerry Delaney, blushing with shame, plucked nervously at his bedfellow's skirt, but Bridget pulled it up more tightly and shouted: 'Awa'! Ye've seen it oaften enough! Are ye ashamed o' it?' while Jerry told her he had always said she had the finest leg in Glasgow and acted as if he had never beheld such a distressing sight. Beside them a very dozy youth gazed dully at Bridget's fat, white thigh, and from the rose-wreathed wallpaper Pope Pius X, in a cheap print, looked sternly at the sinful limb.

Mrs Macdonnel hurried her hysterical sister-in-law into the small bedroom, and the only comment on the incident was, 'Blimey! Wot a lark!' from Mrs Bills. Blind Mary asked excitedly what had happened. Some of the ladies, while affecting shocked modesty, trembled with desire to take up Bridget's challenge; but no one could have explained her hysteria, except, perhaps, Mr Delaney. His one eye always glowed with admiration for a fine woman and he had gazed warmly all evening at Blind Mary. But Bridget's astonishing behaviour was superseded for the moment by the arrival of Wee Danny Quinn 'wi' his melodyin'', whom Jimmy Macdonnel himself introduced as the guest of honour.

The street-musician, a pug-nosed, dwarfish Glaswegian, bow-legged and very muscular, drank two large glasses of whisky, wiped his lips and began playing. The mother-o'-pearl keys of his big Lombardi piano-accordion flashed in the gaslight as his fingers danced skilfully among them, and while he leant his ear to the instrument, his little dark eyes looked up with a set smile, like a leprechaun listening to the earth. He played jigs and reels and waltzes; all the furniture in the kitchen was pushed to the wall and all who could find room to crush around were soon dancing through the lobby and back again.

It was late in the night, when the dancers had paused for refreshment, that Willie McBride the bookmaker, a six-foot red-headed Highlandman, suddenly reappeared arm-in-arm with his wife, he dressed in her clothes and she in his. They had disappeared for fifteen minutes and effected the change with the connivance of Aunt Kate, who slipped them the key of her house. Mr McBride had somehow managed to crush his enormous chest into the blouse of his slim wife; between it and the skirt, his shirt looked out, and from the edge of the skirt, which reached his knees, his thick, pink woollen drawers were visible; Mrs McBride, drowned in his suit, floundered, bowing to the delighted company.

This wild whim of the McBrides heated everyone like an aphrodisiac, and very soon Aunt Kate's but-an'-ben became the dressing-room for the transformation of several ladies and gentlemen. The two Delaneys exchanged clothes and Bridget showed to advantage her splendid legs swelling out her husband's trousers; Aunt Kate retired with a slight youth and reappeared in his fifty-shilling suit as the neatest little man of the evening; then Mrs Macdonnel walked in disguised as her husband, even to his glasses and cap, and was followed by him gallantly wearing the Spanish shawl, in which, after filling out his wife's blouse with two towels, he danced what he imagined was a Spanish dance and sang a hashed-up version of the 'Toreador Song' from *Carmen*.

Danny Quinn's playing became inspired and his volume majestic as he laughed at the dressed-up couples dancing around. The house was throbbing like a battered drum when heavy thumps shook the stairhead door. 'It's the polis,' cried everyone with amused alarm. Mrs Macdonnel rushed to open and a soft Irish voice echoed along the lobby: 'Ye'se'll have to make less noise. The nayburs is complainin'!'

'Ach, come awa in, Tarry, an' have a wee deoch-an'-doris!' cried Mrs Macdonnel, holding the door wide for the portly constable who stood amazed at her masculine garb, while Willie McBride was roaring, 'Do Ah hear me aul' freend Boab Finnegan? Come ben an' have a drink, man! Shure you an' me's had many a dram when yer inspector wisnae lookin'!' and Mrs Macdonnel conducted into the parlour Police-Officer Finnegan followed by a tall, young Highland officer, a novice in the Force, with finger at chin-strap and a frown of disapproval. The two policemen were welcomed with full glasses, and Mr Finnegan, known all over The Gorbals as 'Tarry Bob' because his hair and big moustache were black as tar and his heavy jowls became more saturnine with every shave he had, surveyed the strange gathering with a clownish smile, while Mr McBride, the street bookie, told the company how often he had dodged the Law by giving Tarry Bob a friendly drink.

In five minutes both policemen sat down and laid their helmets on the sideboard among the numerous bottles and fifteen minutes later they had loosened their tunics and were dancing with the ladies, their heavy boots creating a louder rumpus than they had come to stop.

Eddy Macdonnel stood in the crowded lobby craning his head over to watch the lively scene. After a long while he heard his mother say to Tarry Bob, who was protesting he must go: 'Och, hiv another wee nip! Shure a wee nip won't kill ye!' then he saw the good-natured policeman drench himself in beer as he put on his helmet into which some playful guest had emptied a pint bottle.

Eddy's wits were staggering. 'Human behaviour' had muddled his understanding, and he mooned bewildered into the kitchen where Jimmy sat half-asleep with a glass of whisky trembling in his bronzed hand, while opposite him sat a youth gazing in agony at the glass, expecting to see the darlin' drink spilled on the floor.

Eddy took Jimmy's glass and placed it on the mantelshelf, then picked up a postcard that lay face downward on the floor. It was the picture of Meg Macgregor. He had fallen in love with the picture himself and he looked at it again through sentimental eyes that saw her average prettiness as dazzling beauty. He had been nerving himself to ask Jimmy if he had a photo of her to spare and was awaiting with adolescent impatience her sensational arrival. 'Ye've dropped Meg's photo,' he said, holding it up to Jimmy's wavering stare. The sailor thrust it aside. 'Take it away!' he said. 'Her face scunners me!'

'But it's Meg!' Eddy said. 'Meg Macgregor. The girl ye're bringing home to marry!'

' "Take her away!" I said,' cried Jimmy with a royal wave of the hand. 'There's nae wumman 'll run ma life for me!' The youth sitting by the table nodded his approval, then stood up and quickly drank off Jimmy's whisky.

Eddy studied his brother for a moment, desperately failing to remember some part of his book on psychology that would explain Jimmy's sudden jaundiced dismissal of Meg Macgregor. Then he drifted solemnly into the lobby, opened the stairhead door and wandered slowly down to the close-mouth. His confused head was ringing with a medley of folk-songs and music-hall choruses and his heart held the streams and hills and the women of the poetry of Robert Burns. He was thinking of Jeannie Lindsay and wishing he might find her standing at her close in South Wellington Street. But it was very late. He hurried round the corner in a queer, emotional tangle of sexual shame and desire, his romantic thoughts of Jeannie mingled with the shameful memory of his mother and the women dressing up in men's clothes and Bridget Delaney pulling up her skirts to her hips to show her bare legs to the men.

Naomi Mitchison

IN THE FAMILY

It was in the family to be seeing things that are not meant to be seen. And it was not nice for them, not at all. They could have done without seeing the most of what they saw. Mostly all of them had seen the Lights, one way and another, and his mother had seen the Funeral itself coming round the head of the glen, and fine she knew the Bearers, and the Corpse she could guess, and sure enough that was how it was before the week was out, but she herself was sick in her bed for the whole day after it.

If you go far enough back, there was his grandfather's uncle that was a great piper, and he was coming back over the hills from a wedding at the far side. It was a good-going wedding, the way they were in those days, and it had lasted all of four nights, and they would not have been sparing of the whisky for their pipers. And as he was coming back by Knocnashee, the fairies came out from the hill and asked would he come in a whilie and pipe for them. And he would have done it sure enough, for the whisky had made him as bold as a robin, but he was just too drunk to do justice to his own pipes, so he said he would come to them another day. He never did, and indeed, he died in his bed. But he was in a terrible fear all his life afterwards in case they would mind on what he had said. And there was a kind of fear on all the family, in case it might be remembered on one of them, and he would need to keep the promise of the old piper.

His father had a young sister, Janet, a terrible bonny lassie she was, with a high colour on her. But there was a thing went wrong and the doctor could not say right what it was, so he was for sending her to the hospital in Glasgow. Well then, the evening before she was to go, she was walking up by the old well, and who should she see but the fairy woman. And the fairy woman warned her and better warned her not to go to the hospital, walking beside her all the while without movement of her feet, the way it is with the fairy folk. And the lassie came back and she was gey put about and she said she would not go. So they sent for the doctor to tell him of it, but he was wild affronted and said he had it all arranged and go she must or the great doctors in Glasgow would have his head off. So the lassie grat and her mother grat, but the end of it was they could not go against the doctor, and the poor lassie went to the hospital and died there.

So the rest of them said to themselves that if ever they were to get a warning they would bide by it. But for long enough it did not come. His father, Donald MacMillan, had a wee glimpse of the fairies one time; he was under-keeper at the Castle and he was coming back in the early morning from setting his traps on the hill and as he came down by the back road the fairies were riding round the castle, wee dark folk on white ponies with a glitter of gold on the bridle. But he held his tongue about it, for it is not an under-keeper's place to be seeing the fairies belonging to the castle ones. And he did not like it, no, not at all, and after that he volunteered for the Army, and it was ten years before he came back.

But Angus himself had seen not a thing. And he was apt to say there was nothing at all in it, and when his sister Effie came back from a dance one night in a terrible fright and saying that a ghost had walked with her all the way from the cross-roads, he was not believing her. For the thing is this. You may know well enough that something has happened. But, gin the Kirk is against it, and the schools, and the newspapers and the wireless forby, you will find it hard enough to believe your own eyes and ears. And the other thing is, that, with yon kind of sights, it is never the same twice. I will see a thing one way and you will see it another, but maybe it is the same in itself. Yet it might be the Ministers are in the right of it and we should not be speaking of such things at all.

But, however that may be, Angus was a well-doing laddie. He was driving one of the Forestry lorries and he cared for his lorry the same as it was a horse. He was for ever cleaning and oiling it and putting in a wee thing here or there and never once did he have an accident on the road. And he was a Church member and in the choir and he was not drinking scarcely at all except maybe now and then, and he was going with a lassie that was in the choir too, and she was in the alto line and he was in the tenor. And not one of the family had seen an unchancy thing for years now, and his sister Effie married and with three bairns and indeed she was inclined to laugh at the story of her own ghost now. For it had mistaken her surely, the poor thing, since all it had been after from her was the lend of a horse and cart, and it turned out afterwards that it was an old soul from one of the crofts at the head of the glen and he had died more than a year back and terrible put about over this same thing and so he had needed to come back.

He had the Gaelic, had Angus, not so as to read excepting it might be some easy kind of song, but well enough to speak a bit and to know what was said to him. This was mostly because his father and mother would be speaking the Gaelic to one another across the table the way the bairns would not be understanding them, and Angus was that angry at this when he was a wee fellow that he started to learn the Gaelic out of pure devilment to know what his elders would be saying.

Well, the choir had been practising all winter and the time came when they were to go over and give a concert in aid of the church funds at Auchandrum, and there was to be a dance after. They would hire a bus and it would be just fine, with all the folk singing away to pass the time on the road and going back with the lassies, and indeed Angus was mostly sure that Peigi MacLean – for that was his lassie's name – would be sitting beside him at the back, though she would not promise.

Then it came on to two days before, and Angus had finished up and parked his lorry at the saw-mill with a tarpaulin over her, and he was taking the short cut home through the larches and by the old well that nobody went to now, since there was a fine new County Council water supply at that side of the village and some of the houses with bathrooms even. There was a woman sitting by the side of the well and at first he thought she was a summer visitor and maybe a painter or that, the way she had a long green cloak of an old-fashioned kind that our own womenfolk would never be wearing. But as he came nearer she stood, and he saw that she was going to speak to himself and a kind of uneasiness came at him that got suddenly worse when she spoke to him by name and that in the Gaelic. So he got a grip on the monkey wrench that he was taking back to the house and he answered her and she began to walk by his side and he saw that there was no movement of her feet under the green cloak and for a while he could not anyways listen to what she was saying, with the blood pouring in spate through him and the sweat standing out on his forehead and the greatest fear on him lest she should reach out her hand and touch his own.

But after a whilie it came to him that she was speaking about the choir and their journey to Auchandrum and she was warning him, that he must not, above all, let Peigi go on the bus, or there would be no happiness for him all his life long. And he tried wild to speak, but he could not get his mouth round the words for a time. At last he said in the Gaelic: 'How are you telling me this, woman of the Sidhe?'

She said: 'It is because of the friendship between ourselves and your grandfather's uncle that was a good piper and a kindly man, drunk or sober, and I am telling you for your great good, Angus, son of Donald.'

So he said: 'How will I know if it is true?'

She smiled, and some way it was a sweet smile, but far off, since she had the face and body of a young lassie, yet her look was that of an old, old woman, beyond love or hate. She said: 'I will show a sign on the thing you hold in your hand, and believe you me, Angus!'

And he looked full into her eyes, for the fear was beginning to leave him, but as he did that he began to see the young larches behind her on the hillside, and in a short while it was clear through her he was looking and nothing at all to show where she had been, only the sweat cold on his face. So he went home and said nothing, and his mother brought in the tea, and suddenly she laughed and asked him what kind of a job at all had he been doing on his lorry, for there was the monkey-wrench lying over on the press, and it was wreathed round with the bonny wild honeysuckle.

Well, he thought and he better thought, and he worked the talk round till his mother began to speak of her good sister Janet, who had not been let take the warning, but had died in the Glasgow hospital, and he thought it would be a wild thing if the like of thon were to happen to his own lassie through his fault. So when he had washed he went over to the choir practice and there sure enough was Peigi. So on the way back he was speaking to her, begging her not to go to the concert. But she was not listening to him at all, for she thought he was on for some kind of devilment and she said goodnight to him, kind of sharp.

Well, the next day he was hashing and fashing away at it and in the evening again he went over to Peigi's folks' house and he got the talk round to warnings, so that she would be prepared, and then, as she was seeing him to the gate, he told her how it had been. Well, she was terrible put about and at first she was not believing him, and then she was, but she had her dance dress washed and ironed and what would the rest of the lasses say? And there could be nothing in it and nobody believed in such blethers nowadays. And the more Angus pled and swat, the more reasons Peigi was finding not to be heeding him at all and the more she needed to say to herself that he had maybe been drinking and if she were to do what he asked, all the folk would be speaking of it and she was not to be made a clown of by Angus or any other lad, and it would be a great dance after the concert and was Angus not coming to be her partner?

'If you go, I will go, Peigi,' said Angus, 'for if there is a danger coming to you, I would soonest be there.'

So he went to his bed and he tried to tell himself that none of this was real; but it was beyond him not to believe, and indeed in his sleeping he was seeing the fairy woman just as plain, and she speaking to him again. And in the morning it was on him wild to keep Peigi from the concert, yet all the forenoon he could not think of a way. But towards four he was taking back the lorry empty to the saw-mill and he saw Peigi on the road going for a message for her mother. He cried on her to come up beside him and he would give her a lift along, and up she came. But when he got to the cross-roads he put on speed and swung his lorry round and up the glen. 'What in God's name are you up to, Angus!' said Peigi, and held on tight.

'I am taking you away from the concert,' said Angus, and he did not look at her, but only at the road ahead of him.

'Well then, I will scream!' said Peigi.

'It will not help you any,' said Angus, 'and maybe least said is soonest mended. And indeed I am terribly sorry, Peigi, but it is on me to do this. And you had best not try to snatch at the steering wheel, Peigi, for I would need to hit you and I amna wanting to.'

So Peigi sat as far as she could from him in the cab of the lorry, and they never passed another car, but only an old farm cart or so, and Angus hooted and put on all speed and there was nothing she could do, and by and by she cried a little because she was thinking of the dance dress and the nice evening she would be missing, and what in all the world could she say to the rest of the choir?

But Angus was watching his petrol gauge. He was ten miles out of the village now, and he swung round on to a side road that went up past the common grazing towards some old quarries. There would be no chance of Peigi hailing a car and getting a lift back on a road the like of this. And they went bumping up along the old tracks and it was near six and the bus would be starting for Auchandrum in half an hour. At last he stopped the lorry at the mouth of one of the quarries and he said: 'I am that spited, Peigi, but I know well I am in the right of it.'

Peigi said nothing and when he tried to come near her she snatched herself away. So there they sat and no pleasure in it for either of them, but well they knew what would be said of them in the village. And forby that, Angus was thinking how it would be when he did not bring his lorry back to the saw-mill. He liked his job with the Forestry fine, but this way he would be leaving it with no good character. And the more he thought, the blacker things looked ahead of him, and sudden he began to wonder if the fairy woman had played a trick on him. And it was a terrible thought, yon.

So he started up his engine again and he backed and turned and came down cannily in second and Peigi beside him as cross as a sack of weasels. 'Will you no' speak to me at all, Peigi?' he asked, as they came out into the glen road down towards the village.

'I will never speak to you again!' she said, and a terrible hurt feeling came over his heart and he hated the fairy woman and the warning and all the two days and nights of it. So that way they came down to the village. 'Do you not take me to the house!' said Peigi suddenly, 'leave you me here and maybe – och, maybe they'll not know and there could be time to think of a thing to say!'

He stopped the lorry and jumped out to help her down, but she had jumped clear, and when he came to her she gave a cry and started to run down the road. So he did not follow until she was out of sight and he knew she would take the back road by old Donnie's hen house.

As he came down to the post office he saw a ring of folk round the telephone kiosk and his own brother cried on him to stop and he jumped out. 'Is it yourself, Angus!' his brother shouted and seized him by the two hands and there were tears streaming out of his eyes and then he said, 'Did Peigi go with the choir?'

'She did not,' said Angus and there was her father shaking him by the hands as well, and it all came out there had been an accident to the bus and three or four folk hurt bad and mostly all cut with the glass and they had just heard it on the telephone, but they werena just sure who was on it. And Angus found himself going off into a wild silly kind of laughing and he could not stop himself any. So he got back into the lorry and drove off to the saw-mill and parked her, and then he started to clean her and polish her, for he did not know what the Forester would say, and he might be getting his books and he might never be back in the cab of his lorry.

Sure enough, while he was at it, up came the Forester, for he had been terrible put about when Angus MacMillan never brought in the lorry, and he mostly so dependable, and the Forester had his own bosses over him. 'So this is you at last!' said the Forester. 'And what have you to say?'

But Angus found no words for he could not begin to speak of a fairy woman. At last he kicked at the tyre of the lorry and said: 'I am terrible sorry, Duncan, and I have not hurt her any, and – and I will pay for the petrol.'

'I will need to think what to do about this,' said the Forester, 'for I cannot have such a carry-on with my lorries. I will see you in the morning.' So Angus said never a word, but home he went, and his own folk speaking about nothing but the accident and the lucky he was to be out of it. They knew that Peigi MacLean had not been in it, but they did not know yet that she had been with him. One of his chums had a leg broken, and another was bleeding from his inside and the doctor up with him, and Peigi's young sister had a terrible nasty cut on her head and it was a wonder nobody was killed. Angus went off to his bed and he was terrible tired, but some way he could not sleep. And at least he said to himself, it was a true warning, and I took it, and the fairy has not tricked me. So he got out of his bed and felt for his flash, and he walked around in his shirt looking for any one thing that was worth giving as a gift. And there seemed to be nothing. For what would a fairy do with the set of cuff links he won at the Nursing Association raffle or the printed letter that had come with his Welcome Home money or the bottle of port he was saving up for Effie's new bairn's christening, or his good boots, even? But at last he came on a thing and it was a wee kind of medal that his father had worn at his watch chain and his father before him, and it might have belonged to the piper for that matter. He did not know was it silver or not and he gave it a rub on his sleeve. And he went out in his bare feet, and his shirt blowing round his legs, and up to the well, and the queer thing was he kind of half wanted to see the fairy woman, but there was no breath at all of her. So he threw the wee medal into the well and he stood and he said a kind of half prayer, and he came stumbling back down the path with the stones sore on his feet, but after that he slept as quiet as a herring in a barrel.

But the next morning he went down to the saw-mill and the Forester sent for him to his wee office with the papers and the telephone and the bundles of axes and saw blades. But still he could say nothing, and after a time the Forester said in an angry kind of way that if he had no excuse then he was sacked. But at that Angus had to speak and out it came, the whole story, and halfway through the Forester got up and shut the door of his office. At the end he said: 'There is folks that would shut you up in the Asylum for the like of yon, Angus.'

'But it is not touched I am!' said Angus anxiously.

'I know plenty that would think it,' said the Forester. 'So it was a green cloak she was wearing, yon one? Aye, aye. It is fortunate altogether that you have the Gaelic. But I am wondering wild what would the Minister say.'

'You will not tell him, Duncan!' said Angus. But he knew that the Minister was no great favourite with the Forester, on account he had complained that the noise of the saw-mill was stopping him from composing his sermons, and everyone in the place knew that the half of them came out of books.

The Forester said nothing to this, and Angus stood first on one foot and then on the other. At last the Forester said: 'Are you for marrying Peigi?'

'I am, surely,' said Angus, 'but I am no' just so sure of herself. I amna sure if she will speak to me, even.'

'Well,' said the Forester, 'you had better be asking her and that way you will keep this story in the one family and maybe it will stay quietest so, for it doesna do to be speaking of such things.'

'I just darena ask her and that it is the truth,' said Angus.

'Well,' said the Forester, 'if you are marrying Peigi MacLean I will overlook this and keep you on, but if you havena the courage, then you can take your books and off with you and best if you go away out of the place altogether.' And Angus went stumbling out the door of the wee office, and the Forester took two new axe heads out of the store and checked them off.

Word had got about of how Angus and Peigi had passed the evening of the concert, and Angus getting plenty from his mates of what could be done with a nice lassie in the cab of a lorry or in the back of it even, and they all thinking it was for badness he had taken her away and kind of half proud of him. But the accident to the bus had more to it, so the talk went over to that, and glad enough was Angus.

After his tea he went over to the MacLeans' house, and there was father MacLean staking his peas, and Angus asked after Peigi's sister, and the district nurse was in with her, and then he spoke of the great growth on the peas. At last old MacLean said: 'What is this I hear about yourself and Peigi, Angus Mac-Millan?'

Angus said: 'It is true enough she came for a drive in my lorry, but it wasna for anything bad.'

'You are telling me that,' said old MacLean and he began to fill his pipe, 'but you were away for three hours and what could you find to be speaking about? So I must ask you, what were you doing?'

'I was driving the lorry mostly,' said Angus, 'and Peigi wasna speaking to me, she was that cross.'

'Then I will ask you, why did you drive the lorry with my daughter in it?'

Then Angus cleared his throat and said in a kind of loud voice: 'I had a warning that Peigi was not to go with the choir.'

Mr MacLean said nothing for a time, but scraped his boot on the edge of a spade and puffed away at his pipe, and at last he said:

'I was hearing just that. And she would have been killed, likely, if she had been in the bus.'

'I was thinking so,' said Angus in a half whisper. For she would have been next to her sister and most likely on the outside next to the glass. And then the District Nurse came out of the house and said cheerily that the lassie was going on fine, and now she must be off to the others and what a carry-on she was having with them all. And she started her wee car and drove off.

'Well, well,' said Mr MacLean, 'it is in your family to be seeing things. And things are mostly unchancy. But this time it was the great chance for my own lassie. Aye, aye. You will be wanting to see Peigi, likely?'

'It is what I would like most in the world,' said Angus, 'but –'

'Well, come you in,' said Mr MacLean, 'and we will say no more over this matter of the warning.' They went into the house together. Peigi was there, washing her sister's frock that had been spoilt a bit. Her father said: 'I will go through and see your sister.'

Peigi went on slapping and scrubbing away at the dress, letting on she did not see there was a soul there.

After a time Angus said: 'Are you speaking to me, Peigi?'

'Ach well –' she said, 'I might.'

'Duncan was at me over me taking the lorry,' said Angus.

'Was he now? And I am sure he was quite right. You should not be taking things without leave.'

'He spoke the way he might be giving me my books, Peigi.'

Peigi let the frock fall back into the lather. 'The dirty clown! How could he do that on you?'

'Well,' said Angus, 'he was only kind of half believing me, maybe. If he were to believe me right I am thinking there would be nothing said. Ach, Peigi, he would believe me if he thought I had done it because I loved you true! He was asking were you and I to be married, Peigi. But I was saying I daredna ask you.'

'How?' she said.

'Och well, if you hadna been speaking to me, it would have been kind of difficult, Peigi.'

Peigi was flicking the suds off her fingers. She said into the air: 'Isn't it wild now, to think of the nice time we could have been having on the hillside and we just ourselves, if only you had explained the thing right to me at the first!'

'Indeed and I did my best!' said Angus.

'Aye, but I was not knowing then that the bus would have this accident, and how would anyone with a grain of sense believe you, Angus? But we will not speak any more of this warning nor anything to do with it, beccause I am thinking we will have plenty else to speak about.'

Eric Linklater

SEALSKIN TROUSERS

I am not mad. It is necessary to realize that, to accept it as a fact about which there can be no dispute. I have been seriously ill for some weeks, but that was the result of shock. A double or conjoint shock: for as well as the obvious concussion of a brutal event, there was the more dreadful necessity of recognizing the material evidence of a happening so monstrously implausible that even my friends here, who in general are quite extraordinarily kind and understanding, will not believe in the occurrence, though they cannot deny it or otherwise explain – I mean explain away – the clear and simple testimony of what was left.

I, of course, realized very quickly what had happened, and since then I have more than once remembered that poor Coleridge teased his unquiet mind, quite unnecessarily in his case, with just such a possibility; or impossibility, as the world would call it. 'If a man could pass through Paradise in a dream,' he wrote, 'and have a flower presented to him as a pledge that his soul had really n there, and if he found that flower in his hand when he awoke – Ay, and what then?'

But what if he had dreamt of Hell and wakened with his hand burnt by the fire? Or of Chaos, and seen another face stare at him from the looking-glass? Coleridge does not push the question far. He was too timid. But I accepted the evidence, and while I was ill I thought seriously about the whole proceeding, in detail and in sequence of detail. I thought, indeed, about little else. To begin with, I admit, I was badly shaken, but gradually my mind cleared and my vision improved, and because I was patient and persevering – that needed discipline – I can now say that I know what happened. I have indeed, by a conscious intellectual effort, *seen and heard* what happened. This is how it began . . .

How very unpleasant! she thought.

She had come down the great natural steps on the seacliff to the ledge that narrowly gave access, round the angle of it, to the western face which today was sheltered from the breeze and warmed by the afternoon sun. At the beginning of the week she and her fiancé, Charles Sellin, had found their way to an almost hidden shelf, a deep veranda sixty feet above the white-veined water. It was rather bigger than a billiard-table and nearly as private as an abandoned lighthouse. Twice they had spent some blissful hours there. She had a good head for heights, and Sellin was indifferent to scenery. There had been nothing vulgar, no physical contact, in their bliss together on this oceanic gazebo, for on each occasion she had been reading Héaloin's *Studies in Biology* and he Lenin's *What is to be Done?*

Their relations were already marital, not because their mutual passion could brook no pause, but rather out of fear lest their friends might despise them for chastity and so conjecture some oddity or impotence in their nature. Their behaviour, however, was very decently circumspect, and they already conducted themselves, in public and out of doors, as if they had been married for several years. They did not regard the seclusion of the cliffs as an opportunity for secret embracing, but were content that the sun should warm and colour their skin; and let their anxious minds be soothed by the surge and cavernous colloquies of the sea. Now, while Charles was writing letters in the little fishing-hotel a mile away, she had come back to their sandstone ledge, and Charles would join her in an hour or two. She was still reading *Studies in Biology*.

But their gazebo, she perceived, was already occupied, and occupied by a person of the most embarrassing appearance. He was quite unlike Charles. He was not only naked, but obviously robust, brown-hued, and extremely hairy. He sat on the very edge of the rock, dangling his legs over the sea, and down his spine ran a ridge of hair like the dark stripe on a donkey's back, and on his shoulder-blades grew patches of hair like the wings of a bird. Unable in her disappointment to be sensible and leave at once, she lingered for a moment and saw to her relief that he was not quite naked. He wore trousers of a dark brown colour, very low at the waist, but sufficient to cover his haunches. Even so, even with that protection for her modesty, she could not stay and read biology in his company.

To show her annoyance, and let him become aware of it, she made a little impatient sound; and turning to go, looked back to see if he had heard.

He swung himself round and glared at her, more angry on the instant than she had been. He had thick eyebrows, large dark eyes, a broad snub nose, a big mouth. 'You're Roger Fairfield!' she exclaimed in surprise.

He stood up and looked at her intently. 'How do you know?' he asked.

'Because I remember you,' she answered, but then felt a little confused, for what she principally remembered was the brief notoriety he had acquired, in his final year at Edinburgh University, by swimming on a rough autumn day from North Berwick to the Bass Rock to win a bet of five pounds.

The story had gone briskly round the town for a week, and everybody knew that he and some friends had been lunching, too well for caution, before the bet was made. His friends, however, grew quickly sober when he took to the water, and in a great fright informed the police, who called out the lifeboat. But they searched in vain, for the sea was running high, until in calm water under the shelter of the Bass they saw his head, dark on the water, and pulled him aboard. He seemed none the worse for his adventure, but the police charged him with disorderly behaviour and he was fined two pounds for swimming without a regulation costume.

'We met twice,' she said, 'once at a dance and once in Mackie's when we had coffee together. About a year ago. There were several of us there, and we knew the man you came in with. I remember you perfectly.'

He stared the harder, his eyes narrowing, a vertical wrinkle dividing his forehead. 'I'm a little short-sighted too,' she said with a nervous laugh.

'My sight's very good,' he answered, 'but I find it difficult to recognize people. Human beings are so much alike.'

'That's one of the rudest remarks I've ever heard!'

'Surely not?'

'Well, one does like to be remembered. It isn't pleasant to be told that one's a nonentity.'

He made an impatient gesture. 'That isn't what I meant, and I do recognize you now. I remember your voice. You have a distinctive voice and a pleasant one. F sharp in the octave below middle C is your note.'

'Is that the only way in which you can distinguish people?'

'It's as good as any other.'

'But you don't remember my name?'

'No,' he said.

'I'm Elizabeth Barford.'

He bowed and said, 'Well, it was a dull party, wasn't it? The occasion, I mean, when we drank coffee together.'

'I don't agree with you. I thought it was very amusing, and we all enjoyed ourselves. Do you remember Charles Sellin?'

'No.'

'Oh, you're hopeless,' she exclaimed. 'What is the good of meeting people if you're going to forget all about them?'

'I don't know,' he said. 'Let us sit down, and you can tell me.'

He sat again on the edge of the rock, his legs dangling, and looking over his shoulder at her, said, 'Tell me: what is the good of meeting people?'

She hesitated, and answered, 'I like to make friends. That's quite natural, isn't it? – But I came here to read.'

'Do you read standing?'

'Of course not,' she said, and smoothing her skirt tidily over her knees, sat down beside him. 'What a wonderful place this is for a holiday. Have you been here before?'

'Yes, I know it well.'

'Charles and I came a week ago. Charles Sellin, I mean, whom you don't remember. We're going to be married, you know. In about a year, we hope.'

'Why did you come here?'

'We wanted to be quiet, and in these islands one is fairly secure against interruption. We're both working quite hard.'

'Working!' he mocked. 'Don't waste time, waste your life instead.'

'Most of us have to work, whether we like it or not.'

He took the book from her lap, and opening it read idly a few lines, turned a dozen pages and read with a yawn another paragraph.

'Your friends in Edinburgh,' she said, 'were better-off than ours. Charles and I, and all the people we know, have got to make our living.'

'Why?' he asked.

'Because if we don't we shall starve,' she snapped.

'And if you avoid starvation – what then?'

'It's possible to hope,' she said stiffly, 'that we shall be of some use in the world.'

'Do you agree with this?' he asked, smothering a second yawn, and read from the book:

The physical factor in a germ-cell is beyond our analysis, or assessment, but can we deny subjectivity to the primordial initiatives? It is easier, perhaps, to assume that mind comes late in development, but the assumption must not be established on the grounds that we can certainly deny self-expression to the cell. It is common knowledge that the mind may influence the body both greatly and in little unseen ways; but how it is done, we do not know. Psychobiology is still in its infancy.

'It's fascinating, isn't it?' she said.

'How do you propose,' he asked, 'to be of use to the world?'

'Well, the world needs people who have been educated – educated to think – and one does hope to have a little influence in some way.'

'Is a little influence going to make any difference? Don't you think that what the world needs is to develop a new sort of mind? It needs a new primordial directive, or quite a lot of them, perhaps. But psychobiology is still in its infancy, and you don't know how such changes come about, do you? And you can't foresee when you *will* know, can you?'

'No, of course not. But science is advancing so quickly –'

'In fifty thousand years?' he interrupted. 'Do you think you will know by then?'

'It's difficult to say,' she answered seriously, and was gathering her thoughts for a careful reply when again he interrupted, rudely, she thought, and quite irrelevantly. His attention had strayed from her and her book to the sea beneath, and he was looking down as though searching for something. 'Do you swim?' he asked.

'Rather well,' she said.

'I went in just before high water, when the weed down there was all brushed in the opposite direction. You never get bored by the sea, do you?'

'I've never seen enough of it,' she said. 'I want to live on an island, a little island, and hear it all round me.'

'That's very sensible of you,' he answered with more warmth in his voice. 'That's uncommonly sensible for a girl like you.'

'What sort of a girl do you think I am?' she demanded, vexation in her accent, but he ignored her and pointed his brown arm to the horizon: 'The colour has thickened within the last few minutes. The sea was quite pale on the skyline, and now it's a belt of indigo. And the writing has changed. The lines of foam on the water, I mean. Look at that! There's a submerged rock out there, and always, about half an hour after the ebb has started to run, but more clearly when there's an off-shore wind, you can see those two little whirlpools and the circle of white round them. You see the figure they make? It's like this, isn't it?'

With a splinter of stone he drew a diagram on the rock.

'Do you know what it is?' he asked. 'It's the figure the Chinese call the T'ai Chi. They say it represents the origin of all created things. And it's the sign manual of the sea.'

'But those lines of foam must run into every conceivable shape,' she protested.

'Oh, they do. They do indeed. But it isn't often you can read them. There he is!' he exclaimed, leaning forward and staring into the water sixty feet below. 'That's him, the old villain!'

From his sitting position, pressing hard down with his hands and thrusting against the face of the rock with his heels, he hurled himself into space, and straightening in mid-air broke the smooth green surface of the water with no more splash than a harpoon would have made. A solitary razorbill, sunning himself on a shelf below, fled hurriedly out to sea, and half a dozen white birds, startled by the sudden movement, rose in the air crying 'Kitti-wake! Kittiwake!'

Elizabeth screamed loudly, scrambled to her feet with clumsy speed, then knelt again on the edge of the rock and peered down. In the slowly heaving clear water she could see a pale shape moving, now striped by the dark weed that grew in tangles under the flat foot of the rock, now lost in the shadowy deepness where the tangles were rooted. In a minute or two his head rose from the sea, he shook bright drops from his hair, and looked up at her, laughing. Firmly grasped in his right hand, while he trod water, he held up an enormous blue-black lobster for her admiration. Then he threw it on to the flat rock beside him, and swiftly climbing out of the seat, caught it again and held it, cautious of its bite, till he found a piece of string in his trouser-pocket. He shouted to her, 'I'll tie its claws, and you can take it home for your supper!'

She had not thought it possible to climb the sheer face of the cliff, but from its forefoot he mounted by steps and handholds invisible from above, and pitching the tied lobster on to the floor of the gazebo, came nimbly over the edge.

'That's a bigger one than you've ever seen in your life before,' he boasted. 'He weighs fourteen pounds, I'm certain of it. Fourteen pounds at least. Look at the size of his right claw! He could crack a coconut with that. He tried to crack my ankle when I was swimming an hour ago, and got into his hole before I could catch him. But I've caught him now, the brute. He's had more than twenty years of crime, that black boy. He's twenty-four or twenty-five by the look of him. He's older than you, do you realize that? Unless you're a lot older than you look. How old are you?'

But Elizabeth took no interest in the lobster. She had retreated until she stood with her back to the rock, pressed hard against it, the palms of her hands fumbling on the stone as if feeling for a secret lock or bolt that might give her entrance into it. Her face was white, her lips pale and tremulous.

He looked round at her, when she made no answer, and asked what the matter was.

Her voice was faint and frightened. 'Who are you?' she whispered, and the whisper broke into a stammer. 'What are you?'

His expression changed and his face, with the waterdrops on it, grew hard as a rock shining undersea. 'It's only a few minutes,' he said, 'since you appeared to know me quite well. You addressed me as Roger Fairfield, didn't you?'

'But a name's not everything. It doesn't tell you enough.'

'What more do you want to know?'

Her voice was so strained and thin that her words were like the shadow of words, or words shivering in the cold: 'To jump like that, into the sea – it wasn't human!'

The coldness of his face wrinkled to a frown. 'That's a curious remark to make.'

'You would have killed yourself if – if –'

He took a seaward step again, looked down at the calm green depths below, and said, 'You're exaggerating, aren't you? It's not much more than fifty feet, sixty perhaps, and the water's deep. – Here, come back! Why are you running away?'

'Let me go!' she cried. 'I don't want to stay here. I – I'm frightened.'

'That's unfortunate. I hadn't expected this to happen.'

'Please let me go!'

'I don't think I shall. Not until you've told me what you're frightened of.'

'Why,' she stammered, 'why do you wear fur trousers?'

He laughed, and still laughing caught her round the waist and pulled her towards the edge of the rock. 'Don't be alarmed,' he said. 'I'm not going to throw you over. But if you insist on a conversation about trousers, I think we should sit down again. Look at the smoothness of the water, and its colour, and the light in the depths of it: have you ever seen anything lovelier? Look at the sky: that's calm enough, isn't it? Look at that fulmar sailing past: he's not worrying, so why should you?'

She leaned away from him, all her weight against the hand that held her waist, but his arm was strong and he seemed unaware of any strain on it. Nor did he pay attention to the distress she was in – she was sobbing dryly, like a child who has cried too long – but continued talking in a light and pleasant conversational tone until the muscles of her body tired and relaxed, and she sat within his enclosing arm, making no more effort to escape, but timorously conscious of his hand upon her side so close beneath her breast.

'I needn't tell you,' he said, 'the conventional reasons for wearing trousers. There are people, I know, who sneer at all conventions, and some conventions deserve their sneering. But not the trouser-convention. No, indeed! So we can admit the necessity of the garment, and pass to consideration of the mate-rial. Well, I like sitting on rocks, for one thing, and for such a hobby this is the best stuff in the world. It's very durable, yet soft and comfortable. I can slip into the sea for half an hour without doing it any harm, and when I come out to sun myself on the rock again, it doesn't feel cold and clammy. Nor does it fade in the sun or shrink with the wet. Oh, there are plenty of reasons for having one's trousers made of stuff like this.'

'And there's a reason,' she said, 'that you haven't told me.'

'Are you quite sure of that?'

She was calmer now, and her breathing was controlled. But her face was still white, and her lips were softly nervous when she asked him, 'Are you going to kill me?'

'Kill you? Good heavens, no! Why should I do that?'

'For fear of my telling other people.'

'And what precisely would you tell them?'

'You know.'

'You jump to conclusions far too quickly: that's your trouble. Well, it's a pity for your sake, and a nuisance for me. I don't think I can let you take that lobster home for your supper after all. I don't, in fact, think you will go home for your supper.'

Her eyes grew dark again with fear, her mouth opened, but before she could speak he pulled her to him and closed it, not asking leave, with a roughly occludent kiss.

'That was to prevent you from screaming. I hate to hear people scream,' he told her, smiling as he spoke. 'But this' – he kissed her again, now gently and in a more protracted embrace – 'that was because I wanted to.'

'You mustn't!' she cried.

'But I have,' he said.

'I don't understand myself! I can't understand what has happened –'

'Very little yet,' he murmured.

'Something terrible has happened!'

'A kiss? Am I so repulsive?'

'I don't mean that. I mean something inside me. I'm not – at least I think I'm not – I'm not frightened now!'

'You have no reason to be.'

'I have every reason in the world. But I'm not! I'm not frightened – but I want to cry.'

'Then cry,' he said soothingly, and made her pillow her cheek against his breast. 'But you can't cry comfortably with that ridiculous contraption on your nose.'

He took from her the horn-rimmed spectacles she wore, and threw them into the sea.

'Oh!' she exclaimed. 'My glasses! – Oh, why did you do that? Now I can't see. I can't see at all without my glasses!'

'It's all right,' he assured her. 'You really won't need them. The refraction,' he added vaguely, 'will be quite different.'

As if this small but unexpected act of violence had brought to the boiling-point her desire for tears, they bubbled over, and because she threw her arms about him in a sort of fond despair, and snuggled close, sobbing vigorously still, he felt the warm drops trickle down his skin, and from his skin she drew into her eyes the saltness of the sea, which made her weep the more. He stroked her hair with a strong but soothing hand, and when she grew calm and lay still in his arms, her emotion spent, he sang quietly to a little enchanting tune a song that began:

> 'I am a Man upon the land,
>   I am a Selkie in the sea,
> And when I'm far from every strand
>   My home it is on Sule Skerry.'

After the first verse or two she freed herself from his embrace, and sitting up listened gravely to the song. Then she asked him, 'Shall I ever understand?'

'It's not a unique occurrence,' he told her. 'It has happened quite often before, as I suppose you know. In Cornwall and Brittany and among the Western Isles of Scotland; that's where people have always been interested in seals, and understood them a little, and where seals from time to time have taken human shape. The one thing that's unique in our case, in my metamorphosis, is that I am the only seal-man who has ever become a Master of Arts of Edinburgh University. Or, I believe, of any university. I am the unique and solitary example of a sophisticated seal-man.'

'I must look a perfect fright,' she said. 'It was silly of me to cry. Are my eyes very red?'

'The lids are a little pink – not unattractively so – but your eyes are as dark and lovely as a mountain pool in October, on a sunny day in October. They're much improved since I threw your spectacles away.'

'I needed them, you know. I feel quite stupid without them. But tell me why you came to the University – and how? How could you do it?'

'My dear girl – what is your name, by the way? I've quite forgotten.'

'Elizabeth!' she said angrily.

'I'm so glad, it's my favourite human name. But you don't really want to listen to a lecture on psychobiology?'

'I want to know *how*. You must tell me!'

'Well, you remember, don't you, what your book says about the primordial initiatives. But it needs a footnote there to explain that they're not exhausted till quite late in life. The germ-cells, as you know, are always renewing themselves, and they keep their initiatives though they nearly always follow the chosen pattern except in the case of certain illnesses, or under special direction. The direction of the mind, that is. And the glands have got a lot to do in a full metamorphosis, the renal first and then the pituitary, as you would expect. It isn't approved of – making the change, I mean – but every now and then one of us does it, just for a frolic in the general way, but in my case there was a special reason.'

'Tell me,' she said again.

'It's too long a story.'

'I want to know.'

'There's been a good deal of unrest, you see, among my people in the last few years: doubt, and dissatisfaction with our leaders, and scepticism about traditional beliefs – all that sort of thing. We've had a lot of discussion under the surface of the sea about the nature of man, for instance. We had always been taught to believe certain things about him, and recent events didn't seem to bear out what our teachers told us. Some of our younger people got dissatisfied, so I volunteered to go ashore and investigate. I'm still considering the report I shall have to make, and that's why I'm living, at present, a double life. I come ashore to think, and go back to the sea to rest.'

'And what do you think of us?' she asked.

'You're interesting. Very interesting indeed. There are going to be some curious mutations among you before long. Within three or four thousand years, perhaps.'

He stooped and rubbed a little smear of blood from his shin. 'I scratched it on a limpet,' he said. 'The limpets, you know, are the same today as they were four hundred thousand years ago. But human beings aren't nearly so stable.'

'Is that your main impression, that humanity's unstable?'

'That's part of it. But from our point of view there's something much more upsetting. Our people, you see, are quite simple creatures, and because we have relatively few beliefs, we're very much attached to them. Our life is a life of sensation – not entirely, but largely – and we ought to be extremely happy. We were, so long as we were satisfied with sensation and a short undisputed creed. We have some advantages over human beings, you know. Human beings have to carry their own weight about, and they don't know how blissful it is to be unconscious of weight: to be wave-borne, to float on the idle sea, to leap without effort in a curving wave, and look up at the dazzle of the sky through a smother of white water, or dive so easily to the calmness far below and take a haddock from the weed-beds in a sudden rush of appetite. Talking of haddocks,' he said, 'it's getting late. It's nearly time for fish. And I must give you some instruction before we go. The preliminary phase takes a little while, about five minutes for you, I should think, and then you'll be another creature.'

She gasped, as though already she felt the water's chill, and whispered, 'Not yet! Not yet, please.'

He took her in his arms, and expertly, with a strong caressing hand, stroked her hair, stroked the roundess of her head and the back of her neck and her shoulders, feeling her muscles moving to his touch, and down the hollow of her back to her waist and hips. The head again, neck, shoulders, and spine. Again and again. Strongly and firmly his hand gave her calmness, and presently she whispered, 'You're sending me to sleep.'

'My God!' he exclaimed, 'you mustn't do that! Stand up, stand up, Elizabeth!'

'Yes,' she said, obeying him. 'Yes, Roger. Why did you call yourself Roger? Roger Fairfield?'

'I found the name in a drowned sailor's pay-book. What does that matter now? Look at me, Elizabeth!'

She looked at him, and smiled.

His voice changed, and he said happily, 'You'll be the prettiest seal between Shetland and the Scillies. Now listen. Listen carefully.'

He held her lightly and whispered in her ear. Then kissed her on the lips and cheek, and bending her head back, on the throat. He looked, and saw the colour come deeply into her face.

'Good,' he said. 'That's the first stage. The adrenalin's flowing nicely now. You know about the pituitary, don't you? That makes it easy then. There are two parts in the pituitary gland, the anterior and posterior lobes, and both must act together. It's not difficult, and I'll tell you how.'

Then he whispered again, most urgently, and watched her closely. In a little while he said, 'And now you can take it easy. Let's sit down and wait till you're ready. The actual change won't come till we go down.'

'But it's working,' she said, quietly and happily. 'I can feel it working.'

'Of course it is.'

She laughed triumphantly, and took his hand.

'We've got nearly five minutes to wait,' he said.

'What will it be like? What shall I feel, Roger?'

'The water moving against your side, the sea caressing you and holding you.'

'Shall I be sorry for what I've left behind?'

'No, I don't think so.'

'You didn't like us, then? Tell me what you discovered in the world.'

'Quite simply,' he said, 'that we had been deceived.'

'But I don't know what your belief had been.'

'Haven't I told you? – Well, we in our innocence respected you because you could work, and were willing to work. That seemed to us truly heroic. We don't work at all, you see, and you'll be much happier when you come to us. We who live in the sea don't struggle to keep our heads above water.'

'All my friends worked hard,' she said. 'I never knew anyone who was idle. We had to work, and most of us worked for a good purpose; or so we thought. But you didn't think so?'

'Our teachers had told us,' he said, 'that men endured the

burden of human toil to create a surplus of wealth that would give them leisure from the daily task of breadwinning. And in their hard-won leisure, our teachers said, men cultivated wisdom and charity and the fine arts; and became aware of God. – But that's not a true description of the world, is it?'

'No,' she said, 'that's not the truth.'

'No,' he repeated, 'our teachers were wrong, and we've been deceived.'

'Men are always being deceived, but they get accustomed to learning the facts too late. They grow accustomed to deceit itself.'

'You are braver than we, perhaps. My people will not like to be told the truth.'

'I shall be with you,' she said, and took his hand. But still he stared gloomily at the moving sea.

The minutes passed, and presently she stood up and with quick fingers put off her clothes. 'It's time,' she said.

He looked at her, and his gloom vanished like the shadow of a cloud that the wind has hurried on, and exultation followed like sunlight spilling from the burning edge of a cloud. 'I wanted to punish them,' he cried, 'for robbing me of my faith, and now, by God, I'm punishing them hard. I'm robbing their treasury now, the inner vault of all their treasury! – I hadn't guessed you were so beautiful! The waves when you swim will catch a burnish from you, the sand will shine like silver when you lie down to sleep, and if you can teach the red sea-ware to blush so well, I shan't miss the roses of your world.'

'Hurry,' she said.

He, laughing softly, loosened the leather thong that tied his trousers, stepped out of them, and lifted her in his arms. 'Are you ready?' he asked.

She put her arms round his neck and softly kissed his cheek. Then with a great shout he leapt from the rock, from the little veranda, into the green silk calm of the water far below . . .

I heard the splash of their descent – I am quite sure I heard the splash – as I came round the corner of the cliff, by the ledge that leads to the little rock veranda, our gazebo, as we called it, but the first thing I noticed, that really attracted my attention, was an enormous blue-black lobster, its huge claws tied with string, that was moving in a rather ludicrous fashion towards the edge. I think it fell over just before I left, but I wouldn't swear to that. Then I saw her book, the *Studies in Biology*, and her clothes.

Her white linen frock with the brown collar and the brown belt, some other garments, and her shoes were all there. And beside them, lying across her shoes, was a pair of sealskin trousers.

I realized immediately, or almost immediately, what had happened. Or so it seems to me now. And if, as I firmly believe, my apprehension was instantaneous, the faculty of intuition is clearly more important than I had previously supposed. I have, of course, as I said before, given the matter a great deal of thought during my recent illness, but the impression remains that I understood what had happened in a flash, to use a common but illuminating phrase. And no one, need I say? has been able to refute my intuition. No one, that is, has found an alternative explanation for the presence, beside Elizabeth's linen frock, of a pair of sealskin trousers.

I remember also my physical distress at the discovery. My breath, for several minutes I think, came into and went out of my lungs like the hot wind of a dust-storm in the desert. It parched my mouth and grated in my throat. It was, I recall, quite a torment to breathe. But I had to, of course.

Nor did I lose control of myself in spite of the agony, both mental and physical, that I was suffering. I didn't lose control till they began to mock me. Yes, they did, I assure you of that. I heard his voice quite clearly, and honesty compels me to admit that it was singularly sweet and the tune was the most haunting I have ever heard. They were about forty yards away, two seals swimming together, and the evening light was so clear and taut that his voice might have been the vibration of an invisible bow across its coloured bands. He was singing the song that Elizabeth and I had discovered in an album of Scottish music in the little fishing-hotel where we had been living:

> 'I am a Man upon the land,
> I am a Selkie in the sea,
> And when I'm far from any strand
> I am at home on Sule Skerry!'

But his purpose, you see, was mockery. They were happy, together in the vast simplicity of the ocean, and I, abandoned to the terror of life alone, life among human beings, was lost and full of panic. It was then I began to scream. I could hear myself screaming, it was quite horrible. But I couldn't stop. I had to go on screaming . . .

Lewis Grassic Gibbon

SMEDDUM

She'd had nine of a family in her time, Mistress Menzies, and brought the nine of them up, forby – some near by the scruff of the neck, you would say. They were sniftering and weakly, two-three of the bairns, sniftering in their cradles to get into their coffins; but she'd shake them to life, and dose them with salts and feed them up till they couldn't but live. And she'd plonk one down – finishing the wiping of the creature's neb or the unco dosing of an ill bit stomach or the binding of a broken head – with a look on her face as much as to say *Die on me now and see what you'll get!*

Big-boned she was by her fortieth year, like a big roan mare, and *If ever she was bonny 'twas in Noah's time*, Jock Menzies, her eldest son, would say. She'd reddish hair and a high, skeugh nose, and a hand that skelped her way through life, and if ever a soul had seen her at rest when the dark was done and the day was come he'd died of the shock and never let on.

For from morn till night she was at it, work, work, on that ill bit croft that sloped to the sea. When there wasn't a mist on the cold, stone parks there was more than likely the wheep of the rain, wheeling and dripping in from the sea that soughed and plashed by the land's stiff edge. Kinneff lay north, and at night in the south, if the sky was clear on the gloaming's edge, you'd see in that sky the Bervie lights come suddenly lit, far and away, with the quiet about you as you stood and looked, nothing to hear but a sea-bird's cry.

But feint the much time to look or to listen had Margaret Menzies of Tocherty toun. Day blinked and Meg did the same, and was out, up out of her bed, and about the house, making the porridge and rousting the bairns, and out to the byre to milk the three kye, the morning growing out in the east and a wind like a hail of knives from the hills. Syne back to the kitchen again she would be, and catch Jock, her eldest, a clout in the lug that he hadn't roused up his sisters and brothers; and rouse them herself, and feed them and scold, pull up their breeks and straighten their frocks, and polish their shoes and set their caps straight. *Off you get and see you're not late*, she would cry, *and see you behave yourselves at the school. And tell the Dominie I'll be down the night to ask him what the mischief he meant by leathering Jeannie and her not well.*

They'd cry *Ay, Mother*, and go trotting away, a fair flock of the creatures, their faces red-scoured. Her own as red, like a meikle roan mare's, Meg'd turn at the door and go prancing in; and then at last, by the closet-bed, lean over and shake her man half-awake. *Come on, then, Willie, it's time you were up.*

And he'd groan and say *Is't?* and crawl out at last, a little bit thing like a weasel, Will Menzies, though some said that weasels were decent beside him. He was drinking himself into the grave, folk said, as coarse a little brute as you'd meet, bone-lazy forby, and as sly as sin. Rampageous and ill with her tongue though she was, you couldn't but pity a woman like Meg tied up for life to a thing like *that*. But she'd more than a soft side still to the creature, she'd half-skelp the backside from any of the bairns she found in the telling of a small bit lie; but when Menzies would come paiching in of a noon and groan that he fair was tashed with his work, he'd mended all the ley fence that day and he doubted he'd need to be off to his bed – when he'd told her that and had ta'en to the blankets, and maybe in less than the space of an hour she'd hold out for the kye and see that he'd lied, the fence neither mended nor letten a-be, she'd just purse up her meikle wide mouth and say nothing, her eyes with a glint as though she half-laughed. And when he came drunken home from a mart she'd shoo the children out of the room, and take off his clothes and put him to bed, with an extra nip to keep off a chill.

She did half his work in the Tocherty parks, she'd yoke up the horse and the sholtie together, and kilt up her skirts till you'd see her great legs, and cry *Wissh!* like a man and turn a fair drill, the sea-gulls cawing in a cloud behind, the wind in her hair and the sea beyond. And Menzies with his sly-like eyes would be off on some drunken ploy to Kinneff or Stonehive. Man, you couldn't but

think as you saw that steer it was well that there was a thing like
marriage, folk held together and couldn't get apart; else a black
look-out it well would be for the fusionless creature of Tocherty
toun.

Well, he drank himself to his grave at last, less smell on the
earth if maybe more in it. But she broke down and wept, it was
awful to see, Meg Menzies weeping like a stricken horse, her eyes
on the dead, quiet face of her man. And she ran from the house,
she was gone all that night, though the bairns cried and cried her
name up and down the parks in the sound of the sea. But next
morning they found her back in their midst, brisk as ever, like a
great-boned mare, ordering here and directing there, and a fine
feed set the next day for the folk that came to the funeral of her
orra man.

She'd four of the bairns at home when he died, the rest were in
kitchen-service or fee'd, she'd seen to the settling of the queans
herself; and twice when two of them had come home, complain-
ing-like of their mistresses' ways, she'd thrashen the queans and
taken them back – near scared the life from the doctor's wife, her
that was mistress to young Jean Menzies. *I've skelped the lassie
and brought you her back. But don't you ill-use her, or I'll skelp
you as well.*

There was a fair speak about that at the time, Meg Menzies and
the vulgar words she had used, folk told that she'd even said what
was the place where she'd skelp the bit doctor's wife. And faith!
that fair must have been a sore shock to the doctor's wife that was
that genteel she'd never believed she'd a place like that.

Be that as it might, her man new dead, Meg wouldn't hear of
leaving the toun. It was harvest then and she drove the reaper up
and down the long, clanging clay rigs by the sea, she'd jump down
smart at the head of a bout and go gathering and binding swift as
the wind, syne wheel in the horse to the cutting again. She led the
stooks with her bairns to help, you'd see them at night a drowsing
cluster under the moon on the harvesting cart.

And through that year and into the next and so till the speak
died down in the Howe, Meg Menzies worked the Tocherty toun;
and faith, her crops came none so ill. She rode to the mart at
Stonehive when she must, on the old box-cart, the old horse in the
shafts, the cart behind with a sheep for sale or a birn of old hens

that had finished with laying. And a butcher once tried to make a bit joke. *That's a sheep like yourself, fell long in the tooth.* And Meg answered up, neighing like a horse, and all heard: *Faith, then, if you've got a spite against teeth I've a clucking hen in the cart outbye. It's as toothless and senseless as you are, near.*

Then word got about of her eldest son, Jock Menzies, that was fee'd up Allardyce way. The creature of a loon had had fair a conceit since he'd won a prize at a ploughing match – not for his ploughing, but for good looks; and the queans about were as daft as himself, he'd only to nod and they came to his heel; and the stories told they came further than that. Well, Meg'd heard the stories and paid no heed, till the last one came, she was fell quick then.

Soon's she heard it she hove out the old bit bike that her daughter Kathie had bought for herself, and got on the thing and went cycling away down through the Bervie braes in that spring, the sun was out and the land lay green with a blink of mist that was blue on the hills, as she came to the toun where Jock was fee'd she saw him out in a park by the road, ploughing, the black loam smooth like a ribbon turning and wheeling at the tail of the plough. Another billy came ploughing behind. Meg Menzies watched till they reached the rig-end, her great chest heaving like a meikle roan's, her eyes on the shape of the furrows they made. And they drew to the end and drew the horse out, and Jock cried *Ay,* and she answered back *Ay,* and looked at the drill, and gave a bit snort, *If your looks win prizes, your ploughing never will.*

Jock laughed, *Fegs, then, I'll not greet for that,* and chirked to his horses and turned them about. But she cried him *Just bide a minute, my lad. What's this I hear about you and Ag Grant?*

He drew up short then, and turned right red, the other childe as well, and they both gave a laugh, as plough-childes do when you mention a quean they've known over-well in more ways than one. And Meg snapped *It's an answer I want, not a cockerel's cackle: I can hear that at home on my own dunghill. What are you to do about Ag and her pleiter?*

And Jock said *Nothing,* impudent as you like, and next minute Meg was in over the dyke and had hold of his lug and shook him and it till the other childe ran and caught at her nieve. *Faith, mistress, you'll have his lug off!* he cried. But Meg Menzies turned like a mare on new grass, *Keep off or I'll have yours off as well!*

So he kept off and watched, fair a story he'd to tell when he rode out that night to go courting his quean. For Meg held to the lug till it near came off and Jock swore that he'd put things right with Ag Grant. She let go the lug then and looked at him grim: *See that you do and get married right quick, you're the like that needs loaded with a birn of bairns – to keep you out of the jail, I jaloose. It needs smeddum to be either right coarse or right kind.*

They were wed before the month was well out, Meg found them a cottar house to settle and gave them a bed and a press she had, and two-three more sticks from Tocherty toun. And she herself led the wedding dance, the minister in her arms, a small bit childe; and 'twas then as she whirled him about the room, he looked like a rat in the teeth of a tyke, that he thanked her for seeing Ag out of her soss, *There's nothing like a marriage for redding things up.* And Meg Menzies said *EH?* and then she said *Ay*, but queer-like, he supposed she'd no thought of the thing. Syne she slipped off to sprinkle thorns in the bed and to hang below it the great handbell that the bothybillies took with them to every bit marriage.

Well, that was Jock married and at last off her hands. But she'd plenty left still, Dod, Kathleen and Jim that were still at school, Kathie a limner that alone tongued her mother, Jeannie that next led trouble to her door. She'd been found at her place, the doctor's it was, stealing some money and they sent her home. Syne news of the thing got into Stonehive, the police came out and tormented her sore, she swore she never had stolen a meck, and Meg swore with her, she was black with rage. And folk laughed right hearty, fegs! that was a clout for meikle Meg Menzies, her daughter a thief!

But it didn't last long, it was only three days when folk saw the doctor drive up in his car. And out he jumped and went striding through the close and met face to face with Meg at the door. And he cried *Well, mistress, I've come over for Jeannie.* And she glared at him over her high, skeugh nose, *Ay, have you so then? And why, may I speir?*

So he told her why, the money they'd missed had been found at last in a press by the door; somebody or other had left it there, when paying a grocer or such at the door. And Jeannie – he'd come over to take Jean back.

But Meg glared. *Ay, well, you've made another mistake. Out of this, you and your thieving suspicions together!* The doctor turned red, *You're making a miserable error* – and Meg said *I'll make you mince-meat in a minute*.

So he didn't wait that, she didn't watch him go, but went ben to the kitchen, where Jeannie was sitting, her face chalk-white as she'd heard them speak. And what happened then a story went round, Jim carried it to school, and it soon spread out, Meg sank in a chair, they thought she was greeting; syne she raised up her head and they saw she was laughing, near as fearsome the one as the other, they thought. *Have you any cigarettes?* she snapped sudden at Jean, and Jean quavered *No*, and Meg glowered at her cold. *Don't sit there and lie. Gang bring them to me*. And Jean brought them, her mother took the pack in her hand. *Give's hold of a match till I light up the thing. Maybe smoke'll do good for the crow that I got in the throat last night by the doctor's house*.

Well, in less than a month she'd got rid of Jean – packed off to Brechin the quean was, and soon got married to a creature there – some clerk that would have left her sore in the lurch but that Meg went down to the place on her bike, and there, so the story went, kicked the childe so that he couldn't sit down for a fortnight, near. No doubt that was just a bit lie that they told, but faith! Meg Menzies had herself to blame, the reputation she'd gotten in the Howe, folk said, *She'll meet with a sore heart yet*. But devil a sore was there to be seen, Jeannie was married and was fair genteel.

Kathleen was next to leave home at the term. She was tall, like Meg, and with red hair as well, but a thin fine face, long eyes blue-grey like the hills on a hot day, and a mouth with lips you thought over thick. And she cried *Ah well, I'm off then, mother*. And Meg cried *See you behave yourself*. And Kathleen cried *Maybe; I'm not at school now*.

Meg stood and stared after the slip of a quean, you'd have thought her half-angry, half near to laughing, as she watched that figure, so slender and trig, with its shoulders square-set, slide down the hill on the wheeling bike, swallows were dipping and flying by Kinneff, she looked light and free as a swallow herself, the quean, as she biked away from her home, she turned at the bend and waved and whistled, she whistled like a loon and as loud, did Kath.

Jim was the next to leave from the school, he bided at home and he took no fee, a quiet-like loon, and he worked the toun, and, wonder of wonders, Meg took a rest. Folk said that age was telling a bit on even Meg Menzies at last. The grocer made hints at that one night, and Meg answered up smart as ever of old: *Damn the age! But I've finished the trauchle of the bairns at last, the most of them married or still over young. I'm as swack as ever I was, my lad. But I've just got the notion to be a bit sweir.*

Well, she'd hardly begun on that notion when faith! ill the news that came up to the place from Segget. Kathleen her quean that was fee'd down there, she'd ta'en up with some coarse old childe in a bank, he'd left his wife, they were off together, and she but a bare sixteen years old.

And that proved the truth of what folk were saying, Meg Menzies she hardly paid heed to the news, just gave a bit laugh like a neighing horse and went on with the work of park and byre, cool as you please – ay, getting fell old.

No more was heard of the quean or the man till a two years or more had passed and then word came up to the Tocherty someone had seen her – and where do you think? Out on a boat that was coming from Australia. She was working as stewardess on that bit boat, and the childe that saw her was young John Robb, an emigrant back from his uncle's farm, near starved to death he had been down there. She hadn't met in with him near till the end, the boat close to Southampton the evening they met. And she'd known him at once, though he not her, she'd cried *John Robb?* and he'd answered back *Ay?* and looked at her canny in case it might be the creature was looking for a tip from him. Syne she'd laughed *Don't you know me, then, you gowk? I'm Kathie Menzies you knew long syne – it was me ran off with the banker from Segget!*

He was clean dumbfounded, young Robb, and he gaped, and then they shook hands and she spoke some more, though she hadn't much time, they were serving up dinner for the first-class folk, aye dirt that are ready to eat and to drink. *If ever you get near to Tocherty toun tell Meg I'll get home and see her some time. Ta-ta!* And then she was off with a smile, young Robb he stood and he stared where she'd been, he thought her the bonniest thing that he'd seen all the weary weeks that he'd been from home.

And this was the tale that he brought to Tocherty. Meg sat and listened and smoked like a tink, forby herself there was young Jim there, and Jock and his wife and their three bit bairns, he'd fair changed with marriage, had young Jock Menzies. For no sooner had he taken Ag Grant to his bed than he'd started to save, grown mean as dirt, in a three-four years he's finished with feeing, now he rented a fell big farm himself, well stocked it was, and he fee'd two men. Jock himself had grown thin in a way, like his father but worse his bothy childes said, old Menzies at least could take a bit dram and get lost to the world but the son was that mean he might drink rat-poison and take no harm, 'twould feel at home in a stomach like his.

Well, that was Jock, and he sat and heard the story of Kath and her say on the boat. *Ay, still a coarse bitch, I have not a doubt. Well if she never comes back to the Mearns, in Segget you cannot but redden with shame when a body will ask 'Was Kath Menzies your sister?'*

And Ag, she'd grown a great sumph of a woman, she nodded to that, it was only too true, a sore thing it was on decent bit folks that they should have any relations like Kath.

But Meg just sat there and smoked and said never a word, as though she thought nothing worth a yea or a nay. Young Robb had fair ta'en a fancy to Kath and he near boiled up when he heard Jock speak, him and the wife that he'd married from her shame. So he left them short and went raging home, and wished for one that Kath would come back, a summer noon as he cycled home, snipe were calling in the Auchindreich moor where the cattle stood with their tails a-switch, the Grampians rising far and behind, Kinraddie spread like a map for show, its ledges veiled in a mist from the sun. You felt on that day a wild, daft unease, man, beast and bird: as though something were missing and lost from the world, and Kath was the thing that John Robb missed, she'd something in her that minded a man of a house that was builded upon a hill.

Folk thought that maybe the last they would hear of young Kath Menzies and her ill-gettèd ways. So fair stammy-gastered they were with the news she'd come back to the Mearns, she was down in Stonehive, in a grocer's shop, as calm as could be, selling out tea and cheese and such-like with no blush of shame on her face at all, to decent women that were properly wed and had never looked on men but their own, and only on them with their braces buttoned.

It just showed you the way that the world was going to allow an ill quean like that in a shop, some folk protested to the creature that owned it, but he just shook his head, *Ah well, she works fine; and what else she does is no business of mine.* So you well might guess there was more than business between the man and Kath Menzies, like.

And Meg heard the news and went into Stonehive, driving her sholtie, and stopped at the shop. And some in the shop knew who she was and minded the things she had done long syne to other bit bairns of hers that went wrong; and they waited with their breaths held up with delight. But all that Meg did was to nod to Kath *Ay, well, then, it's you – Ay, mother, just that – Two pounds of syrup and see that it's good.*

And not another word passed between them, Meg Menzies that once would have ta'en such a quean and skelped her to rights before you could wink. Going home from Stonehive she stopped by the farm where young Robb was fee'd, he was out in the hayfield coling the hay, and she nodded to him grim, with her high horse face. *What's this that I hear about you and Kath Menzies?*

He turned right red, but he wasn't ashamed. *I've no idea – though I hope it's the worse – It fell near is – Then I wish it was true, she might marry me, then, as I've prigged her to do.*

Oh, have you so, then? said Meg, and drove home, as though the whole matter was a nothing to her.

But next Tuesday the postman brought a bit note from Kathie, it was to her mother at Tocherty. *Dear mother, John Robb's going out to Canada and wants me to marry him and go with him. I've told him instead I'll go with him and see what he's like as a man – and then marry him at leisure, if I feel in the mood. But he's hardly any money, and we want to borrow some, so he and I are coming over on Sunday. I hope that you'll have dumpling for tea. Your own daughter, Kath.*

Well, Meg passed that letter over to Jim, he glowered at it dour, *I know – near all the Howe's heard. What are you going to do, now, mother?*

But Meg just lighted a cigarette and said nothing, she'd smoked like a tink since that steer with Jean. There was promise on strange on-goings at Tocherty by the time that the Sabbath day was come. For Jock came there on a visit as well, him and his wife, and besides him was Jeannie, her that had married the clerk down in Brechin, and she brought the bit creature, he fair was a toff; and he stepped like a cat through the sharn in the close; and when he had heard the story of Kath, her and her plan and John Robb and all, he was shocked near to death, and so was his wife. And Jock Menzies gaped and gave a mean laugh. *Ay, coarse to the bone, ill-gettèd I'd say if it wasn't that we came of the same bit stock. Ah well, she'll fair have to tramp to Canada, eh mother? – if she's looking for money from you.*

And Meg answered quiet *No, I wouldn't say that. I've the money all ready for them when they come.*

You could hear the sea plashing down soft on the rocks, there was such a dead silence in Tocherty house. And then Jock habbered like a cock with fits *What, give silver to one who does as she likes, and won't marry as you made the rest of us marry? Give silver to one who's no more than a —*

And he called his sister an ill name enough, and Meg sat and smoked looking over the parks. *Ay, just that. You see, she takes after myself.*

And Jeannie squeaked *How?* and Meg answered her quiet: *She's fit to be free and to make her own choice the same as myself and the same kind of choice. There was none of the rest of you fit to do that, you'd to marry or burn, so I married you quick. But Kath and me could afford to find out. It all depends if you've smeddum or not.*

She stood up then and put her cigarette out, and looked at the gaping gowks she had mothered. *I never married your father, you see. I could never make up my mind about Will. But maybe our Kath will find something surer. . . . Here's her and her man coming up the road.*

Robert MacLellan

THE MENNANS

The drinkin watter at Linmill had come at ae time frae a wal on the green fornent the front door. The auld stane troch was there yet, big eneuch for playin in, but the pump was lyin amang the rubbish in a corner o the cairt shed, and the hole it had come oot o was filled up wi stanes. The wal had gaen dry, it seems, juist efter I was born, and in my day the watter for the hoose was cairrit up frae the bottom orchard by Daft Sanny, twa pails at a time.

The wal in the bottom orchard was juist inside the Linmill hedge. There were twa trochs there, big round airn anes sunk into the grun, and the ane faurer frae the spoot had a troot in it to keep the watter clean. Through the hedge, tae, in Tam Baxter's grun, there was anither troch, and it was fou o mennans, for Tam was a great fisher and needit them for bait.

I gaed doun to the wal to play whiles, but I didna bother muckle wi oor ain troot. It was aye Tam's mennans I gaed for. I didna try to catch them, I was ower feart for that, but whan I had creepit through the hedge by the hole aside the honeysuckle I lay on my belly watchin them, wi my lugs weill cockit for the bark o Tam's dug.

I was fell fond o catching mennans, but seldom got the chance. I wasna alloued doun to Clyde withoot my grandfaither, for I had to be liftit twa-three times on the wey ower the bank, and in the simmer he was aye gey thrang in the fields, gafferin the warkers. Sae whan I wantit badly but couldna gang I juist gaed through the hedge and had a look in Tam's troch. It helpit me to think o the mennans in Clyde, for they aw had the same wey o soumin, gowpin at the mou and gogglin their big dowie een.

For a lang while I had the notion that Tam foun his mennans for himsell, but ae day whan I was on my wey back to the hoose efter

takin a finger-length o thick black doun the field to my grandfaither I met a big laddie frae Kirkfieldbank wi a can in his haund.

'Whaur are ye gaun wi the can?'

'To the Falls.'

'What's in it?'

'Mennans.'

'Let me see.'

The can was fou.

'What are ye takin them to the Falls for?'

'To sell them to Tam Baxter.'

'Will Tam buy them?'

'He buys them for the fishin.'

'What daes he pey ye?'

'A penny a dizzen.'

'Hoo mony hae ye?'

'Twenty-fower.'

'That'll be tippence.'

'Ay.'

I could haurdly believe it. I thocht o aw the mennans I had
catchit and gien to the cats. I could hae bocht the haill o Martha
Baxter's shop wi the siller I had lost.

Aw I could dae noo was mak a clean stert. The cats could want
efter this.

At lowsin time that day I was waitin for my grandfaither at
the Linmill road-end. It was airly in my simmer holiday, afore the
strawberries were ripe, and he was warkin wi juist a wheen o the
weemen frae roun aboot, weedin the beds. I heard him blawin his
birrel and kent he wadna be lang, for he was in the field neist to the
wal yett, and that was juist ower the road.

The weemen cam through the yett first, some haudin their
backs, for it was sair wark bending aw day, and ithers rowin up
their glaurie aprons. They skailed this wey and that, and syne cam
my grandfaither, wi the weeders in ae hand and his knee-pads in
the tither. I cam oot frae the hedge and gaed forrit to meet him.

'Whan will ye tak me to Clyde again, grandfaither?'

'What's gotten ye noo?'

'I want doun to Clyde to catch mennans.'

'Ay ay, nae doobt, but it's time for yer tea, and syne ye'll hae to
gang to yer bed.'

'Ay, but can I no gang the morn?'

'We'll see what yer grannie says.'

'But she aye says na.'

'What's pat it into yer heid to catch mennans?'

'I like catchin mennans.'

'Ay ay, nae doobt.'

'Grandfaither?'

'Ay?'

'Tam Baxter peys a penny a dizzen for mennans.'

'Wha telt ye that?'

'A laddie frae Kirkfieldbank.'

'Weill, weill.'

'Daes he?'

'I daursay.'

'It wad be grand to hae some mennans to sell him.'

'Ay, weill, we'll see. I'll be weedin aside Clyde the morn.'

'Will ye lift me doun ower the bank, then?'

'Mebbe. I'll ask yer grannie.'

He didna ask her at tea-time, and I was beginning to think he had forgotten, but when he cairret me ower to my bed he gied me a wink o his guid ee, the tither was blin, and I jaloused he hadna.

Shair eneuch, whan he had feenished his denner the neist day, and I had forgotten aboot the mennans athegither, for the baker had come in the mornin and gien me a wee curran loaf, he gaed to the scullery and cam back wi ane o the milk cans.

'Hae ye a gless jaur ye could gie the bairn?'

My grannie soundit crabbit, but it was juist her wey.

'Ye'll fin ane in the bunker.'

He took me to the scullery and foun the gless jaur.

'Come on,' he said.

My grannie cried frae the kitchen.

'Dinna let him faw in, noo, or ye needna come back.'

We gaed oot into the closs withoot peyin ony heed.

On yer wey doun to Clyde ye took the same road as ye did to the wal, and as faur as the wal the grun was weill trampit, but faurer doun there was haurdly mair to let ye ken the wey than the space atween the grosset busses and the hedge, and there the grun was aw thistles and stickie willie. He cairrit me ower that bit, to save my bare legs, and we hadna gaen faur whan the rummle o Stanebyres Linn grew sae lood that we could haurdly hear oorsells. No that I wantit to say ocht, for near the soun o the watter I was aye awed, and I was thinkin o the mennans soumin into my jaur.

We cam to the fute o the brae and turnt to the richt, alang the bank abune the watter, and were sune oot o the orchard aside the strawberry beds. The weemen were waitin to stert the weedin, sittin on the gress aneth the hazels, maist o them wi their coats kiltit up and their cutties gaun.

I didna like to hae to staun fornent the weemen. They couldna haud their silly tongues aboot my bonnie reid hair, and ane o them wad be shair to try to lift me, and as my grannie said they had a smell like tinkers, aye warkin in the clartie wat cley. My grand-faither saw them stertit at ance, though, and syne turnt to tak me doun to Clyde.

The wey ower the bank was gey kittle to tak, wi the rocks aw wat moss, and I grippit my grandfaither ticht, but he gat me to the bottom wi nae mair hairm nor the stang o a nettle to my left fute. He rubbit the stang wi the leaf o a docken, and tied a string to the neck of my jaur, and efter tellin me no to gang near the Lowp gaed awa back up to his wark.

An awesome laneliness cam ower me as sune as he had turnt his back. It wasna juist the rummle o the Linn frae faurer doun the watter; it was the black hole aneth the bank at my back whaur the otters bade, and the fearsome wey the watter gaed through the Lowp. The front o the hole was hung ower wi creepers, and ye couldna be shair that the otters werena sittin ben ahint them, waiting to sneak oot whan ye werena lookin and put their shairp teeth in to yer legs. The Lowp was waur. It was doun a wee frae the otter hole, across a muckle rock, whaur the haill braid watter o Clyde, sae gentle faurer up, shot through aneth twa straucht black banks like shinie daurk-green gless; and the space atween the banks was sae nerra that a man could lowp across. It wasna an easy lowp, faur abune the pouer o a laddie, yet ye found yersell staunin starin at it, fair itchin to hae a try. A halflin frae Nemphlar had tried it ance, in a spate whan the rocks were aw spume, and he had landit short and tummelt in backwards, and they say it was nae mair nor a meenit afore his daith-skrech was heard frae Stanebyres Linn itsell, risin abune the thunner o the spate like a stab o lichtnin.

The sun was oot, though, and I tried no to heed, and trith to tell gin it hadna been sae eerie it wad hae been lichtsome there, for in aw the rock cracks whaur yirth had gethert there were hare-bells growin, sae dentie and wan, and back and forrit on the mossie stanes that stude abune the watter gaed wee willie waggies, bobbin up and doun wi their tails gaun a dinger, and whiles haein a dook to tak the stour aff their feathers.

I didna gie them mair nor a look, for I had come to catch mennans, and as I grippit my can and jaur and gaed forrit ower the rock to the whirlies I could feel my hairt thumpin like to burst through my breist. It was aye the same whan I was eager, and it didna help.

The whirlies were roun holes in the rock aside the neck o the Lowp, worn wi the swirl of the watter whan it rase in spate and fludit its haill coorse frae bank to bank; but whan Clyde was doun on a simmer day they were dry aw roun, wi juist a pickle watter comin haufwey up them, clear eneuch to let ye see the colours o aw the bonnie chuckies at the fute. Noo there was ae whirlie wi a shalla end, and a runnel that cam in frae Clyde itsell, and on a hot day, gin aw was quait, the mennans slippit ben, about twenty at a time, to lie abune the warm chuckies and gowp in the sun. That was the whirlie for me, for gin ye bade quait eneuch till the mennans were aw weill ben, and laid yer jaur in the runnel wi its mou peyntin to them, and syne stude up and gied them a fricht, they turnt and gaed pell mell into it.

I laid doun my can and creepit forrit, and shair eneuch the mennans were there, but I couldna hae been cannie eneuch, for the meenit I gaed to lay my jaur in the runnel they shot richt past and left the whirlie toom. It was a peety, but it didna maitter. I kent that gin I waitit they wad syne come back.

The awkward thing was that if ye sat whaur ye could see the runnel the mennans could see yersell, sae I had to sit weill back and juist jalouse whan they micht steer again. I made up my mind no to move ower sune.

Wi haein nocht to dae I fell into a dwam, and thocht o this thing and that, but maistly o the siller Tam Baxter peyed for the mennans. Syne my banes gat sair, sittin on the hard rock, and I moved a wee to ease mysell a bit. On the turn roun my ee spied the otter hole, and I could hae sworn I saw the creepers movin. I began to feel gey feart, and my thochts took panic, and it wasna lang afore I was thinkin of the halflin that fell in the Lowp, though I had tried gey hard no to.

I lookit up the bank to see if my grandfaither was watchin, and shair eneuch there he was, staunin lookin doun on me to see that I was aw richt. I felt hairtent then, and pat my finger to my mou to keep him frae cryin oot to me, for I kent that gin he did he wad ask me hoo mony mennans I had catchit, and I didna want to hae to tell him nane.

Kennin he was there I grew eager to show him what a clever laddie I was, and I kent I had gien the mennans rowth of time to win back ben the whirlie, sae aw at ance I lowpit forrit and laid my jaur in the runnel, but I was sae hastie that I laid it wrang wey roun. It didna maiter, though, for the mennans were ben, dizzens o them, and they couldna win oot. Quick as a thocht I turnt the jaur roun and geid a lood skelloch. They shot this wey and that, and syne for my jaur, and whan I saw that some o them were into it I poued hard on my string.

I was ower eager, for the jaur gaed richt ower my heid and broke on the rock at my back, and the mennans I had catchit flip-flappit for the watter as hard as they could gang. I grabbit my can and gaed efter them, but they were gey ill to haud, and by the time I had twa o them safe the ithers were back into Clyde.

I stude up. I was richt on the edge o the Lowp.

I couldna tak my een off the glessie daurk-green watter, and I kent the whirlie was somewhaur ahint me, sae I didna daur step backwards. I juist stude still wi my breist burstin, and my wame turnin heid ower heels, till I gey nearly dwamt awa.

I didna, though. I gaed doun on my knees, aye wi my can grippit ticht, and had a wee keek roun. The whirlie was ahint me, but faurer up the rock than I had thocht. I creepit weill past it and lookit up the bank.

My grandfaither wasna there. He hadna been watchin efter aw.

I ran to the bank fute and cried oot, but wi the rummle o the watter he didna hear me, and I stertit to greet. I grat gey sair for a lang while, and syne tried to sclim up the bank, but I slippit and tummelt my can.

It hadna ae bash, but the mennans were gaen. I gied my een a rub wi my guernsey sleeve and stertit to look for them. In the end I spied them, bedirten aw ower and hauf deid. I mindit then that I hadna filled my can wi watter.

Whan they were soumin again they syne cam roun, though ane o them lay for a while wi its belly up, and I thocht it wad dee. Whan it didna I was hairtent again, and began to wish I could catch anither ten.

I had nae gless jaur.

I foun a wee hole in the rock and pat the mennans in, and syne gaed to the whirlie. It was toom, for I hadna keepit quait, but I tried my can in the runnel and foun a bit it wad fit. I wasna dune yet.

I tied my string to the can haunle and sat doun to wait again.

I had a waur job this time to keep mysell in haund, tryin no to think o the horrid end I wad hae come to gin I had fawn ower the edge o the Lowp, but I maun hae managed gey weill, for I didna seem to hae been sittin for a meenit whan my grandfaither's birrel gaed.

It was time to gang hame. I could haurdly believe it.

I gaed forrit to meet him as he cam doun the bank.

'Hoo mony mennans hae ye catchit?'

'Juist twa. I broke my jaur.'

'Dear me. Whaur's the can?'

'It's ower by the runnel. I hae tied my string to the haunle.'

'And whaur are yer twa mennans?'

'In a wee hole.'

'Quait, then, and we'll hae ae mair try. It's time to gang hame.'

He sat doun and cut himsell a braidth o thick black, and whan his pipe was gaun and the reek risin oot o it I gat richt back into fettle. I sat as still as daith, wishin his pipe had been cleaner, for it gied a gey gurgle at ilka puff, and I was feart it wad frichten the mennans. But I didna daur say ocht.

Aw at once, withoot warnin, he lowpit for the runnel wi the can. I lowpit tae.

The can was useless. The mennans saw it and gaed back ben the whirlie. They juist wadna try to win oot.

'Fin a stane,' said my grandfaither.

I ran to the fute o the bank and found a stane.

'Staun ower the whirlie and pitch it in hard.'

I lat flee wi aw my strength. The stane hit the watter wi a plunk. The mennans scattert and shot for the runnel. My grandfaither liftit the can.

Whan my braith came back I gaed ower aside him.

'Hoo mony hae we gotten?'

He was doun on his hunkers wi his heid ower the can.

'I canna coont. They winna bide still.'

My hairt gied a lowp. There wad shairly be a dizzen this time. But I was wrang.

'Eicht,' he said.

I had a look mysell. I coontit them three times. There was eicht and nae mair.

'Come on, then. Fin the ither twa and we'll win awa hame.'

I was fair dumfounert.

'But I hae juist ten, grandfaither. I need anither twa still.'

'Na, na, we're late. Yer grannie'll be thinking ye're drcount.'

'But I need a dizzen.'

'What dae ye want a dizzen for?'

'For Tam Baxter's penny.'

'Dinna fash aboot Tam Baxter. I'll gie ye a penny mysell.'

'But I want to mak my ain penny.'

'Na na.'

'They'll juist be wastit.'

'We'll gie them to the cats. Whaur did ye put the first twa?'

I took him ower to the wee hole. They were still there. He pat them in the can wi the ithers and made for the bank.

'I'll tak the mennans up first.'

He gaed awa up and left me. Whan he cam doun again I had stertit to greet.

'Come on, son. I'll gie ye tippence.'

But it didna comfort me. I had wantit sae hard to mak a penny o my ain, and I juist needit twa mennans mair. It was past tholin.

Whan we cam to the wal I was begrutten aw ower. He stude for a while.

'Haud on, son. Ye'll hae yer dizzen yet.'

He took the tinnie that hung frae the wal spoot. It was there for the drouthie warkers.

'We'll put the mennans in this.'

He had a gey job, for it didna leave them muckle watter, but he managed.

'Bide here and haud on to it. Keep ae haund ower the tap or they'll lowp oot.'

He left me wi the tinnie and took the can through the hedge. I jaloused at ance what he was efter, and my hairt stertit to thump again, but there was nae bark frae Tam's dug. It maun hae been tied at his back door.

My grandfaither cam back.

'Here ye are, then. Put thae anes back.'

I lookit in the can. There were twa in it. I toomed in the ithers.

'That's yer dizzen noo. Ye can tak them to Tam the morn.'

I kent I couldna face Tam the morn.

'Daes he no coont his mennans, grandfaither?'

'Na na, he has ower mony for that.'

'But it's stealin.'

'Dinna fash aboot that. Tam's laddies whiles guddle oor troot.'

It was the trith, and they didna aye put it back, but still I kent I couldna face him.

We cam to the wal yett.

'Grandfaither?'

'Aye?'

'I think we'll juist gie them to the cats efter aw.'

'What wey that?'

'I'm feart. I couldna face Tam Baxter.'

'Nonsense.'

'I couldna, grandfaither.'

'He'll ken naething.'

'He micht fin oot.'

'Deil the fear.'

We cam to the closs mou.

'Grandfaither?'

'What is it?'

'Juist let me gie them to the cats.'

'Aw richt, then. Please yersell.'

J. F. Hendry

THE DISINHERITED

A ray of sun, from behind a cloud, opened out on a small figure in a suit of blue Harris tweed, hastening desperately along the empty streets, between the shadowing tenements, to reach the haven of church before the bell stopped ringing. A pale ghost with blood-less lips sailed past the dark-blue windows of Templeton's the Grocers, Benson's the Newsagents, and the Hill Café, now and then, as it ran, staring backward, appalled, at a reflection in their window-blinds. A cap bit deep into the brow, and a spotted bow-tie pointed to five past seven. There was no time to adjust them.

– Dong! Ding-dong! Ding-dong! – sang the chimes, their echoes washing in waves of monotonous warning up the High Street, where a yellow cat stood lazily stropping itself against a chalk-fringed wall.

– Dong! Ding-dong! – and then, surprisingly, in a sudden giddy recoil, stopped altogether. Sawney broke into a run as he tackled the cobbled hill.

'What's the hurry?' called Big Sneddon, the policeman, from across the street. 'Ye're awfu' religious all of a sudden, or are ye off to a fire? The Bad Fire? –'

He broke down into raucous laughter at his own wit, but the face which was turned on him was so full of savagery, and something else besides, that it would have silenced anyone, let alone Big Sneddon, the handcuff-king. The angular blue figure straightened at once, and gazed thoughtfully after Sawney, now racing uphill, but it was not the expression alone in the latter's face that had sobered him. 'Poor Devil,' he said aloud, 'he's for it all right.'

Panting as he arrived at the door, Sawney paused for a moment or two, feeling as breathless as the bells. He turned to the east, but only for the wind, and, taking off his bonnet, waved it once or twice before his face, to dry the sweat.

'Late! Curse it,' he coughed, then plunged, like a man in a dream, through the open portals of the Kirk.

In their pew, the family were sitting waiting for him. He walked down the aisle, conscious of their hostile stares, and saw his mother's face grow slowly purple. He was wearing high, narrow boots of red ox-hide, which creaked as he walked, and now seemed about to crack, though this was hardly a cause for anger. His father, however, to his surprise, blew his nose loudly in his handkerchief, and Jimmy, his brother, sniggered outright, in the aisle. It was just like Jimmy to snigger. He had neither tact nor sympathy. He needed a doing!

Grinning sheepishly to several of his mother's stairhead acquaintances, he took his place beside her on the cushion, and a long and vicious hair entered his leg. He squirmed.

'How dare ye,' hissed his mother. 'Sawney, how dare ye drag me down like this! Never, never, will I be able to live doon the disgrace ye've brought upon me this day!'

Why this should be so was not immediately clear to Sawney, since, just then, in a river of robes, the Minister entered through a side-door and flowed up the stairs that led to the pulpit. You would have thought he was going to his execution, the majestic way he walked up.

These ruminations were cut short by a fierce dig in the ribs. 'Ye're finished, dae ye hear? I want no part of ye from now on! Oh, wait till I get ye outside,' his mother moaned in whispering, inarticulate rage, one eye on the pulpit where the Minister was opening the Book – 'I'll skivver the liver out o' ye, ye impiddent young deevil! Look at ye, look at your face!'

His father's impassive stare, Jimmy's noble contempt, his mother's passion and the amused glances of young girls, peeping over the tops of their hymn-books, at last forced Sawney actually to feel his face, which had in fact, now that his attention had been drawn to it, begun to seem slightly puffy.

Only then, as the congregation, without warning, stood up like a forest to sing the opening hymn: 'Be Strong in the Fight!' did it dawn on Sawney's horror-stricken conscience that he had come to church, to attend morning service, with two black eyes.

They swelled up till he could scarcely see. Miserably he sat as though in a cage, exposed to amusement, curiosity and scorn, his hands thrust between his knees, out of sight, to still their convulsive bird-like movements of escape.

Whenever he turned to look at her, he met the fixed glare of his mother, or heard the words: 'Vagabond! Scamp! –'

He grued when he thought of the end of the service, when he would have to face her tigerish wrath, out there in the bright sunlight. Surely this enforced silence would do something to calm her down? Instead, it only served to deepen her shame.

'The disgrace!' she said, drawing her breath, and looking round, her back stiff.

Sheepishly, he grinned again and looked at his father, who pushed forward his white moustache and stolidly gazed at the pulpit.

Once more, he was in disgrace. He had always been in disgrace ever since, a boy in striped pants, called 'Zebra' by his unfeeling friends, he had left school for the last time and kicked his books high in the air over the wall into Sighthill Cemetery. The only prize he had ever had in his life was a book called *No and Where to Say It*, and that was for regular attendance at the Highland Society School. It was a good book. It told you about the perils of life for a young man, and how easy it was, after the first weak 'Yes' to evil companions, to go on saying 'Yes', and end up gambling, drinking, going with women and spending your substance, or breaking your mother's heart.

'You'll break my heart!' she hissed now. 'You and your wild hooligan freens! –'

He had learned to say 'No' from that book. Surely *he* could not be breaking his mother's heart? He did not drink. He did not gamble. All he did was box every Sunday morning in the stables behind Possil Quarry.

He was not, Sawney told himself, in the habit of grousing, but what chance had he ever had? Instead of meditating now on his sins, as he should have done, or trying to remember exactly what it was that Joseph had taken with him from Pharaoh's palace, he began to think of his own upbringing. An old man, who had once been an agricultural labourer, wearing a lum hat wanting a crown, had stood like a clown in the cobbled backyard of the house in Grafton Street when he was born, his patron saint, an industrial troubadour, singing in beggared chivalry. In token of the day of infinite jest it was, he played on a flute that through his mother's dreams had drowned the sound of the traffic, and now and then quavered a thoroughly commercial chorus:

'Balloons and windmills for jelly jars!'

Amid that great conglomeration of city streets, blocks of tenements, unsightly factories, and engineering shops, intricate as the network of railways imposed on the town without so much as a by-your-leave, without planning of any sort, and with no principles at all save those of immediate and substantial gain, there was no one to suckle the child except the midwife, a stout buxom woman, timeless as one of the Furies, as it lay blinking in the bed on the wall.

Outside his room lay the rampant scenery of loch and mountain, but Campsie and Lennoxtown were as far away, for the child, as the life his ancestors had once led among these former fields. Their miles had been transformed into money. Nearer were the forests of poverty broken down into the fuel and ash of coal-depots and yards. Nearer were the foliage and sky of hoardings, blossoming enormous letters and pictures, a mythology of commerce, whose gods and demons waited to invade his fairyland. Nearer were the woodland paths of tramlines and railways. An iron song of bells and sirens stilled the birds. He had been born into a cage.

Nomadic crime had settled on these steppes. Where once the total police force had consisted of Sergeant Oliver and Constable Walker, now twenty-six officers and men were required to keep what they called 'the peace', a force larger than that of other equally populated areas further south – such as Ayr.

His self-pity was cut rudely short.

A thunder of shuffling presaged the 'skailing' of the kirk. The congregation relaxed and allowed itself the luxury of starched smiles.

Sawney rose, and filtered, slowly and shamefully, out into the bright sunlight, feeling more forsaken, more forlorn than ever.

Outside, little groups stood discussing the sermon, waiting for friends, inspecting each other's dress, or gossiping. Mrs Anderson sailed past them, her ears burning, imagining that behind her she could hear suppressed laughter, scandalous allegations and even criminal threats.

She waited until she had reached the comparative neutrality of the pavement, then she spun round on her son, who had been dragging behind like an unwilling puppy.

'How did it happen? Who did it to ye? It serves ye right!' she said in one breath.

'It wasna my fault, honest! He hit me first.'

'Who? I'll never, *never* forgive ye for this, I swear!'

'Dukes Kinnaird. He was sparring. He's to fight the English champion tomorrow. They asked me to go a couple of rounds with him.'

'Did ye?' asked the white-haired old man who was his father, stuffing thick black down into his pipe and trying to look angry, in support of his wife.

'It was only supposed to be a spar,' pleaded Sawney, 'but all of a sudden he hit me right between the eyes. I saw he was coming for a knock-out, the dirty dog.'

'Don't dare use that language in front of me. On a Sunday, too!'

'What happened?' his father asked.

'I let go with my left and crossed with my right. He went back over the ropes into a bath of hot water.'

The old man laughed. His wife turned on him. 'That's enough of you! Well, I'm for no more of it. Ye can come hame and pack yer things. I don't want ye in my hoose. Ye'll end up on the end of a rope one day, I tell ye.'

For all his waywardness, Sawney was genuinely appalled. Leave home? Where would he go? He'd be a laughing stock. He knew his mother, the auld wife, was hard, but only now was he beginning to realize just how hard. She seemed to have no affection for him left.

'Ye'll pack your things and away this very night!' she said.

He looked at the auld wife to see if she meant it. Her collar stood high on her scrawny neck, and her hat, with one feather on it, made her seem a comical figure, in her anger.

'Why can't you be liker your brother?' his father asked in a low voice. 'He never gets into any scrapes.'

'We canny all be in the Post Office,' said Sawney.

'He's a well-behaved lad. It's a pity ye werena liker him. He'll do weel for himself.'

Sawney did not doubt it. He had never denied that his brother was a very worthy man, a gentleman, and different altogether from himself. It had seemed natural to him, even as a boy, that he should have to fight Jimmy's battles, although Jimmy was older than he was, in the days when fights really were fights. Many a 'jelly-nose' he had awarded boys at school to save his brother's reputation and the family honour, but it never occurred to him to talk about it, or to think there was any particular merit in it. Jimmy was the meritorious one. He never got into scrapes, never fought, never squabbled. Such things were beneath him. He read books until they wafted him into the Post Office, and now he was a Sorter – to Sawney, one of the intellectuals.

As they walked down Hillkirk Road, Mrs Anderson bowing in enforced silence, and screwing up her eyes in what she imagined to be a smile to her neighbours, he had to step on to the pavement to avoid a horse and cart, which with a great grinding of the brake was proceeding downhill. It reminded him of early escapades, which really, he thought, had been enough to break even his mother's stout heart. Had he been younger, he would almost certainly have jumped on the back of that same lorry. He had always done so, until the fatal day when he slipped and the wheel went over his leg, breaking it. He had then had to spend six weeks in bed. What a delight it had been to get out again!

He could still remember that afternoon as clearly as this one. It had been such heaven to run about with his leg out of plaster of Paris, that he must have gone slightly mad. Another lorry passed, and forgetting his mother's injunctions, he had darted after it as soon as he was out of the close-mouth. Leaning on the back with his stomach, he heaved himself up, putting one foot on the rear-axle as he did so. To his horror, his foot slipped and slid through between the spokes. He had howled, for the bone was broken, for the second time. Then, far more scared of his mother than of what had happened to his foot, he had limped upstairs into the close, and sat for three-quarters of an hour on the stairhead lavatory seat, white and sick, gazing at the blood on his leg and hoping somehow it would heal before he had to go in. It did not heal, and he had had a thrashing on top of the ordeal.

Now they were in Springburn Road and Mrs Anderson could give something like full vent to her fury.

'I've a good mind to belt yer ear!' she said. 'If you were half a man you'd dae it!' she concluded to her husband.

'But he's a man!' protested the latter. 'He's past that!' Then, seeing the ruthlessness in his wife's features, he came to a firm resolve.

'All right,' he said, 'I'll take him in hand myself.'

'You will,' she repeated, 'and he'll go this very night, don't forget!'

'How could you do it? To me? Your own mother? Don't I work and slave for ye? Haven't I always worked and slaved to bring you up in decency?'

She was working herself up into a frenzy, starting a 'flyting', and Sawney sought for a way of escape, any way of escape.

'You told me to come to Church, so I came!' he parried.

'You came! You came did ye? Do ye know what the neighbours will be saying this verry meenit? Do ye?'

'Excuse me, mither,' he said, 'there's Rob across the street. I want to talk to him. See you later!'

As he dashed across the roadway to Rob, he heard his mother's last few words hurtle after him.

'Ye can come and fetch yer things when ye're ready!'

It was late when Sawney finally arrived home, having put off the evil hour as long as he possibly could. The door was locked. But it was not the first time he had been locked out, and he knew what to do. Prising open the bedroom window, he climbed up and firmly grasped the aspidistra plant he knew stood there, so that it should not fall over. Then, stepping in, he advanced with it in his arms, through the darkness, into the middle of the room. There was a loud crash.

He had walked bang into the half-open door. Now the fat was in the fire! For a second there was silence, then:

'Come here!' thundered his father's voice from the kitchen.

Walking awkwardly through, the plant still in his hand, he saw the old man standing firmly by the gas-bracket, in his shirt-sleeves, with his cap on.

'I've come to get my things,' he said sullenly. '– are they upstairs?'

'A fine time to come in I must say! Yer things? I've done all *your* packing, my lad! There's nothing left for you to do. It's all here for you to take!'

He had never seen his father so determined before. It was an unpleasant shock. He had no idea where he would go in the middle of the night, unless to Rob's. He saw his father peer forward, as though to read his mood, and an unreasoning anger took hold of him:

'I'm not going to give up boxing because of her,' he said defiantly. 'Where are my things?'

'Ye can do whatever ye like. It's up to you,' was the answer. 'Your things? How many things dae ye think ye've got, beyond what ye stand up in, ye pauper? There's your things, the lot of them!'

He nodded towards the mantelpiece. Sawney's eyes followed.

'There's only a matchbox there!' he said.

His father's features relaxed. 'I ken that,' he answered, knocking out his pipe, 'but it's big enough to hold a' *you* own!'

They stared at each other, and ruefully smiled.

His father put his fingers on the gas-bracket.

'Try not to upset your mother again!' he said. 'Are you a' right?'

'All right,' said Sawney, about to speak, but his father had already turned down the gas and the little kitchen was in complete darkness.

By the red glare of the fire they made their way to bed.

Fred Urquhart

ALICKY'S WATCH

Alexander's watch stopped on the morning of his mother's funeral. The watch had belonged to his grandfather and had been given to Alexander on his seventh birthday two years before. It had a large tarnished metal case and he could scarcely see the face through the smoky celluloid front, but Alexander treasured it. He carried it everywhere, and whenever anybody mentioned the time Alexander would take out the watch, look at it, shake his head with the senile seriousness of some old man he had seen, and say: 'Ay, man, but is that the time already?'

And now the watch had stopped. The lesser tragedy assumed proportions which had not been implicit in the greater one. His mother's death seemed far away now because it had been followed by such a period of hustle and bustle: for the past three days the tiny house had been crowded with people coming and going. There had been visits from the undertakers, visits to the drapers for mourning-bands and black neckties. There had been an unwonted silence with muttered 'sshs' whenever he or James spoke too loudly. And there had been continual genteel bickerings between his two grandmothers, each of them determined to uphold the dignity of death in the house, but each of them equally determined to have her own way in the arrangements for the funeral.

The funeral was a mere incident after all that had gone before. The stopping of the watch was the real tragedy. At two o'clock when the cars arrived, Alexander still had not got over it. He kept his hand in his pocket, fingering it all through the short service conducted in the parlour while slitherings and muffled knocks signified that the coffin was being carried out to the hearse. And he was still clutching it with a small, sweaty hand when he took his seat in the first car between his father and his Uncle Jimmy.

His mother was to be buried at her birthplace, a small mining village sixteen miles out from Edinburgh. His father and his maternal grandmother, Granny Peebles, had had a lot of argument about this. His father had wanted his mother to be cremated, but Granny Peebles had said: 'But we have the ground, Sandy! We have the ground all ready waiting at Bethniebrig. It would be a pity not to use it. There's plenty of room on top of her father for poor Alice. And there'll still be enough room left for me – God help me! – when I'm ready to follow them.'

'But the expense, Mrs Peebles, the expense,' his father had said. 'It'll cost a lot to take a funeral all that distance, for mind you we'll have to have a lot o' carriages, there's such a crowd o' us.'

'It winna be ony mair expensive than payin' for cremation,' Granny Peebles had retorted. 'I dinna hold wi' this cremation, onywye, it's ungodly. And besides the ground's there waiting.'

The argument had gone back and forth, but in the end Mrs Peebles had won. Though it was still rankling in his father's mind when he took his seat in the front mourning-car. 'It's a long way, Jimmy,' he said to his brother. 'It's a long way to take the poor lass. She'd ha'e been better, I'm thinkin', to have gone up to Warriston Crematorium.'

'Ay, but Mrs Peebles had her mind made up aboot that,' Uncle Jimmy said. 'She's a tartar, Mrs Peebles, when it comes to layin' doon the law.'

Although Alexander was so preoccupied with his stopped watch he wondered, as he had so often wondered in the past, why his father and his Uncle Jimmy called her Mrs Peebles when they called Granny Matheson 'Mother'. But he did not dare ask.

' "We have the ground at Bethniebrig, Sandy," ' mimicked Uncle Jimmy. ' "And if we have the ground we must use it. There'll still be room left for me when my time comes." The auld limmer, I notice there was no word aboot there bein' room for you when *your* time comes, m'man!'

Alexander's father did not answer. He sat musing in his new-found dignity of widowerhood; his back was already bowed with the responsibility of being father and mother to two small boys. He was only thirty-one.

All the way to Bethniebrig Cemetery Alexander kept his hand in his pocket, clasping the watch. During the burial service, where he was conscious of being watched and afterwards when both he and James were wept over and kissed by many strange women, he did not dare touch his treasure. But on the return journey he took the watch from his pocket and sat with it on his knee. His father was safely in the first car with Mr Ogilvie, the minister, and his mother's uncles, Andrew and Pat. Alexander knew that neither his Uncle Jimmy nor his Uncle Jimmy's chum, Ernie, would mind if he sat with the watch in his hand.

'Is it terrible bad broken, Alicky?' asked James, who was sitting between Ernie and his mother's cousin, Arthur.

'Ay,' Alexander said.

'Never mind, laddie, ye can aye get a new watch, but ye cannie get a new –'

Ernie's observation ended with a yelp of pain. Uncle Jimmy grinned and said: 'Sorry, I didnie notice your leg was in my way!'

The cars were going quicker now than they had gone on the way to the cemetery. Alicky did not look out of the windows; he tinkered with his watch, winding and rewinding it, holding it up to his ear to see if there was any effect.

'Will it never go again, Alicky?' James said.

'Here, you leave Alicky alone and watch the rabbits,' Ernie said, pulling James on his knee. 'My God, look at them! All thae white tails bobbin' aboot! Wish I had a rifle here, I'd soon take a pot-shot at them.'

'Wish we had a pack o' cards,' said Auntie Liz's young man, Matthew. 'We could have a fine wee game o' Solo.'

'I've got my pack in my pocket,' Ernie said, raking for them. 'What aboot it, lads?'

'Well –' Uncle Jimmy looked at Cousin Arthur; then he shook his head. 'No, I dinnie think this is either the time or the place.'

'Whatever you say, pal!' Ernie gave all his attention to James, shooting imaginary rabbits, crooking his finger and making popping sounds with his tongue against the roof of his mouth.

The tram-lines appeared, then the huge villas at Newington. The funeral cars had to slow down when Clerk Street and the busier thoroughfare started. James pressed his nose against the window to gaze at the New Victoria which had enormous posters billing a 'mammoth Western spectacle'.

'Jings, but I'd like to go to that,' he said. 'Wouldn't you, Alicky?'

But Alicky did not look out at the rearing horses and the Red Indians in full chase. He put his watch to his ear and shook it violently for the fiftieth time.

'I doubt it's no good, lad,' Uncle Jimmy said. 'It's a gey auld watch, ye ken. It's seen its day and generation.'

The blinds were up when they got back, and the table was laid for high tea. Granny Matheson and Granny Peebles were buzzing around, carrying plates of cakes and tea-pots. Auntie Liz took the men's coats and hats and piled them on the bed in the back bedroom. Alicky noticed that the front room where the coffin had been was still shut. There was a constrained air about everybody as they stood about in the parlour. They rubbed their hands and spoke about the weather. It was only when Granny Matheson cried: 'Sit in now and get your tea,' that they began to return to normal.

'Will you sit here, Mr Ogilvie, beside me?' she said. 'Uncle Andrew, you'll sit there beside Liz, and Uncle Pat over there.'

'Sandy, you'll sit here beside me,' Granny Peebles called from the other end of the table. 'And Uncle George'll sit next to Cousin Peggy, and Arthur, you can sit –'

'Arthur's to sit beside Ernie,' Granny Matheson cut in. 'Now, I think that's us all settled, so will you pour the tea at your end, m'dear?'

'I think we'd better wait for Mr Ogilvie,' Granny Peebles said stiffly. And she inclined her head towards the minister, smoothing the black silk of her bosom genteelly.

Alicky and James had been relegated to a small table, which they were glad was nearer to their Granny Matheson's end of the large table. They bowed their heads with everyone else when Mr Ogilvie started to pray, but after the first few solemn seconds Alicky allowed himself to keek from under his eyelashes at the dainties on the sideboard. He was sidling his hand into his pocket to feel his watch when Tiddler, the cat, sprang on to the sideboard and nosed a large plate of boiled ham. Alicky squirmed in horror, wondering whether it would be politic to draw attention to the cat and risk being called 'a wicked ungodly wee boy for not payin' attention to what the minister's sayin' about yer puir mammy', or whether it would be better to ignore it. But Mr Ogilvie saved the situation. He stopped in the middle of a sentence and said calmly in his non-praying voice: 'Mrs Peebles, I see that the cat's up at the boiled ham. Hadn't we better do something about it?'

After tea the minister left, whisky and some bottles of beer were produced for the men, and port wine for the ladies. The company thawed even more. Large, jovial Uncle Pat, whose red face was streaming with sweat, unbuttoned his waistcoat, saying: 'I canna help it, Georgina, if I dinna loosen my westkit I'll burst the buttons. Ye shouldna gi'e fowk sae much to eat!'

'I'm glad you tucked in and enjoyed yourself,' Granny Peebles said, nodding her head regally.

'Mr Ogilvie's a nice man,' Granny Matheson said, taking a cigarette from Uncle Jimmy. 'But he kind o' cramps yer style, doesn't he? I mean it's no' like havin' one o' yer own in the room. Ye've aye got to be on yer p's and q's wi' him, mindin' he's a minister.'

'Ye havenie tellt us who was all at the cemetery,' she said, blowing a vast cloud of smoke in the air and wafting it off with a plump arm. 'Was there a lot o' Bethniebrig folk there?'

'Ay, there was a good puckle,' Uncle Pat said. 'I saw auld Alec Whitten and young Tam Forbes and –'

'Oh, ay, they fair turned out in force,' Uncle Jimmy said.

'And why shouldn't they?' Granny Peebles said. 'After all, our family's had connections with Bethniebrig for generations. I'm glad they didnie forget to pay their respects to puir Alice.' And she dabbed her eyes with a small handkerchief, which had never been shaken out of the fold.

'I must say it's a damned cauld draughty cemetery yon,' Uncle Andrew said. 'I was right glad when Mr Ogilvie stopped haverin' and we got down to business. I was thinkin' I'd likely catch my death o' cauld if he yapped on much longer.'

'Uncle Pat near got his death o' cauld, too,' Uncle Jimmy grinned. 'Didn't ye, auld yin?'

'Ay, ay, lad, I near did that!' Uncle Pat guffawed. 'I laid my tile hat ahint a gravestone at the beginnin' of the service and when it was ower I didna know where it was. Faith, we had a job findin' it.'

'Ay, we had a right search!' Uncle Jimmy said.

'It's a pity headstone's havenie knobs on them for hats,' Auntie Liz said.

'Really, Lizzie Matheson!' cried Granny Peebles.

Auntie Liz and the younger women began to clear the table, but Alexander noticed that Auntie Liz did not go so often to the scullery as the others. She stood with dirty plates in her hands, listening to the men who had gathered around the fire. Uncle Pat had his feet up on the fender, his large thighs spread wide apart. 'It's a while since we were all gathered together like this,' he remarked, finishing his whisky and placing the glass with an ostentatious clatter on the mantelpiece. 'I think the last time was puir Willie's funeral two years syne.'

'Ay, it's a funny thing but it's aye funerals we seem to meet at,' Uncle Andrew said.

'Well, well, there's nothin' sae bad that hasna got some guid in it,' Uncle Pat said. 'Yes, Sandy lad, I'll take another wee nippie, thank ye!' And he watched his nephew with a benign expression as another dram was poured for him. 'Well, here's your guid health again, Georgina! I'm needin' this, I can tell ye, for it was a cauld journey doon this mornin' frae Aberdeen, and it was a damned sight caulder standin' in that cemetery.'

Alexander squeezed his way behind the sofa into the corner beside the whatnot. Looking to see that he was unnoticed, he drew the watch cautiously from his pocket and tinkered with it. As the room filled with tobacco smoke the talk and laughter got louder.

'Who was yon wi' the long brown moth-eaten coat?' Uncle Jimmy said. 'He came up and shook hands wi' me after the service. I didnie ken him from Adam, but I said howdye-do. God, if he doesnie drink he should take doon his sign!'

'Och, thon cauld wind would make anybody's nose red,' Matthew said.

'Ay, and who was yon hard case in the green bowler?' Ernie said.

'Ach, there was dozens there in bowlers,' Uncle Jimmy said.

'Ah, but this was a *green* bowler!'

Uncle Jimmy guffawed. 'That reminds me o' the bar about the old lady and the minister. Have ye heard it?'

Alexander prised open the case of the watch, and then took a pin from a small box on the whatnot and inserted it delicately into the works. There was loud laughter, and Ernie shouted above the others: 'Ay, but have ye heard the one about –?'

'What are ye doin', Alicky?' James whispered, leaning over the back of the sofa.

'Shutup,' Alexander said in a low voice,. bending over the watch and poking gently at the tiny wheels.

'I dinnie see why women can't go to funerals, too,' Auntie Liz said. 'You men ha'e all the fun.'

'Lizzie Matheson!' Granny Peebles cried. 'What a like thing to say! I thought ye were going to help your mother wash the dishes?'

It was going! Alicky could hardly believe his eyes. The small wheels were turning – turning slowly, but they were turning. He held the watch to his ear, and a slow smile of pleasure came over his face.

'What are you doing there behind the sofa?'

Alexander and James jumped guiltily. 'I've got my watch to go!' Alicky cried to his father. 'Listen!'

'Alexander Matheson, have you nothing better to do than tinker wi' an auld watch?' Granny Peebles said. 'I'm surprised at ye,' she said as she swept out.

Abashed, Alicky huddled down beside the sofa. James climbed over and sat behind him. They listened to the men telling stories and laughing, but when the room darkened and the voices got even louder the two little boys yawned. They whispered together. 'Go on, you ask him,' James pleaded. 'You're the auldest!'

James went on whispering. Beer bottles were emptied, the laughter and the family reminiscences got wilder. And presently, plucking up courage, Alexander went to his father and said: 'Can James and I go to the pictures?'

There was a short silence.

'Alexander Matheson,' his father cried. 'Alexander Matheson, you should be ashamed o' yersel' sayin' that and your puir mother no' cauld in her grave.'

'Och, let the kids go, Sandy,' Uncle Jimmy said. 'It's no' much fun for them here.'

'We're no' here for fun,' Alexander's father said, but his voice trailed away indecisively.

'You go and put the case to your granny, lad, and see what she says,' Uncle Jimmy said. He watched the two boys go to the door, then looking round to see that Mrs Peebles was still out of the room, he said, 'Your Granny Matheson.'

Five minutes later, after a small lecture, Granny Matheson gave them the entrance money to the cinema. 'Now remember two things,' she said, showing them out. 'Don't run, and be sure and keep your bonnets on.'

'Okay,' Alicky said.

They walked sedately to the end of the street. Alicky could feel the watch ticking feebly in his pocket, and his fingers caressed the metal case. When they got to the corner they looked round, then they whipped off their bonnets, stuffed them in their pockets, and ran as quickly as they could to the cinema.

Muriel Spark

THE HOUSE OF THE FAMOUS POET

In the summer of 1944, when it was nothing for trains from the provinces to be five or six hours late, I travelled to London on the night train from Edinburgh, which, at York, was already three hours late. There were ten people in the compartment, only two of whom I remember well, and for good reason.

I have the impression, looking back on it, of a row of people opposite me, dozing untidily with heads askew, and, as it often seems when we look at sleeping strangers, their features had assumed extra emphasis and individuality, sometimes disturbing to watch. It was as if they had rendered up their daytime talent for obliterating the outward traces of themselves in exchange for mental obliteration. In this way they resembled a twelfth-century fresco; there was a look of medieval unselfconsciousness about these people, all except one.

This was a private soldier who was awake to a greater degree than most people are when they are not sleeping. He was smoking cigarettes one after the other with long, calm puffs. I thought he looked excessively evil – an atavistic type. His forehead must have been less than two inches high above dark, thick eyebrows, which met. His jaw was not large, but it was ape-like; so was his small nose and so were his deep, close-set eyes. I thought there must have been some consanguinity in the parents. He was quite a throwback.

As it turned out, he was extremely gentle and kind. When I ran out of cigarettes, he fished about in his haversack and produced a packet for me and one for a girl sitting next to me. We both tried, with a flutter of small change, to pay him. Nothing would please him at all but that we should accept his cigarettes, whereupon he returned to his silent, reflective smoking.

I felt a sort of pity for him then, rather as we feel towards animals we know to be harmless, such as monkeys. But I realized that, like the pity we expend on monkeys merely because they are not human beings, this pity was not needed.

Receiving the cigarettes gave the girl and myself common ground, and we conversed quietly for the rest of the journey. She told me she had a job in London as a domestic helper and nursemaid. She looked as if she had come from a country district – her very blonde hair, red face and large bones gave the impression of power, as if she was used to carrying heavy things, perhaps great scuttles of coal, or two children at a time. But what made me curious about her was her voice, which was cultivated, melodious and restrained.

Towards the end of the journey, when the people were beginning to jerk themselves straight and the rushing to and fro in the corridor had started, this girl, Elise, asked me to come with her to the house where she worked. The master, who was something in a university, was away with his wife and family.

I agreed to this, because at that time I was in the way of thinking that the discovery of an educated servant girl was valuable and something to be gone deeper into. It had the element of experience – perhaps, even of truth – and I believed, in those days, that truth is stranger than fiction. Besides, I wanted to spend that Sunday in London. I was due back next day at my job in a branch of the civil service which had been evacuated to the country and, for a reason that is another story, I didn't want to return too soon. I had some telephoning to do. I wanted to wash and change. I wanted to know more about the girl. So I thanked Elise and accepted her invitation.

I regretted it as soon as we got out of the train at King's Cross, some minutes after ten. Standing up tall on the platform, Elise looked unbearably tired, as if not only the last night's journey but every fragment of her unknown life was suddenly heaping up on top of her. The power I had noticed in the train was no longer there. As she called, in her beautiful voice, for a porter, I saw that on the side of her head that had been away from me in the train, her hair was parted in a dark streak, which, by contrast with the yellow, looked navy blue. I had thought, when I first saw her, that possibly her hair was bleached, but now, seeing it so badly done, seeing this navy blue parting pointing like an arrow to the weighted weariness of her face, I, too, got the sensation of great tiredness. And it was not only the strain of the journey that I felt, but the foreknowledge of boredom that comes upon us unaccountably at the beginning of a quest, and that checks, perhaps mercifully, our curiosity.

And, as it happened, there really wasn't much to learn about Elise. The explanation of her that I had been prompted to seek I got in the taxi between King's Cross and the house at Swiss Cottage. She came of a good family, who thought her a pity, and she them. Having no training for anything else, she had taken a domestic job on leaving home. She was engaged to an Australian soldier billeted also at Swiss Cottage.

Perhaps it was the anticipation of a day's boredom, maybe it was the effect of no sleep or the fact that the V-1 sirens were sounding, but I felt some sourness when I saw the house. The garden was growing all over the place. Elise opened the front door, and we entered a darkish room almost wholly taken up with a long, plain wooden work-table. On this were a half-empty marmalade jar, a pile of papers, and a dried-up ink bottle. There was a steel-canopied bed, known as a Morrison shelter, in one corner and some photographs on the mantelpiece, one of a schoolboy wearing glasses. Everything was tainted with Elise's weariness and my own distaste. But Elise didn't seem to be aware of the exhaustion so plainly revealed on her face. She did not even bother to take her coat off, and as it was too tight for her I wondered how she could move about so quickly with this restriction added to the weight of her tiredness. But, with her coat still buttoned tight, Elise phoned her boy-friend and made breakfast, while I washed in a dim, blue, cracked bathroom upstairs.

When I found that she had opened my hold-all without asking me and had taken out my rations, I was a little pleased. It seemed a friendly action, with some measure of reality about it, and I felt better. But I was still irritated by the house. I felt there was no justification for the positive lack of consequence which was lying about here and there. I asked no questions about the owner who was something in a university, for fear of getting the answer I expected – that he was away visiting his grandchildren, at some family gathering in the home counties. The owners of the house had no reality for me, and I looked upon the place as belonging to, and permeated with, Elise.

I went with her to a nearby public house, where she met her boy-friend and one or two other Australian soldiers. They had with them a thin Cockney girl with bad teeth. Elise was very happy, and insisted in her lovely voice that they should all come along to a party at the house that evening. In a fine aristocratic tone, she demanded that each should bring a bottle of beer.

During the afternoon Elise said she was going to have a bath, and she showed me a room where I could use the telephone and sleep if I wanted. This was a large, light room with several windows, much more orderly than the rest of the house, and lined with books. There was only one unusual thing about it: beside one of the windows was a bed, but this bed was only a fairly thick mattress made up neatly on the floor. It was obviously a bed on the floor with some purpose, and again I was angered to think of the futile crankiness of the elderly professor who had thought of it.

I did my telephoning, and decided to rest. But first I wanted to find something to read. The books puzzled me. None of them seemed to be automatically part of a scholar's library. An inscription in one book was signed by the author, a well-known novelist. I found another inscribed copy, and this had the name of the recipient. On a sudden idea, I went to the desk, where while I had been telephoning I had noticed a pile of unopened letters. For the first time, I looked at the name of the owner of the house.

I ran to the bathroom and shouted through the door to Elise, 'Is this the house of the famous poet?'

'Yes,' she called. 'I *told* you.'

She had told me nothing of the kind. I felt I had no right at all to be there, for it wasn't, now, the house of Elise acting by proxy for some unknown couple. It was the house of a famous modern poet. The thought that at any moment he and his family might walk in and find me there terrified me. I insisted that Elise should open the bathroom door and tell me to my face that there was no possible chance of their returning for many days to come.

Then I began to think about the house itself, which Elise was no longer accountable for. Its new definition, as the house of a poet whose work I knew well, many of whose poems I knew by heart, gave it altogether a new appearance.

To confirm this, I went outside and stood exactly where I had been when I first saw the garden from the door of the taxi. I wanted to get my first impression for a second time.

And this time I saw an absolute purpose in the overgrown garden, which, since then, I have come to believe existed in the eye of the beholder. But, at the time, the room we had first entered, and which had riled me, now began to give back a meaning, and whatever was, was right. The caked-up bottle of ink, which Elise had put on the mantelpiece, I replaced on the table to make sure. I saw a photograph I hadn't noticed before, and I recognized the famous poet.

It was the same with the upstairs room where Elise had put me, and I handled the books again, not so much with the sense that they belonged to the famous poet but with some curiosity about how they had been made. The sort of question that occurred to me was where the paper had come from and from what sort of vegetation was manufactured the black print, and these things have not troubled me since.

The Australians and the Cockney girl came around about seven. I had planned to catch an eight-thirty train to the country, but when I telephoned to confirm the time I found there were no Sunday trains running. Elise, in her friendly and exhausted way, begged me to stay, without attempting to be too serious about it. The sirens were starting up again. I asked Elise once more to repeat that the poet and his family could by no means return that night. But I asked this question more abstractedly than before, as I was thinking of the sirens and of the exact proportions of the noise they made. I wondered, as well, what sinister genius of the Home Office could have invented so ominous a wail, and why. And I was thinking of the word 'siren'. The sound then became comical, for I imagined some maniac sea nymph from centuries past belching into the year 1944. Actually, the sirens frightened me.

Most of all, I wondered about Elise's party. Everyone roamed about the place as if it were nobody's house in particular, with Elise the best-behaved of the lot. The Cockney girl sat on the long table and gave of her best to the skies every time a bomb exploded. I had the feeling that the house had been requisitioned for an evening by the military. It was so hugely and everywhere occupied that it became not the house I had first entered, nor the house of the famous poet, but a third house – the one I had vaguely prefigured when I stood, bored, on the platform at King's Cross station. I saw a great amount of tiredness among these people, and heard, from the loud noise they made, that they were all lacking sleep. When the beer was finished and they were gone, some to their billets, some to pubs, and the Cockney girl to her Underground shelter where she had slept for weeks past, I asked Elise, 'Don't you feel tired?'

'No,' she said with agonizing weariness, 'I never feel tired.'

I fell asleep myself, as soon as I had got into the bed on the floor in the upstairs room, and overslept until Elise woke me at eight. I had wanted to get up early to catch a nine o'clock train, so I hadn't much time to speak to her. I did notice, though, that she had lost some of her tired look.

I was pushing my things into my hold-all while Elise went up the street to catch a taxi when I heard someone coming upstairs. I thought it was Elise come back, and I looked out of the open door. I saw a man in uniform carrying an enormous parcel in both hands. He looked down as he climbed, and had a cigarette in his mouth.

'Do you want Elise?' I called, thinking it was one of her friends.

He looked up, and I recognized the soldier, the throwback, who had given us cigarettes in the train.

'Well, anyone will do,' he said. 'The thing is, I've got to get back to camp and I'm stuck for the fare – eight and six.'

I told him I could manage it, and was finding the money when he said, putting his parcel on the floor, 'I don't want to borrow it. I wouldn't think of borrowing it. I've got something for sale.'

'What's that?' I said.

'A funeral,' said the soldier. 'I've got it here.'

This alarmed me, and I went to the window. No hearse, no coffin stood below. I saw only the avenue of trees.

The soldier smiled. 'It's an abstract funeral,' he explained, opening the parcel.

He took it out and I examined it carefully, greatly comforted. It was very much the sort of thing I had wanted – rather more purple in parts than I would have liked, for I was not in favour of this colour of mourning. Still, I thought I could tone it down a bit.

Delighted with the bargain, I handed over the eight shillings and sixpence. There was a great deal of this abstract funeral. Hastily, I packed some of it into the hold-all. Some I stuffed in my pockets, and there was still some left over. Elise had returned with a cab and I hadn't much time. So I ran for it, out of the door and out of the gate of the house of the famous poet, with the rest of my funeral trailing behind me.

You will complain that I am withholding evidence. Indeed, you may wonder if there is any evidence at all. 'An abstract funeral,' you will say, 'is neither here nor there. It is only a notion. You cannot pack a notion into your bag. You cannot see the colour of a notion.'

You will insinuate that what I have just told you is pure fiction. Hear me to the end.

I caught the train. Imagine my surprise when I found, sitting opposite me, my friend the soldier, of whose existence you are so sceptical.

'As a matter of interest,' I said, 'how would you describe all this funeral you sold me?'

'Describe it?' he said. 'Nobody describes an abstract funeral. You just conceive it.'

'There is much in what you say,' I replied. 'Still, describe it I must, because it is not every day one comes by an abstract funeral.'

'I am glad you appreciate that,' said the soldier.

'And after the war,' I continued, 'when I am no longer a civil servant, I hope, in a few deftly turned phrases, to write of my experiences at the house of the famous poet, which has culminated like this. But of course,' I added, 'I will need to say what it looks like.'

The soldier did not reply.

'If it were an okapi or a sea-cow,' I said, 'I would have to say what it looked like. No one would believe me otherwise.'

'Do you want your money back?' asked the soldier. 'Because if so, you can't have it. I spent it on my ticket.'

'Don't misunderstand me,' I hastened to say. 'The funeral is a delightful abstraction. Only, I wish to put it down in writing.'

I felt a great pity for the soldier on seeing his worried look. The ape-like head seemed the saddest thing in the world.

'I make them by hand,' he said, 'these abstract funerals.'

A siren sounded somewhere, far away.

'Elise bought one of them last month. She hadn't any complaints. I change at the next stop,' he said, getting down his kit from the rack. 'And what's more,' he said, 'your famous poet bought one.'

'Oh, did he?' I said.

'Yes,' he said. 'No complaints. It was just what he wanted – the idea of a funeral.'

The train pulled up. The soldier leaped down and waved. As the train started again, I unpacked my abstract funeral and looked at it for a few moments.

'To hell with the idea,' I said. 'It's a real funeral I want.'

'All in good time,' said a voice from the corridor.

'*You* again,' I said. It was the soldier.

'No,' he said, 'I got off at the last station. I'm only a notion of myself.'

'Look here,' I said, 'would you be offended if I throw all this. away?'

'Of course not,' said the soldier. 'You can't offend a notion.'

'I want a real funeral,' I explained. 'One of my own.'

'That's right,' said the soldier.

'And then I'll be able to write about it and go into all the details,' I said.

'Your own funeral?' he said. 'You want to write it up?'

'Yes,' I said.

'But,' said he, 'you're only human. Nobody reports on their own funeral. It's got to be abstract.'

'You see my predicament?' I said.

'I see it,' he replied. 'I get off at this stop.'

This notion of a soldier alighted. Once more the train put on speed. Out of the window I chucked all my eight and sixpence worth of abstract funeral. I watched it fluttering over the fields and around the tops of camouflaged factories with the sun glittering richly upon it, until it was out of sight.

In the summer of 1944 a great many people were harshly and suddenly killed. The papers reported, in due course, those whose names were known to the public. One of these, the famous poet, had returned unexpectedly to his home at Swiss Cottage a few moments before it was hit direct by a flying bomb. Fortunately, he had left his wife and children in the country.

When I got to the place where my job was, I had some time to spare before going on duty. I decided to ring Elise and thank her properly, as I had left in such a hurry. But the lines were out of order, and the operator could not find words enough to express her annoyance with me. Behind this overworked, quarrelsome voice from the exchange I heard the high, long hoot which means that the telephone at the other end is not functioning, and the sound made me infinitely depressed and weary; it was more intolerable to me than the sirens, and I replaced the receiver; and, in fact, Elise had already perished under the house of the famous poet.

The blue cracked bathroom, the bed on the floor, the caked ink bottle, the neglected garden, and the neat rows of books – I try to gather them together in my mind whenever I am enraged by the thought that Elise and the poet were killed outright. The angels of the Resurrection will invoke the dead man and the dead woman, but who will care to restore the fallen house of the famous poet if not myself? Who else will tell its story?

When I reflect how Elise and the poet were taken in – how they calmly allowed a well-meaning soldier to sell them the notion of a funeral, I remind myself that one day I will accept, and so will you, an abstract funeral, and make no complaints.

Elspeth Davie

PEDESTRIAN

A great patch of scoured and gravelly land at either end marked the approach to the motorway café. Beyond that were flat fields and a long horizon line broken here and there by distant clumps of trees. At no point on this line was there a sign of building. A glass-sided, covered bridge joined the car park to the café, and people if they wished could stand in the middle and look down onto the road below. The four lanes of the motorway carried every sort of traffic. The long vehicles were the most spectacular and there was no limit to their loads – lorries carrying sugar and cement and tanks of petrol went past, carrying building cranes and wooden planks, barrels of beer, cylinders of gas, sheep and horses, bulls in boxes, hens, furniture and parts of aeroplanes. There were lorries carrying cars and lorries carrying lorries.

The café itself was filled day and night with a periodic inrush of people and changed its whole appearance from half-hour to half-hour throughout the twenty-four. It had its empty time and its time of chaos. Habitual tough travellers of the road mixed here with couples stopping for the first time for morning coffee. Here buses disgorged football fans and concert parties, and stuffed family cars laboriously unloaded parents, children, grandparents, for their evening meal. The cars far outnumbered other vehicles. And no pedestrian, as opposed to hitchhiker, was ever seen here, for it would be nearly impossible to arrive by foot. Any person unattached to a vehicle was as unlikely as a being dropped from the skies. There was no place for him on the motorway.

Nevertheless there were still pedestrians in everyday life. A married couple who were queueing at the counter of this café one evening found themselves standing beside a man who admitted to being one himself. The couple had been discussing car mileage with one another and they kindly brought him into it. 'And how about you?' asked the wife. 'How much have you done?' The other smiled but said nothing. He had obviously missed out on their discussion, and she didn't repeat the question. From his blank look she might have just as easily been asking how much time he had done in jail. Behind the counter a woman with a long-armed trowel was shovelling chips from a shelf, while her companion dredged up sausages from a trough of cooling fat. 'Sorry,' said the man suddenly, 'I didn't pick you up just now. No. I'm not in a car. I'm in the bus out there. Long distance to Liverpool.'

'Good idea,' said the woman's husband. 'Good idea to leave it at home once in a while. No fun on the roads these days. No fun at all!'

'No, I haven't got a car.'

'You don't run one?'

'No, never had one.'

'Then you're probably a lot luckier than the rest of us,' said the man after only the slightest pause, at the same time giving him a quick look up and down. He saw a well-set-up fellow, well-dressed and about his own age. Not a young man. This look, however, cost him an outsize scoopful of thick, unwanted gravy on his plate. He slid cautiously on towards a bucket of bright peas. His wife, who had kept her eye on her plate, now bent forward and asked politely: 'Have you ever thought about it?'

'Thought about . . . ?'

'Getting one.'

'No, I can't say I have.'

The woman nodded wisely, blending in a bit of compassion in case there was some good reason for it – a physical or even a mental defect. For a moment the hiss of descending orange and lemonade prevented further talk. The three moved across to a table which had just been vacated by the window. From this point they had a straight view of the bridge and a glimpse of the road beneath. Every now and then, in the momentary silences of noisy places, they could hear the regular swish of passing traffic. On the far side of the bridge glittering ranks of cars filled one end of the parking space with lorries at the other. Long red-and-green buses were waiting near an exit for their passengers.

'You don't mind if I go ahead?' said the man from the bus. 'There's only twenty minutes or so to eat.'

'No, go right on. Don't wait for us,' said the woman. The couple were occupied with some problem about the engine of their car and the unfamiliar sound it had been making for ten miles back. They discussed what kind of sound – tick or rattle or thump – and with almost musicianlike exactitude queried the type of beat – regular or irregular? There was the question of whether to look into it themselves, have it looked into or go straight on. Even now they were careful to include the other in the talk in case he should feel left out. They let him into the endless difficulties of parking, of visiting friends in narrow streets, or of visiting friends in any street, wide or narrow, because of the meter. They told him how much for twenty minutes, how much for forty minutes, how much if you were to talk for an hour. They discussed the price of petrol and of garage repairs and the horrors of breakdown on the road.

'And the hard shoulder can be a very lonely place on the motorway,' said the woman. 'All those cars rushing past you. Have you ever had to pull over yourself?'

'No, I haven't,' the man said, with a hint of apology in his voice.

'Oh no, no – of course you haven't! I absolutely forgot for the moment that you haven't got . . . Excuse me. I am being so stupid.'

The man said no, there was nothing to excuse. It was easy to forget. He added that the hard shoulder did indeed sound a very unsympathetic place to rest on in the night.

The three of them had now finished their first course and had turned towards the door to watch the next group entering. Half a dozen families were coming in, and a carload of men carrying trumpets. Two policemen were moving slowly about among the tables. At the far end of the room a waitress was mopping up the floor where someone had let a plate slide from a tray. The policemen bent and spoke to a man at a table, then sat down, one on either side of him while he put ketchup on a last wedge of steak pie and ate it with seeming relish. The three of them left the café together. 'This is where you find them,' remarked the car-owner to his wife and the passenger from the bus. They had now started on their squares of yellow sponge cake with a custard layer between. The custard too had been sliced into neat and solid squares, and their plates when they had finished were as dry and clean as when they had started. 'One job less for the staff, I suppose,' said the husband examining his dish with distrust.

The other man – seeing they had confided in him – began to tell them what it felt like to walk along the edge of an ordinary country road while the cars went by. The husband looked vaguely aside. It was not a believable thing for a grown man to do and he did not hear it beyond the first sentence. But the woman said: 'You mean hitch-hiking?'

'No, no – just getting about from one place to another, sometimes by bus and train, naturally, and sometimes walking.'

'As a pedestrian?'

'Yes, I suppose so. In cities naturally one walks a good deal.'

'Yes, I see – a pedestrian,' said the woman, looking at him with a vague interest.

Her husband had now brought coffee for the three of them and the man drank his quickly, for the time was up.

'I'm sorry to rush,' he said, 'but the bus leaves in eight minutes, and they don't wait long. Thanks for the coffee – and a very good journey!'

'And the same to you!' They watched him go, weaving between the tables, and a few minutes later saw him hurrying down the glass bridge and starting to run as he reached the far end.

'A pedestrian,' murmured the woman musingly.

'Well, a bus-traveller.'

'But he tells me he walks a lot of the time, in country as well as city.'

After a while her husband looked at his watch. 'Shall we get on then?'

'Might as well. We can take our time.' They wandered slowly away from the windows, looking back to see one of the buses moving off. '*His* bus, I expect,' said the woman. 'Careful and don't slip on that chip,' she added as they passed the spot where the plate had fallen.

The glass bridge over the motorway was the only viewing-point for miles. The man and woman paused in the middle and looked down onto the great streams below. Four or five chains of long vehicles happened to be coming up on one side with a second line going down on the other. Great grey roofs slid beneath them in opposition like extra roads moving along on top of the others. At this time of day the cars too were coming one after the other with scarcely a second between them, and – seen from above – scarcely an inch.

'I can't say I've met many non-drivers in my time,' said the man broodingly, 'but there's usually a perfectly legitimate reason for it. Certainly not money in his case though.'

'Physical disablement, maybe,' said his wife. 'Remember Harry Ewing. *He* didn't drive. He had one short leg.'

'You'd never have known. Anyway, with all the dashboard gadgets these days, what's a short leg, or arm for that matter?'

'Some people have bad eyes,' suggested the woman.

'Funny thing, but I've seen cross-eyed people driving about and nobody stopped them yet. And as for one eye at the wheel – that's common enough, believe me!'

Watchers on the bridge, or any persons not in a hurry, invariably attracted others. Something about the static bridge, sealed in above the speed, made company acceptable. So, before long, the two who had been standing there found that another couple had joined them – a man in a blue summer jacket and his wife in a cream coat. For a while the four of them stood comfortably together, silently watching. Then the first man said, 'My wife and I were speaking about non-drivers – their reasons, I mean, for not having a car. Most disabilities can be overcome, you know.'

'Maybe it's nerves,' said the man in the blue jacket. 'Or more likely psychological.'

'You mean,' said his wife, 'like that woman who'd never let her boy touch a machine – not even a child's scooter. So he never had a car all his life, not even when she was dead. Well, I suppose he loved his mother.'

'Well, I've heard that story the other way,' said her husband. 'His mother *wants* him to own this super-car since ever he opened his eyes. Nagged him all his life. And he won't do it, not even when she's dead.'

'Sure,' said the other man, 'because he *doesn't* love his mother.'

They turned and sauntered slowly along the bridge together like old acquaintances, looking down at the motorway to the left and right of them as though it was still a long, long way off.

'That man in the café – maybe he just didn't want one,' said the first wife. Her husband looked aside again with his vague and unbelieving smile. The four of them now seemed reluctant to reach the end of the bridge. They began to walk more and more slowly as they neared the opening. In front the great gravelled space was, if anything, more closely packed than ever – some cars edging out, others slowly burrowing in like beetles into hidden corners. The two couples paused and stared intently at this space, searching for their own. 'Well, nice to have met you,' they said to one another, 'very nice indeed to have the pleasure . . .' For one more moment they hesitated on the sloping ramp of the bridge. An overpowering whiff of loneliness reached them from the fumy air beyond. Then they stepped down and out into the narrow lanes between the cars and the glittering maze of metal divided them.

George Mackay Brown

THE WIRELESS SET

The first wireless ever to come to the valley of Tronvik in Orkney was brought by Howie Eunson, son of Hugh the fisherman and Betsy.

Howie had been at the whaling in the Antarctic all winter, and he arrived back in Britain in April with a stuffed wallet and jingling pockets. Passing through Glasgow on his way home he bought presents for everyone in Tronvik – fiddle-strings for Sam down at the shore, a bottle of malt whisky for Mansie of the hill, a second-hand volume of Spurgeon's sermons for Mr Sinclair the missionary, sweeties for all the bairns, a meerschaum pipe for his father Hugh and a portable wireless set for his mother Betsy.

There was great excitement the night Howie arrived home in Tronvik. Everyone in the valley – men, women, children, dogs, cats – crowded into the but-end of the croft, as Howie unwrapped and distributed his gifts.

'And have you been a good boy all the time you've been away?' said Betsy anxiously. 'Have you prayed every night, and not sworn?'

'This is thine, mother,' said Howie, and out of a big cardboard box he lifted the portable wireless and set it on the table.

For a full two minutes nobody said a word. They all stood staring at it, making small round noises of wonderment, like pigeons.

'And mercy,' said Betsy at last, 'what is it at all?'

'It's a wireless set,' said Howie proudly. 'Listen.'

He turned a little black knob and a posh voice came out of the box saying that it would be a fine day tomorrow over England, and over Scotland south of the Forth-Clyde valley, but that in the Highlands and in Orkney and Shetland there would be rain and moderate westerly winds.

'If it's a man that's speaking,' said old Hugh doubtfully, 'where is he standing just now?'

'In London,' said Howie.

'Well now,' said Betsy, 'if that isn't a marvel! But I'm not sure, all the same, but what it isn't against the scriptures. Maybe, Howie, we'd better not keep it.'

'Everybody in the big cities has a wireless,' said Howie. 'Even in Kirkwall and Hamnavoe every house has one. But now Tronvik has a wireless as well, and maybe we're not such clodhoppers as they think.'

They all stayed late, listening to the wireless. Howie kept twirling a second little knob, and sometimes they would hear music and sometimes they would hear a kind of loud half-witted voice urging them to use a particular brand of tooth-paste.

At half past eleven the wireless was switched off and everybody went home. Hugh and Betsy and Howie were left alone.

'Men speak,' said Betsy, 'but it's hard to know sometimes whether what they say is truth or lies.'

'This wireless speaks the truth,' said Howie.

Old Hugh shook his head. 'Indeed,' he said, 'it doesn't do that. For the man said there would be rain here and a westerly wind. But I assure you it'll be a fine day, and a southerly wind, and if the Lord spares me I'll get to the lobsters.'

Old Hugh was right. Next day was fine, and he and Howie took twenty lobsters from the creels he had under the Gray Head.

It was in the spring of the year 1939 that the first wireless set came to Tronvik. In September that same year war broke out, and Howie and three other lads from the valley joined the mine-sweepers.

That winter the wireless standing on Betsy's table became the centre of Tronvik. Every evening folk came from the crofts to listen to the nine o'clock news. Hitherto the wireless had been a plaything which discoursed Scottish reels and constipation advertisements and unreliable weather forecasts. But now the whole world was embattled and Tronvik listened appreciatively to enthusiastic commentators telling them that General Gamelin was the greatest soldier of the century, and he had only to say the word for the German Siegfried Line to crumble like sand. In the summer of 1940 the western front flared into life, and then suddenly no more was heard of General Gamelin. First it was General Weygand who was called the heir of Napoleon, and then a few days later Marshal Petain.

France fell all the same, and old Hugh turned to the others and said, 'What did I tell you? You can't believe a word it says.'

One morning they saw a huge gray shape looming along the horizon, making for Scapa Flow. 'Do you ken the name of that warship?' said Mansie of the hill. 'She's the *Ark Royal*, an aircraft carrier.'

That same evening Betsy twiddled the knob of the wireless and suddenly an impudent voice came drawling out. The voice was saying that German dive bombers had sunk the *Ark Royal* in the Mediterranean. 'Where is the *Ark Royal*?' went the voice in an evil refrain. 'Where is the *Ark Royal*? Where is the *Ark Royal*?'

'That man,' said Betsy 'must be the Father of Lies.'

Wasn't the *Ark Royal* safely anchored in calm water on the other side of the hill?

Thereafter the voice of Lord Haw-Haw cast a spell on the inhabitants of Tronvik. The people would rather listen to him than to anyone, he was such a great liar. He had a kind of bestial joviality about him that at once repelled and fascinated them; just as, for opposite reasons, they had been repelled and fascinated to begin with by the rapturous ferocity of Mr Sinclair's Sunday afternoon sermons, but had grown quite pleased with them in time.

They never grew pleased with William Joyce, Lord Haw-Haw. Yet every evening found them clustered round the portable radio, like awed children round a hectoring schoolmaster.

'Do you know,' said Sam of the shore one night, 'I think that man will come to a bad end?'

Betsy was frying bloody-puddings over a primus stove, and the evil voice went on and on against a background of hissing, sputtering, roaring and a medley of rich succulent smells.

Everyone in the valley was there that night. Betsy had made

some new ale and the first bottles were being opened. It was good
stuff, right enough; everybody agreed about that.

Now the disembodied voice paused, and turned casually to a
new theme, the growing starvation of the people of Britain. The
food ships were being sunk one after the other by the heroic
U-boats. Nothing was getting through, nothing, nor a cornstalk
from Saskatchewan nor a tin of pork from Chicago. Britain was
starving. The war would soon be over. Then there would be
certain pressing accounts to meet. The ships were going down.
Last week the Merchant Navy was poorer by a half million gross
registered tons. Britain was starving –

At this point Betsy, who enjoyed her own ale more than anyone
else, thrust the hissing frying pan under the nose – so to speak – of
the wireless, so that its gleam was dimmed for a moment or two by
a rich blue tangle of bloody-pudding fumes.

'Smell that, you brute,' cried Betsy fiercely, 'smell that!'

The voice went on, calm and vindictive.

'Do you ken,' said Hugh, 'he canna hear a word you're saying.'

'Can he not?' said Sandy Omand, turning his taurine head from
one to the other. 'He canna hear?'

Sandy was a bit simple.

'No,' said Hugh, 'nor smell either.'

After that they switched off the wireless, and ate the bloody-
puddings along with buttered bannocks, and drank more ale, and
told stories that had nothing to do with war, till two o'clock in the
morning.

One afternoon in the late summer of that year the island
postman cycled over the hill road to Tronvik with a yellow corner
of telegram sticking out of his pocket.

He passed the shop and the manse and the schoolhouse, and
went in a wavering line up the track to Hugh's croft. The wireless
was playing music inside, Joe Loss and his orchestra.

Betsy had seen him coming and was standing in the door.

'Is there anybody with you?' said the postman.

'What way would there be?' said Betsy. 'Hugh's at the lobsters.'

'There should be somebody with you,' said the postman.

'Give me the telegram,' said Betsy, and held out her hand. He
gave it to her as if he was a miser parting with a twenty-pound note.

She went inside, put on her spectacles, and ripped open the envelope with brisk fingers. Her lips moved a little, silently reading the words.

Then she turned to the dog and said, 'Howie's dead.' She went to the door. The postman was disappearing on his bike round the corner of the shop and the missionary was hurrying towards her up the path.

She said to him, 'It's time the peats were carted.'

'This is a great affliction, you poor soul,' said Mr Sinclair the missionary. 'This is bad news indeed. Yet he died for his country. He made the great sacrifice. So that we could all live in peace, you understand.'

Betsy shook her head. 'That isn't it at all,' she said. 'Howie's sunk with torpedoes. That's all I know.'

They saw old Hugh walking up from the shore with a pile of creels on his back and a lobster in each hand. When he came to the croft he looked at Betsy and the missionary standing together in the door. He went into the outhouse and set down the creels and picked up an axe he kept for chopping wood.

Betsy said to him, 'How many lobsters did you get?'

He moved past her and the missionary without speaking into the house. Then from inside he said, 'I got two lobsters.'

'I'll break the news to him,' said Mr Sinclair.

From inside came the noise of shattering wood and metal.

'He knows already,' said Betsy to the missionary. 'Hugh knows the truth of a thing generally before a word is uttered.'

Hugh moved past them with the axe in his hand.

'I got six crabs forby,' he said to Betsy, 'but I left them in the boat.'

He set the axe down carefully inside the door of the outhouse. Then he leaned against the wall and looked out to sea for a long while.

'I got thirteen eggs,' said Betsy. 'One more than yesterday. That old Rhode Islander's laying like mad.'

The missionary was slowly shaking his head in the doorway. He touched Hugh on the shoulder and said, 'My poor man –'

Hugh turned and said to him, 'It's time the last peats were down from the hill. I'll go in the morning first thing. You'll be needing a cart-load for the Manse.'

The missionary, awed by such callousness, walked down the path between the cabbages and potatoes. Betsy went into the house. The wireless stood, a tangled wreck, on the dresser. She brought from the cupboard a bottle of whisky and glasses. She set the kettle on the hook over the fire and broke the peats into red and yellow flame with a poker. Through the window she could see people moving towards the croft from all over the valley. The news had got round. The mourners were gathering.

Old Hugh stood in the door and looked up at the drift of clouds above the cliff. 'Yes,' he said, 'I'm glad I set the creels where I did, off Yesnaby. They'll be sheltered there once the wind gets up.'

'That white hen,' said Betsy, 'has stopped laying. It's time she was in the pot, if you ask me.'

Ian Hamilton Finlay

THE MONEY

At one period in my life, as a result of the poverty I was suffering, it became impossible for me to tell a lie. Consequently, I became the recipient of National Assistance money. But it all began when I applied for Unemployment Benefit money at the little Labour Exchange in the nearest town.

As I entered the building, the typist turned to the clerk and I heard her whisper, 'The artist is here again.' No, she gave me a capital – 'Artist'. The clerk rose, and, making no attempt to attend to me, crossed to the door marked 'Welfare Officer' and gave it a knock.

The clerk was seated. Presently the Welfare Officer appeared. He is, or I should say, was then, a rather stout, unhappy looking person in his early forties. This afternoon, as if he had known I was coming to see him, he wore a fashionable sports jacket and a large, arty and gaudy tie. My heart went out to him as he advanced towards the counter saying: 'I've told you before. We have no jobs for you. You are simply wasting our time.'

Somehow, I had got myself into a ridiculous *lolling* position, with my elbows on the counter and my hand supporting my chin. I gazed up at the Welfare Officer and replied timidly, 'I haven't come about a job. I have *been* in a job. Now I have come to ask you for Unemployment Benefit money.'

As I spoke, I could not help glancing at the large, locked safe that stood in the far corner of the room. Out of it, distinctly, a curious silence trickled, rather as smoke trickles out of the stove in my cottage. I had no doubt it was the silence of The Money I had just referred to.

'What!' exclaimed the Welfare Officer, raising his black, bushy eyebrows. 'You have been in a job!'

I nodded. 'I was editing a magazine.'

'And may I ask what salary you received?' he said, his tone disguising the question as an official one.

'One pound, three and sixpence,' I answered, for, as I explained, I could not tell a lie.

'Per month?' he suggested.

'Per week,' I replied with dignity. 'And it was only a part-time job.'

'Hum! In that case, assuming that you have been in part-time employment and did not leave it of your own accord you will be entitled to claim part-time Unemployment Benefit money from this Labour Exchange,' he informed me, all in one breath.

'What? But that isn't fair!' I retorted. My cheeks crimsoned; I took my elbows off the counter and waved my hands. 'That isn't just! I paid *full-time* National Insurance money. So I should draw *full-time* Unemployment Benefit money from this Labour Exchange!'

My impassioned outburst brought a nervous titter from the typist and an astonished rustle from the young clerk. The Welfare Officer, however, only glanced at me for an instant, turned his back on me, strode into his office and shut the door.

I waited a few moments. Then, 'Do you think I have offended him?' I asked the clerk. 'Am I supposed to go away now? Do you know?'

But before I had received an answer to my unhappy question, the Welfare Officer appeared once more, bearing two large volumes – no, *tomes*, in his arms. CRASH! He dropped the tomes on the counter, right under my nose.

Then he opened one of the tomes; and slowly, silently, with brows sternly knitted, he began to thumb his way through the thick and closely printed sheets. Page 100 . . . Page 250 . . . And he still had the second of the tomes in reserve.

I moistened my lips, and said weakly, 'Very well, I give in. I am only entitled to draw part-time Unemployment money from this Labour Exchange.'

'That is correct,' observed the Welfare Officer. Closing the tome, and flexing his muscles, he bent to push it aside. Then he took a step or two towards the safe. That, at least, was my impression. Looking back on the incident, I see that he was really going to the cupboard to fetch forms.

But the sight of his too-broad figure retreating to fetch me The Money touched my heart. True, he had won a hollow victory, but I did not mind, and I wanted him to know I did not mind.

'Thank you,' I said, in low, sincere tones.

The Welfare Officer stopped at once. He turned to face me again. 'Thank you? Why are you saying thank you? You haven't got the money yet, you know,' he warned me.

'I know that,' I said, and I apologized to him. He appeared to accept my apology, and, turning, took another step or two towards the cupboard – or, as *I* thought, the safe.

Again I was touched. It was the combination of my poverty, his pathetic appearance in his rich clothes, and the thought of The Money he was about to give me. It was as if he was generously giving it to me out of his own pocket, I felt.

'But honestly,' I sighed, 'I'm awfully grateful to you. You see, if you give me The Money, I'll be able to work . . . I'll be free to work – at last!'

'Work? What work?' exclaimed the Welfare Officer. He halted, flew into a rage, and once more turned to face me. 'If you are going to be working you cannot claim Unemployment Benefit money! Don't you understand that!' he shouted.

At this moment, the typist intervened, saying, 'He doesn't mean work. What he means is, taking pictures. Like that one – I forget his name – who cut off his ear.'

I, too, flew into a rage, and not only at this mention of *ears*.

'*Taking* pictures? TAKING pictures? PAINTING pictures if you don't mind!' I fixed the typist with my eye, and as a sort of reflex action, she bent forward and typed several letters on her machine. Then, looking at the Welfare Officer, I asked: 'Just tell me, yes, do tell me, how is a person to work when they are in a job? I can only work when I am NOT in a job? When I am in a job I CANNOT work, do you understand?'

'Are you working or are you not working?' shouted the exasperated Welfare Officer at the very top of his voice. 'Think it over will you, and let me know!'

So I thought it over, and that very night, by the light of my oil lamp, I wrote a polite letter to the authorities in the Labour Exchange. In effect, what I said was: 'I resign.' And the following morning, I handed the letter to the postman when he delivered the bills at my mountain-cottage.

But in the afternoon, when I was painting in my kitchen, I happened to look through the window, and I saw a neat little man. Clothed in a pin-striped office-suit and clasping a brief-case, he was clinging rather breathlessly to the fence. Several sheep had ceased to crop the hillside and were gazing at him with evident surprise.

As he did not look like a shepherd, I at once concluded that he must be – could only be – an art-dealer. Overjoyed, I thrust my hairless brushes back in their jam-pot, threw the door open, and ran out into the warm summer sunshine to make him welcome.

My collie dog, swinging the shaggy pendulum of his tail, and barking furiously, preceded me. 'Don't be afraid!' I shouted to the art-dealer. However, he had already scrambled back over the fence, and was standing, at bay, in the shade of the wood.

Calling the dog off, I opened the gate, and, smiling, advanced to meet him with outstretched hand. 'Good afternoon. I'm very glad to see you,' I said. The art-dealer took my hand, shook it warmly, and replied, 'I am from the National Assistance Board. Good afternoon.'

It was then I noticed he had been holding *forms*. The collie still bounded about us, leaping up on the stranger so as to sniff his interesting office-y smells. 'Fin McCuil,' I ordered, 'you mustn't touch *those*. Bad. Go away, now. Chew your bone instead!'

Then I turned to the National Assistance man, and I explained to him, with many apologies, that I had resigned.

He listened sympathetically, but when I had finished speaking, he came a step nearer to me, placed his arm around my shoulder, and said softly, 'Son, there is no need to feel like that, you are perfectly entitled to take this money.'

He tapped his brief-case. He meant, of course, the National Assistance money.

'But I don't feel *like that*,' I assured him. 'Believe me, I feel grateful . . . I mean, ungrateful . . . bringing you all this way . . . But I have resigned . . . I don't think I fit in very well, you see . . .'

'Son,' said the National Assistance man, speaking as no art-dealer ever did, 'I understand your position. No, don't look surprised. I do understand it. For you see, my own brother is a violinist . . .' And breaking off for a moment, he gazed thoughtfully down the steep and rickety old path up to my house. Here was a green, ferny landing; there a hole in the bannisters of bracken where a sheep had crashed through. 'He lives in a garret,' he continued. 'He is in the same . . . er . . . position . . . you see, as you are. He sits up there all day playing his violin.'

So there had been a mistake. It was just as I thought, and almost as bad as if I had told a lie. 'But I don't play the violin,' I pointed out. 'I don't play anything. You see, there's been a mistake.'

'No, no, I understand. You don't play the violin. You paint pictures,' said the National Assistance man soothingly. 'By the way,' he added, 'what do you do with them?'

'Do with them?' I repeated, at a loss. 'Ah, do with them: I see. Well, the big ones I put upstairs, in the attic. The little ones I put downstairs, in the cupboard.'

'You don't ever think of selling them?' he asked gently.

'Selling them! HA, HA! No, I don't,' I said, delighted by the fantasy of the question.

There was a pause. Suddenly he looked me straight in the eye, and he asked me, point-blank, 'Son, do you want this money?'

I could not tell a lie. 'I do,' I said.

So he thrust his hand into his brief-case. He offered me The Money, and, without looking at It, I put It in my pocket as fast as I could. Money is a great embarrassment when you are poor.

'Just fill those in,' he explained.

So, I thought to myself, they are not pound notes; they are postal-orders. But when we had shaken hands and said good-bye to each other, I found they were not postal-orders, either; they were forms . . .

And I filled them in. And thereafter, till my truthfulness got me into fresh trouble (for, of course, I had been brought up to look on charity as trouble) they sent me a regular weekly cheque. For my part, I was requested to fill in a form stating what Employment I had undertaken during the week and how much money I had earned by it. As painting was not Employment, though it was Work, I very carefully wrote the words 'None' and 'Nil' in the appropriate columns. After five or six weeks they gave me a seven-shilling rise.

Then I sold a picture. And I was inspected at the same time by an unfamiliar National Assistance man.

It was a breezy, blue and golden day in early autumn when he arrived at the door of my cottage. No sooner had I answered his knock than he cheerfully apologized. 'Sorry, old chap. Can't wait long today. Two ladies down in the car . . .'

'I expect you are going out for a picnic,' I observed, wondering if I ought or ought not to return his wink.

'Ha, ha, old boy, you are quite right there!' he answered.

'Well, do come in for just a moment,' I said. 'I shan't keep you, I promise.'

Lifting my easel out of the way, and hastily removing my wet palette from a chair, I invited him into my kitchen, and he sat down. On my palette, as it happened. He had sat on the chair on to which I had removed it; I at once ran for the turpentine and the cloth.

When we had cleaned him up, I put in tentatively: 'There is something I wanted to ask you. It's er . . . it's about those . . . er . . . forms . . .'

'Forms?' His bright face clouded over. I was spoiling his picnic with my Prussian Blue paint and my silly questions.

'Those . . . er . . . weekly forms that you send me . . .'

'Oh, those. You mean that you complete those, do you?' He seemed astonished that I did.

But I could not tell a lie. 'I'm afraid I do,' I confessed. 'Do you think it matters very much?'

'Ah, well, no harm done, I suppose.'

'Then there is a difficulty,' I announced. And quickly, so as not to keep the ladies waiting, I mentioned the awful problem I was now faced with. Painting, I explained, was not Employment, though it was *Work*. And even if I stretched a point and called it Employment, still it was not employment undertaken *this week*. The picture I had sold had been painted a whole year ago . . . How was I to inform them of the money I had received for it?

'I want to be quite truthful, you see,' I added. 'The form applies only to the present week . . . So, you see, it is difficult to be truthful.'

'If you want my advice, old boy, *be* truthful,' he answered. 'Yes, be truthful, that is always best. Or nearly always best, eh? HA, HA! Ah, hmm . . .' He rose, and moved to the door. 'I say,' he whispered to me, 'do I smell of turpentine?'

I sniffed at him, and assured him that he did not. 'The very best of luck then, old chap.' We shook hands. Halting to wave to me at frequent intervals, he hurried down the path, and I returned to the house.

There and then, determined to be truthful at all costs, I set about filling in my weekly form. 'Employment Undertaken – None.' And under 'Money Earned' I carefully wrote – '£5. 5. 0.' It had, I reflected, that slight suggestion of paradox one expects with the truth.

I posted the form, and, by return of post, I was sternly summoned to the central office of the National Assistance Board.

When I entered the building, and gave my name at the desk, I was at once led, like a very special sort of person, down several long passages and into a room. There, I was awaited. Several men, all of whom, it was plain, were awaiting me, were seated rather grimly around a table. On the table lay my form. Strange to say, it looked completely different there; *absurd*.

On my arriving in the room, one of the men – their spokesman or perhaps the head one – pointed to my form, and said, 'What is *that*?'

'That? Why, it's my weekly form,' I replied.

'Can you explain it to us?' another asked me.

'Yes, easily,' I answered. And I proceeded to explain it to them. Time. Money. Work. Truth. When I had completed my explanation, one of them got up from his chair and fetched a tome. It was a signal, for, at this, they all left their chairs and fetched back tomes. They threw them open on the table.

I grew nervous. After a while, I looked at the one who had first addressed me, and, pointing to his tome, I said, 'You are wasting your time. *I am not in it.*' He looked at me, but he did not smile or reply.

'Gentlemen –,' I began, interrupting them. 'Gentlemen, I think it would be best if I gave up The Money. I don't quite fit in, I quite see that. I sympathize with you. So I resign.'

At this, there was a sudden and very noticeable change in the atmosphere. They were obviously relieved at my decision. They smiled at me. But one of them said: 'There is no need to be hasty.' And another added: 'We wish you well.'

'Then I am to go on taking The Money, am I?' I asked.

But once more there was a change in the atmosphere. The men became grim again, and put on frowns.

'I see,' I said. 'Then I have no alternative but to resign.'

Smiles. Relief. Opening of silver cigarette-cases. 'There is no need to be hasty.' 'We wish you well.'

'I believe you,' I assured them. 'Will you send on the forms or shall I just fill them in now?'

'Now!' said the men, speaking all at once.

So I completed the forms of resignation, and I left the building a free man.

Iain Crichton Smith

SURVIVAL WITHOUT ERROR

I don't often think about that period in my life. After all, when one comes down to it, it was pretty wasteful.

And, in fact, it wasn't thought that brought it back to me: it was a smell. To be exact, the smell of after-shave lotion. I was standing in front of the bathroom mirror – as I do every morning at about half past eight, for I am a creature of habit – and I don't know how it was, but that small bottle of Imperial after-shave lotion – yellowish golden stuff it is – brought it all back. Or, to be more exact, it was the scent of the lotion on my cheeks after I had shaved, not the colour. I think I once read something in a *Reader's Digest* about an author – a Frenchman or a German – who wrote a whole book after smelling or tasting something. I can't remember what it was exactly: I don't read much, especially not fiction, you can't afford to when you're a lawyer.

So there I was in the bathroom on that July morning preparing to go to the office – which is actually only about five hundred yards or so away, so that I don't even need to take the car – and instead of being in the bathroom waiting to go in to breakfast with Sheila, there I was in England fifteen years ago. Yes, fifteen years ago. Exactly. For it was July then too.

And all that day, even in court, I was thinking about it. I even missed one or two cues, though the sheriff himself does that, for he's a bit deaf. I don't often do court work: there's no money in it and I don't particularly care for it anyway. To tell the truth, I'm no orator, no Perry Mason. I prefer dealing with cases I can handle in my office, solicitor's work mainly. I have a certain head for detail but not for the big work.

I suppose if I hadn't put this shaving lotion on I wouldn't have remembered it again. I don't even know why I used that lotion today: perhaps it was because it was a beautiful summer morning and I felt rather lighthearted and gay. I don't use lotions much though I do make use of Vaseline hair tonic as I'm getting a bit bald. I blame that on the caps we had to wear all the time during those two years of National Service in the Army. Navy-blue berets they were. And that's what the shaving lotion brought back.

Now I come to think of them, those years were full of things like boots, belts and uniforms. We had two sets of boots – second best boots and (if that makes any sense) first best boots. (Strictly speaking, it seems to be wrong to use the word 'best' about two objects, but this is the first time I've located the error.) Then again we had best battle dress and second best battle dress. (Again, there were only two lots.)

We always had to be cleaning our boots. The idea was to burn your boots so that you could get a proper shine, the kind that would glitter back at you brighter than a mirror, that would remove the grain completely from the toes. Many a night I've spent with hot liquefied boot polish, burning and rubbing till the dazzling shine finally appeared, till the smoothness conquered the rough grain.

We really had to be very clean in those days. Our faces too. In those days one had to be clean-shaven, absolutely clean-shaven, and, to get the tart freshness into my cheeks, I used shaving lotion, which is what brought it all back. The rest seems entirely without scent, without taste, all except the lotion.

I went to the Army straight from university and I can still remember the hot crowded train on which I travelled all through the night and into the noon of the following day. Many of the boys played cards as we hammered our way through the English stations.

I am trying to remember what I felt when I boarded that train and saw my sister and mother waving their handkerchiefs at the station. To tell the truth, I don't think I felt anything. I didn't think of it as an adventure, still less as a patriotic duty. I felt, I think, numbed; my main idea was that I must get it over with as cleanly and as quickly as I could, survive without error.

About noon, we got off the train and walked up the road to the camp. It was beautiful pastoral countryside with hot flowers growing by the side of the road; I think they were foxgloves. In the distance I could see a man in a red tractor ploughing. I thought to myself: This is the last time I shall see civilian life for a long time.

After we had been walking for some time, still wearing our bedraggled suits (in which we had slept the previous night) and carrying our cases, we arrived at the big gate which was the entrance to the camp. There was a young soldier standing there – no older than ourselves – and he was standing at ease with a rifle held in front of him, its butt resting on the ground. His hair was close cropped under the navy-blue cap with the yellow badge, and when we smiled at him, he stared right through us. Absolutely right through us, as if he hadn't seen us at all.

We checked in at the guardroom and were sent up to the barracks with our cases. As we were walking along – very nervous, at least I was – we passed the square where this terrible voice was shouting at recruits. There were about twenty of them and they looked very minute in the centre of that huge square, all grey and stony.

In any case – I can't remember very clearly what the preliminaries were – we ended up in this barrack room and sat down on the beds which had green coverings and one or two blankets below. There must have been twelve of these beds – about six down each side – and a fire-place in the middle of the room with a flue.

Now, I didn't know anything about the Army though some of the others did. One or two of them had been in the Cadets (I remember one small, plump-cheeked, innocent-looking youngster of eighteen who had been in the cadet corps in some English public school: he looked like an angel, and he was reading an author called Firbank) but the rest of us didn't know what to expect. Of course, I'd seen films about the Army (though not many since I was a conscientious student, not patronizing the cinema much) and thought that they were exaggerated. In any case, as far as my memory went, these films made the Army out to be an amusing experience with a lot of hard work involved, and though sergeants and corporals appeared terrifying, they really had hearts of gold just the same. There used to be a glint in the sergeant's eye as he mouthed obscenities at some recruit, and he would always praise his platoon to a fellow sergeant over a pint in the mess that same night. That was the impression I got from the films.

Well, it's a funny thing: when we went into the Army it was at first like a film (it became a bit more real later on). We were sitting on our beds when this corporal came in (at least we were told by himself that he was a corporal: I was told off on my second day for calling a sergeant major 'sir' though I was only being respectful). The first we knew of this corporal was a hard click of boots along the floor and then this voice shouting, 'Get on your feet.' I can tell you we got up pretty quickly and stood trembling by our beds.

He was a small man, this corporal, with a moustache, and he looked very fit and very tense. You could almost feel that his moustache was actually growing and alive. He was wearing shiny black boots, a shiny belt buckle, a yellow belt and a navy-blue cap with a shining badge in it. And when we were all standing at a semblance of attention, he started pacing up and down in front of us, sometimes stopping in front of one man and then in front of another, and coming up and speaking to them with his face right up against theirs. And he said (as they do on the films),

'Now, you men are going to think I'm a bastard. You're going to want to go home to mother. You're going to work like slaves and you're going to curse the day you were born. You're going to hate me every day and every night, if you have enough strength left to dream. But there's one thing I'm going to say to you and it's this: if you play fair by me I'll play fair by you. Is that understood?'

There was a long silence during which I could hear a fly buzzing over at the window which was open at the top, and through which I could see the parade ground.

Then he said,

'Get out there. We're going to get you kitted out at the quartermaster's.'

And that was it. I felt as if I had been hit by a bomb. I had never met anyone like that in my life before. And it was worse when one had come from a university. Not even the worst teacher I had met had that man's controlled ferocity and energy. You felt that he hated you for existing, that you looked untidy, and that he was there to make you neater than was possible.

*

All this came back to me very quickly as a result of a whiff of that shaving lotion and, as I said, even during my time in the court I kept thinking about that period fifteen years before so that the sheriff had to speak to me once or twice.

The case itself was a very bad one, not the kind we usually get in this town which is small and nice, the kind of town where everyone knows everybody else and the roads are lined with trees. The background to the case was this:

Two youths were walking along the street late at night when they saw this down-and-out sitting on a bench. He had a bottle of VP and he was drinking from it. The two youths went over and asked him for a swig, but he wouldn't give them any so, according to the police, they attacked him and, when he was down, they kicked him in the face and nearly killed him. In fact, he is in hospital at this moment and close to death. The youths, of course, deny all this and say that they never saw him before in their lives, and that they don't know what the police are on about.

They are a very unprepossessing pair, I must confess, barely literate, long-haired, arrogant and contemptuous. They wear leather jackets, and one has a motor bike. They have a history of violence at dance halls, and one of them has used a knife. I don't like them. I don't like them because I don't understand them. We ourselves are childless (Sheila compensates for that by painting a lot), but that isn't the reason why I dislike them. They don't care for me either and call me 'daddy'. They are more than capable of doing what the police say they did, and there is in fact a witness, a young girl who was coming home from a dance. She says that she heard one of the youths say,

'I wish the b . . . would stop making that noise.' They are the type of youths who have never done well in school, who haven't enough money to get girls for themselves since they are always unemployed, and they take their resentment out on others. I would say they are irreclaimable, and probably in Russia they would be put up against a wall and shot. However, they have to have someone to defend them. One of them had the cheek to say to me,

'You'd better get us off, daddy.'

They made a bad impression in the court. One of them says,

'What would we need that VP crap for, anyway?' It's this

language that alienates people from them, but they're too stupid or too arrogant to see that. As well as this they accuse the police of beating them up with truncheons when they were taken in. But this is a common ploy.

Anyway, I kept thinking of the Army all the time I was in court, and once I even said 'sergeant' to the judge. It was a totally inexplicable error. It's lucky for me that he's slightly deaf.

I was thinking of Lecky all the time.

Now, I suppose every platoon in the Army has to have the odd one out, the one who can never keep in step, the one who never cleans his rifle properly, the one whose trousers are never properly pressed. And our platoon like all others had one. His name was Lecky. (The platoon in the adjacent hut had one too, though I can't remember his name. He, unlike Lecky, was a scholarly type with round glasses and he was the son of a bishop. I remember he had this big history book by H. A. L. Fisher and he was always reading it, even in the Naafi, while we were buying our cakes of blanco, and buns and tea. I wonder if he ever finished it.)

Funny thing, I can't remember Lecky's features very well. I was trying to do so all day, but unsuccessfully. I think he was small and black-haired and thin-featured. I'm not even sure what he did in Civvy Street, but I believe I once heard it mentioned that he was a plumber's mate.

The crowd in our platoon were a mixed lot. There were two English ex-schoolboys and a number of Scots, at least two of them from Glasgow. There was also a boxer, who spoke with a regional, agricultural accent. One of the public schoolboys had a record-player which he had brought with him. He was a jazz devotee and I can still remember him plugging it into the light and playing, on an autumn evening, a tune called 'Love, O, Love, O, Careless Love'. The second line, I think, was, 'You fly to my head like wine'. The public schoolboys were very composed people (certain officers), and the chubby-cheeked one was always reading poetry.

Lecky stood out from the first day. First of all, he couldn't keep in step. We used to march along swinging our arms practically up to our foreheads and then this voice from miles away would shout across the square, 'Squad, Halt!' Then the little corporal would march briskly across the square, and he'd come to a halt in front of

Lecky and he'd say (the square was scorching with the heat in the middle of a blazing July), his face thrust up to close to him, 'What are you, Lecky?' And Lecky would say, 'I don't know, Corporal.' And the corporal would say, 'You're a bastard, aren't you, Lecky?' And Lecky would say, 'I'm a bastard, Corporal.' Then the marching would start all over again, and Lecky would still be out of step.

It is strange about these corporals, how they want everything to be so tidy, as if they couldn't stand sloppiness, as if untidiness is a personal insult to them. I suppose really that the whole business becomes so mindlessly boring after a few years of it that the only release for them is the manic anger they generate.

Of course, Lecky got jankers. What this involved was that after training was over for the day (usually at about four o'clock) he would put on his best boots, best battle dress, best tie, best everything and report to the guardroom at the double. Then, after he had been inspected (if he didn't get more jankers for sloppiness), he would double up to the barrack room again, change into denims, and go off to his assigned fatigue which might involve weeding or peeling potatoes or helping to get rid of swill at the cookhouse.

Continual jankers are a dreadful strain. You have to have all your clothes pressed for inspection at the guardroom; as well as that, boots and badges must be polished and belts must be blancoed. You live in a continual daze of spit and polish and ironing, and the only time you can find to do all this is after you have come back from your assigned task which is often designed to make you as dirty as possible. There is rapid change of clothes from battle dress to denims and back again. For after your fatigues are over you have to change back into battle dress to be inspected at the guardroom for a second time. I must say that I used to feel sorry for him.

His bed was beside mine. I never actually spoke to him much. For one thing his only form of reading was comics, and we had very little in common. For another thing – though this is difficult to explain – I didn't want to be infected by his bad luck. And after all what could I have done for him even if I had been able to communicate with him?

The funny thing was that as far as the rest of us were concerned the corporal became more relaxed as the training progressed and treated us as human beings. He would bellow at us out on the square, but at nights he would often talk to us. He'd even listen to the jazz records though he preferred pop. All this time while the others were gathered round the record-player, the corporal in the middle, Lecky would be rushing about blancoing or polishing or making his bed tidy. Sometimes the corporal would shout at him, 'Get a move on, Lecky, are you a f . . . snail or something?' And Lecky would give him a startled glance, before he would continue with whatever he was doing.

I never saw him write a letter. I have a feeling he couldn't write very well. In fact, when he was reading the comics, you could see his lips move and his finger travel along the page. Once I even saw the corporal pick up one of the comics and sit on the bed quite immersed in it for a while.

At the beginning, Lecky seemed quite bright. He even managed to make a joke out of that classic day when he was first taught to fire the bren. Instead of setting it to single rounds, he released the whole batch of bullets in one burst and nearly ripped the target to shreds. I saw the corporal bending down very gently beside him and saying to him equally slowly, 'What a stupid uneducated b . . . you are, Lecky.' He got jankers for that, too.

But, as the weeks passed, a fixed look of despair pervaded his face. He acted as if his every movement was bound to be a mistake, as if he had no right to exist, and that carefree open-faced appearance of his faded to leave a miserable white mask. Sometimes you wonder if it was right.

The more I see of these two people in the court, the more I'm sure that they really are guilty of hitting that old man, though they themselves swear blind they didn't do it. They keep insisting that they are being victimized by the police and that they were even beaten up at the station. They even picked on one of the policemen as the one who did it. He very gravely refuted the charges. One of them says he never drank VP in his life, that he thinks it's a drink only tramps use, and that he himself has only drunk whisky or beer. He is quite indignant about it: one could almost believe him. They also accuse the girl of framing them because one of them had a fight with her brother once on a bus. But their attitude is very defiant and it isn't doing them any good. My wife was away yesterday seeing her mother so I had to go to Armstrong's for lunch. Armstrong's is opposite the court which is in turn just beside the police station. As I was entering the restaurant I was passed by the superintendent who greeted me very coldly, I thought. He is a tall broad individual, very proud of his rank, and you can see him standing at street corners looking very official and stern, with his white gloves in his hands, staring across the traffic, one of his minions, usually a sergeant, standing beside him. I wondered why he was so distant, especially as we often play bowls together and have been known to play a game of golf.

It struck me afterwards that perhaps he thought I had put them up to their accusations against the police. After all, we mustn't undermine the authority of the police as they have a lot to put up with, and, even if they do use truncheons now and again, we must remember the kind of people they are dealing with. I believe in the use of psychology to a certain extent, but the victim must be protected too.

There was the time, too, when Lecky nearly killed off the platoon with a grenade. After a while it got so that hardly anyone in the hut spoke to him much. At the beginning they used to play tricks on him, like messing up his blankets, but that was before the corporal got to work on him (no, that's not strictly true, the Glasgow boys were doing it even after that). Most of the time we didn't see him at all, as he was so often on jankers. I don't know why we didn't speak to him. I think it was something about him that made us uneasy: I can only express it by saying that we felt him to be a born victim. It was as if he attracted trouble and we didn't want to be in the neighbourhood when it struck. We didn't want to have to do that spell of ten weeks' training all over again as Lecky was sure to do.

One morning we had an inspection. We had inspections every Saturday: the C.O. (distant, precise, immaculately uniformed) would come along, busily accompanied by the sergeant major, the sergeant, and corporal of the platoon. Oh, and the lieutenant as well (our lieutenant had been to Cambridge). We would all be standing by our beds, of course, rifles ready so that the C.O. could peer down the barrel, followed in pecking order by all the members of his entourage. If there was a single spot of grease we were for it. Our beds had all our possessions laid out on them, blanco, fork, knife and spoon, vest, pants, and much that I can't now remember. All, naturally, had to be spotlessly clean.

So there we were, standing stiff and frightened as the C.O. stalked up the room followed by the rest of his minions, the corporal with a small notebook in his hand. Unwavering and taut, we stared straight ahead of us, through the narrow window that gave out on the outside world which appeared to be composed of stone, as the only thing we could see was the parade ground.

Our hearts would be in our boots as we took the bolt out of the rifle and the C.O. would squint down the barrel to see if there was any grease. Mine was all right, but a moment later I heard a terrifying scream from the C.O. as if he had been mortally wounded. I couldn't even turn my head.

'Take this man's name. His rifle's dirty.' And the sergeant major passed it down to the corporal who put the name in the notebook. The C.O. proceeded on his tour round the room poking distastefully here and there with his stick, and staring at people's faces to see if they had shaved properly. I remember thinking it was rather like the way farmers prod cattle to see if they are fat and healthy enough. On one occasion he even got the sergeant major to tell someone to raise his feet to see if all the nails in the soles of his boots were still present and correct. Then he went on to the next hut, his retinue behind him.

And the corporal came up to Lecky, his face contorted with rage, and, punching him in the chest with his finger, said, 'You perverted motherless b . . . , you piece of camel's dung, do you know what you've done? You've gone and stopped the weekend leave for this platoon. That's what you've done. And don't any of you public school wallahs write to your M.Ps about it either. As for you, Lecky, you're up before the C.O. in the morning, and I hope he throws the book at you. I sincerely hope he gives you guard-duty for eighteen years.'

Now this was the first weekend we were going to have since we had entered the camp five weeks before. We hadn't been beyond the barracks and the square all that time. Blancoing, polishing, marching, eating, sleeping, waking at half past six in the morning, often shaving in cold water – that had been the pattern of our days. We hadn't even seen the town: we hadn't been to a café or a cinema. All that time we hadn't seen a civilian except for the ones working in the Naafi. So, of course, you can guess how we felt. I wasn't myself desperate. I wasn't particularly interested in girls (though later on when I was in hospital I got in tow with a nurse). I didn't drink. All I wanted was to get that ten weeks over. But I also wanted to put on my clean uniform just for once, and walk by myself, without being shouted at, down the anonymous streets of some town and see people even if I didn't talk to them. I would have been happy just to look in the shop windows, to stroll in the cool evening air, to board a bus, anything at all to get out of that hut.

There were two Glasgow boys there, and they went up to Lecky when the corporal had left and said to him, 'You stupid c . . . , what do you think you've done?' or words to that effect. They were practically insane with rage. For the past weeks all they had talked about was this weekend and the bints they would get off with, the dance they would go to, and so on. In fact, I think that if either of them had had a knife they would have run him through with it. And all this time Lecky sat on his bed petrified as if he had been shell-shocked. He was so shell-shocked that he didn't even answer. He didn't even cry. I had heard him crying once in the middle of the night. But there was nothing I could do. What could anyone do? I must say that I felt these Glasgow boys were going too far and I turned away, feeling uncomfortable.

Lecky was trying to pull a piece of rag through his rifle in order to clean it. One of the Glasgow boys took the rag from him (Lecky surrendered it quite meekly as if he didn't know what was happening, and indeed, I don't think he did know), rubbed it on the floor and then pulled it through the rifle again. The other tumbled Lecky's bed on to the floor, upsetting everything in it. (All this time the chubby-cheeked boy was reading Firbank.)

'You'd best keep in tonight,' the Glasgow boy said. 'If I get you outside . . .' and he made a motion of cutting Lecky's throat. Lecky sat on the floor looking up at him, deadly pale, his adam's apple going up and down in his throat.

'And no help for this bastard from any of you, anymore,' said the Glasgow boy, turning on us threateningly. The boxer, I remember, grinned amiably like a big dog. I think even he was afraid of the Glasgow boys, but I don't know. He was pretty hefty too, and the corporal spoke more softly to him than to any of the rest of us.

So Lecky went up next morning and got another three weeks of jankers, and on top of that he had trouble from the Glasgow boys as well. I would have said something to them, but what would I have gained? They would just have started on me. The sergeant was a placid family man and he left everything to the corporal. The sergeant was pretty nice really: a nice stout man who was very good at handing out the parcels any of us got and making sure that he got a signature. It was funny how Lecky never wrote any letters.

So the time came for our passing-out parade, to be inspected by a brigadier, one of those officers with a monocle, and a red cap, and a shooting stick. Of course, our own C.O. would be there as well.

I remember that morning well. It was a beautiful autumn-morning, almost melancholy and very still. We were up very early, at about half past five, and I can still recall going out to the door of the hut and standing there regarding the dim deserted square. I am not a fanciful person but, as I stood there, I felt almost as if it were waiting for us, for the drama that we could provide, and that without us it was without meaning. It had taken much from us – perhaps our youth – but it had given us much too. I felt both happy and sad at the same time, sad because I had come to the end of something, and happy because I would be leaving that place shortly.

I don't know if the others felt the sadness, but they certainly felt the happiness. They were skylarking about, throwing water at each other from the wash-basins and singing at the tops of their voices. The ablutions appeared on that day to be a well-known and almost beloved place, though I could remember shaving there in the coldest of water, in front of the cracked mirror. Today, however, it was different. In a few hours we would be standing on the square, then we would be marching to the sound of the bagpipes.

And after that we would all leave – all, that is, except Lecky. We were even sorry to be leaving the corporal, who had become more and more genial as the weeks passed, who condescended to be human and would almost speak to us on equal terms. He had even been known to pass round his cigarettes and to offer a drink in the local pub. Perhaps after all he had to be tough; one must always remember the kind of people with whom he often had to deal. For instance, there was one recruit who was in his fourth year of National Service; every chance he got he went over the wall and the M.Ps had to chase him all over the north of England. That's just stupidity, of course. You can't beat the Army, you should resign yourself. Rebellion won't get you anywhere. I believe he had a rough time in the guardroom every time they got him back, but he was indomitable. You almost had to admire him in a way.

Anyway, I found myself standing beside Lecky at the wash-basin. I could see his thin face reflected in the mirror beside my own. There was no happiness in it, and one could not call what one saw sadness: it was more like apathy, utter absence of feeling of any kind. I saw him put his hand in his shaving bag, look again, then become panicky. He turned everything out on to the ledge but he couldn't find what he was looking for. I looked straight into the mirror where my face appeared cracked and webbed. He turned to me.

'Have you a razor blade?' he said. To the other side of him I saw the two Glasgow boys grinning at me. One of them drew an imaginary razor across his throat, a gesture which in spite of his smile I interpreted as a threat.

I knew what would happen to Lecky if he turned up on parade unshaven. I looked down at my razor and remembered that I had some more in my bag. I looked at the grinning boys and knew that they had taken Lecky's blade.

I said to him, 'Sorry I've only got the one blade, the one in the razor.' After all, one must be clean. It would be a disgusting thing to lend anyone else one's razor blade: why, he might catch a disease. It is quite easy to do that. There's one thing about the army: it teaches you to be clean. I was never so fit and clean in my life as during that period I spent in the Army.

I turned away from the grinning Glasgow boys and looked steadily into the mirror, leaning forward to see beyond the cracks as if that were possible. I shaved very carefully, because this was an important day, cutting the stubble away with ease under the rich white lather, the white towel wrapped round my neck.

I should like to describe that parade in detail, but I can't now exactly capture my feelings. I began very clumsily, not quite in tune with the music of the pipes, but, as the day warmed, and as the colours became clearer, and as the sun shone on our boots and our badges, and as I saw the brigadier standing on the saluting platform, and as my body grew to know itself apart from me, I had the extraordinary experience of becoming part of a consciousness that was greater than myself, of entering a mysterious harmony. Never before or since did I feel like that, did I experience that kinship which exists between those who have become expert at the one thing and are able to execute a precise function as one person. It was like a mystical experience: I cannot hope to describe it now. Perhaps one had to be young and fit and proud to experience it. One had perhaps to feel that life was ahead of one, with its many possibilities. Today I think of Sheila and a childless marriage and a solicitor's little office. Perhaps, for once in my life, I sensed the possible harmony of the universe. Perhaps it is only once we sense it. Not even in sex have I felt that unity. It was as if I had fallen in love with harmony and as if I was grateful to the Army for giving me that experience. And after all, at the age I was at then, it is easy to believe in music: I could have sworn that all those men were good because they marched so expertly to the bagpipes, and that anyone who was out of step was bad, and that it would be intolerable for the harmony to be spoilt. I began to understand the corporal, and to be sorry for those who had never experienced the feeling that I was then experiencing.

At that moment all was forgotten, the angry words, the barbaric barrack room, the eternal spit and polish, the heart-break of those nights when I had lain sleeplessly in bed watching the moonlight turn the floor to yellow and hearing the infinitely melancholy sound of the Last Post. All was forgiven because of the exact emotion I felt then, that pride that I had come through, that I was one with the others, that I was not a misfit.

When the parade was over, I ran into the barrack room with the others. There was no one in the room except Lecky who was lying on his bed. I went over to him, thinking he was ill. He had shot himself by putting the rifle in his mouth and pulling the trigger. The green coverlet on the bed was completely red and blood was dripping on to the scrubbed wooden floor. I ran outside and was violently sick. Looking back now I think it was the training that did it. I didn't want to be sick on that clean floor.

Of course, there was an inquiry but nothing came of it. No one wrote to his M.P. or to the press after all, not even the public schoolboys. There was even a certain sympathy for the corporal: after all, he had his career to make and there were many worse than him. The two public schoolboys became officers: one in the Infantry and the other in education. I never saw them again. Perhaps the corporal is a sergeant major now. Anyway, it was a long time ago but it was the first death I had ever seen.

The sheriff leaned down and spoke briefly to the two youths after they had been found guilty. He adjusted his hearing aid slightly though he had nothing to listen for. He said,

'If I may express a personal opinion I should like to say that I think the jury were right in finding you guilty. There are too many of you people around these days, who think you can break the law with impunity and who believe in a cult of violence. In sentencing you I should like to add something which I have often thought and I hope that people in high places will listen. In my opinion, this country made a great mistake when it abolished National Service. If it were in existence at this date perhaps you would not be here now. You would have been disciplined and taught to be clean and tidy. You would have had to cut your hair and to walk properly instead of slouching about insolently as you do. You would not have been allowed to be idle and drunk. I am glad to be able to give you the maximum sentence I can. I see no reason to be lenient.'

The two of them looked at him with insolence still. I was quite happy to see the sheriff giving them a stiff sentence. After all, the victim must be protected too: there is too much of this mollycoddling. I hate court work: I would far rather be in my little office working on land settlements or discussing the finer points of wills.

It was a fine summer's day as I left the court. There was no shadow anywhere, all fresh and new, just as I like to see this town.

A CHOICE OF PENGUINS

☐ **Small World** David Lodge £2.50

A jet-propelled academic romance, sequel to *Changing Places*. 'A new comic débâcle on every page' – *The Times*. 'Here is everything one expects from Lodge but three times as entertaining as anything he has written before' – *Sunday Telegraph*

☐ **The Neverending Story** Michael Ende £3.95

The international bestseller, now a major film: 'A tale of magical adventure, pursuit and delay, danger, suspense, triumph' – *The Times Literary Supplement*

☐ **The Sword of Honour Trilogy** Evelyn Waugh £3.95

Containing *Men at Arms, Officers and Gentlemen* and *Unconditional Surrender*, the trilogy described by Cyril Connolly as 'unquestionably the finest novels to have come out of the war'.

☐ **The Honorary Consul** Graham Greene £2.50

In a provincial Argentinian town, a group of revolutionaries kidnap the wrong man . . . . 'The tension never relaxes and one reads hungrily from page to page, dreading the moment it will all end' – Auberon Waugh in the *Evening Standard*

☐ **The First Rumpole Omnibus** John Mortimer £4.95

Containing *Rumpole of the Bailey, The Trials of Rumpole* and *Rumpole's Return*. 'A fruity, foxy masterpiece, defender of our wilting faith in mankind' – *Sunday Times*

☐ **Scandal** A. N. Wilson £2.25

Sexual peccadillos, treason and blackmail are all ingredients on the boil in A. N. Wilson's new, *cordon noir* comedy. 'Drily witty, deliciously nasty' – *Sunday Telegraph*

A CHOICE OF PENGUINS

☐ **_Stanley and the Women_ Kingsley Amis** £2.50

'Very good, very powerful . . . beautifully written . . . This is Amis _père_ at his best' – Anthony Burgess in the _Observer_. 'Everybody should read it' – _Daily Mail_

☐ **_The Mysterious Mr Ripley_ Patricia Highsmith** £4.95

Containing _The Talented Mr Ripley, Ripley Underground_ and _Ripley's Game._ 'Patricia Highsmith is the poet of apprehension' – Graham Greene. 'The Ripley books are marvellously, insanely readable' – _The Times_

☐ **_Earthly Powers_ Anthony Burgess** £4.95

'Crowded, crammed, bursting with manic erudition, garlicky puns, omnilingual jokes . . . (a novel) which meshes the real and personalized history of the twentieth century' – Martin Amis

☐ **_Life & Times of Michael K_ J. M. Coetzee** £2.95

The Booker Prize-winning novel: 'It is hard to convey . . . just what Coetzee's special quality is. His writing gives off whiffs of Conrad, of Nabokov, of Golding, of the Paul Theroux of _The Mosquito Coast._ But he is none of these, he is a harsh, compelling new voice' – Victoria Glendinning

☐ **_The Stories of William Trevor_** £5.95

'Trevor packs into each separate five or six thousand words more richness, more laughter, more ache, more multifarious human-ness than many good writers manage to get into a whole novel' – _Punch_

☐ **_The Book of Laughter and Forgetting_
Milan Kundera** £3.95

'A whirling dance of a book . . . a masterpiece full of angels, terror, ostriches and love . . . No question about it. The most important novel published in Britain this year' – Salman Rushdie

A CHOICE OF PENGUINS

☐ **_The Philosopher's Pupil_ Iris Murdoch** £2.95

'We are back, of course, with great delight, in the land of Iris Murdoch, which is like no other but Prospero's . . .' – *Sunday Telegraph*. And, as expected, her latest masterpiece is 'marvellous . . . compulsive reading, hugely funny' – *Spectator*

☐ **_A Good Man in Africa_ William Boyd** £2.95

Boyd's brilliant, award-winning frolic featuring Morgan Leafy, overweight, oversexed representative of Her Britannic Majesty in tropical Kinjanja. 'Wickedly funny' – *The Times*

These books should be available at all good bookshops or newsagents, but if you live in the UK or the Republic of Ireland and have difficulty in getting to a bookshop, they can be ordered by post. Please indicate the titles required and fill in the form below.

NAME _____ BLOCK CAPITALS

ADDRESS _____

_____

_____

Enclose a cheque or postal order payable to The Penguin Bookshop to cover the total price of books ordered, plus 50p for postage. Readers in the Republic of Ireland should send £1R equivalent to the sterling prices, plus 67p for postage. Send to: The Penguin Bookshop, 54/56 Bridlesmith Gate, Nottingham, NG1 2GP.

You can also order by phoning (0602) 599295, and quoting your Barclaycard or Access number.

Every effort is made to ensure the accuracy of the price and availability of books at the time of going to press, but it is sometimes necessary to increase prices and in these circumstances retail prices may be shown on the covers of books which may differ from the prices shown in this list or elsewhere. This list is not an offer to supply any book.

This order service is only available to residents in the UK and the Republic of Ireland.